Bindis & Brides

NISHA MINHAS

POCKET
BOOKS

LONDON • SYDNEY • NEW YORK • TORONTO

First published in Great Britain by Simon & Schuster, 2005
This edition first published by Pocket Books, 2005
An Imprint of Simon & Schuster UK
A Viacom company

1 3 5 7 9 10 8 6 4 2

Simon & Schuster UK Ltd
Africa House
64–78 Kingsway
London WC2B 6AH

www.simonsays.co.uk

Simon & Schuster Australia
Sydney

A CIP catalogue record for this book
is available from the British Library.

ISBN 0 7434 6881 3
9780743468817

Typeset in Sabon by M Rules
Printed and bound in Great Britain by
Cox & Wyman Ltd, Reading, Berkshire

For the love of my life, Dave
∞OX9!

Tusi mera zindagee hai

Acknowledgements

To my wonderful partner, Dave – a whopping thank you for your endless support. For making this book possible. For the sick jokes, poems, ideas, twisted story-line, and for taking me to the top of a multi-storey car park to help me research heights, in an endeavour to understand mountaineering. Thanks also for your mountaineering expertise. And a double thank you for being you.

My family with all my love and all my heart, my thoughts are always with you.

Kate Lyall Grant – many thanks once again for your brilliant editing. As always your expertise has improved the book no end; taking the manuscript to a fit enough state to be let loose on the public. A big huge thank you.

Lorella Belli – thanks, thanks as ever to you my agent. My book writing is so much easier when I know that they are in safe hands. What's more on top of your agent skills you're a great friend to boot. Thank you.

Emma Noel – thanks for all the help you have given me, thanks for all your enthusiasm, and thanks for taking me round London in the p***ing rain. It's been fun working with you.

All at Simon & Schuster – thanks for your continuing support for the books.

Thank you to my readers and a kind thank you to those who have sent me such lovely and encouraging e-mails.

And finally thanks to the person who invented the word 'thanks' as I've used it quite a lot on these acknowledgements. Cheers.

Brown-Winged Angel

All who leave their motherland of
India so fine
will kneel and pray for re-acquaintance
in the future sometime.

All who kneel and pray to their Gods
Hindu, Muslim, Buddhist, Sikh
will hear the simple message given
will understand we're all unique.

And all who feel the pull of home
and all who feel the pain of heart
will see a brown-winged, brown-eyed angel
and will know that land and people will never
    truly
        part

By Dave Bell Carney

Chapter One

Everyone would know which woman Joel Winters had chosen for his latest love-making marathon because, by morning, a metallic thud could be heard just outside the house of the woman in question. The distinctive sound of a female throwing away her vibrator, knowing full well that the orgasm she'd received the night before from Joel could never be replaced by a Super Rabbit Orgasmatron 2000. One lady, in a state of confusion, threw out her Hotpoint washing machine, shouting, 'Won't be needing you any more,' only to remember later that she used it for washing her clothes as well.

Joel stared down the packed aisle in the supermarket waiting for the opportune moment. It was Saturday morning and he had until this evening to become an expert Indian chef. He was beginning to regret telling beautiful Claudia that his talents extended way beyond the bedroom and into the kitchen. A kitchen that had dished up recipes that Madhur Jaffrey herself would pay millions of rupees just to have the barest of tastes. Claudia was definitely expecting more tonight than boil-in-the-bag Uncle Ben's rice and a jar of Uncle Ben's Chicken Korma.

The plan was simple: he'd wait until someone filled their trolley or basket with a packet of curry powder. He would then walk casually up to them and ask, 'How do you cook Indian?' Simple. Joel patiently watched the curry powder shelf, completely aware that a security camera was now trained on his position. Trying not to draw attention to himself from the other shoppers but at the same time keen to let the security staff know he wasn't a shoplifter, Joel smiled up at the camera, winked and pulled out his jeans pockets, lifted up his T-shirt and opened his mouth wide to prove he wasn't hiding smuggled goods in there. He gave the camera the thumbs-up to seal the deal. Not quite the behaviour one might expect of a thirty-year-old, strikingly handsome, perfectly toned, fabulously rich, love-making expert, who was noted within mountaineering circles as possibly the best and most disciplined climber that Britain had ever produced. Not quite the behaviour one might expect of such a man, but friends who knew him better would always say, 'Expect the unexpected with Joel.'

'What's he doing now?' the senior security guard asked his colleague, squinting at the CCTV monitor.

'He's pretending to read a jar of tandoori paste – upside down.'

'Zoom in on his basket. Let's see what the nutcase has picked up so far.'

'It looks like . . . hang on . . . er, still that pink economy

2

bra we saw him trying on earlier, and a pack of Red Bull.'

'Just keep an eye on him, Jim.'

Just like Joel was keeping an eye on the Indian spices. Finally, after learning by heart what additives went into Patak's Poppadoms, Joel watched a hand reach out for the curry powder and pop it in a basket. He was upon the young woman before the packet had time to settle.

'Making an Indian, are you?' Joel asked, pointing to her ingredients. 'Either that or you must make the weirdest shepherds pies.' He laughed, but she didn't. 'Anyway, I'll be clear about this, I'm not trying to chat you up. I just need some help to cook an Indian.' He counted to three in his mind. 'Well, are you going to help me or not? The truth is that I want to impress a woman tonight. She thinks that I can cook, but I can't. I told her that I'm a bit of a whiz in the kitchen but all I can really dish up is a huge feast of lies. I *really* need your help.'

The lady looked him up and down, as though scanning his image into her processors. Her lips became so thin that Joel was tempted to swipe his credit card through them and charge her for her rude manner. She eventually spoke: 'Get yourself a cookery book and learn the hard way like I had to. I don't appreciate being interrupted on my Saturday shop.' With a flick of her hair and a tut from her mouth, she disappeared from view.

'Nice to meet you too,' Joel mumbled, wondering if he should just do the noble thing this evening and order an Indian takeaway instead (palming it off as his own creation, of course).

He viewed the selection of aromatic spices and tantalizing pastes before his eyes. In the right hands these ingredients were taste-bud dynamite, flavour neutron bombs. And in the wrong hands, they were spicy suicide. But whether you cooked them right or wrong, you could always be sure of one thing, your backside would explode.

'I couldn't help overhearing your conversation with the lady just now,' murmured a female voice behind Joel. 'But cooking Indian isn't that hard, if you're pointed in the right direction.'

And what would you know, Miss Nosy Boots, thought Joel, before turning around to see a stunning Indian woman staring at him. Without thinking, he hid the pink bra under the Red Bulls. Quite a feat considering the bra's size and colour.

She continued, 'I think it's really romantic that you're trying to make an effort to impress a woman tonight. You must really love her. I'm Zarleena, by the way.'

Love her? He'd only just met her. Joel's mind wandered back to last week, the day he'd spotted Claudia. She worked at Colchester Zoo as a nutritionist. Joel had asked her if she wouldn't mind taking a quick photograph of him in front of two mating elephants. He liked the fact that she never asked 'Why?' And she hadn't had the heart to tell him that they were two bull elephants with the names Graham Norton and Boy George. One thing led to another. Names were swapped, telephone numbers were swapped, even e-mail addresses. All that needed swapping now was their bodily fluids. It was extremely important that tonight ran smoothly.

He replied to the Indian woman, 'Love? I worship the very ground she walks on. My life is a mere empty shell without her. I am lost without my Claudia. Love is too small a word to describe what I feel about her. So you can help me cook Indian, then? I'm Joel, by the way. But my mates just call me "Joel".'

Zarleena saw in Joel all that was missing from her husband. Love and caring for his woman. Qualities not to be sniffed at in the world where she came from. A world devoid of romance and love. She read the small writing on his T-shirt and giggled. CLIMBERS ALWAYS TREAD IN DOG SHIT, BECAUSE THEY NEVER LOOK DOWN. Well, Zarleena thought to herself, as she wasn't a climber she'd take the opportunity of looking Joel both up and down – and boy was he scrumptious-looking. Claudia was a very lucky woman. *Of course* she'd help him with his cooking.

Ready, steady, shop. Zarleena darted up and down the aisles with Joel, explaining as she went, filling his basket with essential Indian spices. It grieved her to see beautiful Indian recipes stuffed into jars and labelled as 'traditional'. As far as she could remember, her mother had never used spices such as E621, E635, colourings, flavouring enhancers and preservatives for her dishes. Although once, in her memory hall of shame, Mum did admit to using an OXO cube in desperation for a dish she then labelled 'Chicken Gravy Masala'.

Time soon passed and finally the shopping, queueing and paying was done.

Joel pulled out a seat for Zarleena in the supermarket's coffee shop. 'You've been so helpful; the least I can do is buy you a coffee.' His eyes couldn't help but be drawn to the bunch of red roses in one of the bags, and he couldn't help but ask, 'Do Indians really use flowers in their recipes?'

She laughed. 'The flowers are to decorate the table. Not for the balti. You really have no idea, have you?'

And he didn't. Joel listened as Zarleena explained how to cook the dish. She jotted down the step-by-step instructions on a piece of paper. Just at the bottom she left her phone number – only to be used in an emergency – and bid him farewell. Joel proffered his cheek for her to kiss him goodbye, but she must have missed it.

Result! Only a fool could screw up now. If things went well tonight, he would broaden his horizons, and it would only be a matter of time before he was hunting for a Chinese person in the supermarket. It had taken him an awful amount of self-restraint, and one look at Zarleena's wedding ring, to steer clear of chatting her up. There was no denying her beauty, even Pinocchio couldn't lie about that, and her sweet friendly charm was so warming it could defrost a cheesecake in seconds. He gave himself a high-five for his discipline then took the shopping bags to his black Range Rover. Extra dark tinted windows, extra wide chunky tyres, extra shiny alloy wheels, two huge chrome exhausts, personalized number plate K2 PEAK and one extremely proud owner. Enough money spent on the outside extras to have bought another Range Rover. And the inside? Well, just your usual DVD player and screens, 5000-watt sound system, Internet link-up, satellite navigation, seat warmers etc. It was no surprise that Joel had even spent money on the boot.

In the boot of Joel's 4×4 sat two small fridges powered by the car battery. One he kept for Red Bulls, the other was kept free and topped-up with ice in case his finger or knob dropped off. In his line of work it paid to be smart. And in his line of work it also helped if you were slightly nuts. After loading the boot with the bags, he jumped into the driving seat and headed away from Colchester in Essex and towards Hunterslea, his home town, just ten minutes' drive east.

Joel loved Hunterslea. He'd lived here all his thirty years and was unable to pick fault with the place. As yet it remained unspoilt by the military boys from Colchester Barracks who deemed all pubs and clubs within bombing range their own. Just a short drive from the coast, it was hard to feel claustrophobic here. The fresh air and the surrounding countryside made it a perfect retreat for the snobbier families down this neck of the woods. Which left Joel surprised when his parents decided to leave Hunterslea four years ago and make their new roots in Florida. Surprised and disappointed. If there was any family member he wanted shot of then it was his older brother, Dylan; he was the trouble-maker of this family, and seeing him at any time was seeing him too much.

To pinpoint the moment Dylan and Joel became disgusted at the sight of each other, it was the day Joel was born. Things got steadily worse after that. Five-year-old Dylan waited patiently for his mother to leave a sleeping one-month-old Joel unattended and then stuck a nappy pin in his bottom. 'You are costing this family a lot of money by being born,' he'd hissed in Joel's tiny ear, ignoring his wails. 'Watch yourself or I might accidentally pour a kettle full of steaming water over you.' The bad vibes reverberated through their years together. It was never sibling rivalry with these two, more like sibling cavalry – they were at constant war.

The Range Rover drove into the luxurious grounds of Forest Falls Apartments, up a short road decorated on either side with flowers and trees, then, after a quick wave from Joel to the uniformed doorman on duty, down the ramp that led to the underground car park half-filled with Mercs and Jags. Joel switched off the engine and wondered about the consequences of what he was hopefully going to be doing with Claudia tonight. His conscience was ordering him to look at the photograph of his girlfriend, Candy, tucked in his wallet. On the back of her picture Joel had written some words to himself just for occasions like this.

He slid out her photo and admired her beauty. Blonde, blue eyes, model looks, amazing. Nothing short of a work of art. And the words:

Do you want to lose the best thing that has ever happened to you?
Don't sleep around. Don't hurt her. Have a wank instead.

The message was supposed to be the verbal equivalent of a cold shower, or the visual equivalent of looking at Tracey Emin. But after three years of cheating its power had diminished and its impact was negligible.

The message was about as useful in preventing Joel having sex as a slice of garlic bread would be to Dracula biting someone's neck. Maybe it was time for Joel to change the words.

Or maybe it was time for Candy to change her boyfriend.

He kissed Candy's picture and said his usual, 'Sorry, I'll never do it again after tonight. I miss you.'

But missing each other was a huge part of their relationship so far. Candy lived in Cornwall, Joel lived in Essex. Her job, working as a leader in an Outdoor Pursuit Centre, took her around the world for weeks at a time, as did his job as a climber (sometimes for months). Finding periods to see each other was a matter of getting out their diaries and searching for matching empty days. It hardly bore the hallmarks of a relationship destined for a ruby wedding anniversary. That was the negative. But on the positive side, when they were together, it seemed like nothing could tear them apart.

And then there was this business of dealing with death. The rudest interruption of them all. Ever since he was a young lad of five Joel had felt the need to climb. His first major summit was when he climbed St Nicholas Infant School's assembly hall roof. 'You could have died up there, Joel,' his mum had shouted after being informed by the teacher of Joel's precarious ascent. 'Get used to it,' Joel had replied. 'I do not fear death.' They'd been 'getting used to it' ever since. The school roof, to the tallest trees, to climbing walls and finally the mountains. Snowdon, Ben Nevis, Kilimanjaro, Mont Blanc. Then came the Himalayan peaks. The giant 8000-metre range. Lhotse, Makalu, Cho Oyu, Dhaulagirl, Manaslu, K2 and, the best of them all, Mount Everest. Joel knew that to succeed at the very top of his chosen sport/profession, he must not bow to the fear of death. He'd seen countless dead bodies on his climbs. Women, men, friends and lovers all taken by the mountains and frozen in their last moments. Their lifeless forms leaving one final message to those following in their footsteps: treat the mountains with respect. Candy worried that Joel's fearless attitude would someday be punished by the mountain's fearful altitude. An avalanche or a broken leg too high for rescue, or just a simple fall. Each slippery step up a mountain, as Candy often told Joel, was a step nearer your grave.

Another car entered the underground car park and drove to its allocated slot, increasing the worth of the car park by a further one hundred grand. Joel waited for Mr Lewis-Jones, the resident millionaire, to depart before venturing out to collect the shopping. Mr Lewis-Jones had made his fortune by selling new-improved Open Sesame Laxatives. The last thing Joel needed right now was yet another lengthy discussion regarding his bowel movements. Mr Lewis-Jones had been pestering Joel for a faeces sample ever since Joel had moved in six years ago. Maybe, after tonight's experimental Indian cookery, Joel might rush round to Penthouse Four and ask Mr Lewis-Jones if he could donate his sample down his toilet. At least that way Joel would avoid stinking out his own Penthouse.

It was the neighbourly thing to do.

Chapter Two

The first time Zarleena's husband, Armin, made love to her, he made her feel cheap. No words, no kind gestures, no passion. Just a grunting man lying on top of her, sweating and pounding, until he was satisfied; Zarleena not daring to cry out that he was hurting her, afraid he would blame her for wrecking the moment. What moment? Her bridal sari lay in a heap on the floor next to his underpants, discarded, just like any romantic thoughts that this would be a special evening had been discarded. She should have realized when his hand had felt for blood on her inner thigh, after which he'd said, 'At least I know I'm your first. I had my doubts,' that this man, her new husband, was not quite the man she had been led to believe he was. On her first meeting with him, he was all give, give, give. Now, he was just take, take, take, and she didn't feel like she'd given away her virginity, rather it was taken; and if he'd left some money on the side it wouldn't have shocked her. For a husband to make his wife feel like a prostitute on her wedding night doesn't make for a very auspicious start to a blissful marriage. More like the start to a bad dream.

And if bad dreams were films, then Zarleena's was an epic; one that started three years ago, one she'd been struggling to come to terms with right up until now.

Now it was Sunday, dragon-breath hot, a typical June day – for Africa. Zarleena smiled in admiration at the latest poster her younger sister, Honey, had felt compelled to stick to their maisonette's living-room window. Passers-by had seen numerous slogans over the last nine months or so. SAVE OUR TRANSPORT SYSTEM – IMPORT RICKSHAWS; DROP VIAGRA NOT BOMBS. MAKE LOVE NOT WAR, and today's poster, BUILD BRIDGES, NOT BARRIERS. SAY GOODBYE TO THE CASTE SYSTEM! Honey had notched up an impressive 793 miles of marches in the last year alone. That's Land's End to John O'Groat's, shouting at the top of her lungs all the way. She hated being a spectator of the wrongs in this world and wished to play a part in righting some of them. Zarleena loved the fight in her sister. It would take a lot to make her crumble.

The opposite, in fact, of Zarleena who was more crumbly than a Flake. Already she'd worked her way through half a toilet roll looking through her wedding photos. Each smiling portrait gave little clue to the horror that would soon follow. A family joined by blood, strengthened by history and held secure by tradition was just a short, perilous step away from devastation in those photographs. If only cameras could take pictures of the future, then her family would have kept Zarleena a million miles away from her husband. One snapshot of her future hell was all that would have been needed.

She placed the album beside her on the sofa, wondering if she was a misfit in life. Maybe all men would treat her like her husband had. Was there something in her smile, or her eyes maybe, that gave off the signal that she wouldn't fight back? Is that why he continued? Because she just curled up in a ball and prayed for it to finish. Was she so weak that she couldn't stand up for herself? Not even once. If only she had Honey's strength.

'Oi, fatty.'

Zarleena looked towards the stepper machine in the corner. She was sure the blasted thing spoke to her at times.

'Oi, fatty, it's 11.30, get your arse over here and start losing that lard. Thunder thighs!'

Zarleena obeyed the voice. Whether it be her conscience, or whether she had a talking stepper machine, it didn't matter, the truth was no metabolic rate in the world should have to cope with the amount of chocolate she devoured. Her stomach was in danger of turning into a chocolate fondue.

Mmmm, chocolate fondue, thought Zarleena, working away on the squeaky machine, climbing an imaginary hill, pretending to enjoy the burning in her thighs. It had taken Honey and herself nearly two exhausting hours to put the stepper machine together. Suspicion that it had been assembled incorrectly arose when it collapsed into a heap of metal and plastic after just four steps. It was at that point they realized what the forty 'spare' screws were for.

Zarleena upped the tempo on her stepping, focusing on the goldfish swimming in its bowl. The whole room had been decorated to complement Orangeina, the goldfish. With cream-coloured walls and sofa, and a polished wooden floor, the sisters had added bright orange curtains, throws and cushions. A fiery orange lava lamp did its thing in the corner, whilst a glass wind chime sprinkled the air with notes. Much like the rest of the maisonette, the living room was warm, modern and relaxing. Besides that, it was very, very tidy. From their childhood, they'd been encouraged to be ship-shape, and the habit had stuck, no clutter was visible, no mess was allowed. Even Orangeina felt guilty when a pooh trailed him in the bowl. If only there was another fish to blame.

Fifteen minutes later and Zarleena was still stepping, hoping for the interruption of a phone ringing, or maybe the smoke alarm sounding, even some young kid kicking his football through the window. Any excuse to stop. And here was the punchline to Zarleena's weight-loss routine: she was as skinny as a rake, weighing just eight stones soaking wet. Her relatives used to call her *Dalchini Danda* (cinnamon stick) when she was younger, which was infinitely better than being called *Haithi* (elephant) as her eighteen-stone (dry) cousin, Heera, had been called. Nicknames in India are commonplace, and rarely is anyone referred to by their real name. Even Gandhi was called Nappy Man by some of his closer friends. (And Nappy Filler by his enemies.)

Zarleena's heart was now pumping madly. Like being chased. Like being scared. Like being worried.

Like being in love? She wondered how that gorgeous-looking gentleman she met in the supermarket yesterday had got on with her balti-cooking advice. He was obviously love-struck, was Joel. Zarleena smiled, wiping her brow of sweat: quite a nice name too. How she envied those people who had experienced the awesome power of love. What she wouldn't do to sample that wondrous feeling. Did Joel's heart ache for his woman? Did he spend every spare minute daydreaming about being with her? Zarleena sighed. Why couldn't her parents have matched her up with someone like Joel? Forget the fact that he was white and she knew nothing about him, and his family most likely didn't have ties with Dad's village in Jammalamadugu. Forget the fact that he wasn't a Hindu and most probably had slept with half a nation. Forget all that. He was cooking for a woman, wasn't that enough?

The orange neon phone sprang to life, ringing and flashing until Zarleena jumped off the stepper and answered it. Up until that moment she'd never considered herself psychic. But now she wasn't so sure. It was Joel on the phone. Had she made him call her by thinking about him? She couldn't wait for the mid-week lottery now.

'Sorry to disturb you on this glorious Sunday,' he said. 'I'll keep it short and sweet as you're probably dying to get back to whatever you were doing before I rang.' He laughed. 'You're puffing nearly as much as she was last night. Honestly, I don't know what ingredients you made me put in that meal, but it gave her amazing energy in the sack.'

'I beg your pardon?'

'Two hours we were at it. I just wanted to thank you for making the evening ... erm ... spicy.' He laughed again. 'Anyway, thanks. You're tops. Cheers.' And he hung up.

Zarleena stared at the mouthpiece in disbelief.

MEN!

Gorgeous, hunky, blue-eyed men.

Chapter Three

Just after Claudia left the apartment that morning, Joel scraped the leftover Indian sauce from the bottom of the saucepan and bottled it in a jam jar labelled SPICY SEDUCTION. He placed it in the fridge and decided to try it out on Candy next time she was down. No wonder Indian families were so massive, he thought, one spoon of that stuff and sex becomes an act of necessity.

Joel viewed his messy but mighty kitchen. Granite worktops, hand-built wooden cupboards, an American-style double-fridge, mod-cons galore. He wondered if there was enough room to fit in a *tandoori* oven. He wanted to make sure he had all his bases covered if he was going to be taking this Indian cooking seriously. The only other alternative he could think of which would guarantee authentic home-cooked Indian cuisine would be to hire a discreet Indian chef every time he wanted to entertain a woman. Joel thought back to last night as he loaded up the dishwasher. Surely the sex wasn't so amazing that he was thinking about hiring a chef? He remembered howling like a wolf, the clawing and rolling across the room; he remembered her standing over him in just her high heels like a dominatrix demanding he obey her every command. And after the foreplay things just got out of control. It had to be the Indian spices; he'd never known a woman behave so ... dirty before. Hire a chef? He'd hire a fucking restaurant if he had to.

But first he had to let someone go. Claudia was both sweet and pretty but never a replacement for his girl-friend. Already the guilt at betraying Candy *again* was beginning to tighten its screws. He would have to make his position clear with Claudia immediately. It had been a glorious one-night stand but nothing more than that. He was about to pick up his mobile and dial her number when Eloise, his sister, emerged from her bed-room and eyed Joel holding his address book. She walked across the wooden floor, snatched the book away, glanced at the open page then handed it back.

'You won't be needing that,' Eloise stated, rummaging in the fridge. 'I've already dumped Claudia for you this morning. I followed her out of the apartment when she left.' She opened the raspberry yoghurt, dipped her finger in the pot, then pushed it into Joel's open mouth. 'Lick!'

'You dumped her?' This wasn't the first time Eloise had seen fit to push Joel's women out of his life. 'I hope for her sake that you did it with a degree of sensitivity, Eloise, she's a very nice girl.'

She smiled. 'Of course. I mentioned that you were into animals – that's why you went to the zoo – and that you couldn't believe your luck when an animal agreed to come home with you. She hardly cried at all.'

'Eloise,' Joel was disgusted, 'just stay out of my personal life.'

My sister, thought Joel, such a joy. He glared at her while she ate her lunch. Little Miss Protection herself. He loved her like crazy although she drove him crazy. Not so much a heart-breaker, more like a heart-attack maker. Although what did one expect with a name like Eloise? After naming Dylan after Bob Dylan, Joel after Billy Joel, their parents had decided to change track and instead of naming their next child after a singer, chose to name her after a record. Dad particularly liked the single 'E=MC^2' by Big Audio Dynamite. But Mum liked the Damned at the time and so ... Eloise was born. Joel's mates Brent, Clovis and Jay thought she was a knock-out, or in their word, 'Shaggable'. Long chestnut-coloured hair, brown eyes, extremely slim, every young man's desire. A twenty-year-old beauty. But trouble since day one.

And day one began when Eloise reached sixteen and turned up on his doorstep with seventeen suitcases and fifteen hat boxes. She was moving in whether Joel liked it or not – she didn't have a job, for God's sake. It was the least he could do; it was what big brothers were for. Four years later, with Eloise still unemployed, Joel realized that big brothers were for other things too. Like paying for little sister's designer clothes, paying for her bills, her food, her make-up, mobile phones, holidays abroad with her friends. Being big brother meant paying for her dental care, sunbeds, her French manicures, her waxing and facials. She even asked for a 'sexual toys' expense. Oh, being big brother to Eloise was such a privilege it almost made him wish that she was one of a twin . . . and then he could be bankrupt.

After clearing up the mess in the kitchen, Joel fetched his personal records from his bedroom. It was the day before he was due to fly to the Garden of the Gods in Colorado. His agent had fixed him up with another climb promoting Red Bull. These jobs were the bread and butter of his living. Well paid, highly dangerous, short duration. Nothing like an expedition to the Himalayas which might involve months and months of preparation and a team of climbers, but every bit as exciting in its own way. Joel would normally write a short account of his climb for his website on his return. His fans waited eagerly for the next instalment of Joel's life because he always concluded his climbing accounts with a new sexual tip on making love at altitude. On top of promotional climbs and expeditions Joel's ever-growing wealth was supplemented by small parts in films (where mountaineers were needed), TV adverts, payment for lectures, advice to the military, climbing-club talks. Then there were the fees for magazine articles he wrote. And because the life expectancy of a climber is pretty low, his agent, who had already sold the rights to a publisher, had him writing his autobiography. Climbing was his world. Could be the title of the book, it was certainly the title of his life.

But right now Joel had to sit down and think seriously about death. AGAIN. Reviewing the terms of his will was part of his pre-climb ritual. The will was a morbid reminder of the unnecessary dangers Joel took whilst edging his way up a cliff-face, or across a 7000-metre high crevice. His mountaineering buddies over the years had shaken their heads in despair as Joel refused to climb up a mountainside using fixed ropes left behind from a prior ascent. They'd asked him why he declined to use bottled oxygen when scaling above 8000 metres. As far as the climbing community was concerned, Joel might be one of the best around, but he wouldn't be around for too long. He was too suicidal for that. Rumour had it that Joel had a death wish. But for every yin there is a yang. Joel also had a life wish too. Over the years his charity work could only be described as beyond generous. Risking his life to climb certain mountains to raise money for orphanages, cancer research, the homeless and even the Aids crisis in Africa. On his many trips to India, Pakistan, Nepal and Tibet he'd seen poverty on a scale that filled his heart with tears. Families clinging to life by a crust. Their tormented bodies ravaged by injustice. To ignore their pain would be to damn them. And Joel could never be accused of damning anyone.

An hour and a half of careful deliberation later and the will was complete. Joel sat back on his vibrating chair facing the enormous floor-to-ceiling window as the sun flooded the living room and drowned the shadows. He knew, as he'd known last time, that the will was guilt-driven. Apart from leaving the odd knick-knack to his mates and Eloise, and a fair amount of money to charity; everything else went to Candy. Joel trawled his eyes down the inventory of items left to Candy. Christ, that was a lot of guilt.

And if he felt this bad for betraying Candy, sleeping around, then why the hell did he do it? Joel hoped the vibrations in his chair might shake the answer from his brain. Because for the life of him the only answer he had so far was: he was a man, with manly urges, and manly needs. Pathetic, thought Joel; if that was the case then why couldn't he just make do with a porno magazine? Well, there was a good reason for that. He was never too keen on masturbating over one of those things; watching others have sex never rocked his boat, Joel preferred the real article – despite what the lady at Snappy Shots 1 Hour Photos said when she handed him back his Colchester Zoo pictures of animals mating. Getting the real article had rarely been an issue either. With his striking looks, piercing blue eyes, pine cone-coloured hair and healthy shiny aura, he never had a problem attracting women. And once they'd seen his fantastic mountain-built body naked, they never wanted to let him go. Eloise often said that an evening out with Joel in the vicinity of women was like watching flies around shit. Of course, Eloise was the FlyZap fly spray. And of course, the women in question would never describe a hunky, handsome man like Joel as 'shit'.

'You're a real shit, Joel,' Eloise said, red-faced after reading his will. 'Yet again you give everything worthwhile to that cow you call your girlfriend. What about me, the number-one woman in your life? Okay, so I don't give you blow jobs, but you've never asked. I wish sometimes you'd think about me for a change, we came from the same womb, for God's sake. I'm worth nothing to you, am I?' She stormed out of the front door, a camera clasped in her hand, shouting, 'Change the fucking will, Joel, or I might tell the taxman about your sneaky, secret bank accounts. Remember, I know how much you're really worth.'

But how much was Joel worth? Most of the details were written down on his latest will and testament. Monetary-wise the amount was quite substantial. He was rich. In real terms? Was it really possible to quantify what you were worth? Wasn't that judged by how much you would be missed when you were gone? Joel wondered about that for a moment. How many people would miss him when he was gone? He fished out his calculator to deal with the huge figure, then realized just a couple of hands would do. God, it was quite humbling to know that only nine people would *really* miss him when he slipped off the mountain to his death. Jesus Christ, he thought, it was time he made an effort to be extra nice to people. NINE! He'd had more friends in nursery school.

With his common sense playing hookey at the moment, Joel's conscience was tickled quietly by an idea. A feather of guilt regarding his brother, Dylan. Was it too late in the day to add him to his list? Was it possible, after all that had been said and done, for Dylan to be the tenth person on Joel's list of people who would miss him when he was dead? The situation for the last eleven years had been ugly, maybe it was time it had a facelift.

Tucked away in a drawer in his bedroom, hidden amongst a scrapbook of newspaper cuttings, was Dylan's final letter to Joel before communications between the two brothers had been more or less severed. The odd polite hello and goodbye in front of family was all that had been uttered over the past decade. Joel steeled himself and read the letter once again:

> Joel,
> Mummy and Daddy have asked me to 'fix' things with you. I don't suppose they realize how grave things are between us. We can never fix this. So, I will keep it simple. Don't ever phone me, don't ever try to see my son, never talk to my wife. I don't consider you my brother. STAY AWAY.
>   In return, I will be civil towards you when we are in the company of Mummy and Daddy and Eloise.
>   Dylan

'Fuck you,' said Joel, throwing the letter back in the drawer. 'Fuck you, Dylan. I can live with nine; or rather . . . I could die with nine.'

Chapter Four

An Indian man's ego could be referred to as his hymen. If he sleeps around before wedlock, it will be his ego that exposes his secret, rather than a torn hymen. Even if he lies about sleeping around, his world could come tumbling down. Suddenly that porky pie about the 'gangbang' in Majorca isn't so funny. Or how he'd slept with every leading lady from Bollywood since 1995. (Yes, they used to fly him out there specially.) A virginal Indian man could well do without bedroom brags. Especially in the Indian community where family gossip is more prevalent than oxygen.

Take Salam, for instance, he regretted lying to his best mate, Raza, about sleeping with a woman. Secretly he was still proud of being a virgin. Unfortunately for Salam, by the time would-be-writer Raza had tarted up Salam's story, the woman had turned into one woman a week, and Salam's sexual prowess was worthy of its own website. Raza unleashed the rumour on the Indian community. Raza told Sumil told Amina told Preeya told Bobby told Karim told Sangeeta who told Namita.

Namita was Salam's bride-to-be.

And Namita, Salam's bride-to-be-no-more, came bursting into Bindis & Brides shop with her entourage of friends, flinging her boxed bridal sari onto the counter; 'refund' written all over her screwed-up face.

Zarleena and Honey swapped looks. Oh no, another wedding break up. The third this month. May as well call the shop Bindis, Brides & Bust Ups.

'Bastard! Lying feeble bastard,' Namita stated, collecting looks of sympathy from everyone in the shop. 'Men have lost their honour these days. Our mothers took the last of the good Indian men, yar? I'm not marrying a man with a busy *danda*. Who needs it?'

'Not me,' said Honey, opening the box and examining the exquisite hand-stitched sari. 'Such a shame. You would have looked like a princess in this.' Sunlight sparkled from every sequin and bead.

'I know,' replied Namita, tears beginning to roll down her cheeks. 'Bastard.'

It wasn't the first time this shop had heard such expletives either. Sitting midway up Hunterslea High Street, Bindis & Brides, Zarleena's and Honey's daring venture, was turning into a twenty-four-carat goldmine, attracting Asians, tourists and anyone interested in an Indian-style wedding from miles around. The odd swear word was to be expected. Nearly a year into business and already the shop's reputation had spread, with the till making more noise some days than the *bhangra* music coming from the speakers. The atmosphere was just right, enhanced by the smoking incense sticks, bright spicy-coloured walls and hand-carved wooden statues. And most importantly, two beautiful Indian women with welcoming smiles to see to your every need. Besides wedding outfits, the shop also stocked a wide variety of Indian gifts and knick-knacks. If one walked in with money, it was nearly impossible to walk out again without at least one item of Eastern sway. Some days, when a rare hunk walked in, both sisters wanted that Eastern gift he walked out with to be them. He could even choose which material he wanted them gift-wrapped in.

Zarleena handed Namita a tissue for her tears. She knew about bastard men. 'At least you found out before,' she said, a hint of sadness in her voice. 'It's always better to find out their bad points *before* you marry.'

'How? We don't get the luxury of dating. The last time I looked my parents were Indian. And the last time I checked, Indian parents don't allow us to date men, yar?'

'Amen,' chorused her friends. Amen indeed.

Honey pulled from under the counter a sheet of A4. 'This is a list of questions that a bride should feel free to ask her future husband before she even thinks about marrying him.' She handed it to Namita. 'The sexual questions at the bottom are not compulsory.' She stared at the girl sternly. 'But if he refuses to answer them, my guess is he's a pervert.'

Namita looked to the bottom questions as her friends crowded around. Question 35 was regarding goats. Question 37 was in relation to hygiene and general cleanliness of the genital area. Over the page was a free space to write, in as descriptive a way as possible, about any weird fetishes that he might expect his partner to partake in. And even though the questionnaire was written in a jovial manner, its content was of extreme importance to girls who were about to embark on the journey of an arranged marriage. What if, after the wedding, the bride found out that he wanted bondage, or he liked role-play sex, or even, heaven forbid, he got his kicks watching her go for a number two.

'You're mad, you are,' Namita said, giggling.

'I know,' Honey replied. 'Zarleena was thinking about designing an Indian-style straitjacket for me with sequins and itsy mirrors. At least if I'm going to be a loony I want to be a stylish loony.'

Laughs all round; Zarleena shaking her head at her sister, Honey keeping up the charade that this was a normal day, when, in fact . . . it was far from normal. Mum had secretly phoned her earlier explaining that Zarleena's husband had been at her house yesterday evening, when Dad was out, demanding to know where Zarleena now lived. He said he still carried a torch for her and would like to burn her with it. Mum had threatened him with the police to which he laughed, 'Just tell my second-rate wife that I'm looking for her. Tell her I'll find her.' Mum's panic down the phone had sent fear into Honey's heart. Surely they hadn't expected the snake to shed its evil skin, but what were they to do? Honey needed time to think before burdening Zarleena with yet more worry.

But how much time? Honey glanced at her sister. She would have to tell her soon.

The refund was sorted, Namita and her friends departing in a much better mood than they had entered. Zarleena tucked away the questionnaire while Honey made lunch upstairs in their maisonette. A few customers browsed, quietly. Zarleena sat on a stool, dressed in her beautiful lilac *shalwar kameez*, munching on a Bounty, leafing through a few thoughts. Thoughts that normally jumped into bed with her and kept her up half the night.

What kind of questionnaire would have helped her see the truth in her husband, wondered Zarleena. What answers would have made her flee away from him? What possible words from him would scare even the bravest woman witless? Try this: *I will make you black and blue with my fists. You will wake up to a nightmare each day. I will control you in this arranged marriage.*

Arranged marriage, ha! Arranged horror more like.

But no warning was given about his violence. No questionnaire was filled in. Zarleena had walked unknowing into a relationship full of terror and tears and the sterile smell of First Aid boxes. The only sugar on this otherwise bitter pill was that her sister, Honey, had been born after her. The first-born daughter had been destined by the Gods for many, many years to marry this man. It could so easily have been Honey. Tears welled in Zarleena's eyes; she wouldn't have been able to cope if it had been her little sister hurt by this monster. If that had been the case, she would most likely have murdered him.

A shout from across the shop broke her day-nightmare. 'Excuse me, young lady, is this the only size you do?' A middle-aged English woman held a mushroom-coloured silk sari aloft.

Zarleena joined her. 'One size fits all,' she stated, suddenly wondering about the legitimacy of that statement now that she'd seen the woman's huge belly. 'Is it for you?'

'This is true.' A nervous laugh followed. 'I'm attending a dinner party next week and would like to be different, to stand out a little. I thought a sari would be perfect.' She laughed again. 'I take it that it comes with fitting instructions? Imagine it unravelling amongst a hundred guests.'

No thanks, thought Zarleena, visualizing a hundred guests pissing themselves with laughter. 'Ooh imagine, terribly embarrassing to say the least. If you follow me to the changing rooms at the rear I will gladly show you the correct way to wrap a sari. It's quite painless.'

Honey returned with the sandwiches while Zarleena helped the customer learn the intricate skill of sari-fitting. It took four attempts to teach her, the woman's mind obviously elsewhere – most likely on those scrummy-looking sandwiches that Honey had brought down. But fitting saris on non-Indian women was a trend that seemed to be gathering pace lately, much to Zarleena's and Honey's delight. Fingers crossed and David Beckham might wear one soon. The Real Madrid Sari Football Kit was a sure winner. And if by bad luck a thread fell off David's No. 23 sari, his wife could wear one too.

The till filled quickly, its greedy drawer hungry for notes. As ever in a busy environment, the hours raced past, and before the girls had time to realize how tired they were, the six o'clock chimes came. Closing time in Bindis & Brides was always a spiritual affair with both girls circling the area with candles, humming their own mantra, 'Un-curse our purse and fill our till,' over and over. It brought closure to the day and, like Night Nurse, aided restful sleep; another day done and dusted.

Up a short flight of stairs and they were in the maisonette. The girls had always dreamed of sharing a place together, never thinking for one moment that they actually would. It seemed like only yesterday when they were plaiting each other's hair in Mum and Dad's house in Colchester. Dressing the same, talking the same, pretending they were the same. And Zarleena was sure that if Honey hadn't been such a rebellious egg, fighting for her right to stay in the ovaries until she wanted to leave, then they would have been born twins. Twins, how magnificent that would be, they told each other. Imagine knowing what the other was thinking.

And to this day some people mistook them for twins. Both extremely beautiful, slim and elegant with light tanned skin, almost honeycomb in colour, large, delving brown eyes, envy-inducing cheekbones and smiles that would light up Blackpool Tower in a power cut. The only marked difference these days was the length of their hair: Zarleena, at twenty-eight, wearing hers short, in a bob, with Honey, at twenty-six, keeping hers long.

Only a fool would think that these two were separable.

But wasn't love life's biggest fool?

And sometimes, wasn't love life's biggest let-down too.

Chapter Five

Joel didn't die on the mountain in Colorado. Maybe the Grim Reaper was scared of heights that day, or he packed the wrong climbing boots; whatever the reason, Joel cheated death, and his Red Bull sponsors were impressed with the photographs, and rightly so. The shots of Joel hanging from just two fingers at one thousand feet, without safety ropes, helmet or harnesses, while drinking a can of Red Bull were pretty damn impressive. If it gave most people wiiings it gave Joel a rocket-powered engine with anti-gravity boots.

Seven days later, after collecting his baggage at Heathrow Airport, Joel was waved goodbye by Pete, his agent. 'Just before you split, Joel, Dougie asked me to ask you why you always have an unlit cigarette in your mouth when you climb. You don't even smoke.'

'In case I fall,' Joel said, slinging his holdall over his shoulder.

Pete screwed up his face. 'Talk sense, Joel.'

'I couldn't live with the fact that I died because my skills weren't up to scratch. The papers would have a field day. Much rather the press headline read: TOP CLIMBER DIES TRYING TO LIGHT A FAG or SMOKING KILLS CLIMBER.'

'I worry about you, Joel; maybe the lack of oxygen up there has taken its toll. You know you made one of the female photographers cry last week? Handing her a dustpan and brush just in case she had to sweep up your remains. It's sick!'

'Real life is sick and the sooner you realize it the better. Wake up, Pete. Anyway, who's the real sicko here? Just a couple of months back I nearly lost my left hand's fingers to frostbite and your first question to me was, would I still be able to climb with a metal hook as a hand. That's sick!'

'Point taken.' And they went their separate ways.

The M25 is officially Britain's most dangerous road, and therefore, by definition, Joel's favourite. The perfect end to the day would be a near miss with an articulated lorry. After scaling the highest ridges, then being buffeted in a turbulent plane, it would be a shame for the danger level in his life to reduce to 'safe'. This death-wish attitude began in the womb where Joel deliberately got his head tangled up in the umbilical cord. Well, this is what he told the psychiatrist his mother took him to when he was just ten years old. 'I like to jump out of high windows,' he explained to Dr Freshman, who was busy signing Joel's latest plaster cast. 'Tall trees are my favourite though. I climb up as far as I can, then leap across to the next tree like a monkey. I normally wait until the fireman has got his ladder in position to save me before I dive to the next tree. You should see how angry they get. I shout across, "Don't get your pants on fire". They don't understand though, I need the practice. One day I will climb Mount Everest like Tenzing did. My hero. My middle name *is* Sherpa you know?'

Sherpa Joel parked his Range Rover in the underground car park of the luxury penthouse where he lived. Surveillance cameras kept watch down here, while up top a security guard-cum-doorman kept an eye on the twelve apartments and premises, either on patrol or via a bank of monitors from Reception. Two guards shared the shifts, one talked too little, the other talked too much. Tonight's guard was Arthur, the talker; Joel didn't mind Arthur, in some ways he was quite fond of him.

As Joel entered the building, Arthur turned down the volume to his Steps CD and asked 'Did you get my message?' 'I told Sammy to tell you before you left for the States.'

'Nope. No message, Arthur.'

Arthur's face turned an angry red. 'That useless piece of shit. Why I ever thought he would tell you.' He tutted. 'It's too late now. It's pointless, absolutely, f for fucking pointless.'

'And the message was?'

'To watch *Cliffhanger*. ITV were showing it.'

Joel sniggered, remembering that hilarious scene where the woman lost her grip and fell to her demise. He had been the only person in the cinema cheering at the time. If she had simply used a clove-hitch knot, she might have lived. Arthur and Joel continued chatting for a few minutes until Joel's jet lag tugged on his eyelids. He bid Arthur 'goodnight' then rode the lift to his top-floor apartment.

Inside, Hurricane Eloise had visited. The once immaculate abode now looked like the setting for *Twister 2*. This was all the proof he needed: women were the messier sex. And not only the messier either, the noisier. Eloise's screams could be heard coming from his bedroom. About to make his presence known, Joel heard the words, 'Come on, big boy, give it to me harder.' More screams, then, 'You'd better untie me after this, Johan, if Joel finds out his climbing gear is being used for bondage I'm in deep stook. We've already got to change the sheets and tidy the place before he gets back tomorrow morning. And gracious me, would you please stop kerfuffling with that climbing helmet and see to my womanly needs . . .'

At this point Joel tuned off, no brother wants to hear his sister have sex. Watching her moan in the future as she struggled to open a jam jar would never be the same. He rammed his headphones on, lay back on the sofa listening to U2's 'Hold Me, Thrill Me, Kiss Me, Kill Me', and drifted off to a welcome sleep. It was the perfect relaxant.

Even in the land of nod, Joel never left the mountains. His mind was decorated with images of his climbs over the years, and his fantasy was decorated with visions of mountains yet to be conquered. On his apartment walls hung huge framed photographs of untamed mountain peaks. If one sat at the oak table in the vast dining room, a picture of Mount Annapurna peered down. In the living room, with its gigantic, floor-to-ceiling windows, hung an immense picture of the Nepalese Himalayas. Everywhere, photographs of some of the earth's oldest rocks. Probably the same pictures the FBI have on their walls with the heading: POSSIBLE BIN LADEN HIDEAWAYS.

After many attempts of waking Joel the previous night by shouting, water drips and rubbing chilli seeds on his cheeks, Eloise had decided to let him sleep through until morning. She sat on the vibrating chair watching Joel gently snore. Most people, after sleeping the night on the sofa, wake up looking like the leftovers of a Chinese takeaway. Joel on the other hand, in the opinion of the women he'd slept with over the years, appeared gourmet appetizing. His naked upper body was the perfect visual starter and main. And for the dessert? There was not a black-cherry gateau, or an apple tart, or even a sponge pudding that could compete with the dessert that Joel kept tucked away in his boxer shorts. And what's more, you couldn't get fat on it either (unless you swallowed his custard).

Eloise lit a match and held it under the living room's smoke alarm. The squealing noise brought Joel's dream of playing chicken at Silverstone F1 race track to an abrupt halt, his arm reaching out to switch off the non-existent alarm clock.

'Greetings, sloth,' Eloise said, handing Joel a mug of coffee and a Jordans breakfast bar. It was 11 a.m.

'Has big boy gone?' he asked, referring to her boyfriend, Johan, noting the rope burns on her wrists.

'Gone for today. He said you looked quite cute asleep, for a criminal. Although he did have trouble imagining that you had been in prison for manslaughter.' She picked up a Pizza Hut box and stuffed it in the bin liner. 'Until I showed him your climbing axe and demonstrated how you cracked someone's head open with it.'

'Manslaughter?'

'I had to get rid of him somehow this morning, Joel, you know how he likes to hang around. My life doesn't revolve around a man; it revolves around me and Natalie going shopping. Besides, he was talking of flying me out to the Czech Republic to meet his parents. I hate discussing that with him. You know how I hate flying. Ever since . . .' She stopped.

Ever since a family holiday to Florida, where Joel managed to shit up an entire Boeing 737 by claiming he had had a vivid premonition of the plane exploding into a ball of fire in mid flight. So convincing was his act, the rolling of the eyes, the shaking limbs, the crying, the praying (he even poured water on his Bermuda shorts to pretend he'd wet himself) that the crew refused to leave their seats for most of the flight, strapping themselves in at the slightest sign of turbulence.

Joel hung his head in shame. 'I still feel bad about that, you know? I was only a kid having a laugh . . . at other people's expense.' He unzipped his holdall and pulled out his wallet. 'Here you go, buy yourself something nice.' He handed her £200. 'For all those package holidays you've missed out on.'

She grabbed the notes and grinned internally. Joel was such a sucker. 'Cheers, bro.'

After returning the flat to its former glory, mess free and smelling fresh, Eloise flopped into the black, leather vibrating chair, and began to vibrate. It was hard to pin down what her brother was thinking sometimes. Part of his fascination was his unpredictability. That edge he lived on. Perversely she'd often thought that a man willing to risk his life up a mountain was a sure bet to being dangerous in the bedroom. But where does one go to get a date with a mountaineer? Up Everest? She'd seen the faces of the women who'd left Joel's apartment. Smug in the knowledge that as orgasms go, Joel had reached their summit. Eloise had often wanted to shout out after them, 'I taught him everything he knows, my brother.' But no, she got her sweet justice in other ways. Like helping to persuade Joel to dump them. You had to be cruel to be kind sometimes. And one of the first rules of mountaineering is to travel light. Nothing was heavier than a woman imposing herself on a man's freedom. All Eloise did was help him lose the excess baggage, that's all. Except Candy. She daren't interfere with her. Candy was one bag that was to be left alone, or, in Joel's kind words, 'So help me, Eloise, I'll throw you out on the streets if you upset Candy in any way.' Don't go there.

Back from a shower, Joel gazed into the living room. A tall, pink candle flickered on the coffee table. Eloise stood poised with the candle snuffer. This could only mean one thing.

'While you were away, Brandy phoned a number of times,' Eloise began, on spotting her brother. 'She didn't believe me when I said you were in the States. She didn't trust me, Joel, your own sister. She seemed to think that she knew you better than I did. As if. Anyway, the crux of the matter is this: I dumped her for you. And don't worry, I didn't say you had Aids or anything like that this time.' She held up the snuffer. 'Will you or will you not be phoning her again?'

Joel couldn't even remember a Brandy. 'Did I sleep with her?'

Eloise shook her head disapprovingly. 'Once. You don't know who I'm talking about, do you? That's it.' She snuffed out Brandy's flame. 'Fancy being called Brandy anyway. I mean, she had blonde hair, for God's sake; should have named her Egg Nogg.'

The June sun burst through the huge living-room window, threatening to melt the snow on the white-capped peaks of the Nepalese Himalayas photograph. Joel stood looking out on the magic views that surrounded his apartment. He loved to think about women from this spot – especially Candy. They were as mysterious as the landscape. His eyes searched as far as they would go. When he'd first shown Joel round, the estate agent had listed all the mod-cons that Forest Falls Apartments boasted. The air-conditioning, the wooden floors, the immense square footage, the fully kitted-out gymnasium on the ground floor, the security. The blah, blah, blah. 'Just show me the view, please,' Joel had demanded. And he was hooked the moment he saw it. The horizon was a thick shadow of trees encompassing a huge flower-filled park. Horses rode the bridleway that cut through the centre of the magnificent green, and to the left was an old castle ruin – just visible on a clear day. One could get lost dreaming of the past from here – Hobbits must have lived in these parts once – and one could definitely get lost thinking about women here, that's for sure! Lost and lazy. Joel raised his arms above his head and stretched, knowing he should head downstairs for a fitness session. Living on top of a gym left little room for excuses. And in the world of mountaineering, along with paying close attention to your diet, if you didn't spend enough time working out, building up your grip strength, stamina, suppleness and general robustness, then no mountain in the world would pay heed to the line, 'I didn't realize extra training was necessary,' as you plummeted to the ground below. No, there were no excuses.

Eloise joined him at the window. 'I'm going to mention another girl's name. She phoned a few days ago. Holly. You've not slept with her . . . yet. She confirmed that Saturday night is good for her and that "yes" she loves Indian food. And don't worry, I'll make myself scarce.'

Joel smiled, Saturday should be fun, and with a name like Holly he just hoped she wasn't too prickly in bed. He chuckled at his own joke.

Now, where did he leave Zarleena's cooking instructions? His record for losing something in his apartment was two days (how his car keys got in Eloise's Prada handbag, he'd never know); today was Monday, surely his record would remain intact. From Monday until Tuesday evening Joel tried the 'It will turn up' technique of location. By Tuesday night, Joel was onto the 'I will remember where I left it in my sleep' technique. By Wednesday morning Joel was on to the 'You can stick it up your backside, because I don't give a shit any more' technique. If only Joel had tried the 'Have you got it, Eloise?' technique, he might have been more successful. It wasn't the only thing of Joel's that she hid under her pillow.

Wednesday was traditionally half day down Hunterslea High Street. A letter of condemnation from a few shops had been presented to Zarleena and Honey a few months back, berating them for flouting the town's 200-year-old tradition by remaining open all day. Mr Turnsdale, the butcher, even went so far as to write:

> *In consideration for your religion I had the whole pig removed from our window display. As you seem to ignore our own traditions, the pig will be returning (this time with an apple in its mouth).*

Unfortunately for Mr Turnsdale, both Zarleena and Honey loved pork. It was the cow that was sacred to Hindus, not the pig; but the chances of Mr Turnsdale having a whole cow displayed in the window (mouth stuffed with a melon) were pretty slim. Although, from time to time, his fair wife, Mrs Turnsdale, could be seen behind the glass stocking up on sausages.

Zarleena stood at the till, the shelves beneath looking more like an armoury each day. Since Honey had mentioned that Zarleena's husband, Armin, was out to make a nuisance of himself again, weapons had been stashed. One large carving knife, two barbeque skewers, a brick, a small jar of battery acid, one picture of Lesley Ash, another picture of a fish, and a heavy metal statue of the peace-loving God, Parvati. Oh yeah, and an air rifle. A woman's imagination acknowledges no boundary when working out revenge on a wife-beater.

Mrs Lorena Bobbitt lacked artistic integrity as far as Honey was concerned; she should have made him cut off his own willy – while she gave him encouragement by rubbing a blade against his throat. Zarleena had to put her foot down, though, when Honey phoned the RSPCA enquiring about guard dogs, rattlesnakes and killer bees.

A police siren wailed outside and Honey and Zarleena skidded to the window, shoving a sari-clad mannequin to one side; their noses pressed tight to the pane, eyes searching down the High Street for a disturbance.

'Can't see anything,' Honey said, annoyed. 'This town is too well behaved for trouble.'

Zarleena nodded. From the time they moved here from Colchester nearly a year ago and opened the shop, the closest thing to trouble in the town was a broken water main. Boy, how the street talked about that burst pipe. People went out panic-buying Evian, just in case. Mothers took their children for extra jabs. Swimming pools were only half filled. Could it be Armageddon?

Suddenly Zarleena gasped, pointing to the right. 'Smoke, blimey, look!'

Sure enough, smoke could be seen billowing upwards in the near distance. Another siren sounded as a fire engine shot past. Honey had a thing about men in uniform (she also had a thing about men *not* in uniform as well), and her knees nearly gave way.

'Look at them, Zarleena, rushing to the unknown, risking their lives to save others. I marched outside

43

Downing Street for their wages, I spent hours making banners – FAIR PAY FOR FIREMEN – but it doesn't make the flames less hot, does it?' She put her hand on her sister's shoulder. 'I think it's time we cooked the station a meal again. Cheer them up.'

Zarleena tutted. 'You mean it's about time you saw your fantasy men again? Remember it's not the length of the hose, it's what he does with it.'

Various gags about what a fireman could do with his hose were interrupted by the sound of coughing in the shop. Standing near the till, holed up inside a huge sari, was a middle-aged Indian woman. The forgotten customer. She smiled sweetly, fearful of imposing, but also eager to leave the shop; she waved a packet of bindis in the air keen to let the girls know that with her huge expenditure their business would never go under.

'That will be ninety pence, Aunti-ji.' Zarleena keyed in the amount. 'And sorry about keeping you waiting.'

'Nonsense, it's a pleasure to wait in such a shop,' she replied, dropping the ten-pence change in a charity box: ASIAN WOMEN'S HOSTEL. 'I must be off now, *namaste*.'

'*Namaste*.'

Sometimes the shop seemed full of Indian women just like aunti-ji, browsing around, enjoying the Indian home from home. Zarleena had even installed a second clock on the wall displaying the correct time in Delhi. Purses and wallets emptied more readily when under the influence of India's gravity. The pull of their homeland fuelled their nostalgia, which in turn encouraged them to spend more. And even on this quiet Wednesday afternoon, the till groaned with a full belly.

The quiet was soon broken by an excited Honey, who was still standing at the shop window, but now punching the air, screaming, 'Pink turban, pink turban.' Her eyes were wide with joy at spotting this rarest of rare sights.

Zarleena confirmed the finding and shook Honey's well-deserving hand. 'Congratulations, sis, top marks.'

Out of view of the customers – well out of view – was a chart. Its name: THE TURBAN RAINBOW. It was a sort of I-Spy for turbans. Pink was an extremely sought-after colour and put Honey ahead in the ratings.

'I would split the points but I only need a gold and a chequered blue and I've won. The only way I can see you taking the title is by a visit to a temple, either that or . . .' Honey stopped talking, her words transformed to dribbles. She became as still as the mannequin she was standing next to, transfixed by the man walking up the street towards their shop. There were two reasons he looked out of place. One, he was far too gorgeous to be in this town. Honey held her breath as he stood at the shop window staring right at her. Did he know she was real? She dared not move a muscle as his eyes explored her body. And, she wasn't an expert by any stretch of the imagination, but she was sure this would have been the first mannequin that this hunky man had ever seen with nipples becoming harder as he watched. He knocked on the window, but it was too late to be a real person now – she would have to stay a statue.

He shook his head and entered Bindis & Brides, stamping his feet hard on the welcome mat. 'Sorry about the ash,' he said, taking a few steps in.

Zarleena eyed him up and down. Here was the other reason he looked out of place in Hunterslea: the man appeared to have come straight off a bonfire and he smelled like a used firework. She guessed that the original colour of his T-shirt had been white; and finally here was someone wearing a pair of combat bottoms who looked as though they'd seen some. Despite the Guy Fawkes overtones he was still the best-looking man she'd ever seen – and more importantly, it wasn't the first time she'd seen him either.

'Hello, Joel,' Zarleena said, wondering why, considering the state Joel was in, she felt badly dressed. 'Have you been involved in some sort of fire?'

Joel studied his melted Nike trainers. 'No, why do you ask?'

Honey struggled not to giggle. Her back was becoming sore standing like she was, if only Zarleena could take the hunk to the back of the shop she could slip from the mannequin position. It beat her how Zarleena knew him anyway. And if he thought that partially cremating himself Hindu-style was going to impress her sister, he had a lot to learn.

'I don't suppose you get many white people in here?' supposed Joel, following Zarleena to the middle of the shop.

'We don't get many grey people, either,' she replied, which set the mannequin off giggling again. 'Would you like me to fetch you a towel?'

Joel looked puzzled. 'You want me to cover my head? Like a turban?'

Zarleena explained patiently that the towel was to wipe away the soot covering his face. Honey slipped from the window, hid behind a rack of shawls, and threw on a bright green sari. She didn't want Joel to know she was the mannequin. She then scrambled on all fours to the other end of the shop, and appeared like magic from under the counter a few feet away from Zarleena and Joel. As usual when talking to a man, her first words did not make this her proudest moment.

'Crikey you stink,' she said, then felt awash with rudeness. 'I mean, er, what happened to you?'

After being introduced, Joel explained about the fire. It hadn't even occurred to the sisters that the smoke they'd seen earlier might be connected to Joel's burnt image in some way. He described how an innocent car journey had turned into a journey from hell. Dante's worst nightmare. As he'd minded his own business on one side of the road, a caravan exploded on the other. An inferno called his name.

'I didn't stop to think, for all I knew someone was in there.' Joel thought back to the adrenalin rush of kicking down the caravan door and diving inside. 'I was scared shitless, but I couldn't just leave them to fry.'

Zarleena stared at this selfless man. 'But you could have died.'

He smiled. 'Exactly. I could have died.'

'But no one died?' Honey asked, concerned.

'Nope, it was empty. An insurance job most likely. I even checked the cupboards for kittens. I've never given mouth-to-mouth to a kitten before but I would have if I had to.'

The girls were overwhelmed by Joel. His heroics were something they hadn't come across since Uncle-ji Jugderpreet, while on a cheap cruise, agreed to sleep on the bottom of a bunk bed, while his twenty-stone wife slept on top. Honey offered to fetch Joel a T-shirt from round the back of the shop, just to borrow until he got home. It was a spare from a peace rally over the Iraq war and showed a picture of Bush and Blair smiling, with the words THE REAL WEAPONS OF MASS DESTRUCTION! printed above them. Joel whipped off his singed top and flung on the spare.

'It doesn't fit,' Zarleena stated, almost dribbling with lust. 'You'll have to take it off and stand there for about forty-five minutes while we look for another one. Come on.' She held out her hands for his T-shirt, desperate to see his fit, fit, fit fuck-me body again. 'Quick, quick.'

Honey had other ideas, preferring the hands-on approach, tugging and yanking, ripping if necessary, frenzied. 'Great Durga in heaven, how did you get a body like this?'

'Climbing mountains and a lot of sweat in the gym,' he replied, holding tight to his combat bottoms, his mountaineering grip coming in handy. 'And the top fits fine, thank you.' He stepped backwards. 'Just fine.'

The sisters felt slightly cheated, and even slightly worried at their own behaviour. During the T-shirt battle, Honey had even suggested, in Hindi, that Zarleena should fetch the air rifle and force Joel to undress. Slightly ashamed of their antics, the sisters returned to being good Indian girls, leaving the nymphomaniacs to fester inside their heads. It was only good fortune that had kept customers from entering the shop during Joel's spontaneous strip, or goodness knows what excuse they would have had to think up.

'So, what can we do for you, Joel?' Zarleena asked, pretending to be busy with a calculator.

'I would like to discuss a proposition with you,' he replied, turning Zarleena's calculator up the right way for her.

'And what is this proposition? Nothing to do with matches, I hope?'

'I was wondering if you've got time for a coffee? Ned's Fried Fill Ups is open. The steak sandwich he does is ace.' He winced. 'Sorry, I mean the bacon sarni is ace. I know you're allergic to beef.'

The girls giggled, how romantic. Ned's Fried Fill Ups. This man had class.

Zarleena pondered for a while. 'Would you mind if my sister and I talked in Hindi for a moment? We need to discuss whether you might be a rapist or a weirdo.'

Joel agreed and watched an animated discussion take place. Most of the words were gobbledygook with the odd 'Peter Sutcliffe', 'Jason Voorhees', 'Pinhead The Lead Cenobite' and 'Michael Myers' thrown in for good measure. This was a tough decision for the sisters. From their eyes, a gorgeous man they hardly know waltzes into their shop and asks to discuss a 'proposition' over a coffee. And it was true that Zarleena had helped him out once before with instructions for cooking a traditional Indian meal for his girlfriend, Claudia, but could he be trusted? And now he was here smelling like a bush fire. Instincts told the sisters that Joel was harmless. A coffee in a public place – what could possibly go wrong?

Zarleena spoke to Joel. 'Well, if we're eating at Ned's, I'd better wear something designer. Honey, do you know where I left my Gucci bin liner?' She grabbed her handbag from under the counter and kissed her sister on the cheek. 'Back soon.'

Joel smiled at Honey. 'When we're gone, I take it you'll be returning to the window display as a dummy. If so, may I make a suggestion? Don't chew on your chewing gum.'

'May I make one as well?' Honey thinned her eyes. 'Next time you're in a burning caravan, don't bother coming back out. Goodbye.' She giggled noticing the back of Joel's T-shirt. It read: ASIAN WOMEN AGAINST BOMBS. It's a good job, she thought, he wasn't wearing any of her other masterpieces. One of her favourites read: WOMEN HATE WARS. THE ONLY BLOOD THEY SPILL IS PERIOD.

Chapter Six

The walk from halfway up Hunterslea High Street to the end would normally take fifteen minutes when sober. In high-heeled *chappals* and a draping beetroot-coloured *shalwar kameez*, it took for ever. Joel sighed with relief as Zarleena crossed the finishing line just in front of Ned's Fried Fill Ups, the very last building on the road. The café had been in business for years, catering for truckers and holiday makers passing through. Like Bindis & Brides it stayed open all day on Wednesday. Unlike Bindis & Brides the money in Ned's till always smelled of smoky bacon – as opposed to ylang-ylang joss sticks.

'What does the Ned's Special include?' Zarleena asked, pointing to the blackboard on the pavement. 'Eat all you want for *fifty pence*. Sounds a bit cheap.'

Joel led her inside, promising to reveal all about the 'Ned's Special' once they had found a table. They sat by the window looking out to Jesus Christ church diagonally across the road.

During the thirty-five-minute walk to Ned's, Joel had

51

explained that even though he had lost Zarleena's number the whereabouts of her workplace wasn't a mystery, considering she'd answered the phone a week or so ago with the words 'Bindis & Brides Shop'. He was ashamed to admit that he actually thought one could purchase an Indian bride from there. A bit like a mail-order bride from the Philippines.

'It's a good job we were open, or it would have been a wasted journey,' Zarleena said, sipping her coffee. 'I think only this café and us are open on a Wednesday.'

Joel whispered, 'Ned's such a stingy bastard, there's no way he would close on Wednesdays. He's a modern-day Scrooge, Dickens would be proud.' He rubbed his fingers through his hair, loosening the ash and soot onto the table. 'Are my eyebrows still there?'

She giggled. 'Yes, both of them. So . . . are you implying that my sister and I are stingy then?'

'No, you're different. Different rules apply to you. Everyone knows Indians work seven days a week, fifty-three weeks a year. It's normal. It's in your blood. And to be honest, I would have felt a bit let down if I'd found you closed today. You must hold on to your culture.' He washed down his huge smile with a gulp of Red Bull. 'Good stuff this. You're a very successful race of people. And fucking good cooks as well.'

Ned heard that, and assumed the comment was being directed at him. He'd make sure that table got an extra helping of lard in their lunch. This is why he loved being a chef, the generous compliments from satisfied customers made it all worth while. He wiped the spatula on his dirty apron and tossed in another lump of pig's fat.

Joel had noticed a couple of soldiers tucked away in a greasy corner, who were occasionally glancing their way and he tried his hardest not to whistle a Status Quo song, 'We're in the Army Now'. More than likely they were from the Colchester Barracks, and more than likely they took their inspiration from Rambo films. The moment they signed up for the army, they swapped all their expletives for one word: 'Civvy'. The number of times Joel and his mates had been called a 'Civvy' he'd lost count. He always thought fuckface was so much better as an insult. Two plates arrived, one toasted bacon sarni for Joel and a fried egg sandwich for Zarleena.

About to tuck into his meal, Joel became aware of Zarleena staring towards the kitchen, a slight grimace across her face. 'What's up?' he enquired. 'Checking that the eggs are halal eggs?'

She laughed. Was this man serious? Halal eggs? 'No, I was wondering why Ned was fishing out bits of left-over food from that brown bucket and placing them on a clean plate.'

Joel smirked. 'If you wait a second you'll find out.' He watched Ned shake off some beans stuck to half a sausage.

Sure enough, a few seconds later, Ned heated up the plate in the microwave oven then served it to a gentle-man a few tables away. It was the 'Ned Special'. All the leftover food you could eat for fifty pence.

Zarleena felt sick and handed her partly bitten egg sandwich to a grateful Joel.

'Anyway,' Joel began, 'back to my proposition. My love life improved radically because of you the other

53

day. Claudia did things to me in the bedroom that . . .'
Joel noticed Zarleena's embarrassment. 'You get the
picture. I know for sure she wouldn't have done half
what she did if I hadn't cooked that meal. You're to
thank for that. Now, my proposition is this. I pay *you*
to cook Indian meals for *me*.'

'Excuse me?'

'Think of it as your contribution to romance. I
noticed your shop has a charity box on the counter,
think of my bedroom as your new charity. I'm sure
Holly is the one for me, I just need to prove to her I can
cook.'

'Holly? I thought I was helping you with Claudia the
other day. You said in the supermarket that love wasn't
a strong enough word to describe how you felt about
Claudia. Now it's *Holly*?'

Joel stuffed in the egg sandwich. Shit! Women's
names were the bane of his life. Think, think, think.
He'd forgotten how convincing he had been back in the
supermarket that day, laying it on thicker than peanut
butter, explaining to Zarleena how much he loved
Holly, no, how much he loved Claudia, just so she
would help him with the Indian meal.

'Holly,' Joel said, deliberately, nervously, 'is her
handle for the chat room I met her in.' He gave himself
an internal high-five. 'Claudia is her real name. I love
her so much. If I could impress her just that little bit
more – maybe we could do a starter this time, or something with less garlic – then I'm sure she will say yes
when I ask her to marry me. If she says no, then I may
as well be dead.'

Zarleena felt goose bumps marching up her spine.

This was a genuine call for help here. A cry in the dark. For a man to want a woman's hand in marriage so much that he is willing to pay a virtual stranger to cook a . . .

'How many courses do you want?' she asked.

'Three.'

. . . to cook a three-course meal, he must be head over *chappals* in love. She couldn't let him down now. Love might not have visited her marriage, but if she could help someone else with love, then she would. A deal was brokered. She would come to his place on Saturday morning and prepare a three-course Indian meal for his date with Claudia. She asked for no cash just an invite to the wedding.

'Obviously, you'll clear it with your husband first?' Joel said, looking at her wedding ring.

She nodded. 'Obviously.'

A loud cheer erupted as the café door burst open. Three more soldiers entered and searched around for an empty table. Unsuccessful, they lumbered over to the corner where they squatted on the floor by the other squaddies.

'Oi, Civvies,' one shouted out to no one in particular. 'Where's your manners? Where's your respect?' No response was forthcoming. 'Someone get me a fucking chair! I risked my life for you lot, I risked my fucking balls in Afghanistan. And I come back here and no one can get off their fat arses and offer me their chair.'

Another soldier spoke. 'Leave it, Spud, have mine.' He stood up and pushed a red-faced Spud into his seat. 'Come on, not today, just one day without a fight, hey?'

Spud made growling noises, his fists opening and clenching, itching for trouble. His dad had fought for Britain, his granddad had fought for Britain; his family had nothing to be ashamed of. They had red, white and blue flowing through their veins. Unlike that bastard sitting over there with the Indian woman. Spud eyed him with hatred. How dare he sit there with combat bottoms on? Had he ever witnessed heads being blown off on the battlefield? When was the last time he sucked on the barrel of a gun? When was the last time he wrote a will? His anger got the better of him and he strode over to Joel and Zarleena's table . . .

Armin, Zarleena's husband, loved the power he felt behind the wheel of a motor. His testosterone doubled as soon as his foot hit the accelerator. Prem, his cousin, sat beside him in the car, fearful of what mood Armin might be in if things turned out badly today.

'Pay attention, Prem, let me show you how fickle women can be.' Armin eyed the two blondes driving just in front. 'Watch their mood change as I ram them.'

Prem prepared himself for the collision and felt the car swerve sharply into the back of the blondes who suddenly turned their heads, slightly shocked, slightly whiplashed. Armin rammed them aggressively again and again and again, enjoying the women's screams, enjoying the fear in their eyes. There was no let-up. And he was correct: the women's mood *had* now changed; their swearing could be heard in Frinton.

'That's enough! Out, you're wrecking the fun for everyone else.' The hippy-looking man, who ran the bumper car rides on Clacton-on-Sea's pier, shook his head. There was always one. But normally he was too young to vote.

Grudgingly Armin and Prem left the ride, snapped on their shades, and walked to the end of the wooden pier where bearded anglers were casting out to sea. Armin breathed in the salty air as the sun beat down on his head.

'You'll need this.' Armin passed a photograph of Zarleena across. 'See how false she is? Smiling in the photo, but ten minutes later she's back-chatting me in the kitchen. She had it easy with me, Prem, maybe I should have been stricter on her. In India she would have been burnt alive for the behaviour she adopted.' Armin bent down, picked up a crab and tossed it to the sea below – it had taken the poor critter two years to get up there.

Prem tucked the picture in his jacket pocket. He'd heard every story there was to hear of Armin's two-year marriage (three years if one included this last year of being separated) and how Zarleena had become too Westernized. No doubt about it, Armin had struggled to keep her happy. But how long can a man continue to lavish his wife with gifts and love when she won't even show him affection in the bedroom? How hard it must have been for poor Armin to come in late from work to find a note on the table: *Dial yourself dinner*. What torture Armin must have gone through to discover telephone bills listing numbers he never recognized? The final insult was to find a pregnancy test in the bin, knowing full well he hadn't slept with her in months? How much could an Indian man take? And all those rumours that Armin used to beat her, Prem never believed those for one second. He'd only ever seen Armin behave like a gentleman towards Zarleena. He asked him now, 'Why are you so keen to find her again, Armin? Especially after all she has put you through.' And his answer, the only answer really, left Prem deeply moved. 'I love her, Prem, she is my wife.'

But there was one other answer that Armin might have given. The real reason why he wanted to meet up with his feeble wife again. The truth.

Armin lobbed another crab into the sea, then apologized to the fisherman for throwing back his catch. 'Come on, we have a long day ahead of us.'

The two cousins walked back along the pier to their car. It shouldn't be too hard locating Zarleena. She was a creature of habit, most likely still frequenting the same shops and restaurants that she had before she and Armin had married. One thing was as certain as death though, Zarleena would never move too far from her mother and sister. The Indian men drove along the sea front, keeping an eye out for cheap B&Bs then took the road that would lead them to Hunterslea.

Armin throttled it down the dual carriageway, his heartbeat a steady 180. A cold and nasty smile crept along his lips. It had been a couple of weeks since he'd turned up at Zarleena's parents' house. For the life of him he couldn't understand why Zarleena's mum looked so terrified that he was back. He was hardly going to hit the mother now, was he?

It was her daughter he wanted.

Spud stared down at Joel. 'Civvy!'

'Fuckface,' Joel replied, his voice a loud echo in

Ned's Fried Fill Ups. Was this the start of the Colchester soldiers invading Hunterslea? He hoped not.

Spud tensed up. 'You know what you are, sitting there with a Muslim woman? You're a traitor. It's us against them; the world's changed since 9/11. You do know we're at war now, don't you?'

'You mean with Alka Seltzer?'

Spud turned to his posse in the corner. 'Got a joker 'ere.' He faced Joel. 'Al-Qaeda. The unseen enemy. I don't like the tone of your clothes either.' Spud could read reasonably well. 'I drive a fucking tank and you wear a T-shirt that supports Asian women against bombs. I come home a hero and see shit like that it makes me want to—'

Joel interrupted, 'Just fuck off! I'm trying to talk Weapons of Mass Destruction with my Muslim informer here. Do you know how hard it is to get good weapons-grade plutonium nowadays? It's a bitch, I can tell you. Even getting hold of the aluminium pipes was a headache.' He eyed the soldier. 'Are you still here, Action Man?'

Action Man was, but he wasn't listening any more. It was Zarleena's attention he wanted now. What he considered the true grime in this café. 'Don't you feel ashamed wearing that colour skin? It's funny how brown keeps cropping up when war is mentioned, don't you think? Think Iraq, think Iran, think Zimbabwe, think Kashmir, think Sri Lanka.' He sneered, with an up-turned chin. 'Lost your voice, Brownie? Left it in your mud hut?'

Yes, Zarleena *had* lost her voice. It was crawling around somewhere with her courage. This wasn't the first time she'd been at the receiving end of man's most dangerous weapon, and it wasn't the first time she'd prayed for the ground to open and swallow her either. And yet, one might think an Indian woman would be prepared for such abuse. Ready with a quick poison-tipped comment to blow back in their face. Practised and primed for the moment some sod tried to make her feel three-foot tall when she would be ready to answer the ugly mouth back. And Zarleena *was* always ready in her mind, but when it came to the delivery, her vocabulary had gone AWOL. With her bravery some-where missing in action.

Joel stood up and faced Spud. 'Leave her alone, you racist twit. It's people like you who make me ashamed of my colour, and yet you're so proud of your white skin, aren't you? The colour that travelled half the globe, sacking villages, pillaging whole com-munities. Or maybe the white race that stole the Red Indians' land in America. Or even the white-skinned lot that fucked around with India until it had had enough, then left leaving their bloody footprints on an entire people.' He paused. 'And let's not even go into Hitler.'

'But we invented everything.'

'And we destroy everything. Heard of the Atom Bomb?'

A voice shot out, 'Come on, Spud, drop it, you're making an arse of yourself again.' One of the soldiers gave Zarleena and Joel a look of apology. 'Sorry about him. It's just Spud being a spud.'

And this small skirmish ended with the soldiers departing for their afternoon roll call.

'Thanks,' Zarleena said, still shaking slightly. 'It goes in one ear and out the other though.'

Joel knew that not to be true. 'Exactly, who listens to root vegetables anyway?'

She smiled. 'Exactly.'

The wall clock above the counter showed 2.15 p.m. Joel and Zarleena had been together for over an hour and a half, and Saturday's menu hadn't been discussed yet. It was time to get down to the nitty gritty. Zarleena listed the Indian dishes she could cook and asked Joel to select the ones he thought Claudia would like. Ned listened in jealously, thinking about adding an Indian dish to his menu now. He just hoped that lard would suffice instead of *ghee*; his customers were pretty finicky when it came to quality food, he thought, rinsing the ketchup off the bacon and laying it carefully on a plate.

'So, how much garlic is in the Garlic Chicken?' Joel asked. 'I'm a bit concerned that we won't want to kiss each other after that.'

'Well, if you both eat the same, you'll both smell the same. It shouldn't affect any kissing, Joel.'

He wasn't convinced. 'And another thing, just stop me when you think I'm being too fussy but what if, after the *saag*, she has spinach stuck in her teeth. It's quite a turn-off, you know?'

She huffed, watching a lorry park outside. 'If you love her like you say you do, surely a little bit of green spinach stuck between her teeth won't matter.'

'No, you're right. I'll just get her to brush it off. It's no big deal. It's better than having a fucking great tiger prawn stuck there like I might have if I was cooking a

Chinese. And anyway, her teeth are so perfect, I don't think she's got any gaps. It shouldn't be a problem, you're right.' Joel glanced at a picture of Ned's wife hanging on the wall. A sure advocate of lard if ever there was one. 'So, let's work out wages.'

'No.' Zarleena thought back to the cheap pink bra she'd seen him buy in Tesco – obviously a present for this Claudia (poor girl). His scruffy jeans that day spoke of the DSS. How could she demand money from him? 'Look, like I said before, just a simple invite to your wedding would be nice—'

He interrupted, 'How does £200 sound? That's for cooking and nothing else. I wouldn't expect you to carve a carrot into a flower or anything like that.'

'That's Chinese food.'

'Chinese?'

'Yes, we Indians carve mangos into elephants,' Zarleena said, holding a straight face. 'Anyway, I'll be happy if you just made a donation to the Asian Women's Hostel. It's a foundation I feel very strongly about and . . .' Suddenly Zarleena ducked under the table.

Joel was reminded of a similar situation. A few years ago, while on a small climbing expedition in the Himalayas, tragedy had struck. One minute he had been talking to his mate on Mount Kanchenjunga. The next his mate was gone. The only word he'd heard, as his mate tumbled below him, was 'Avalanche!' Joel had jumped sideways, nearly breaking his leg, but saving himself. People only disappeared that quickly in an emergency. But what kind of emergency was Zarleena's? He peered under the table and was shocked to see Zarleena had, figuratively speaking, turned white.

'Fit? Are you having a fit?' He examined her wide eyes. 'Don't you go dying on me now, you hear?'

Even though Zarleena was shaking anyway, she shook her head at Joel. Fear knotted up her body as nerves ran riot. Not only was she having trouble digesting a nibble of Ned's egg sandwich, but now she was having trouble digesting what she had just seen outside the café. Prem, her husband's cousin, was standing just a few metres away. And Zarleena knew wherever Prem was, her husband was not too far behind.

She spoke quietly, 'Can you tell me when the Asian man has left, please? He was hanging around by the church a second ago.'

Joel obliged. Across the road, sure enough, stood an Asian man. It looked as though he was holding a photograph in his hand. Joel watched as the guy stopped a passer-by and showed him the picture. No joy as the passer-by shrugged and walked on down the street. Joel relayed the man's movements to Zarleena as she stayed hidden under the table.

Zarleena felt the teeth of her wedding ring bite hard on her finger. Married Indians were not supposed to split. 'To death do us part' never meant more than in an Indian coupling. Such is the stigma of separation that dying is the only honourable way to split up. Bringing Zarleena to her next worry. Maybe Armin wanted her dead now. Maybe Armin had found another woman for a punch bag and had decided it was high time Zarleena hit the high road for good.

'He's sitting on the church wall looking down the road,' whispered Joel. 'Looks like he's talking to himself.

Maybe he's got a hands-free mobile. I'd strangle him just for that. I see them on the tube sometimes—'

She switched off from Joel – if he could just stick to the facts! – and thought deeper about what might be happening. Okay, the warning had come a couple of weeks ago. Since then, both Honey and she had been up late some nights planning what to do if Armin came banging on the shop door. This shouldn't be a total surprise. But what could he want? Reconciliation? A divorce? Was he here just to wreck her life some more? The last present from her husband was a delivery of a small package to her parents' house. She'd opened it to find a sheep's eye weeping on a bed of cotton wool. The accompanying note said: *Happy 3rd Wedding Anniversary. I'll be seeing you.*

'He's crossing the road right now, Zarleena. He's coming towards the café.'

Her heart tightened like a fist. 'Okay, thanks.'

'I think he's coming in. Just stay there.'

When the Indian guy had spotted the café, he reminded Joel of a cat clocking a bird's nest. He'd watched as the man crossed the road, a new swagger in his step, a sense of purpose in his eyes. And Joel wondered. He wondered why a lovely woman like Zarleena would be frightened of such a man. Casually Joel turned his head as the café door opened. Many faces stared towards the Asian man at the doorway. Within a second Joel had joined him.

'What's up? I saw you loitering outside, looking for something?' Joel stood awkwardly in the way, legs wide apart, hands on hips. He would be a difficult man to pass.

Prem handed Joel the picture. 'I'm looking for my sister. I haven't seen her in years but I know she lives down this way.' He eyed Joel. 'Been in a fire?'

Joel studied the photograph of Zarleena. 'Very pretty. I think I'd remember seeing someone like that down here.' He took a quick scan round the café, then pointed to the roughest-looking customer. 'That's the pedigree we get in this town. It's only a small town. Everyone knows everyone down here. Travelled far have you?'

'Far enough. So, you haven't seen her then?'

'Like I said, I never miss a pretty woman's face. Try Ipswich. It's rife with Indians. You can't move five feet without bumping into one. You go in smelling of Echo aftershave and by the time you come out you stink of curry.'

Confidently, Joel returned to his seat, unwittingly giving Prem a perfect view of the back of his T-shirt: ASIAN WOMEN AGAINST BOMBS. Prem sneered at Joel before departing for the street outside. The sooner the old rules returned for Asian women the better, he thought; they had far too much voice these days.

And in a very rushed voice, Zarleena, still under the table, phoned her sister at the shop telling her to close up for the day. Prem was one customer that Bindis & Brides could well do without.

Chapter Seven

America achieved independence in 1776
Iceland achieved independence in 1944
Pakistan achieved independence in 1947
India achieved independence in 1947

Zarleena achieved independence in 2004. The year Armin packed his bags and left her.

And independence for any child born to Asian parents is the proverbial pot of gold at the end of the rainbow. Unfortunately for Zarleena, her pot of gold came with a hefty price tag. Two years of misery and abuse. Keeping the bruises a secret was sometimes more painful than the bruises themselves. Dying to tell her parents that the fine gentleman they chose to be her husband was a monster. Afraid to tell her parents that the man they chose *was* a monster, for fear of dying.

'We have let you down, Zarleena,' her mum had sobbed, when at last finding out the truth about Armin. 'We have brought great misery into your life. And to think we turned down two other candidates because we thought they looked cruel and uncaring. What's that old saying? "You can never trust a book by its blurb."'

With their confidence in choosing partners stripped away, Zarleena's parents decided to do away with arranged marriages. From that moment on both daughters would be free to find the partner of their desire. Hard as it was to toss away Indian tradition, harder still was it to visualize Zarleena kneeling on her kitchen floor begging Armin to stop kicking her.

So, in 2004, Zarleena became independent and she hadn't looked back. Until now.

Zarleena parked the small white van in a guest bay of Forest Falls Apartments just as Joel had asked, and smiled proudly at the van's logo, BINDIS & BRIDES. The future was bright: the harder Honey and Zarleena grafted, it seemed, the higher the wattage. The girls worked alternate Saturdays in the shop, with extra help by way of a shop assistant called Shimla. Honey normally chose to spend her free Saturdays organizing marches and Zarleena normally spent her free Saturdays eating chocolate and burning the calories on the stepper. Normally.

But today was far from normal. Zarleena took in the amazing building; each brick, each balcony, each huge window said one thing: rich people live here. It was in one of the most sought-after areas in Hunterslea, and something within was wishing she had made more of an effort with her clothes. A pink and white tracksuit with matching trainers looked quite cool on an athletics field, but in a luxury apartment, with her hair tied back in a small ponytail, she most likely resembled the cleaner. She headed inside with a large cardboard box under her arm.

In Reception, Sammy, the guard who rarely talked, was stuck on a crossword puzzle and had promised himself that the next person who came through the door he would ask for help.

'Morning,' uttered Sammy to Zarleena as she entered.

'Morning.'

'And how can I help you on this most wonderful of warm days?'

'I'm here to see Joel Winters.'

Sammy nodded knowingly. Another hussy for Joel. 'I see he's got you spellbound, has he? Just because he does a little bit of TV and stars in the odd Hollywood movie. It doesn't make him more of a man by the mere fact that he can climb higher than me, you know. And while we're on the topic of records, do you happen to know the British Queen's first name?'

Zarleena noted the *Sun* newspaper in the security guard's hand. 'Elizabeth. Queen Elizabeth.'

The guard scribbled on the paper. 'No, you're wrong, it doesn't fit. I've been struggling all morning with this one. Any other ideas?'

'Freddie Mercury!' And she left the guard floundering with his puzzle, as she caught the lift to Joel's penthouse, wondering what Sammy meant by Hollywood movies. Slowly but surely Joel was becoming something of a puzzle himself.

Standing in the plush-carpeted corridor outside the apartment, Zarleena felt like she was on the gangway of a luxury liner, about to embark on a cruise to who knows where. For some reason she knew romance wasn't a cargo of this ship. But it didn't stop her wanting to know Joel a whole lot better. The man who had stuck up for her in Ned's café two days ago.

Underneath Joel's ignorant exterior was a deeper man. An intelligent, kind and caring person. His throwaway comments about Indians were just that, throwaway comments; tongue-in-cheek remarks; harmless and mostly innocent. How would Joel know that eggs did not come in the halal variety? Or did they? She didn't even know herself.

One thing for sure though, Joel seemed a lot more mature than most men she'd met. He didn't camouflage his emotions in ego. How many straight men would happily divulge their inner thoughts about love? She had sat engrossed as Joel explained his deep love for Claudia. And when he had described how he'd nearly died making a blood pact with her by accidentally severing a vein in his wrist, tears had appeared in Zarleena's eyes. If only a man could love her like Joel loved Claudia. She would be proud to cook a meal that helped set the scene for his marriage proposal to Claudia tonight. Dead proud.

She pressed the doorbell and a huge farting noise exploded (ten seconds long). Zarleena hoped that she didn't have to press it again. Luckily she didn't and the door opened, presenting a spacious-looking living room.

'Come in,' Joel said, taking the heavy box off her, checking out her clothes. 'Did you jog up here?'

'I sprinted actually. I was running away from the smell of garlic until I realized it was in the box.'

Zarleena assessed the room. It scored very highly; huge, modern, clean and manly. She then assessed Joel. She didn't know about huge, he'd have to drop his jeans for that, but he was definitely manly and most certainly clean. 'Nice place. I don't want to sound rude but I had you down as poor. It just shows you, doesn't it?'

'And I had you down as polite,' Joel replied. 'A lady. It just shows you, doesn't it?'

Expecting a grand tour, Zarleena was dismayed to be shown the enormous fitted kitchen, while Joel popped out to talk to a man about a dog. Claudia was expected in seven hours. To cook the meal would require three. Joel had asked what she would do with the remaining four and she had replied as sexily as possible, 'You tell me, Joel.' To which he had said, 'The bath plughole is blocked with my hair. Fancy a challenge?' Not quite what she had in mind. Far more preferable would have been a harmless chat with him, digging a bit deeper with her curious claws, uncovering another piece to his puzzle. And even though the whole purpose of Zarleena being here was to help solder Claudia and Joel's relationship together with Indian spices, she was beginning to feel a small amount of envy poisoning her good nature. So much so in fact that when she heard Joel's phone ringing from the living room, for one small moment she hoped that it was Claudia calling to cancel. It was her duty as a woman to try to listen in. Zarleena stood over the answerphone, a bunch of coriander in one hand.

The machine switched on, '*By the time you hear the end of this message you will be that much nearer to your death. Ask yourself, am I that important in your life that you need to leave a message? Of course I am. Please leave your message and I will try to live long enough to receive it. Cheers, Joel.'*

A well-spoken man's voice began, 'Eloise, it's Dylan, sorry to ring you on *this* phone, you know how I hate ringing here, but your mobile is switched off. I had no choice in the matter. I wish you wouldn't live with him, I really do, it makes my life so complicated. And I know he is my brother and yes we both have the same parents but . . . you know my feelings on this. Even the thought of him listening to my message brings me to boiling point. Please call me as soon as you can. Hugs and kisses.'

So engrossed in listening, Zarleena failed to realize that Joel had returned and was now standing behind her, *Climbing* magazine in his hand.

He coughed. 'Busy?'

Zarleena jumped and dramatically waved the bunch of coriander in Joel's face. 'I need a vase for these. I thought you might have one by your phone. Flowers are a must for a romantic dinner.'

He viewed the droopy green herbs. 'I'll have to empty the vase from last time. It's filled with parsley at the moment.' He walked towards the kitchen. 'I didn't catch the message, who was on the phone?'

'It wasn't for you.'

'It bloody well wasn't for you either.' He paused. 'Sorry. So, who was it?'

'Dylan.' She began snapping the stalks off the spinach leaves. 'You know, your brother?'

Joel's eyes said it all. Hurt. Anger. Betrayal. Regret? And he changed subjects quicker than an Atlantic wind. 'So, did you manage to shake that Indian guy off? I expect if your husband is anything like I am he would have hounded him right out of town.' Joel whistled the tune to a Spaghetti Western. 'Then again, it's none of my business. If you want to tell me who he is, you will. If you don't, you won't.'

And she did want to tell him. Not because he was the Hunterslea version of Clint Eastwood, but because on occasion he talked sense. Instinctively she felt there was something honest and open about him, it was hard to explain; but even though she'd only known him for a short while, he'd already made inroads into her trust. Besides, Joel was obviously smitten with this Claudia, it was clear he only looked upon Zarleena as a friend. She glanced at her wedding band. A married friend. Zarleena thought back to a moment when she had innocently said to Armin that the ring felt a little loose. He'd struck her hand with the handle of a bread knife until it swelled then asked her, 'Does the ring feel loose now?' It had fit tightly ever since. But why did she still wear it after all the bastard had done? A question Honey asked at least once a week. Her answer was simple, even if understanding it was not: I will wear the damn thing as long as Armin and I are still married.

Time pressed on as preparations became more complicated. Joel's offer to help peel the potatoes was ignored. There were no potatoes in tonight's dishes. After receiving the knock-back with the spuds, he decided not to offer any more help and simply stood by the microwave drinking can after can of Red Bull, each crack of a new tin followed by a huge gulp, then a belch, then a comment, 'Good stuff this.' Cooking under these conditions was quite a challenge.

Crack. Gulp. Buuurrrp. 'Good stuff this,' Joel said, reading the back of the can as though he'd never seen one in his life before. 'It's got taurine in it and a hefty shot of caffeine. Who won't be sleeping tonight?' He rummaged in the fridge, eventually pulling out an opened can of tuna. He hoped the tuna tasted better than it smelled. With a fork Joel tucked in, ignoring the back taste, trying to remember how many weeks it had been sitting there. 'If I go into a coma, tell the paramedics it's probably botulism. Okay?'

Zarleena tried to concentrate. 'Joel, could you pass me a couple of cloves of garlic, please.'

Two bulbs were tossed across, narrowly missing her head. As she caught them expertly, Zarleena explained the difference between a 'bulb' of garlic and a 'clove' of garlic. Joel thought back to the Indian dish he had cooked from Zarleena's instructions a couple of weeks ago. If only he had known back then the difference between a bulb and a clove, poor Claudia wouldn't have had to eat the balti flavoured with six bulbs of organic garlic.

And here was the rub with Joel. Making trivial mistakes was quite a big part of his life down here on earth, but up in the mountains, where mistakes mean death, Joel performed perfectly. Reliant on a quarter of an inch precipice, without safety ropes, helmet or harness, one slippery error and Joel would fall to his highest peak – heaven. Cloves and bulbs seemed insignificant at times. Death was such a huge part of Joel's life that practising to avoid it was a must. Bitten by a snake, Joel knew what to do. Electrocuted by a lawnmower, drinking anti-freeze, falling into a diabetic coma, Joel knew what to do. Only last month he was swallowing fish bones, in the hope he would get one caught in his throat, just so his climbing mate could practise the Heimlich manoeuvre on him. Death was a very serious matter in Joel's books.

So was life. Lying back on the vibrating chair, living the life of a king, Joel listened to his beautiful maid singing in the kitchen. Zarleena was proving to be a major plus in his life. After she had finished cooking, Joel had promised to tell her all about the kidney operation he was willing to undergo for Claudia if she ever needed a spare. He'd already told her of the list of body parts he was happy to donate to various friends and relatives while he was still alive if they needed them. He even offered Zarleena his left foot, the only part not reserved, if she lost hers; and explained not to worry about the colour difference, they had great bleaching techniques nowadays. She replied that if she did accept his foot, even though it was four sizes too big, she would not be bleaching her entire body like he had suggested just to match it. Instead, she would spray his donated foot with brown car spray – only then would she chuck it in the bin.

Joel flicked on the TV. ITV and Channel 4 were his favourites, there was always a chance an advert would appear with him in it, up some mountain, advertising some product that had nothing to do with mountaineering. 'Ashamed of your mobile?' said Paul Merton on the screen. Ashamed of myself, more like, thought Joel. How many lies had he told Zarleena to get her here? He'd conned her with trickery of the highest calibre. Or lowest! Innocently cooking a romantic meal for a woman he dumped two weeks ago. If she knew that her culinary skills were being abused just so he could get a shag out of Holly, he doubted she would be here. God, did he feel guilty. Guilty for Zarleena and guilty for Candy.

Zarleena shouted through, 'Do you fancy another Red Bull?'

'Cheers!' So very guilty.

Crack. Gulp. Buuurrrp. 'Good stuff this,' Joel said to a departing Zarleena.

The wonderful smells wafting through the apartment promised a masterpiece of cuisine at the dinner table. Indian food had always tickled Joel's taste buds ever since his first experience of their spices many years ago on a trek in ... Southall. Three of his climbing buddies and he had decided that in order to acclimatize themselves for their Himalayan expedition, Southall was a must. Unfortunately for them, their publicity stunt of walking down the High Street – The Broadway – with oxygen masks on, to raise funds for their Everest trip, did not go down too well with the locals, digging up memories of the police riot gear worn in the 1979 Southall Riots. It's times like that when a white man wishes he was brown.

Joel popped his head in the kitchen. 'Look, I'm going to take a long shower. I know you're probably going to snoop so I've left all the drawers in my bedroom open. Is that okay?' He smiled. 'And, before you ask, the naked pictures of me on the wall were done for charity. I'm not vain, but I looked pretty good, as you'll see.'

She tutted. 'You've got me all wrong. I was only looking for a vase, I was not, as you would love to imagine, listening in to your dreary answerphone. Anyway, what am I going to get out of sneaking through your drawers? Probably find you don't even wash you pants.' She turned on the food processor. 'Must get on. This is taking longer than I thought.'

Zarleena waited until she was sure Joel was in the shower.

Right! Where to begin? She galloped to the bedroom area, leaving the food processor whizzing up mint. In case any visitor was in doubt as to who the female was in Joel's apartment, he had screwed a large sign on Eloise's door: SISTER'S ROOM. Zarleena pushed it to and gasped. A six-foot clay sculpture of a naked man stood by the window. His erect penis was at least a foot and a half long. It had to be really in order for Eloise to hang her clothes off it. Christmas tree lights pulsed around the ceiling casting a rainbow of colours across the walls. And on her walls was the biggest photo collection Zarleena had ever seen. Climbing magazine covers featuring Joel up various mountains. Snapshots of Joel caught in a variety of actions, making the tea, standing at the window, eating KFC; pictures of Joel hanging with his mates, birthday bashes, wedding parties, seemingly catching every movement Joel had ever made. Zarleena had one thought, 'Strange!' She then viewed the other photographs. Thousands upon thousands of people decorating every spare space. If these were her friends, Eloise was Miss Popular. If they were her enemies, it was time to leave town. Quickly, Zarleena left the gallery, walked a few feet, then pushed open Joel's bedroom door. A massive pile of thick socks took centre stage on the messy wooden floor and Zarleena was reminded of a scene in *Close Encounters*. If she remembered rightly the mountain in the film was called Devil's Tower. If men's socks were anything to go by, that pile smelled like devil's breath. Clinging to the window's curtain rail was a piece of string tied at intervals with small, tatty, fading pieces of coloured material covered in script. Zarleena couldn't tell what they were but guessed them to be of some religious significance. The walls were much like most of the walls in the apartment, covered with pictures and paintings of mountains. Disappointingly, no naked picture of Joel. Although, if she stared long enough at his king-sized bed, she was sure her imagination would muster up a naked Joel for her to drool over. Immediately she smothered that hot thought with a fire blanket and turned her attention to the closed drawers. Maybe Joel had said they were open because in his subconscious mind he wanted her to open them.

Stepping over the various ropes, pulleys, boxes of Red Bull, mountaineering books and boots that littered the floor, Zarleena arrived at the bedside drawers. Just a quick look could do no harm. But what if he came in and caught her? Permission given wasn't always permission granted. Problem solved: Zarleena cracked open a Red Bull can and poured a few drops on her hand, dabbing her face and forehead with the pinky liquid. If Joel came in, Zarleena would pretend she had suddenly come over all flushed and sweaty and needed to lie down. The freedom to nose was worth the tacky face.

Inside the top drawer a photograph lay picture-side down. Written on the back were the words:

> *Candy,*
> *My heart bleeds for her internally*
> *it bleeds for her eternally.*

Zarleena flicked it over and stared at the blonde beauty smiling into the lens. Who the hell was Candy? Zarleena thought the photo to be fairly new because it was still sticky, then she realized that the stickiness was coming from her gummy Red Bull fingers. The rest of the drawer held a scattering of romantic snaps, all showing Candy, and most showing Candy with Joel. Good times captured, then hidden away. This was classic behaviour of remorse. It was pretty obvious to Zarleena that the reason Candy had never been discussed was because Candy was dead. The love of his life lost to the thieving hands of *La Mort*. No wonder Joel lived with a death wish. Each day on this world was another spent apart from Candy in her world. It was at times like this that Zarleena wished Indians were known for great puddings as well as tasty main courses, and then she could have made tonight even more special for Joel and his new love. As it was, a fruit salad would have to do.

An hour later, Joel was still showering. Zarleena laid the table, set the candles and warmed up the plates. It was only forty minutes until Claudia was due. Finally he emerged wearing a tight-fitting shirt and a pair of jeans.

'I fell asleep in the shower. Well, more like the bath really.'

'You look gorgeous,' Zarleena said without thinking, then grabbed Joel, giving him a huge hug for the loss of Candy. 'You make sure you have a great evening.'

Taken back, Joel appeared flustered. 'Erm, what wine should I serve with the food? Or maybe just a can of Red Bull each? It's good stuff you know.'

'Good enough to toast your engagement? I don't think so, Joel.'

Oh yes, the engagement. They were so easy to forget these days. It would be quite prudent at a time like this, especially after all the effort Zarleena had invested, to appear excited at the prospect of getting down on one knee. As usual, when in doubt, Joel went over the top.

'You're bloody right, Red Bull isn't worthy enough for my engagement. Even the most expensive champagne in the world would not be good enough for Claudia. I just pray that she says "yes". I don't know if I could cope if she rejected me tonight.' Joel turned and headed into the dining room. 'Wow!' He couldn't believe how beautifully Zarleena had laid out the table. Then he noticed something. 'Erm, why have you set the table for three?'

Zarleena appeared sheepish. 'I thought I could be your host, at least for the first course and then I—'

'NO!'

'I was thinking, I could borrow something of your sister's to wear and serve up drinks and be your personal Indian waitress. Think how impressed Claudia would be; she's bound to say "yes".'

But Joel was saying 'No' and the extra place setting

was hastily removed. Zarleena went through the re-heating instructions for the meal one more time then collected her handbag to leave. In a way she felt almost tearful. Next time she spoke to Joel he would be engaged. And all because of her.

'Before I go, Joel.' Zarleena stood by the door. 'It would mean a lot to me if we took the next step in our friendship and opened up a bit more. Exchanged a few things.'

'Like bodily fluids?'

'No,' she said, giggling. 'You're very secretive, it wouldn't do you any harm to loosen up a little and trust people.' *And tell me all about Candy, she thought.* 'I'm a very good listener.'

He had a little think, then spoke. 'Okay, I'll tell you something. I once left a good friend of mine up a mountain and when I came back nearly a year later he was still there.'

'Oh, that's really sweet, he waited a whole year for you.'

He shook his head. 'No, Zarleena, he was dead. We had to leave him up there or we would all have perished. Is this the sort of thing you want to know? My secretive past.' He walked over to the CD collection and riffled through the discs. 'Now your turn, you tell me something.'

'Okay, right, this is really bad. You mustn't tell a soul.' She waited for Joel to look up. 'A few times when I've run out of clean underwear, I've turned my knickers inside out and worn them dirty.' There, she'd said it.

He stared with an open mouth and wide eyes. 'You what?'

'I have –' Zarleena felt her body heat up with pure embarrassment – 'I have . . . got to go. Bye.' And she opened the door and legged it down the corridor, cringing.

Joel viewed the CD he was about to play and thought: how appropriate. It had been a while since he'd listened to *The Best of The SKIDS*.

Chapter Eight

Most Indian girls who live with their parents have one arm bigger than the other. Constantly stirring *dhal* and chopping coriander causes this lop-sided disability. Some parents wise to this phenomenon encourage their daughters to alternate the arms and thus create equal thickness in their limbs. Many Indian men daren't arm-wrestle a woman with her *dhal* stirring arm for fear of losing credibility in the family.

Giggling, Honey measured Shimla's arms with the tape measure. It had been three years since the nineteen-year-old Bindis & Brides shop assistant had run away from home and her arms were equal at last. She could even wear a T-shirt without provoking laughter now. The girls cheered loudly in celebration. And some of the T-shirts Honey had in mind for her to promote needed to be noticed for the slogan, not because the Indian girl wearing them had a freaky-sized right arm. This is what the two girls had been telling each other since shop closing time, as they slowly became more sloshed with the Bombay Sapphire Gin.

On the maisonette's living-room floor, materials for banners waited to be put together. The girls were due on a march outside Downing Street tomorrow, and suffering from a hangover was all part of the fun. It made the girls shout more angrily.

Zarleena was expected back from Joel's any time soon. Both Honey and Shimla hoped that she would be in the mood to rustle up something in the kitchen. Maybe she might even come back with her lipstick smeared. It was high time Zarleena had a bit of love in her life.

'This is why our marches are so important, Shimy, for people like my sister, abused by their husbands. Just because she was beat up doesn't mean she will shut up.' Honey paused. 'I like that, write it down.'

Shimla added the quote to her growing list. 'I've got one. "You can cut me with a knife but you ain't wasting my life".'

'Not bad. Jot it down anyway, but I don't think we'll be using it.'

She tried again. 'What about, "I may be brown and smell kinda funny but don't treat me bad 'cos I ain't no dummy"?'

They laughed and gulped down more gin. Lately, not a day had gone past without Zarleena's husband, Armin, being mentioned. Was it a cause for concern that he was back? Or wasn't it? Why was he back? One thing for sure though, like a leopard with acne, Armin would never change his spots. But how did he get them in the first place? What makes a man bully his wife? How could someone get thrills from causing fear in others? Honey sometimes felt guilt tapping on her shoulder. An awareness that because of Armin's treatment of Zarleena she now lived without the dread of an arranged marriage. Simply put: because Zarleena got hit, Honey got saved. Was that fair? She would find her conscience doing a whistle-stop tour of her emotions (Buckle up, we're going for a ride!), through sadness, pain, hope and happiness, stopping finally at sisterhood. It reminded Honey of a news programme where one young girl gave up a kidney to save her sister. Zarleena had given up two years of her life to save her. She put up with a monster husband, and not once did she ever complain how he hurt her. Not once did she ever explain how rotten her life had become. And not once did Armin ever show he loved her. And most painful of all for Zarleena's family, she never told them about any of it.

Not once.

'Pass the staple gun, please, Shimy,' Honey asked, spreading out the A2 sized poster boards. The slogan was being directed at one man:

> TONY BLAIR
> ABOLISH FORCED MARRIAGES.
> WOULD YOUR PARENTS HAVE
> CHOSEN CHERIE FOR YOU?

A rattle of keys broke the girls' concentration, and they watched as Zarleena opened the door, an envelope in her hand. Honey could tell immediately that something was wrong.

'Do you mind waiting in the kitchen, Shimy, I've got a feeling she's just been raped.'

A shocked Shimla made herself scarce, leaving Honey to comfort her sister.

'It was bad, Honey. I don't think I will ever be able to see Joel again.' Zarleena slumped down on the sofa and helped herself to the gin. 'What a mess. He looked at me like I was a dog.'

Honey blamed herself. They had discussed at length whether it was safe for Zarleena to meet with Joel in his apartment after only knowing him for such a short time. It was Honey who had encouraged Zarleena to think positive. And now, she had forced her own flesh and blood into a man trap where she was raped. Honey straightened a few stray hairs in Zarleena's fringe, noting how sticky it was. It was all over her forehead as well. What had he done to her? What gross act had Joel made her perform?

'Tell me, Zarleena, did he ejaculate over your head?'

'Pardon?'

'After he raped you, did he, you know, force you to kneel down while he—'

Zarleena stood up. 'NO, he did not. What are you talking about? Rape?' Zarleena lifted up the bottle of Bombay Sapphire. 'How much of this have you drunk?'

'But your head is all sticky.'

'It's Red Bull. Good stuff you know.'

She went on to explain what had happened. No rape. No ejaculating. No forcing down on her knees. He was the perfect gentleman who had just had his dinner cooked by someone who reverses her underwear when dirty.

'The thing is, Honey, I don't do that with my knickers. You know that. I only said it to impress him. His mountain story was so shocking that I had to come up with something to top it. I could only think of Dirty

Jenny at school, she used to do that all the time. You remember Dirty Jenny?'

She nodded. 'So why the funeral face?'

'You should have seen how he looked at me. He was disgusted. Why did I say it? I've never felt so impure in all my life,' Zarleena said, slapping her hand against her forehead.

And as the evening unfolded, the three girls' blood became yet more impure as the laughter-inducing alcohol rinsed out their veins. Leaning against Orangeina's goldfish bowl was the envelope that Zarleena had picked up off the maisonette's front mat earlier. It could have been a bill. Or it could have been a bank statement. It could even have been an order for twenty pink and yellow saris.

Zarleena grabbed the envelope and cut through it with her index finger. It could have been any of those things. But it wasn't.

It was a typed threat:

> *Dear Bindis & Brides,*
> *We don't want your sort here.*
> *Pack your bags and go.*
> *Before things turn nasty.*

This time, all three needed to change their underwear. It was a 'Here's Johnny' moment and they were kacking their pants.

Joel, however, was having a whale of a time. At first, he couldn't remember for the life of him who Holly was, but he knew that in order to have invited her round,

87

there must have been some kind of connection with her. Beyond her fabulously long legs and pretty face, that is. A couple of glasses of wine later, his memory of Holly had returned. Esso garage. Pump 3. He'd filled up his Range Rover with diesel, while she'd chatted him up with four-star innuendoes. But today she seemed different in some way and he couldn't put his finger on it.

'You've had something done since I last saw you, haven't you?' Joel asked, ripping up naan bread and dunking it into his garlic chicken.

Holly smiled as she poked out her newly pierced tongue. 'Thlike it?'

'Pardon?'

'Thlike the thongue thstud?'

Oh that's what's different about you, thought Joel; *I can't understand a fucking word.* 'Very fetching. Makes you sound like Jamie Oliver.'

'Thhanks.' She giggled. 'And it's not the only plathce I've had pierthced either.' Her eyes dropped below.

Joel's eyes followed hers, leaving him guessing: belly button or . . .

So after *tandoori* chicken for starters, garlic chicken, *saag* and rice for main, then fruit cocktail for dessert, Holly was beyond impressed with Joel and was all starry eyed.

'Come with me.' He grabbed her hand and pulled her into the kitchen. 'Now check the bin. Make sure I haven't cheated by ordering a takeaway. I've got a few mates who would stoop that low to impress a woman. But I can assure you I cooked the whole meal all by myself. Just for you.'

Holly rummaged through the bin. Just onion skins, chicken bones, spinach stalks and twenty empty cans of Red Bull. Not a takeaway container in sight.

'I am gobthsmacked. Totally.' She laced her hands behind his back and kissed him on the lips. 'You are a dream man.'

'Thanks,' he said, grinning. 'It all seems so calm here now, Claudia, but you should have seen me earlier. I was frantic. Chopping up spices, grinding up herbs. And marinating the onions in *saag*. I'm just pleased you liked it, that's all. Bit of a shame about the fruit cocktail though, but I'd forgotten the recipe for *kulfi* ice cream.'

'Did you just call me Claudia?' she asked, unlacing her hands from behind his back.

'Claudia? Who the hell is Claudia? I said coriander. Chopping the coriander seeds, *Holly*.' He pushed his tongue in her mouth hard, mentally repeating the word 'Holly, Holly, Holly' over and over. 'You're okay actually, I thought your breath was going to stink after the garlic. But it's fine.'

Holly laughed. Joel was not normal. But in a good way. She would love to think that she'd discovered Joel all by herself, but she was sure a thousand other women would have spotted him first. He was that rare kind of man you just knew your parents were going to love, your friends were going to love, even your brother, if you had a brother, would love Joel. Unfortunately with a man like him, the question would always be, would Joel love you? Pure, refined hunk, bursting with life, brimming with confidence. And with those ice-cool blue eyes, mischievous and daring, hiding a darker side, what woman could fail to be won over? Not this one. It was about time she showed him her other piercing.

A sign above Joel's bed had Holly laughing again:

PLEASE SWITCH OFF ALL MOBILES

And she obliged.

If Joel didn't believe in God before, he did now. The God of Indian Food. Could it really be this easy? One cooked Indian meal and luscious, pretty women were in his bed begging for it before the meal had come out the other end. If he had known this when he was a lad he would have brought a bag of Bombay Mix to school on Valentine's Day. Alternatively, he could have coaxed Miss Kilmartin, the young, beautiful, blonde, busty, biology teacher, to remove her clothes with a strategically placed vegetable *samosa* in her desk drawer. The possibilities were endless. The science must be in the spices, he thought, working their way into the bloodstream and firing up the pheromone furnace, turning the quintessential English woman into a fully raging nymphomaniac. Long live Chicken Tikka Masala.

Long live the horny woman!

Joel was about to ask Holly if she fancied being tied up, when he noticed a climbing rope on the floorboards that had belonged to Candy. Lifeless it lay, like a dead snake, wrecking the mood, putting a dampener on the proceedings, reminding him of the woman with whom his loyalties ought to lie. He was about to ask for a time out when he caught the wonderful sight of Holly's naked body reclining on the bed. A sudden rush of hormones brought Joel back to the moment. There was no point getting hung up on guilt – especially if you were well hung. Joel stripped bare and knelt over Holly on the bed.

'Let's see it then . . . your piercing.' She obliged. 'Very impressive.' Joel wondered if they made stainless-steel condoms to protect men confronted with such a hazard. 'I look forward to making contact.'

And they were off. Making love hotter than the food they'd eaten. Holly seemed nice, good in bed, a woman most blokes would love to be around. But to Joel, she was a million miles away from Candy.

But then again, all women were to him.

Chapter Nine

Money can't buy you everything, thought Armin, but it could certainly buy you colour sometimes. The landlord of Sea Rock B&B in Clacton had no rooms available. And yet the sign on the window read: ROOMS VACANT. Maybe the sign should have read: ROOMS VACANT (EXCEPT FOR ASIANS). It was only when Armin produced a bundle of fifty-pound notes that his skin miraculously changed colour and an available room miraculously appeared. The landlord's racist joke, 'I trust you haven't got another hundred Indians stashed in your suitcase', left Armin promising himself that on vacating the room he would defecate on the mattress. He doubted that the landlord would have any uncertainty with the colour 'brown' after that.

It was Wednesday, a week since Prem and Armin had scouted Hunterslea looking for Zarleena. Much energy had been spent for little return until a bright fluorescent yellow poster pasted to a bus shelter had caught their eyes:

STAMP OUT SLAVERY
UNCHAIN INDIAN WOMEN
JOIN OUR MARCH (If husband gives permission).
HONEY'S BRITASIAN CAUSE!
STOP BY BINDIS & BRIDES SHOP FOR DETAILS.

Well, well, well, he'd thought. Armin had most likely found not only his wife's whereabouts, but also the new HQ of the Anti-Indian Way Movement. And by the sound of its President, Honey, it appeared she'd been eating too much Royal Jelly lately. He should have known Honey wouldn't have become a shrinking violet, she was always buzzing around Zarleena, always causing trouble.

And now it was Armin's turn again – to cause trouble.

After a quick celebratory drink in a local pub, Armin and Prem had headed back home to London to plan their next move. It soon became apparent that in order for Armin to achieve success with his wife, he would need to return to Hunterslea alone. It was no use having straight-laced Prem in the background if he wanted to scare Zarleena properly.

Armin stared at the four walls of his poky bed and breakfast room as he threw his suitcase on the floor (God, those Indian stowaways were heavy). If he didn't know any better, judging by the water-marked ceiling, the tide came in here. But he was assured by the landlord it was just a leaky pipe. Not to let it dampen his stay. Don't let bad plumbing or any other petty moan wreck the room's glory. Like the petty cigarette burns on the bed sheets, or the petty chewing gum stamped in the carpet, or, Armin walked to the en-suite bathroom, even the petty mildew on the tiles. Judging by the purple hair clogging the sink, Armin guessed that old people normally stayed here. Petty old people. But he could put up with this grotty hole. No problem. It was a sacrifice he was willing to make.

It would be worth it, just to watch his wife beg for mercy once more.

Right now, Zarleena was begging for mercy of a different kind. She held up the colourful knickers that Joel had sent her through the post. Having to sign for a package marked clearly SPARE KNICKERS was humiliating enough, but to open the parcel to find a sachet of Persil Automatic and instructions on 'Skid Cleaning' was taking the biscuit. Although she was grateful for the huge box of Thank You choccies, and the generous cheque donated to the Asian Women's Hostel.

Zarleena sat on her bed admiring the lacy panties. Joel had taste, and a good eye for detail; he'd guessed her size 8 correctly. A man this expert on lingerie had to be pretty damn good with what went in the lingerie too. She giggled to herself. But a man this naive with relationships was hardly destined to stay in one long. How many men, already in a relationship with another woman, would send a married woman racy knickers through the post? It bordered on romantic suicide.

And speaking of romance, she wondered how Joel was getting along with his girlfriend. It was so tempting to pick up the phone and ask him whether he had proposed to Claudia. And if not, why not? He was so easy to talk to and with Honey out at her martial arts class,

Zarleena could think of nothing better. Well, she could, but it was X-rated.

After receiving the threatening letter on Saturday and deciding not to go to the police for now, the sisters had been dubious about being apart from each other for any length of time. Safety in numbers and all that. It would take a brave person to ignore such a threat. Or someone madly in love with their martial arts instructor. 'Just go,' Zarleena had said. 'I couldn't bear your sulking if you stayed. And don't worry, I'll triple-lock the door.'

So, with the front door triple-locked, Zarleena tucked into the Belgian chocolates, forcing her pancreas on overtime for the next hour or so, wallowing in the simplistic surroundings of her bedroom. Honey had often mentioned that Zarleena's room was too plain. With only a double bed and a wardrobe to keep the walls company, she wasn't far wrong. But Zarleena liked the minimalism of the room, with its cream walls and Victoria plum-coloured duvet, curtains and cushions; it seemed to project a natural feeling of Zen, with a sense of calm that engulfed her as soon as her head hit the pillow.

Like it was hitting the pillow now, except instead of calm, a turbulent storm brewed, with thoughts of Armin tossing thunderbolts her way. What an awful husband he had turned out to be. How ironic was it, that every time someone treated her nicely, she would think of Armin? When someone smiled and said thank you, she would think of Armin, because he was never polite. When someone complimented her on her looks, she would think of Armin, because not once, not even on their wedding night, did Armin compliment her. And when someone gave her gifts – Zarleena popped in another chocolate – she thought of Armin. Because not once, not even for her birthday, did Armin ever give her gifts.

Unless one classes a purple bruise as a present.

Zarleena thought of her horror-video collection. *The Exorcist. A Nightmare on Elm Street. Halloween*. Even *Scream*. But none of these compared with *Zarleena's & Armin's Marriage* video. It should have been banned, and so should the wedding.

Mum and Dad had found Armin by networking. A friend of a friend of a cousin knew of him and everything about Armin seemed perfect. He was the correct age, caste, height, even his shade of skin was perfect. (A light shade of caramel mixed with a nutty nutmeg. Quite in fashion at the time.) And to top it off, his family were well thought of; they mixed in the right circles and chinked glasses with the right businessmen. Not quite the high society of Asians, but not far off either. Not bad for a family who came to Britain with just fifty pence in their pocket but now owned a string of cash 'n' carry stores in London and throughout the Midlands: Golden Karmas Cash 'n' Carry.

Zarleena remembered her first meeting with Armin, or rather her first *unchaperoned* meeting with him. Up until that point, their get-togethers had been under the careful eye of the elders. Alone for the first time, they had sat in a dimly lit Italian restaurant in Colchester. Armin was full of stories and fun to be around. Nothing in his handsome looks hinted at the vile animal that hid beneath his perfect smile. At one point he handed Zarleena a small leather pouch. Inside, he said, she would find clues to his vices. If she still wanted to marry him after that then his conscience was clear. Zarleena had fumbled with the string pull. Did she really want to know the contents of the bag, the list of someone's weaknesses? Encouraged to open it, she eventually did. To her shock, instead of finding a small bottle of alcohol, or a stash of hash, or a business card belonging to some prostitute, she found a credit card.

'This is my only vice, Zarleena,' Armin had said, taking her hand in his. 'I spend too much money on the people I care about. I basically spoil everyone. If you have trouble with generosity then I suggest you don't marry me.'

Zarleena was bowled over. But looking back she should have known better. Armin? Generous? That deserved a real belly laugh. He was tighter than an ant's back passage, more like. Even in the restaurant that evening, the signs had been there when he'd asked Zarleena if she wanted to go Dutch (so as not to insult her independence). She'd replied, 'No it's okay, you pay,' (so as not to insult his generosity).

But Armin's generosity never showed. The closest he came to buying her chocolates was when he picked up a box of Coco Pops. And the nearest he got to buying her flowers was of the self-raising kind.

It was enough to drive any woman wild with lust.

Which was exactly what Scotsmen boasted about their kilts. Eloise had laughed when Joel said he was off to Scotland for a few days, climbing with a couple of Scotsmen in the Outer Hebrides. She imagined Joel trying to ignore what was dangling under the climbers' kilts as he followed them up the mountains. Joel had explained that Scotsmen don't wear kilts for climbing. Or for hang-gliding, pole-vaulting or even the trampoline for that matter.

'Well, when do they wear them?' she'd quizzed.

'When they come to England, just to prove how Scottish they are. That's when!' Joel had replied, packing the bright pink bra in his rucksack. 'And to prove to them how English I am, I show them my Indian takeaway menus.'

Oh take him away, thought Eloise, warmly cuddling him goodbye; please take him away. And he would be away, from now until Saturday. Four days without Joel was going to be hard work. Four whole days to occupy herself was not going to be easy.

She grinned, fondling the envelope that he'd left her. The £500 spending money might just make it bearable though. Even more bearable if she could swindle some readies from her other brother as well.

Within minutes of Joel leaving, and after lighting a candle for his safe return, Eloise was on the phone.

'What am I supposed to do, Dylan? He's gone off again and left me with nothing. I think a hundred quid should just about cover me for food and necessities.' She paused. 'How are you fixed for dinner? Fancy taking your little sister out for a meal? Even better than that ...'

... And by the time the phone call had ended, Dylan was on a promise to escort Eloise to the Staunton Art Gallery in Hunterslea, followed by a slap-up meal in the Dragon's Oven Cantonese restaurant in Colchester.

Dylan, dressed immaculately in a designer suit, arrived at the art gallery with a full wallet, whilst Eloise arrived with an ulterior motive. A quick formal hug was followed by a rare, but noticeably uncomfortable silence. Somehow, today was not about viewing pictures. They walked through the revolving doors and onto the echoing marble floor of a long corridor as Beethoven's 'Moonlight Sonata' greeted them. Eloise smiled, listening to a father explaining to his young son that unfortunately the gallery did not display paintings by Rolf Harris.

'It was fiendishly difficult to get Lilly's permission to come today,' Dylan began, as he strolled with Eloise down the passageway, 'it's my turn to bath and bed the children. So please, let's not have a row like last time.' He passed his eyes over her clothes, mentally passing judgement as he did so. A partially see-through elegant lace top, baring her slim, tanned and pierced midriff. A short, black satin mini-skirt. Prada knee-length suede boots. And a selection of jewellery, gold crucifixes, bangles and earrings, tying the sexy explosion together. For a woman who claimed to be hard up, Eloise certainly dressed with a flair that put most Hollywood stars to shame. 'Still unemployed?'

'Hardly. I'm pursuing my photography career. You know I'm after that one shot that will rocket me to fame.'

Flash! Eloise snapped a picture of Dylan with her camera. He looked like Joel in many ways, except Dylan's face had far more mileage on the clock than his extra years would indicate. He blamed his kids, wife, work and mortgage (and the day he bought his Enron shares). Without all these factors, of course, he would look younger, act younger; anyone could be as much fun as Joel without responsibilities. But someone in the family had to make the parents proud. Someone had to justify all that money they had spent on his private schooling.

And here was the main difference between the brothers' upbringing: schools. Money was on the up when Dylan was at school so his education was a private one. But money was on the slide when Joel was at school so his education came via a craprehensive school. Different schools, different expectations, even a different way of speaking. The differences were vast. Dylan said, 'Mother', Joel said, 'Mum', Dylan said, 'Yar', Joel said, 'Yep'. And Dylan said, 'Do you mind?' Joel said, 'Will you just fuck off?' Quite vast.

Walking through the gallery, Eloise hoped she would find a spot where she could discuss an important issue with Dylan. She watched people drifting like seeds in a wind until they came to rest in front of various pieces of art. Although 'art' was a debatable description considering some of the items on display. She smiled ironically as she took a photo of a sign:

NO CAMERAS PLEASE

Upstairs they found the seclusion of the 'modern' section. Eloise and Dylan sat on a bench that faced a living painting called 'GUM'. Beside the work was a wooden table with countless sticks of chewing gum. The idea was to chew on a stick then add it to the canvas, thus involving oneself in the 'living painting'. It was a simple idea. Hideous, but simple.

'Joel's dying of cancer,' Eloise said, her voice a dull croak. 'And yes, it's incurable.'

'What?'

'Prostate. A bit young for prostate but still, he's dying all right.' Eloise sniffed, dragging up a memory of watching *Watership Down* when she was a young girl. Her tears began to fall. 'Our brother is dying and there's nothing we can do about it. It kind of puts things into perspective, you know.'

Dylan was in shock, his face a collection of worry lines. What a grand photo that would make, thought Eloise, refraining from destroying the delicate moment with her camera. She watched Dylan stand and slowly pace up and down the marble floor, an internal battle raging inside his head.

At last he spoke. 'How long has he got? Surely there's a treatment for prostate cancer. It's quite common.' He paused. 'You were entertaining me with your jokes a minute ago and all the time you knew this?'

'It's my way of dealing with tragedy.'

Eloise explained that Joel would love to be buried up Everest and could Dylan arrange for a group of Sherpas to transport the coffin to the summit. Their parents were only to be informed when Joel's body weight had diminished to less than three stone. Joel's last wish was to beat David Blaine's record of being buried in ice. He should achieve this up Mount Everest.

Something clicked with Dylan as Eloise hummed the tune to 'Bright Eyes'. Her actions were not those of a worried sister. And when she began to text dirty messages to her best friend, Natalie, while he was trying his hardest to hold back tears, his suspicions were aroused some more.

'He's not dying at all, is he?' Dylan announced.

'We're all dying, Dyl, from the moment we are born. Now, how do you spell gonads?'

'But we're not all dying of prostate cancer, are we? There's nothing wrong with Joel, is there?'

Eloise stuffed another stick of chewing gum in her mouth, then switched off her mobile phone. 'No.'

'Good God, Eloise, what possessed you to say it then?'

And Eloise began her explanation. She'd seen what she'd wanted to see in Dylan. She had witnessed a man distraught at the thought of losing his brother to cancer. It proved beyond doubt that he cared about Joel. It proved beyond doubt that now was the time to patch up their differences; before Joel really did die on one of his mountains. A man can only live with a death wish for so long until his wish comes true.

'I don't think you would be able to forgive yourself if Joel died with this not sorted out. And the way Joel is behaving lately, all erratic, it really could happen any time. He's losing control, Dyl, he honestly thinks he's invincible. He still likes walking on top of multi-storey car parks. He eats out-of-date food. I'm serious, Dylan, he'll be dead before he reaches thirty-five. You know he still climbs those stupid mountains without oxygen? There's no air at the top of those things, it's just suicide.'

'I can't forgive him, you know that. I nearly lost my son because of him.'

'Oh come on: Joel was only nineteen then.' She stood up and held his shoulders, looking directly into his blue eyes. 'I think if it wasn't for you and it wasn't for Candy, Joel would be normal. You're partially to blame for the way he behaves. He just wants his older brother to love him, that's all. And as for Candy, if she really loved him, like she pretends she does, then she'd ask him to stop his madness. She's a cow.'

Dylan breathed in heavily. 'Does he still stick his fingers and toes in the deep freeze?'

'Yes, and the tip of his nose. He even stuck his knob in there once. He says it helps him get used to frostbite. He likes to fight the freeze.'

And Dylan liked to fight the thaw. His heart had become cold towards Joel. Although if Dylan were to be true to himself, his heart had always been slightly frosty towards him from day one, Joel's birth, when Dylan became relegated to number-two son. Now it was past day 10,950, thirty years later, and Eloise was rightly worried that her family had entered a new ice age. At least it would explain Aunty Jennifer's woolly mammoth hair-do.

Dylan grappled with Eloise's plea. Maybe she was right, maybe it was time to fix the broken links. Maybe it was time to have a brotherly chat with Joel. Before he really did die of prostate cancer, or worse, before Joel lost his knob to frostbite.

He spoke. 'I'm in agreement here, Eloise, I *do* think Joel needs help and I'll certainly give the matter some thought. But, I hasten to add, from what you tell me of Candy, there is nothing you or I can do about her.'

Eloise smiled sweetly. It was a shame Candy wasn't around today, she was in the mood to kick her off the pedestal Joel had placed her on.

Chapter Ten

Dressed in black, Armin looked like the man from the Milk Tray advert. (The Bombay version.) He liked the image, and guessed it would send chills down Zarleena's spine. Not that she had much of a spine, the weak, frightened, pathetic excuse of a wife. And not that Armin would be giving her a box of Milk Tray either. Armin laughed to himself as he glanced down to the passenger seat. But he would be giving her a box of something else, now, wouldn't he?

It was Monday. For three days Armin had been watching Bindis & Brides from across the road. Far enough away not to be obvious, but close enough to keep a watchful eye on the comings and goings of the shop. And boy, was it busy. And boy, did that make Armin angry. He'd seen customer after customer leave his wife's shop with full bags and fuller grins. And he guessed his wife was grinning the fullest.

Armin opened the car door and picked up the large box. It was time for the grinning to stop. He eyed the shop entrance from his station. Honey was due to leave any second now. At 4 p.m. Honey would scamper out of Bindis & Brides and head down to the Post Office. She was always gone at least half an hour. Armin chuckled to himself as Honey barged out of the shop with her parcels. Half an hour . . . that was more than enough time to shit up his wife.

Looking back from the car window was a reflection of Armin that he approved of. Sleek and slick. They didn't make villains like they used to. He twisted his body around and stood on tiptoes staring at his behind in the window. Black made his bum seem smaller. He hated it when his mates said he had a fat arse. With one further nod of approval, Armin crossed the road towards Bindis & Brides.

In the shop Zarleena unwrapped beautiful hand-crafted models of the Taj Mahal as she ate her late lunch. She smiled proudly at her people's wonderful craftsman-ship, then shuddered with shame when she saw the 'Made in Japan' labels. Were cultures losing their identities? Were the crafts of different races being diluted by modern advances? Was this evolution? Zarleena leaned across and picked up a cold chip; was nothing sacred any more? She dunked the cold chip in her hot mango pickle; were all the borders coming down?

This time in the afternoon was generally flat, the only thing left from the hustle and bustle of earlier was a headache. But rather a headache for too much money than a migraine for too little. She had never quite got over the thrill of working for herself. The feeling of freedom was worth the lack of security any day. She dunked in another chip, and let out an 'mmm', for even cold chips tasted better when the bills were all paid for.

And so did chocolates. Normally.

The huge box of choccies that Joel had sent her lay half-eaten upstairs in the maisonette. Half-eaten because she couldn't bring herself to finish them since nearly killing Joel on Saturday. Just an innocent phone call to thank him for the knickers and Belgian box had almost cost Joel his life. Because of her, he nearly slipped off the Scottish mountain ledge. When he had answered, 'Not right now, Zarleena, I'm up a mountain,' she'd assumed he was joking. Until she heard his shouts of 'I've lost my fucking grip. Someone, please help me, my footing's gone, I'm fall—' and then the phone line had died. For two hours Zarleena had agonized over Joel's fate, fretting over crazy images of Joel joining Candy on that great mountain range in the sky. And what about Claudia, did Joel get to propose to her? Had he passed away leaving her a love widow? And even a selfish thought intruded, what did Joel think of her cooking? Zarleena remembered slaving over his hot stove. Was it too garlicky?

All was revealed when Joel finally called her back. He explained it was just a joke. And did she get it?

Oh she got it all right; her cursing down the phone could have caused an avalanche. And so, in an act of martyrdom like no other, Zarleena refused to eat any more of the chocolates that Joel had sent her. But it was kind of too late not to wear the knickers.

The doorbell tinkled, and Zarleena screwed up the chip bag, lobbing it in the bin. She put on her 'customer is always right' face and made her way down the shop to greet the shopper. A familiar smell of Joop aftershave brought grey memories to the surface. Violence. Hurt. Shame. Fear. HUSBAND. Zarleena felt the cold creep of misery about her as Armin, all in black, placed a box on the floor, slamming the door behind him. He flicked the sign from 'Open' to 'Closed' then heaved a fire extinguisher in front, preventing anyone from entering.

'Call me a bit cynical, Zarleena, but isn't opening a bridal-wear shop stretching the imagination a bit? You weren't exactly a model bride, were you?' Armin examined his wife, unhappily noting that she looked well. 'Crap in the kitchen, crap in bed, pretty crap all round I'd say. You know how the first cooked *chapatti* is thrown in the bin because it never cooks right? That's how I think of you. You were never right.'

'And I suppose . . .' Zarleena was about to be brave, but she saw Armin's jaw clench. 'What do you want?'

'I want the gold back. All the gold that was given to you on our wedding.'

And I want my virginity back, and everything else I gave to you on our wedding, thought Zarleena. God this man was a creep. Single-celled organisms had more moral fibre than this low life. She never remembered having to sign a form stating that a failed marriage would require the bride to hand back all her wedding gifts. And from an Indian's point of view, the gold was more than just a gift, it was an important part of tradition.

In Indian marriages it's traditional for the groom's family to honour the bride with twenty-two-carat gold. Rich families give a lot; poor give what they can. Stingy families give a box of Terry's All Gold. Armin's family had presented Zarleena with a treasure trove of gifts. Bangles, necklaces, earrings, rings, even a diamond-encrusted head decoration called a *tikka*. Enough gold to sink a ship.

Enough gold to start a business.

When Armin left Zarleena he left her with three things. A wedding album full of false photos. A drawer full of unpaid bills. And a body full of scars and bruises. But in his rush to abandon her in their rented luxury flat in Birmingham, Armin had forgotten to take with him the passbook for the bank vault where the jewellery was stored. With plenty of persuasion from her parents, Zarleena decided to sell the jewellery and use the money, along with a joint loan with Honey, to start Bindis & Brides. A plaque on the shop wall commemorated this:

A Golden Key Opens Every Door
But Behind Each Door Lies a Risk

Perhaps her risk was now being unlocked. The last thing she ever expected was for Armin to show up, demanding his gold back. And why would she? As far as she was concerned, Armin was loaded, from a wealthy family.

Zarleena edged backwards, eyes fixed on Armin, mind zeroed on the weapons stash under the counter. If she could predict one thing about her husband's actions it was how unpredictable they were. He could lash out at any given moment.

'The gold is in the bank,' Zarleena said, nearing the counter. 'Where it's safe.'

'Not a problem, fetch your coat, we'll get it now.'

'But I can't leave the shop unattended.' Her voice was shaking.

Armin smirked. 'Oh, believe me, Zarleena, you wouldn't be leaving the shop unattended.' He chuckled to himself.

'Besides,' she continued, ignoring his last comment, 'I have to make an appointment with my bank before I can view the box.' Her hands fumbled blindly beneath the counter as a warm bead of sweat trickled down her spine. 'It's a silly rule.'

Suddenly Armin exploded. 'Excuses, excuses, EXCUSES!' He picked up the ASIAN WOMEN'S HOSTEL charity box and threw it across the shop floor. 'Someone is getting angry, Zarleena. Someone is getting *really* angry.' He brought his face directly up to hers, sneering as if he was looking at a dog turd. 'There's something about seeing you that makes me want to hurt you. You're so pathetic, so feeble, so—'

Zarleena brought the knife right up to Armin's face, holding it as rigid as her shaking limbs would allow her to. 'Get out, or so help me I'll gut you like a fish.' She'd heard someone say that in a movie once. 'Get out.'

Armin stared at the silver stapler just inches from his nose and prayed it wasn't loaded. In her panic Zarleena had mistaken the harmless piece of office equipment for the carving knife. He could see the headlines now: STA-PLED TO DEATH. Immediately he batted the stapler away, and with a firm shove pushed Zarleena to the floor.

'I'll give you three days to get my gold. Call me on my mobile when you have it. The number's the same. *Namaste.*'

Armin walked towards the entrance, picked up his box, opened the flap with his penknife, and threw it towards Zarleena.

He added one last comment before departing in a fit of laughter. 'Hope you don't suffer from arachnophobia.'

If she didn't before, she certainly did now. A gang of huge, hairy tarantulas scurried away from the box and into the shadows of the shop. Zarleena screamed as she jumped onto the counter, tasting her own heart as it beat in her mouth. But the news wasn't all bad. At least she had chosen to wear shoes today instead of sandals, because right now, as a multitude of yellow eyes watched her from their hiding places, she was standing in a puddle of her own wee.

Where was Joel when you needed him, thought Zarleena, another pair of spare knickers wouldn't have gone amiss right now.

Chapter Eleven

Joel lifted the sleeping bag out of the airing cupboard and shook out his emergency batch of pornography magazines. *Mayfair*, *Penthouse*, *Playboy* and *Fat Housewives with Big Uns*. It was extremely important that his female visitor today thought he was being faithful to her. What better way to explain how he got rid of his sexual urges than porn? And if she decided to look for condoms – ah ha! – he was already one step ahead of her; he'd hidden them inside the vacuum-cleaner bag – God were they a bugger to hoover up, especially the used ones.

Next up was sperm prep. Without wanting to provide his own sample, Joel began mixing flour and water in a small glass bowl. He spooned it onto the magazine pages and tissues, wondering how the hell women could swallow this stuff. Lumpy as fuck and slimy to boot. He hoped that it dried by this afternoon or Candy would think he'd been busy all morning. All that was needed now was a careful placement of the props and when she walked into his bedroom the evidence that Joel had been faithful would be dripping down the walls and – he threw a sticky wad of tissue on the door – dripping down the door.

Men rule at deceit, he thought proudly, tossing on a blood-red Thaw T-shirt and a pair of black combat bottoms. They were kings of the little white lie. Joel took a last look at the little white lies stuck all over his bedroom, then deposited himself on the vibrating chair in the living room.

'Ahh, lovely,' he said, upping the vibration. 'Just luxurious.'

And to think that only three days ago the most luxurious happening up The Big Lick, a frozen mountain in Scotland, was when Joel did a warm fart. One appreciated the advantages of a high-fibre diet when one was freezing one's bollocks off. And one would have also appreciated bottled oxygen when someone else was letting them go in your face too (except The Big Lick was too low for the requirement of bottled oxygen). It was a fact that never seemed to get a mention in climbing guides. Along with 'What to do when you're halfway up a mountain and your mobile phone rings'. Joel felt a little guilty for messing with Zarleena's mind at the weekend. Pretending he had slipped off The Big Lick when she phoned was pretty low. It would need to be corrected. An apology of some sort was definitely in order.

But for now, he was having his bottom massaged. He snapped open a Red Bull and gulped it down in one. Joel remembered overhearing a Red Bull rep trying to convince a head honcho that it was pointless worrying about Joel's seemingly never-ending consumption of the drink, because he would soon get fed up with the taste. That was four thousand cans ago. Part of Joel's fee to advertise their pick-me-up was a five-year supply of the product. He fully intended to fulfil his obligation to drink it. And even with all the free cans of Red Bull lying around, Joel still felt inclined to buy one from time to time just for the thrill of it. On top of Red Bull, Joel's apartment and lock-up were littered with other freebies. Boxes of hair gel, crates of body lotions, deodorants, motorbike gloves, even dog food (the advert had Joel undoing a can of dog food four thousand feet up: DOGS WILL EVEN CLIMB K2 TO GET THEIR K9S ON THE K9 FOOD). Everything that had been advertised up a mountain by Joel ended up in his man pad. And if it wasn't for the apartment's strict anti-pet rules he would have bought a dog by now. Someone had to eat the pet food. Eloise had asked him what would happen when the food ran out, his answer, 'Get rid of the dog.'

'Good stuff this,' said Joel to himself as he crunched up the can. 'Real good.'

So good, in fact, that as usual Joel drifted off to sleep. A dreamland where vertical is horizontal and gravity is propulsion. Where mountains grow and heights are without peaks. For forty-five minutes Joel slept wearing a contented smile, until he awoke with a jolt, screaming out the words, 'I'm scared of heights.' He jumped off the vibrating chair, realizing that a nightmare had taken him. A moment later he was in the bathroom splashing his face with water, washing away the bad dream. He took a quick look at the small wipe board next to the bathroom cabinet. Each week Eloise would jot down items of toiletries that she needed money for. This week it read:

1 Babyliss Dry & Shine hair dryer.
1 Purple Ronnie bath towel.
Liz Collinge make-up (£100 should cover it).
1 Amor Amor perfume (50ml).
And £10 Boots Gift voucher (treat yourself).

Joel rubbed out the writing and wrote:

GET A JOB!

Even though Eloise found it hard to make herself useful, she was pretty good when it came to making herself scarce. Today she was in Blackpool with her boyfriend, Johan, testing out the opposite of Newton's theory – what goes up must come down – with their cooked breakfast, after taking the rollercoaster ride. Her advice to Joel this morning before she left was, 'Don't tell Candy about your other women or you're dumped.' Hence the tissues stuck to the wall next door.

Hence the boxed gift hidden under the coffee table.

Instructions had already been given to Arthur, the doorman downstairs, as to what to do when Candy arrived. Arthur, always keen to shine Joel's boots – ever since Joel had stunt-doubled, up a cliff, in a Hollywood movie – had been practising his one line all morning. As soon as the female visitor appeared at Reception he was to say, dramatically, 'Thank God you're back. Joel has been going out of his mind without you; he has become a recluse.' And just to help matters along, Arthur was going to impress Joel by adding a line of his own. 'And,' Arthur was going to say, 'he has not had one single woman up in that penthouse either; not one.'

The doorbell farted and Joel laughed. God, he loved that noise. Chuckling, he walked to the door, yanked down his combat bottoms, and wondered to himself whether it might be a good idea to open it and greet Candy with an erection. What better way to prove to a woman that you've missed her? Of course, there were other ways, his sensible side argued, like, maybe, a hug for instance? He tugged up his combats. Yeah, a hug should do it.

He opened the door and admired Candy for a few heartbeats. 'Oh, what a relief. I imagined your hair mounted with heavy curls. You said the perm was frosty and thick.' Joel pulled her in, shoved her suitcase to one side, and hugged her tight. 'But it's still straight; we're going to be okay.'

'I said the permafrost on Mont Blanc du Tacul was too thick, you nit-wit, not that I was having a thick perm.' Candy saw Joel smiling, and realized once again, he was joking. 'You bugger.'

Inside it wasn't about perms or permafrost. It was about two people who had missed the pants off each other. Joel eyed Candy, the woman of his heart, the captivator of his dreams. When writers wrote of princesses, they had Candy in mind. But could she sleep for a hundred years? Or turn a frog into a prince? Or even keep a gang of dwarves happy? NO! But she could climb pretty well, and that was good enough for Joel. Plus she did this thing with her tongue that Joel was sure even nymphomaniac Snow White wouldn't be able to do. And that's saying something for a woman who was willing to go down on her knees for seven dwarves.

But Candy's beauty was more than just her appearance, it was more than her long, blonde locks, more than her wide, blue eyes, more even than her fabulous figure that seemed to look good in anything but looked even better without. Her beauty really took hold when you knew what went on inside her head. A place three-quarters dedicated to kindness, and one quarter dedicated to shoes. Joel, much to his credit, fell in love with Candy before he'd even seen her face.

Three and a half years ago on a climbing expedition in the French-Italian Alps to raise money for *Children in Need*, it had all gone horribly wrong when a murderous blizzard had descended upon Mont Blanc. Groups were split in the confusion, and Joel found himself climbing blindly with this strong, confident, funny woman called Candy Greenwood. It was just the two of them and their red noses without another soul in sight. And when darkness fell, Joel suggested that they find a sheltered area to see out the storm. Huddled together for body heat in their refuge, nibbling on Kendal Mint Cake for their sustenance, Joel and Candy swapped stories. Every hour they massaged each other's feet and hands, keeping the blood flow going, keeping themselves alive in the biting cold. It was the longest night of their lives.

By sun up the storm had died, but their romance had been born. Making their way back down to Base Camp, Joel, who had now fallen for Candy big time, prayed that underneath her balaclava, there lay a stunning woman – for all he knew, Candy was a Queen Victoria look-alike. As she removed the face mask, Joel knew his prayers had been answered. Candy was too beautiful for words. Although Joel did have a few that nearly stopped the relationship before it had even begun. He'd said, just as she was about to leave the mountain camp, 'Next time we meet, Candy, I wouldn't mind having a go at your two peaks.'

SLAP!

But all was forgiven – especially after a twenty-minute goodbye roll in the snow. Joel could now say he'd officially reached first base with Candy and, fittingly, he'd reached it at Base Camp.

Splayed out on the couch drinking wine, Joel and Candy talked shop. Mountains, peaks and ravines. A common thread that neatly tied their lives together. Although, if the truth was to be known, Candy's love for mountaineering and mountains had faded the moment she lost her first friend to one. She too used to dream of conquering Mount Everest. Of achieving a goal that God had put out of most people's reach. But now her kicks came from other activities, low-key compared to 8000-metre peaks, but dangerous all the same. River rafting, mountain biking, sailing, hiking and climbing smaller mountains, attainable peaks without the risk of death. Her job as a leader of an Outdoor Pursuit Centre filled her thrill bank and the high interest came from the smiles of underprivileged children when they achieved something they thought was beyond them.

And on her many adventures, whether it be climbing the great Kilimanjaro or rafting down the Trisuli River or even taking a balloon flight over the Kathmandu Valley, more likely than not she'd bump into people she knew or people Joel knew. And without fail each person would always ask the same question, 'Is Joel still alive?' To begin with, Candy was amused by their flippant questions. As time wore on, her amusement wore away. 'Is Joel still alive?' It just wasn't funny any more. In fact, over the last year or so, most of Joel and Candy's above-thirty-decibel arguments had been about Joel's apparent death wish. His refusal to follow basic safety procedure for no good reason she could see, other than his ego, was ridiculous. She'd begged Joel over and over to climb with pre-fixed ropes and bottled oxygen (when needed). She'd cried as she explained she lived in fear of the day she had to answer, 'Yes, Joel is dead now, he slipped off a mountain because he didn't want to use another climber's leftover rope. What a waste.' A widow at only twenty-eight. What a fucking waste.

The wine bottle was empty and Joel placed his arm around Candy's shoulder and closed his eyes, enjoying the feel of her once again. Was he really willing to risk losing all of this just for a few shags? Maybe this wasn't the time to analyze his wrongdoings. He brushed a hair from her eye and watched her smile contentedly. Jesus, how could he have been such a bastard to her? How . . . maybe this wasn't the time for guilt either. Maybe now was the time to enjoy the few days they had together and do the things couples do when they're in love. Now where had he put the Monopoly board?

Before long the time came for them to get out their address books. The evening could only continue once all the paperwork had been completed.

'You go first,' prompted Joel, pen at the ready.

Candy took a deep breath. 'Okay, here goes. There's Todd.' She watched Joel shake his head sadly as he struck a line through Todd's name. 'Fell off K2. And then there's the Anderson Twins.' She paused in reflection. 'Not twins any more. Marcellus froze to death up Everest; poor soul. Andreas was beyond consoling and—'

Joel interrupted. 'Actually, Candy, would you mind if we did this later? No offence, but thinking of dead bodies in ice kind of spoils our romantic evening a bit. I was really looking forward to our shag.' He reached under the coffee table and handed her the present. 'Here, it's just a little something that Eloise helped me choose. And unless you've had a few toes amputated since we last met, they should fit.'

Candy smiled as she shook the box. 'Oh, I wonder what it is.' This was turning into a lovely evening.

Which was more than could be said for Zarleena's.

In fact, Zarleena's whole morning, noon and now night was like a blueprint for a day in hell. A Big Fat Hairy Spider Hell. Since yesterday, when Charlotte's overgrown steroid-using brother spiders had been let loose in Bindis & Brides, the 'Closed' sign had been up. And today, two terrified shop owners had huddled upstairs in their maisonette while a brave warrior from the RSPCA worked his way through the premises collecting all four of the beasts. Of course, this would have been great, a job well done, if it wasn't for the sneaky, fifth tarantula which Zarleena had failed to spot leaping into a stainless-steel *kahari*. She'd been convinced only four spiders had come out of the box.

The first two were responsible for her screams, and the second two were responsible for her peeing her knickers. Maybe it was a good thing the fifth spider never caught her eye, or the shop might have had to be renamed Bindis Bowels & Incontinent Brides.

Keeping the shop invasion a secret was a must. People tended to be a bit finicky these days with establishments that harboured Satan's pets. And if customers were to ask why they had closed for a day and a bit, their reply was simple: 'We were waiting for Ziggy to collect his Spiders.' Or, that ol' high street favourite, 'Stock Check'. Better a little brown lie than to keep the business open and find Aunti-ji Julginder undressed in the shop's changing room and screaming to high heaven because a tarantula tried to mate with her hairy leg. Much better.

And screaming was exactly the response from Zarleena's mother, as she was told of the way Armin had barged into Bindis & Brides and left her daughter frigid with fear. Suddenly her parents' belief in Gandhi's teachings flew out of the window. Peaceful protest was not going to work with someone like Armin. Dad compared him to a creature from the underworld: a living ghost, a parents' choice of husband forever there to haunt them. And he would not sit idly by while his son-in-law wrecked his daughter's life again. 'We haven't travelled from India to be treated as a lower caste,' Dad had said, fuming, 'especially by one of our own. We could quite easily be treated like that back in Bombay.' (Dad refused to call Bombay by its new name, Mumbai, for reasons known only to him, but most likely he kept forgetting the name had changed in

1995. Although, strangely, he now asked for Mumbai Potatoes when eating in Indian restaurants, but that was probably just to annoy the chef.)

Zarleena thanked her parents for their advice and willingness to help, but decided that she should confront this on her own. If she didn't stand up to Armin now, she never would. And the thought of looking over her shoulder for evermore was about as welcome as giving John Prescott a bed bath – after he'd been down his local balti house.

So here she stood, alone in her maisonette, staring at the orange neon phone, trying to put off the un-put-off-able. Zarleena brushed a tear of frustration from her eye. She had never believed the story about *Jack and the Beanstalk*, or the one about *Hansel and Gretel*, even *Cinderella* had its flaws, so why, oh fucking why, had she believed the one about *The Good Little Indian Girl Marrying the Man of Her Parents' Dreams*?

. . . and then Sunil helped his wife, Neena, with the washing up. They laughed the evening away, playing backgammon, until it was time for bed. Sunil kissed his wife goodnight and she smiled. Oh, how contented they were. And they all lived happily ever after. The End.

BOLLOCKS! How about Sunil coming in drunk, smacking Neena round the head for not cooking his favourite curry dish, then ripping off her sari as he raped her on the kitchen table, ignoring her swollen belly from her eight-month pregnancy, whilst whispering in her ear, 'If you don't give me a boy, you'll see what happens.' The End.

The End? And it is the end, the end of so many things. Dreams die young for some Indian girls. The day they move in with their new husband and mother-in-law, reality takes a knife to their hopes, grabbing their fantasy around the jugular and slipping the blade through its windpipe. Nothing is as it should be. Not the husband, not the marriage, not even the wedding.

Wedding talk stalks Indian girls through their whole childhood. Wedding this and wedding that. It's all they live for. It's all the parents can talk about. No holidays, no treats, no luxuries. 'NO back-chat! We're saving for your wedding and dowry.' Save, save, save, sacrifice, sacrifice, sacrifice. 'NO back-chat! You can go on holiday and have your luxuries when you're married. Now empty your pockets and pop your wages in your wedding fund.' And the years go by, and your hair grows longer (you can get it cut when you're married), and your moustache begins to sprout (you can wax/bleach it when you're married), and your eyebrows now meet in the middle (you can get them plucked when you're married), and your bush needs a trim (you can get a Brazilian when you're married), and your armpits need . . . (forget it, no one wants to marry a wolf-girl freak). And the fairy tale gets closer. Seventeen passes, then eighteen, by nineteen you're raring to go on holiday with your future husband, by twenty you can't wait for your hair to be cut, trimmed, waxed, etc. and twenty-one comes, the wedding is here, and before you know it . . . you're a modern-day slave, stuck in the kitchen, freedom-less, pregnant, bored, lonely, moaned at and MARRIED! Most Indian girls would rather have climbed the beanstalk and tried their chances with the giant than this. This was not what they had been promised. Fee, Fie, Foe, Fum, I smell bullshit.

'WE HAVE BEEN RIPPED OFF! All in the name of tradition,' they chant. And maybe they had.

Zarleena gobbled up one last bar of Fruit & Nut for courage, then, after glancing at the A4 sheet in front of her, she dialled Armin's mobile. To hear his creepy phone voice once again tied the string of nerves in her stomach into a knot. She was thankful that she'd written a speech in advance, for putting together a coherent sentence right now was near impossible. Even down a phone line Armin wielded the power to scare.

With a trembling mouth she began, 'Please do not interrupt. Firstly, and I think you knew this was coming, I want a divorce. I'm seeing my solicitor next week and I suggest you do the same. My parents have given me their full backing on this. Secondly,' Zarleena paused, amazed Armin wasn't interrupting, 'secondly, the gold was given to me as a present and as such it was mine to do with as I wished. So I did, I sold it.' A small gasp could be heard at the other end. 'And lastly, you're extremely lucky I never called the police yesterday regarding the spiders. It was both cruel to me and the spiders. If you come anywhere near me or my shop, next time I *will* call the police, and I'll have a court order delivered before you can blink.' Zarleena repeated a comment she'd heard in a Mafia movie: 'And if you think this is a joke, then I had better tell you the punchline.'

'Go on.'

'Mess up and I'll let the whole Indian community know how you used to beat me. News like that will spread quicker than the Internet. You would be shamed and shunned!' She paused, frozen by his silence, and did what she normally did when faced with nerves the size of mangos, she made a mockery of the situation. In her best American accent she said, 'Go on, punk, make my day!' And she hung up feeling drenched with foolishness.

Armin shook his head as he switched off the mobile. God gave women one too many holes, he thought. As if Zarleena's mouth hadn't already caused enough damage in his past, now she wanted to use it to wreck his future. He sat down on the bed, careful to avoid the half-eaten cheese and tomato pizza, and switched on the portable black and white TV, hoping it would drown out the noisy guests next door. What sort of riff-raff did Sea Rock B&B cater for, he wondered, letting out a twenty-decibel cheese and tomato pizza belch . . . To which a thirty-decibel greasy kebab belch answered back through the thin walls, followed by some boisterous laughter.

That sort of riff-raff.

Not wanting to go down that dangerous road of fifty-decibel belches, Armin turned up the volume on the TV and set about preparing his next move. It was at times like this he wished his family tree hadn't pruned him from their branches. How was he to have known that separating from Zarleena would have caused so much strife? The backlash was force ten. At family gatherings he was vilified by relatives. He was considered bad luck and thus banned from all Indian weddings. His father repossessed the company car. And lastly, to top it all, he was demoted from a director of Golden Karmas Cash 'n' Carry, to a mere sales rep. Which in real terms, in real money, meant he now earned a measly wage as opposed to a huge never-ending supply of dosh.

But whose fault was it? Armin blamed his parents. They chose Zarleena to be his wife knowing full well that he was not ready to marry. So, like a good Indian boy, he went along with the whole shebang. To please his parents. He settled down in a luxury flat in Edgbaston, Birmingham. To please his parents. He said the right thing, did the right thing, turned up at the family dos, invested all his free time in the family business. To please his parents.

And he beat the shit out of his wife ... to please himself. He remembered the awful guilt he'd felt after slapping Zarleena for the first time. Just a clip round the ear really, for not ironing a shirt correctly. It was hardly his fault; she'd known he was meeting an important client that day, and that it was imperative he turned up smartly dressed. The next slap was when she taped over the Mike Tyson v Lennox Lewis match with an episode of *Horizon*. They had their own boxing match that night. And this time the slaps were not followed by guilt. Soon everything about Zarleena annoyed him. But most annoying of all was the fact she wouldn't leave him; no matter how hard the slaps, no matter how frequent the beatings. He felt like a trapped monkey in a cage. Why she wouldn't go was beyond him. She was like a dog that kept coming back for more.

And more.

If she had simply left him he could have said to his parents those immortal words, 'At least I tried.' Instead it was Armin who left, and the only words on offer from his parents were: 'You have shamed the whole family.' And a shamed family folds its arms, shakes its head, and closes its doors. No more handouts, no more loans, no more credit-card bills paid for. You're on your own.

Which was why Armin had wanted the gold from Zarleena. The plan was to melt it down, sell it off and give two fingers to his parents. He didn't need their crummy money. Let them choke on their own greed. But now the gold was gone. Or was it? Armin had a theory that Einstein would have been proud of. Gold was like matter. It never really disappeared. It just changed into something else. This time, gold had changed into the Bindis & Brides shop. How the hell else had Zarleena raised enough capital to open that shop? He'd heard a rumour that Zarleena had had a windfall and now he knew where that windfall had blown in from – the hurricane force of gold.

Armin drizzled a pizza slice with chilli sauce then balanced the dough over a lampshade, warming it through via the bulb. He smiled at his own inventiveness. It would take a creative man like him to tackle the next problem. How to get back the money he was owed.

He bit into the reheated pizza, excited at where his brain was taking him. Oh boy was it going to be fun getting that bitch of a wife back – nearly as much fun as counting the money she would soon be handing over.

Armin grinned like a released chimpanzee.

Chapter Twelve

Candy was proud of the fact that out of all her female climbing companions, she was the only one still able to wear sandals. Toe and finger loss was a hazard that went hand-in-hand with the sport, with some climbers proudly displaying their disfigured limbs as if they were trophies. It has been said that there are enough toes and fingers up Mount Everest alone to keep a family of four cannibals fed for a year. Both Joel and Candy always began a text message to each other with 20. Indicating they were still attached to all their digits. (Although when feeling frisky Joel would sometimes text 21.)

After ripping off the silver wrapping paper, Candy looked in awe at her new Nicole Farhi sandals. Joel sure knew which buttons to press and she almost swallowed him in a hug.

'They are gorgeous,' she declared, checking the sole. 'And you even remembered to take off the price tag. How much were they?'

Nearly enough to take away the guilt for sleeping

with those other women, he thought. 'Oh, you know . . . a few quid.'

'You're making it so easy to say yes when you ask me to marry you, Joel.'

Joel suddenly stood up and walked out to the kitchen. 'I'll get some more drinks.' He returned shortly with another bottle of wine. 'Look, about marriage, we—'

She interrupted him, laughing at his worried expression. 'I was joking, Joel, I haven't forgotten what you said.'

Nor had he.

It was all about dreams. Ever since being struck with the mountain bug in his youth, Joel had made a pact with himself. He would not let a woman interfere with his goals. Too many men had forsaken too many ambitions just for a piece of skirt – that was probably too short. But what were Joel's goals, his ambitions, what dreams did he have that would have him put off marriage until he'd achieved them? Just a simple matter of climbing all fourteen of the world's highest mountains. That's all. One of his heroes, Reinhold Messner, was the first mountaineer to do all fourteen. In climbing circles, it was the ultimate prize.

And many had paid the ultimate price.

No marriage until he'd completed all fourteen? Some might say that he was pretty selfish. Candy certainly thought that he was being pretty selfish. But Joel knew that he wouldn't be able to give Candy the one hundred per cent she deserved until he'd given his dreams the one hundred per cent they were promised. Selfish? Possibly.

After reading an article when he was ten, entitled 'Why Climbers Need to be Selfish', Joel had tried to adhere to the 'selfish' rules. Christmas couldn't come quickly enough for Joel the year he became selfish. He'd told everyone that he was a bit strapped for cash and instead of buying them all individual presents he'd bought them all a joint gift instead. The time came for Joel's present to be unwrapped from around the Christmas tree. Dylan, Mum and Dad all drew straws to see who would have the honour of opening it. Mum won and was quite disappointed to find that Joel's present to all the family was a book: *Mountaineering*.

Joel soon realized that he only needed to be selfish when it came to his ambitions, not his wallet. Buying his family a book on mountaineering was an act that Joel still cringed at today. (Although the book came in very handy.)

Joel watched Candy wobbling in her new sandals. For someone who relied on perfect balance for most of her outdoor pursuits, she was sure having trouble with a simple pair of heels. About to make a ridiculous comment, he spotted the wine bottles they had consumed. He decided to make the comment anyway.

'I thought after sleeping with me you would easily be able to handle four inches,' Joel said sniggering.

She replied, 'After my last boyfriend I could handle stilts, it's you who brought me down to four inches, Joel.'

They both laughed, Joel less enthusiastically than Candy. He was going to remind her that her ex-boyfriend lay frozen up K2 and what use was an enormous willy when it was stuck up a mountain; but then he thought better of it. There were enough stiff jokes going around as it was. Suddenly a warning light ignited in his head. If he remembered correctly, Candy became sleepy with too much wine. And for some of the positions that he had planned for tonight she needed to be wide awake.

'Fancy a strong coffee?' Joel asked. 'Or a couple of Red Bulls? It's good stuff you know.'

'Trying to sober me up? Most men do the opposite.' Candy hobbled over in her new shoes and joined him on the sofa. 'But you're not like most men, are you?' She kissed him on the lips.

Joel thought about the time when he electrocuted his testicles with a gas lighter in preparation for the torture he might receive if captured by the Pakistanis for trespassing on their mountain in the Himalayas – no, Joel wasn't like most men.

They snuggled up, enjoying the harmony that they felt with each other, the feeling that somehow their destinies were bound together. Cupid had turned out to be quite a character. Not only could he shoot arrows, but he could bring two people together via a blizzard. And it was the strength of Joel and Candy's beginning that made the periods apart easier to bear. How many couples could survive a month apart, let alone three? Wouldn't Cupid's enemy, Adulterer, make a visit? Wouldn't he turn up with a beautiful, leggy woman, kick Loyalty in the nuts, and tempt Joel, whispering, 'Don't worry about Candy finding out. My mate, Liar, will help you out'? You bet he would.

And boy, would Joel have to rely on Liar tonight, and tomorrow, if he wanted to keep hold of Candy. In fact, Joel would have to continue the act right until the moment he slammed her suitcase in her boot and waved her goodbye. Only then would he receive his Oscar for Domestic Bullshit.

Right now, he deserved an award for Romantic Foreplay, he thought, judging by the moans Candy was emitting. She was almost singing, but most likely the kind of sound that Simon Cowell would never have heard before. Joel stared into Candy's blue eyes with even bluer thoughts, slightly annoyed at a stray feeling that was intent on interfering: had Candy forgotten to take her contraceptive pill? They'd had a close call once before, Candy missing her period, Joel missing his heartbeats. She even went as far as naming the unborn baby. Hillary for a girl. And Edmund for a boy. He didn't want to go through that palaver again. To be on the safe side he wanted to slip on a condom, but that would mean opening up the Hoover bag; it would spoil the mood and everything – plus he'd have to de-fluff it and rinse it through. NO THANKS! But to ask her about her pills would be to insult her. He'd have to hope his sperm got caught in a current and were swept away down her uterus before they could complete their mission.

It was only a matter of time before all thoughts were lost to the feeling of passion. Like a deprived drug addict Joel took his fix of Candy's naked beauty as though he were filling his veins with heroin itself. The high of knowing that soon he would be inside her was immense. And to watch her take small gasps of air, as he touched her dangerously, as she forced him back, not quite ready, turned him on in ways other women couldn't. And those other women, why? Why the need? Joel kissed Candy, her eyes begging him to fuck her, her earlier resistance now just a weak press against him. He didn't have the answers. Only a fool would risk losing all this, Joel thought, just for a quick shag. Candy lifted her hips up – Joel didn't need a second invite – and he gently pushed himself inside her.

'Base Camp, this is Joel, I have reached the summit,' he said, expecting a laugh from Candy. 'The view from here is . . . ouch. Sorry.'

For the next two hours Joel and Candy expended 4000 calories between them, the equivalent of running a half marathon, living up to their mountaineering logo: CLIMBERS DO IT UNTIL THEY FALL.

And both Joel and Candy had fallen. Fallen asleep. On the sofa, exhausted.

Sex on the sofa was pretty tame for people who prided themselves on their love of danger. But men quickly get to know that safe sex is always better than dangerous sex. (And besides, how would the men get to boast to their mates of their conquests if they died while in the throes of passion?) It was 10 p.m. before the two lovers stirred. Joel was pinching himself for not getting Zarleena to cook extra food the other week; a defrosted Indian meal would have gone down a treat. He was also dying to find out what effect Zarleena's spices would have on Candy's love-making skills. She already performed to a standard of someone who had consumed a couple of Chicken Tikka Masalas. It was unfortunate that the jar of Spicy

Seduction he'd placed in the fridge had grown a film of moss, so he couldn't test out the theory. He would have placed a few quid that Madhur Jaffrey's husband walked around with a constant smile on his face, that's for sure.

'Fancy a Red Bull sandwich?' Joel said, peering into the fridge. 'It's—'

'Good stuff, I know, Joel.'

He smiled at Candy in her candyfloss-pink silk dress. Underneath that aura of femininity lay an armoured core. A woman not afraid to get her hands dirty. Someone like Candy deserved a down-to-earth kind of meal.

'I was planning on us going out to eat. How does McDonald's sound?' he joked.

'Joel! You said wear something posh. I didn't dress up like this for Ronald McDonald.'

'And you won't be going to McDonald's. How does Indian food grab yer? A little taste of the Orient.' She nodded. 'Okay, let me go and wash this stink off my body and we'll get going.'

Candy shook her head, hoping he wasn't referring to their smells of passion. His turn of phrase wasn't exactly poetic. Although when Candy moved to the cork noticeboard tucked away in the corner of the kitchen, pinned underneath a collection of photos, takeaway menus and business cards was Joel's version of poetry. A set of lines that, on first reading, had Candy questioning Joel's sanity. Surely a man who didn't fear his own death was dangerous to be around. With an impulse to look at the poem again, Candy pulled it off the noticeboard.

MEET MY MAKER

I ain't gonna die from suicide.
And I ain't gonna die from no gun.
I ain't gonna pop my clogs from drugs.
And I don't want to die on my bum.

I know it's coming and I don't fucking care.
I'll take my death and I'll take it anywhere.
But I'll try for an ending that's as sour as
   it's sweet
Cos I hope when I meet my Maker, I meet
   him on a peak . . .
. . . a mountain peak!

Loving Joel was the hardest challenge of Candy's life. Her heart had been thrown in at the deep end the moment she'd fallen in love with him, and it had been trying not to drown ever since. Some days were easier than others, but every day was filled with fear. Fear she might lose him to another mountain. Fear she might lose him to another woman. But most of all: fear she might lose him because of herself. Her mum sometimes said, 'A good many women have driven away many a good man because many a good woman loves a good man too much.'

But some men are bastards.

Joel returned from the shower with just a towel round his trim stomach. A man like him could give a good many women the wet look; and really, when circulating amongst members of the opposite sex, he should come ready with a bag of spare knickers. And even though we live in a 'Hands off He's Mine' world, some women would still go to great lengths to put their hands on him.

Some women are bitches.

Candy was finding it progressively harder to believe that Joel didn't fill some of his spare time filling other women. Paranoia? Gut instinct? Fear? Stupidity? She hoped it was stupidity. Lately, on her visits to Hunterslea, Joel had been very cagey about going to certain pubs. His excuse that they were too rough sounded reasonable, but to the paranoid girlfriend, they sounded like a man worried he might bump into one of his lovers there. Then there was this woman who had sidled up to her while she was in Scotland taking a group of kids on a trip. In the middle of nowhere, halfway up a mountain, a woman climber trekking the other way, greeted her with the words, 'You're one of Joel's girlfriends, aren't you? Say hello to him for me, I'm Bianca. He's a right dish.' Paranoid?

You betcha.

'Joel, I don't trust you.' Candy launched into her statement. 'I find it hard to believe that in all the three months we have been apart you haven't slept with anyone.'

Joel nodded, he knew this was coming. 'Is that what *you* do? Sleep with other blokes in between our visits? Pretty low, Candy, pretty damn low.' He snapped open a Red Bull and hid his grin in the can.

'Erm. Of course not, I'm in complete control of my sexual urges. You, however, can't claim that, can you?'

He slammed the can down on the table, faking annoyance. 'That's why I wank, *Candy*, I do it for you. To take away my sexual urges.'

She stared at him with revulsion. 'You wank for me? I've never heard so much crap in all my life.'

Suddenly he shot across the kitchen, grabbed her hand and dragged her all the way down to the bedroom. He kicked open the door. 'Take a look in there and see how much masturbating goes on. I dare you to say I don't bash the bishop a lot.'

Deftly she snuck her head round the door. What greeted her eyes was beyond normal behaviour for a group of spotty teenage boys, let alone a grown man. Dirty magazines were strewn everywhere, pages stuck to one another, clumps of tissue on all walls and furniture. A blow-up doll on the bed, porn movie playing on the TV in the background on mute, and a selection of photographs of animals mating.

Joel folded his arms, grinning. 'Feeling a bit stupid? I *told* you I jerk off. I don't need a woman, I can quite happily entertain myself, thank you very much.'

She shook her head, her stomach feeling a little queasy; it was either the wine, or the view of the blow-up doll wearing a climber's helmet. 'I feel sick, Joel, I don't know what to say.'

'How about sorry for doubting me.'

A huge ball of semi-wet tissue fell off the ceiling, landing with a thud just by Candy's stilettos. Which was ironic considering she now needed tissues for her tears. Her sobbing was uncontrollable.

Joel's plans didn't go wrong that often, but when they did, they went wrong big style. He glanced at the far wall covered in naked women, surely there was a better way to convince Candy that his lies were true. What a tosser, he thought, what a complete tosser.

'Look, Candy, would you believe me if I said that all this, the masturbation, the tissues, all the props, it was all done because I'm paranoid that you might think I sleep around? When I don't. I genuinely thought you would be pleased that I wanked.'

'Please stop saying it, it sounds disgusting. You were paranoid? So you turn your bedroom into a sperm bank,' she sniffed, her tears now abating.

'NO! I used flour and water to make it look like sperm. What d'you take me for?'

'Oh, I wish you hadn't told me that.'

So did he.

But how had he made such a boo-boo in guessing Candy's reaction? He'd even had visions of her helping him tidy up the 'love suite'. She'd be so relieved that he was monogamous that clearing up soggy tissues would be a total pleasure. And now she thought of him as Hunterslea's biggest pervert. Maybe it was time to cut his losses and tell her the truth. At least end this relationship with some dignity. Thinking about it now, it was a bloody good job he hadn't ordered that penis-shaped cake with the words 'Cream Filled' on it. Surely that would have been the final nail in his coffin.

He began the defence. 'I've dug myself into quite a hole here, Candy, and the only way I can see out of it is by telling you the truth.' He paused to delay the guillotine. 'I know this will end our relationship, but you deserve to know what a shit I am. Many times I have been raped by women. It's like my hormones have been spiked by date rape drugs.' He looked up.

And Candy looked away. 'So, how many of these "date rapes" have you had to endure?'

He whispered, 'I've lost count.'

'You bastard, Joel.'

An awkward atmosphere descended like fog. Joel afraid to say any more, Candy trying to ignore her instincts to kill him. If this was the silence before the thunder, Joel thought, then he had better batten down the hatches. Candy had hurricane force anger when needed and people who knew her learned quickly to avoid the eye of her storm. To try to placate her now was riskier than removing a thorn from a tiger.

As if kicked, Candy shot forward, grabbed a climbing rope, some pitons and a hammer from the messy floor, barged past Joel and sped across the apartment to the front door. Two seconds later she was gone.

Five seconds later Joel was tipping wine down his throat. He knew exactly where she was going and took a gamble that Candy needed her own space at the moment. There wasn't a rule book that denoted what to do when a woman ran off like that. Maybe it would be a good idea to read Warren Beatty's autobiography (that's if Warren had had the energy to write one in between his women) then next time he would be wiser. He lumbered into the bedroom and began to dress; he'd give her half an hour to calm down.

Which was something Zarleena's parents had been trying to do since listening to Zarleena reveal that Armin was back on the scene. Accepting that Armin was trying to interfere in their daughter's life was bad enough, but worse was the fact that Zarleena had requested that they were not to get involved. To stay out of it. Not to interfere. Appeals that no parent wants to hear from their children.

Especially parents who liked to take control of their daughters.

Namely, Indian parents.

'If we move to England,' Zarleena's father had announced to his young wife in the early seventies over a cup of milky *chai*, in the stinking heat of an Indian summer, 'then let it be said now, that no matter how hard things get, we never give in and return back home to India. If we go, we go for good.'

No matter how hard things get. Hardly worrying words to a couple from a poverty-stricken village who had never had it easy. *If we go, we go for good.* Not exactly disturbing words to a couple desperate to provide a better life for any children they might have. So with more excitement than trepidation the two brown newly-weds flew to England to seek their future in the land of the white man.

And boy, was it cold. After shivering away in the English summer, someone introduced them to an item called 'the Jumper'. It was amazing. As soon as it was worn over the *shalwar kameez* then the goose bumps disappeared or 'jumped away' (Mum's first attempt at an English joke). It was their first true lesson in adapting to a new country. But why buy them when one could quite easily knit them at home? Zarleena's father found employment at a local paper factory via his older brother who had moved to Colchester three years before them. The money was good and the people were friendly and it left Zarleena's mother with plenty of time to knit.

By the time she'd worked her way through four thousand balls of wool, with most of the Asian community now wearing hideous colourful stripy jumpers, Zarleena and Honey had been born and were both in nappies (not knitted). The trials of living in a foreign land had taken their toll, but had not withered their determination to stay. The racism, the weather and the thousands of miles separating them from their relatives still in India. Then there was the worry of bringing up two girls in a society whose rules regarding sex were, let's say . . . very open. And that was a good description of most of the young female disco-goers' legs after midnight.

Which was a good reason why, when both Zarleena and Honey became of age, their outdoor activities were restricted to the temple, school and library. Hardly the hang-outs of the local studs. Which was just the way Mum and Dad preferred it. Strict. Strict. Stricter. It was the only way with Indian girls. Besides, they had an arranged marriage to look forward to. Surely they trusted their own parents when it came to picking their future stud.

And both Zarleena and Honey did. Why would their parents fix them up with anything but the best? The crème de la crème of Indian men. It was a great day for everyone when Armin was introduced to the family. He was the perfect gentleman, with the looks of a Bollywood film star, the manners of a prince and a family background that was squeaky clean. On paper he was fantastic, in the flesh just sensational. No wonder agreement to the wedding was almost instant-aneous.

But so was the change in Armin's personality the moment Zarleena became his wife – or rather, the moment Zarleena became *his*. It put a new slant on the arranged marriage; Zarleena had become the arranged 'punch bag' instead. Their decision would haunt her mother and father for evermore. It's every parent's nightmare to know that their children are in pain. But to know that because of your decision your own child suffered in unimaginable ways, well, night-mare didn't quite cover that. It was a feeling of extreme guilt tied up with extreme regret. Enough of a feeling to question the very roots of your traditions. Reason to ask yourself the question, 'Are arranged marriages really the best way?' Handing your daughter over to a man who was a virtual stranger.

Zarleena's parents weren't naive enough to believe that all arranged marriages turn out to be arranged marriages from hell, but they weren't gamblers enough to risk going through the traditional process again. From that moment on, the custom blinkers were off. Any man whom either Zarleena or Honey wanted to marry would be blessed by them. Whether he be black, white, brown or green.

No one wanted a repeat of what had happened with Armin – except, maybe, the people who had stocks in ibuprofen pain relief.

Chapter Thirteen

The evening was warm enough for nocturnal animals to star bathe and the gibbous moon cast soft shadows on the dry grassy field. Candy leaned against the castle ruins, slightly puffing, peering up to the Forest Falls Apartment lights five hundred yards away. If she was raped tonight it would be Joel's fault. If some greasy axe murderer spilt from the nearby woods and chopped her into pie filling, Joel would be held *responsible*. Which was a word that definitely didn't apply to Joel.

She didn't know whether her heart palpitations were from the mad sprint up here, or from Joel breaking it, but slowly the cooling breeze began to calm her. Sense and reason were items most women carried around with them in the same way they did their mascara (although some women can live without either sense or reason), and it was important to apply them only when the eyes were dry of tears. Trying to decipher a man's behaviour in the midst of a full-on crying session was nigh impossible. Which was why, for now, Candy refused to cry.

She had been raised the old-fashioned way: when a man cheated, you severed his penis. Then you dumped him. (What good is a penis-less man?) But which one of Joel's penises would she amputate? Candy was convinced that Joel was three men. Climbing Joel. Romantic Joel. And Lad About Town Joel. Up a mountain he was steadfast. In a bed he was a turn-on. About town he was a let-down – sleeping around.

Candy watched a couple of bats flapping about the ruins. If it was kiss chase they were up to, Candy hoped they weren't vampire bats. She turned her attention to the stone wall and, under the moonlight, could just make out some marker-pen graffiti:

> *Call this a school trip? It's crap*
> *Billy from Form 3b*

She almost laughed. Poor old Billy, he had probably been expecting moats and drawbridges. She almost cried. Poor old Candy, she had been expecting much more from Joel. Certainly she never had him down as the 'affair' type; admittedly, she did goad him from time to time about flings and affairs, but that was just to keep him on his toes, and even though Joel was tanked up with good looks and sex appeal, somehow, she thought he would always say 'no' when approached by other women. And these women who stay with their cheating men, how do they cope? Is it making the best of a bad situation? Would living without them, the scummy, weak-minded men, who can't help but cheat, be harder than living with them?

Candy removed her sandals and hitched up her

dress. She was a Cornish lass through and through, Joel was an Essex boy froo 'n' froo. Surely Cornish pasties with Pie 'n' Mash were a no-no. God planted those two counties two hundred miles apart for several reasons. And one of those reasons was for men like Joel not to take up with women like Candy. She peered up at the seven-metre high wall, made a swift calculation, and flung her safety rope to the ground. Unwanted.

Just like Joel was?

Foot-by-hand-by-foot Candy ascended the ancient relic, her expertise hardly challenged, her bravery barely explored. Up here on the wall's ledge, as a soft wind tussled her long hair, Candy looked out on the grounds below with her bird's eye view. Sometimes the world looked so much better when the details were too small to see. Mountaineering gave a view of life that cleared the mind of unwanted weeds. She knew why Joel loved the great heights, she just didn't understand why he took the great risks.

A shadow slowly worked its way down the field towards the ruins like a cancer stain moving down an X-ray. It was decision time. Did she give Joel the chance to explain? Or did she give him the push? Candy's own father had played away; Mum kicked him out; Mum seemed to cope. With her Valium, booze, bitter views on men, and acupuncture, she coped extremely well.

The cancer stain arrived and opened its malignant mouth. 'I thought I would find you here,' Joel shouted up, noting she was barefoot. 'Lost your shoes?' His eyes caught sight of her sandals by the base of the wall, along with the safety rope, pitons and hammer. He glared up angrily. 'You stupid idiot, what are you trying to do, kill yourself?' Climbing at night, half drunk, alone, without equipment or shoes, was considered by most sane climbers to be totally insane. 'I'm stupefied!'

Her voice dropped down. 'If you want to discuss stupidity I suggest you climb on up, Lad About Town.'

A few minutes later Joel was perched on the ledge next to her. He pulled out a Red Bull from his combats, cracked it open and handed it to Candy. This seemed like the ideal place to make an apology. If she didn't like it, she could always push him off. A twenty-five-odd-foot drop would certainly teach him a lesson or two about penis etiquette. Joel knew that what came out of his mouth in the next few seconds would determine whether or not Candy forgave him. The excuse had to be perfect.

He took a deep breath. 'If I lose you because of this' – Joel was about to tug out his plonker, and slap it hard to teach it a lesson, but thought better of it – 'if I lose you because of my penis, then I'm the biggest dick going. It's like I've thrown away the winning lottery ticket for a cheap bonk.' He produced an SOS flare and lit it. 'I'm not going to lie to you and pretend I didn't enjoy the shags.'

'Well, you can just fuck off then,' she spat. 'God, Joel, when you cut you really cut deep, don't you?'

'I'm just saying it was purely physical. No emotional attachment whatsoever.'

'Gee thanks.'

He held the flare as close to his face as he dared, to let Candy see how sincere his expression was. 'I fucking hate myself at the moment, I've hurt you and I've made you feel like shit, and all because I couldn't control my urges. How could I have done this to you?' He rose to his feet then began walking down the narrow ledge. 'This is what losers do just to inflate their ego.'

'You are the weakest of the weaker sex.'

Joel closed his eyes and continued to walk across the wall, wobbling at each step, his balance in question. Candy saw the crazy edge in Joel's make-up rear its ugly, bandaged head. Maybe this wasn't the place to be having this discussion. The maybe became a definitely when Joel dropped his flare seven metres below and began to pirouette on the spot. Next up were hand-stands, followed by cartwheels; he was just about to attempt a back flip (his first at this height) when it became too much for Candy.

'Stop it, Joel, please. This is not a cool height to die from.' He continued to spin, now with one leg out like a ballerina; seven metres high was child's play. She said firmly, 'If you want me to forgive you, this is blackmail. Please stop.'

The spinning stopped and the real apology began. Joel sat next to Candy explaining how much he loved her. How his mistakes would never be repeated. She questioned his sincerity. If dicks could talk, what would Joel's say? Would it whisper in Candy's ear, 'Don't believe a word, Candy, Joel and I are on shag duty the minute you head back to Cornwall'? It was hard enough to trust a man at the best of times, but how did Candy go about trusting a man who had, quote, 'lost count' of the women he'd slept with behind her back. She couldn't.

But she couldn't lose him either. It was a pig-shit sit-uation, with only one solution that didn't stink. Candy would have to move in with Joel. It wasn't ideal, she had her own life back in Cornwall helping the disabled children go on activity holidays, but the next step in their relationship had to be taken one day. Didn't it? Besides, for the relationship to really stand a chance of survival in this modern world, it helped if the couple actually saw each other more than they did.

So it was decided, in six months' time, in the New Year, Candy would move in with Joel. Time enough for him to finish his autobiography, give Eloise advance warning that he needed her to move out, and time enough for Candy to find a replacement activity leader in Cornwall and set up a disabled scheme in Hunterslea. Suddenly her life had nipped into the fast lane.

Back at the apartment Joel sat with Candy on the sofa, drinking strong coffee, their faces barely illuminated by the flickering candles. Apart from the ghostly quiet, the only thing out of the ordinary was the bin liner stuffed with pornography, tissues and a blow-up doll resting by the front door. It was a testament to the quality of the blow-up doll that it took Joel seven stabs of the kitchen knife before it went down. It was the last time Juicy Lucy went down on any man.

It was also a testament to the quality of a couple's relationship if they could comfortably sit silently in a room for any length of time. Either that or one of them was sulking. Joel placed his arm round Candy's shoulders and she sank her face into his chest. Heads were gonna roll in his hormone department for this. Either his testicles or his pituitary gland were going to take the rap for this one. Today had been a lesson in soulsearching. Seeing Candy in tears had sent Joel deep into his soul to find the words to dry them. They say you hurt the one you love, but what about Demoralize, Deceive, Distress, Dispirit the one you love, all the Ds . . . Except for Deserve.

No woman can surely Deserve a man who treats her like she was Dirt.

Candy began. 'I know I originally said that we should have an open relationship when we first went out, but I never thought you'd take me literally – especially after you confessed that you loved me. And anyway, "open" doesn't mean every time a woman opens her legs you have to dive in. If I had done the same to you, Joel, if I had slept with so many guys that I lost count, what would you do?' Candy said, sobbing into his T-shirt.

'I think I would have dumped you.'

'That's what I thought. It makes me a sucker, doesn't it?'

It was the wrong time for a blow-job joke. 'Well, get down on your knees and prove it then.'

She gently smacked him. 'You won't hurt me like this again, Joel, will you? Promise me.'

He kissed her on the lips. No way was he going to hurt her again. Not in this life. The fear of losing Candy had knocked some sense into him. Next time a woman other than Candy opened her legs for him, he'd politely ask her to close them.

Case closed.

More like case adjourned.

Candy still had questions that needed answering, but they could wait until morning, she was far too tired to ask Joel how pretty the women were, etc. For now, just the two of them watching the candles burn down was all the excitement she needed. The flames were a slow dance in the room to the background music of their hearts.

Suddenly the candle flames jived as the front door swung open. Before Joel could yell out, 'Mind the bin bag,' Eloise had tripped on Juicy Lucy's deflated head and skidded halfway across the living-room floor, landing face down, spreadeagled beside Candy's stilettos. It beat Blackpool's rides any day.

'I'm such a klutz,' Eloise said, rising to greet Candy with a warm hug. 'And before you joke about another woman falling at your feet, Joel, remember I know how upset you've been lately.' She made herself at home between Joel and Candy, shunting him along. 'He has missed you soooo much, Candy, he's been horrible to live with.'

Joel elbowed Eloise in the ribs. Now was not the time for sisterly help.

'Really?' Candy said, amusement creeping into her voice box. 'How very interesting.'

'Yeah,' Eloise continued, 'if I didn't know you two slept together, I'd think he was gay. He's like this zombie who doesn't even know pretty women exist. Except you that is, Candy.' She pinched Joel's cheek as she shouted, 'ONE OF A KIND. What a result, hey, Candy, you get the only decent bloke in the world who doesn't sleep around. Well done!' She stood, kissed Candy goodnight, then walked out of the room whispering, '*Candyman, Candyman, Candyman,*' knowing that Joel owed her at least £200 for helping him out just then.

Candy stared at 'the only decent bloke in the world who doesn't sleep around'. She said with an edge of disappointment, 'You lie so much, Joel, I'm beginning to wonder: is Eloise really your sister? Or is she your live-in lover? It's very noble of her to lie on your behalf. Was that the plan? For her to burst in at the last minute and make out that you don't sleep around. You're a low-life sick worm, Joel. I'm off to bed.' She scurried away growling, 'Alone.'

Joel picked up his imaginary voodoo doll of Eloise and stuck some imaginary pins in her. 'You stupid cow, Eloise, you stupid, stupid cow. Thanks for nothing.'

After snuffing out the candles Joel lay back on the sofa as his emotions switched back and forth from anger to regret to anger. And there was nothing imaginary about how crap he was feeling right now. How could he have hurt Candy this way? Over the next few days Candy would see a much shorter Joel than she was used to. He would be crawling on his knees that much!

Chapter Fourteen

Dear Bindis & Brides
Fuck off back to India!

Honey held the typed note under Zarleena's nose for her to read. It was not the greatest of starts to a Friday morning. The Union Jack writing paper it was printed on only heightened the feeling of anger. Weren't Zarleena and Honey just as British as anyone else born on these shores? Weren't they schooled and ruled by this country? Zarleena was shocked to see the remnants of a white powdery substance on the paper and was about to yell out 'ANTHRAX' when she noticed Honey's lips were covered in the very same substance.

'Don't worry,' Honey began, pleased with herself, 'I've already tasted it; it's only icing sugar. No need to ring MI5.'

'You tasted it? And what if it was anthrax? What then?'

Honey shook her head as if it was Zarleena who

was the idiot. 'Der! I'd be dead, wouldn't I? Anyway, I don't know what anthrax tastes like.'

'Well, if you read the newspapers, you would have known it tastes like icing sugar.'

Honey screamed as she ran to the back of the shop to wash off the powder.

But in a way the printed note was related to anthrax. It was both poisonous and evil. Although it's doubtful Senator Dashall would worry too much if he received a letter saying, 'Fuck off back to India'. If he was like most Americans, he wouldn't even know where India was.

The sisters tried to put the note out of their minds, knowing that Fridays were normally as busy as a hive; a mad rush to buy presents and clothes before the weekend weddings. It was no good worrying about Icing Sugars of Mass Destruction when a client wanted advice on henna tattoos. Indian customers treated shopping as a social event, nattering to other customers, passing the time of day. Zarleena and Honey even served up cardamom *chai* and sweetmeats to keep the women happy. For a happy customer is a buying customer.

'This letter stinks of Armin,' Zarleena uttered to Honey, as they stocked up a sari rail. 'He's trying to scare us again. We'll just ignore it; men like him hate to be ignored.'

'We could go to the police, it's about time we cooked for them. That okra dish went down a treat last time. The guys said they'd get out their truncheons for us any day of the week.' Honey admired a stunning silk sari, covered in sequins, holding it against her body. 'I much prefer the written threat as opposed to the eight-legged one, don't you?'

Memories of hairy tarantulas came creeping and crawling back, sending a shiver down both sisters' spines. In some cultures, evil folk are said to be reincarnated as spiders. The girls agreed with amusement that Armin was sure to come back as one, and the web of deceit that he was weaving now would soon be the web he used to catch flies.

But a threat was a threat and it left you on edge. It didn't help when customers almost kicked open the door to enter the premises. Both girls jumped as Joel made his entrance; but not nearly as high as Mrs Chowdrey who was glancing through the wedding stationery catalogue halfway up the shop and hadn't been that frightened since she'd seen the quote for her daughter's wedding, but high enough to qualify for the prestigious Tandoori House Games.

Joel removed his shades and marched towards the back of the shop. He passed an old Indian lady, who smelled of curry, then a young couple who smelled of curry, then up to Zarleena and Honey who smelled of . . . garlic. You are what you eat. He just prayed to God he didn't smell of shepherd's pie.

'Good morning, Zarleena, good morning, Honey. Firstly I want to apologize for pretending to fall off The Big Lick Mountain, it was a sick joke and I should have known better.' Joel rubbed his unshaven chin. 'Secondly, I'm in a bit of a pickle to tell you the truth. My girlfriend, Candy, thinks I've been sleeping around which is hurtful really, because I'm not that sort of guy. Anyway, to make the peace, I thought I'd buy her a present. Something special. I know she loves all this spiritual stuff that you sell. I was hoping you could suggest something different that I could give her.'

Zarleena thought back to the photos of Candy hidden in Joel's bedside drawer, she nudged Honey and whispered in her ear in Hindi, 'Bless him, Candy's dead. He means Claudia. His new fiancée.' Zarleena turned her attention to Joel. 'I think you mean Claudia, Joel, not Candy,' she said softly.

'Yeah, I mean Claudia.'

Joel was in cringe heaven. Yet again he'd forgotten that it was Claudia who Zarleena had believed she was cooking for. It was Claudia, Zarleena believed, he was now engaged to. And it was Claudia, Zarleena believed, who was thinking about having his children (on one condition) – *only* if Joel could cook another beautiful Indian meal like he did last time. God, Zarleena believed a lot of crap, but why did he tell so many lies, Joel asked himself; what was the point? Well, at least he didn't lie to himself he thought, scratching his twenty-inch cock.

Soon Joel found himself amongst a selection of Hindu statues, hand-carved bead necklaces, small water features, books on yoga, shiatsu massage and reiki, and even crystals shaped as elephants.

'You haven't got a leather-bound *Kama Sutra*, I take it?' Joel asked sincerely. 'With colour photographs.'

'That would be a no. Bad gift idea,' said Zarleena.

'I understand.' Joel felt slightly ashamed. 'I'm against pornography myself; it's so degrading for women. I found out one of my mates was reading a *Penthouse* once, and I was so upset with him that I never spoke to him again.' He paused. 'Actually that was a lie. Sorry.'

Zarleena and Honey giggled. What was he on?

There was a good reason for Joel's behaviour. Since Tuesday's confession, Joel had hardly slept. What had begun as a niggling worry in his subconscious brain had multiplied and swollen into a full-scale panic throughout his entire being. Men never survived in a relationship once they had committed sin. They postponed the inevitable, but as sure as night followed day, as regret always followed affairs, the women always left them in the end.

To lose Candy . . . To lose Candy . . . Joel wouldn't know what to do if he lost Candy. He'd probably lose his mind. Or maybe he'd become the first person to climb Mount Everest just to throw himself off. He might even do what most members of the 'I fucked up' club did, drink himself into oblivion and then join the exclusive 'cirrhosis' club where instead of 'bring a bottle' to a party, it was 'bring your own liver'.

Joel was about to ask a daft question about hypnotherapy when the shop door banged open, a young kid of about ten yelled, 'Smelly Pakis', threw a string of limp pork sausages across the shop floor, then legged it out, followed speedily by a cursing Honey, leaving the customers in Bindis & Brides speechless (for a nanosecond).

'Is this normal?' Joel asked, staring at Zarleena in astonishment.

Quite clearly annoyed, she replied, 'No!', then retrieved the bangers off the model of the Taj Mahal. 'They normally lob pork pies.' She looked up at him.

'Actually, I think you're a jinx. The racist gremlins only seem to come out to play when you're about. First there was Spud in the café and now this.'

He nodded in agreement. 'Zarleena, just like I wouldn't expect you to apologize on behalf of all Indians if I was served a bad curry, then I won't apologize on behalf of the ignorant white people with their racist comments. But,' he lifted up his index finger to make a point, 'I will stand here ashamed of them.' He slumped his shoulders and lowered his head. 'Bad people.'

Zarleena smiled. God, he was cute at times. And devilishly handsome. It was either a stroke of genius or a stroke of luck that God gave Joel all the good genes. Weren't hunky men supposed to be bastards? Womanizers? Adulterers? Joel was a breath of fresh air (and believe me, thought Zarleena, that's hard in a shop full of Indians), a one-off, or as the AA breakdown advert said, 'A very nice man.'

But what made a nice man? Someone who waited for the woman to orgasm before him? A helper with housework? A PMT sympathizer? What about a man who talked make-up and hairstyles? Did all these attributes a nice man make?

Or did they make him a right poof?

Zarleena studied Joel, still looking pitiful with his head lowered. No, what made Joel a nice man was his ability to make her laugh, the love he showed for his fiancée, Claudia, and the fact that he would rescue a kitten in a fire if he had to. Most men she'd met over the years would think twice about rescuing their own grandmother, even using the opportunity to chuck all those unwanted hand-knitted sweaters on the bonfire for kindling.

Finally Joel's head rose – the period of shame was over. But still he had to find a suitable present for Candy. Zarleena led him to a small selection of ornaments at the back of the store. Bronze statuettes of Hindu Gods. Stone slabs engraved with Indian proverbs. Finely sculptured glass figurines, elegant and expensive. Each item the result of hundreds of painstaking hours of labour.

Joel picked up a marble tablet boldly carved with a copy of a seventh-century stone relief of Vishnu cavorting with a naked Shri. Vishnu was an Indian Hindu God, the protector of the world. And Shri was a symbol of a loyal Hindu wife.

'I want this,' Joel said, stroking Shri's breasts. '"A loyal and submissive wife", I think Candy will love it.' He winced. 'I mean Claudia. This beautiful marble thing shows my future wife, Claudia, exactly where I see the pair of us in the future. It shows us together. In fact, I can't think of anything better. Unless you sell spiritual dildos?'

Zarleena elbowed him – customers were within earshot. 'I'll gift-wrap it for you then.'

Back at the counter, Zarleena went about packaging the present. Ribbons and bows, sparkle and glam. There was always something rewarding in wrapping, Zarleena explained to Joel, knowing that the next time someone saw the gift, hopefully, that person would be smiling.

'Unless you're wrapping a parcel bomb,' he replied, signing the credit-card slip. He felt someone breathing down his neck and turned to see a middle-aged Indian woman. '*Namaste*,' Joel said, holding his hands together and bowing his head in greeting.

'*Namaste*,' Mrs Chowdrey replied, nearly knocked off her *chappals* with surprise.

He continued, '*Mera nam Joel hai. Kya hal hai?*'

'*Main thik hun. Mera nam Mrs Chowdrey hai.*' Mrs Chowdrey looked to Zarleena for an answer to Joel's fluent Hindi, but Zarleena only shrugged. It was the first time in her life that a white man had introduced himself to her in her first language then asked her how she was. Bloody show off. She decided to raise the standard. '*Tusi bafiut sofiani Hindi bolde fio.*'

Joel nodded knowingly. It was obvious that Mrs Chowdrey Hai was trying to make him look stupid. Well, two can play at that game. Let's see if she knew English as well as she thought. He stared straight into her confident brown eyes then spoke quickly, 'Ah biggedy biggedy bong, ah biggedy biggedy bong, dipedy dopedy dipedy dopedy dipa—'

Zarleena put her hands on her hips. 'Oh, Joel, grow up, would you?'

Joel had picked up his basic Hindi knowledge on his many excursions to Nepal. Survival wasn't always about crampons, ropes and pulleys, sometimes survival relied on communications. Especially with the locals. Although it is a safe bet that throughout all the world, when it came to being pinched hard on the cheek by a weighty middle-aged Indian woman, everybody emitted the same sound.

'Ahhhhhhh,' Joel emitted, rubbing his cheek.

'That vill teach you vor being rude to your elders. HA!' Mrs Chowdrey said.

It was time for Joel to leave. Leaning across the counter he kissed Zarleena on the cheek. 'Thanks, you've been a great help.' He walked down the shop and shouted, 'If she doesn't like the present, can I return it?'

'Of course,' Zarleena shouted back, blushing slightly.

'But at the price you've just charged me, I'm expecting Claudia to love it so much that she will get down on her knees and give me the best blow job I've ever had. See ya!'

Zarleena dropped to the floor, laughing at Joel's unabashed crudity out of sight of the other customers but particularly out of sight of Mrs Chowdrey. Indian girls are supposed to keep their sense of humour to themselves in front of men – especially when their elders are present; letting out a small giggle would be frowned upon in the same way as if the Indian girl had just ripped off a huge fart in a busy temple. As such, Zarleena was dreading coming back up from below the counter. No one frowned harder than Mrs Chowdrey.

The shop door tinkled and Zarleena jumped up; her hopes that Honey had returned were dashed on spotting the paperboy dropping off the local rag. Mrs Chowdrey was stuck rigid to the floor. She wasn't going anywhere until she'd put some wrongs to right. In this case the wrong was Zarleena.

Mrs Chowdrey began in her native tongue, Hindi: 'You have beautiful skin, Zarleena, as pretty as the sun. Have you ever seen how ugly skin burnt by boiling *ghee* becomes? Suddenly a perfect princess becomes a disfigured untouchable.' She lowered her voice to a whispering hiss, 'You could have pulled away when that Englishman kissed you. But you stood there and shamed all of India. You let this man caress our motherland with his sly lips. A kiss on you is a kiss on us, Zarleena, now go and wash him off your body.' Mrs Chowdrey let a thin smile climb onto her mouth. 'I know you are young and find it hard to keep to the right path, but kissing men, especially the white man, is virtually irredeemable. I suggest you go to the temple this Sunday and pray for some forgiveness.' She noisily placed a one-pound coin in the ASIAN WOMEN'S HOSTEL charity box, eyed Zarleena for a good few seconds, and left the shop.

Over the top?

Zarleena had had worse. Schooling for any Indian girl continues until way after they've left college. A headmistress in every town, at least five teachers for every pupil. A whole wave of grandmothers, mothers and aunts at the ready to rain down their wisdom on the young Indian women of today. But surely these great teachers don't just walk up to young girls, whom they don't know, in the street and lecture them on the rules of life?

Wanna bet. It's one of the great pleasures of being an elder, knowing they can stick their oar in wherever they see fit. Zarleena and Honey used to joke that the Indian women would go on excursions, day trips, hunts, to find Indian girls breaking the rules. Minibuses of ageing women in camouflage saris on the look-out for girls smoking, sipping, snogging, or swearing. They used to joke about it . . . until they got caught.

Zarleena shuddered, thinking back to her youth. Both she and Honey had been caught with fags in their mouths, bottles in their mouths, but thank God, no cocks. Mum and Dad had been informed by various Asian Super Grasses as to what their daughters got up to. Mrs Balwinder Punderper, from across the road, didn't let her rickets, shin-splints, arthritis or her partial blindness prevent her from following the sisters and noting their wrongdoings. It was her duty as a teacher.

And it was Zarleena's duty as a pupil to learn. To disregard common sense sometimes and follow the path of history. Arranged marriages are born to Indians as clearly as the colour of their skin. Those who choose a different path, in the eyes of many Indians, are snakes who have shed their brown skins. Zarleena was proud of her skin, proud of her history and proud of her parents. As a child she'd watched her parents closely, asking herself the question: did they seem happy? And always they did. But was that enough to base her future on? She trusted them when they told her that they would pick Mr Right for her husband. She trusted them when they said love would eventually blossom. She trusted them when they explained the advantages of the Indian way of marriage compared to that of the West.

She trusted them.

So why did arranged marriages seem so wrong? Was it because it took the 'free' out of freedom and replaced it with 'thral'? Thraldom. Slavery. Bondage. A life of subservience. Was it that, after all the years of being banned from talking about men and sex, suddenly Mum and Dad were choosing the man with whom you have to 'do it'? Or was it simply that every time Zarleena had spoken to a cousin or an Asian friend, news was that yet another Indian girl, shitting herself over her looming arranged marriage, had run away from home?

Was it because the Indian way was splitting up families?

But was not wanting to risk splitting up her family a good enough reason for Zarleena to have gone along with what her parents had wished?

Back in school, boys had asked Zarleena on dates; in college, teenage lads had tried to feel her up; and at work, men had tried to seduce her. 'I'm sorry, but I really don't fancy you,' was easier to say than, 'I'm having an arranged marriage and my parents choose which boy will fill me up, thank you.'

If romance was a battlefield, then there were many dead egos lying around because of Indian women. But if weddings were a battlefield, then there were many dead romances lying around because of the Indian way.

So what did all this have to do with burnt faces? Mrs Chowdrey was from a different era, almost another dimension, where acid outsold *ghee* as the chemical of choice to throw over a misbehaved Indian girl. But what construed misbehaviour? Being kissed on the cheek by a white man was definitely in that category. Flirting, showing too much skin, entering Miss Wet Sari competitions. Misbehaviour in Indian society covered so many situations that the safest way for an Indian child to not misbehave was to copy David Blaine and have themselves frozen in a block of ice. Even then some Indian granny would complain that each time the child was needed for *chapatti*-making duty, they took too long to defrost. It was all about rules . . . and a suitable punishment for breaking them.

Unfortunately what some people might consider suitable, others would consider barbaric. Zarleena had seen pictures of Asian women whose faces had been stolen by nitric acid. She'd stared in horror reading newspaper articles of poor Bangladeshi women who had upset their husband for some feeble crime, maybe innocently looking at another man or not producing a son, and paid for it with a disfigurement which children would run from. Many crimes go on behind closed doors, Zarleena knew that, but wasn't it about time the huge doors of India, Pakistan and Bangladesh were heaved open for all to see the evil suffering that many women are living with. A newspaper article is tomorrow's fish and chip paper, but make no mistake, a scarred face is for life.

The telephone rang, unburdening Zarleena from her thoughts. Honey was on the line, she'd caught the sausage thrower nearly half a mile down the road.

'Whatever you do, Zarleena, don't eat the bangers, they're off,' Honey puffed down the mouthpiece. 'The little toe rag said his father made him do it.'

'Just let him go, Honey.'

'Spoilsport. Oh, guess what your observant sister spotted while running after this little twit. Stop struggling, you worm. Sorry, Zarleena. I only saw a chequered blue turban, didn't I? So cross it off the Turban Rainbow chart.'

Zarleena was dumbfounded. Not the chequered blue. 'I don't believe you. You're making it up.'

'Am I?' A second later and a young lad's voice was on the line. 'She's telling the truth. She saw a chequered blue turban. Now let me go, you're hurting me.' Honey returned to the conversation. 'Satisfied?'

'S'pose. Anyway, hurry back, I need to speak to you about something.'

An excitable yelp. 'Tell me.'

'I'll tell you when you get back. But it's about Joel.' The phone line went dead.

Chapter Fifteen

Already Candy was regretting promising Joel that she would carry his present with her at all times. The fucking thing weighed a tonne. Yesterday had been a good day for her; all her demons had been laid to rest when Joel handed her the stone tablet and proposed over a beautiful Greek meal. His eyes spoke of devotion, the wonderful diamond engagement ring shouted of commitment, and the triple orgasm which followed screamed of excitement. A date for their wedding was set, 30 April the following year – in tribute to the day Sir George Mallory's frozen body, missing for seventy-five years, was rediscovered clinging to the side of Mount Everest (obviously dead). Enough time for Joel's permit to come through enabling him to conquer another one of his magic fourteen mountains (continuing with the challenge he'd set himself when he was younger). And enough time for Candy to organize the wedding in the fashion that she'd always dreamed. Expensive.

The shock of Joel's sudden proposal had banished Candy's fears to her subconscious wasteland. A deep pit where she dropped her nightmares and regrets. To turn him down would have been to turn happiness down; how could she even think about living without him? She certainly couldn't live without thinking about him. Even right now, while he was having his urine tested for his annual insurance medical, her thoughts were with him, smiling at the futility of Joel having a drug test, heart test, liver, kidney, asthma and lung tests, when all they had to do was read what Joel had cheekily written on the form under Hobbies: Death Wish. But after the noises that he'd made in the bedroom last night, maybe the health test wasn't so futile after all. She wouldn't be surprised if the urine sample came back as: Rutting Bull.

With Joel out of the picture, Eloise and Candy had decided to go to a place where men weren't needed. The shops. Nothing quite beat the buzz of barcodes being scanned on the tills, or arms being stretched by countless bags, or that welcome sit down in the café at the end for tea and scones.

Eloise and Candy sat surrounded by their shopping haul in the trendy Taste Box Café. If only Candy hadn't insisted on bringing her stone tablet, she might have been able to carry another six bags. As it was, there were only a mediocre twenty. Not including the bags within bags.

'It's really beautiful,' Candy said, holding it out for Eloise to view. 'I'll never get used to it.'

Eloise stared jealously at Candy's platinum credit card. 'It's lovely. Suits you perfectly.'

'It's the one advantage of parents splitting up; you get to play them off against each other. I'm a bit like a timeshare daughter; Daddy is paying into me all the time, but only gets me for part of the year.' Candy sipped her Darjeeling tea. 'Payback for him sleeping around.'

Silence became a guest at the table; conversation shooed away by the words 'sleeping around'. As far as Eloise was concerned all men who cheated on their partners deserved castration – except for her lovely brother Joel. She was a bit biased, of course, but still, a castrated brother was an unhappy brother and an unhappy brother was hardly likely to give her money for a pair of Jimmy Choo suede boots. Eloise watched Candy bite into her third scone, wondering where she stored all her calories, promising herself that next time Candy popped to the loo, she'd follow her in and peep under the cubicle door; it was her duty to find out if her sister-in-law-to-be was bulimic. But bulimic or not, Eloise was mildly fond of Candy and was still reeling that Joel had nearly destroyed his relationship with her over something as trivial as honesty. What the hell was a man doing admitting to affairs? Especially when Candy was none the wiser. What the eye don't see the eye don't know, wasn't that the rule all men loved by?

Eloise had many things in common with Joel, her competitive nature being one of them. She glanced down at her fourth scone, undid her jeans' belt a notch, then began to munch, praying to the Lord above that Candy didn't order another. Yes, Candy was the one for Joel, which was why Eloise spent so much energy in persuading his one-night stands that he had Aids and various other diseases. The really eager ones, who didn't care what diseases Joel had allegedly picked up, needed a firmer approach, which was where Eloise's other trait in common with Joel came in handy: her psycho nature. Being called the Sister From Hell didn't dampen her resolve with the bimbos, only added to her anger and determination to push them out of Joel's life. Violence had been quite successful over the years. Yes, Eloise was very proud to be the Sister From Hell. She lifted up her camera and took a shot of Candy smiling. Happiness clung to Candy like a second skin. Joel was sure to like this photograph.

'Now that you're getting married, Joel stands a good chance of seeing his fortieth birthday. I had doubts that he'd live through his thirties, you know?' Eloise said, placing the camera on the table. 'I suppose he'll change his will in favour of you now, you'll get everything, including the vibrating chair.'

'If he died I'd kill myself anyway.'

'Oh.' Eloise paused. 'Any chance of putting me on your will then?'

Silence returned for a minute until Candy began again. 'He's promised me that he'll keep his daily life-threatening risks to a minimum. No more speeding, or balancing on multi-storey car parks, he's even given me his word that he won't eat "off" food any more. No more indulgence in food that's past its sell-by date.'

Eloise giggled, he'd been doing that since he was a kid, eating 'off' food, and had had his stomach pumped only the once.

Candy continued, 'It's hard to believe after all Joel's been through that he's turned out so well balanced,' she said, taking off her lacy, pink cardigan. 'I know all about the psychiatrist.'

'We don't talk about that episode in our family,

172

Candy,' Eloise said firmly, fingering the small flower-filled vase in the centre of the table. 'We prefer to look to the future.'

Silence returned yet again. It was obvious that any chat that involved Joel could come to a halt quicker than a David Blunkett speech in a Mosque. Both girls had many things in common. Both were protective of Joel; both had seen Joel naked and both claimed Joel as their best friend.

Fortunately only one of them had slept with Joel. And the other one just listened in when they had sex.

'For such an expensive penthouse,' Eloise began, 'the walls seem extremely thin.'

A warm, red glow appeared on Candy's neck and face as she thought back to last night's mattress marathon. 'Do they? Sorry.'

'"I'm about to avalanche, quick, the avalanche." Hmm, Joel's very descriptive, most blokes just say, "I'm coming."' Eloise paused, plucking petals off the table flower. 'Amazing really, do you know that I counted seven avalanches last night? Seven! I'm surprised there was any snow left on the mountain.'

Candy's head lowered under the weight of her extreme blushing. Talking openly about sex, even to a close friend, was something she was never comfortable with.

'Given him a blow job yet?' asked Eloise, oblivious to Candy's unease. 'Expect so. Who wouldn't?' Like a huge flea, Candy's embarrassment jumped across to Eloise. 'I mean, of course I wouldn't. It's not natural. Sisters don't go around giving their brothers blow jobs, however gorgeous they are.'

Silence again, but this time all the tables in the café were listening. Either the two greedy scone-eating women were discussing an episode of *Hollyoaks* or there was a very incesting conversation going on here. Whatever the situation, it was worth ordering another cup of coffee just in case the topic of bestiality reared its aphrodisiac-laden ivory-horned head.

Candy's mobile rang to the tune of 'Mad World'. It was Joel asking her to grab one of the urine samples from the apartment fridge because the one he'd given at the lab was showing up positive for steroids.

'Steroids?' Candy screamed, much to the enjoyment of the listeners. 'You're on steroids? Of all the idiotic—'

'Calm down. I need your help on this; my job is on the line, Candy. Now go to the fridge and look under sample May 2001, I was totally clean then, bring it to the lab, will you, a.s.a.p. Per-lease!'

A flash went off, then another. Eloise stood in front of Candy, taking photographs of her horrified face. What awesome pictures these were going to be.

Whispering now, Candy held the phone close to her mouth. 'I'll get the sample but I'm not happy about this. Why would you ever need to use steroids? You climb the mountains, Joel, not lift them.'

'I need them to help me recover from my heroin addiction. Which I used to help me with my alcohol problem. Which started because of . . . YOU!' He laughed. 'Got yer! It's the first wind-up you've fallen for since we got engaged. I'd love to see your face right now.'

And he could, when Eloise proudly showed him the photos.

It took a while for Joel's joke to seem funny. Eloise looked on jealously. It wasn't so long ago that Joel had been playing wicked jokes on her. Now . . . Candy was the butt. Not fair.

'I really envy you, Candy,' Eloise said, a few minutes later as they walked out of the Taste Box Café towards Candy's car.

'And why's that?'

'You've got what all women dream about morning, noon and night.' Eloise sighed. 'It really proves that God is up there somewhere watching over you. How lucky you are to have a platinum credit card, how very lucky.'

Candy just shrugged, then began to load her bags in the car's boot. After a moment, she could sense Eloise watching her and turned. 'What's up?'

Eloise smiled securely to herself, knowing what she was about to reveal next would leave Candy feeling selfish. 'It's a good job I remembered to buy Joel a little present, he so hates people who go shopping, spending huge amounts of money on themselves, without even sparing a thought for him. You must have something for him amongst all those clothes, shoes and accessories, Candy, surely you must.' Grinning, Eloise pulled out the DVD she'd bought Joel, from the HMV bag.

My, my, thought Candy, what have we here? A bitch without the disguise? Or was this the first sign of fear from Eloise that she was being pushed to one side by Joel? A sister who lived out of her brother's pockets was bound to feel insecure when he became engaged. But, Jesus, did she really expect Joel to be her roommate for the rest of his life? Some say to fight fire with fire; Candy preferred to fight fire with ice.

She pointed to a La Senza box in the boot. 'I think Joel would favour my present, of me in sexy lingerie, than watching *Touching the Void* on DVD, thank you very much, Eloise.' Candy mumbled to herself out of earshot, 'As if he hasn't seen the bloody thing a million times already.'

Eloise fake laughed. 'Yeah, right, like sex with you is better than his favourite film of all time. I think not, Candy, don't you know anything about my brother? Mountains are first and mountains are second, you are way, way, way down somewhere at the bottom, at Base Camp, in Joel's list of priorities. Get over it.' Eloise stormed to the front of the car, yanked open the door, slung herself in the passenger seat then banged the door shut. Two more days then Candy would be heading home to Cornwall – and good riddance!

Two more days until Eloise had Joel all to herself again. Eloise lost herself in deep thought. Why did she feel so protective towards her Joel? He was only a brother after all. Eloise shook her head. No, he was more than that; he was the man who looked out for her, who made her feel safe. He was the one person she could totally rely on when life was giving her a good kicking. She remembered how hard it had been when her parents moved to Florida, how abandoned she had felt when they packed their bags and left. Joel was there, like Joel was always there (except when he was up a mountain) to take away her tears and mend her hurt. He made her feel like the number-one woman in his life. Sure he had his one-night stands, or his mid-week flings, but never anything to interfere with their brotherly/sisterly relationship. It was the perfect scenario.

And then Candy had come along. 'Hello, everyone, I'm sickeningly nice, bucket-filled beautiful, with charity-driven conscience, polite, sensible, happy, funny, gorgeous, and every other fucking word that goes with "perfect" Candy.' Eloise felt her heart tighten just thinking about the first time Joel had spoken of her: 'I've found my soul-mate. She's not only beautiful but the best shag ever! Oh, yeah, and she loves mountains. What a result!' Eloise had felt a link in her ties with Joel snap. From that moment Eloise couldn't wait to meet this 'Result!' just so she could scare her off. But life had its surprises for Eloise just like it has for everyone else. As soon as Eloise came face to face with Candy, she couldn't help but like her. Deep down she knew she was perfect for Joel. And that's what hurt the most.

Being number two in Joel's life was a hard fact to accept after being his number one for so long. No one likes relegation, least of all siblings. And slowly, but surely, as Joel became more fond of Candy, he began to push Eloise away, preparing her, almost, for the inevitable day that he asked his sister to move out. Eloise felt her eyes water over . . . she could feel that her day of reckoning was approaching fast. Her replacement was scratching at the door. It was only a matter of time now.

Eloise watched Candy get into the car. She had oodles of class. Knowing exactly what to wear to keep a man's attention – and most likely knowing what *not* to wear to keep a man's erection. And judging by the lingerie Candy had bought to wear for Joel today, it wouldn't be a game of Scrabble or *Touching the Void* that would be keeping the pair up late tonight. Joel made no secret of the fact that he loved sex. Once, when a very satisfied lover asked him after intercourse where he found his energetic passion, he said romantically, 'I treat each shag as if it is my last. Death is around every corner, Babe.' Eloise didn't want to face reality, but if she were to be totally truthful with herself right now, then she would have to admit that she was jealous of Candy. Jealous of the hold she had over Joel, jealous that her brother loved her like he did. She could remember the days when Joel would tell *her* how pretty she looked, how this dress or that skirt looked perfect on her; now when she spun in the apartment with a new outfit on, the most she would get out of Joel would be, 'That's a nice get-up, it would look stunning on Candy.'

CANDY! Eloise was sick of her. She had not only stolen her brother but she had stolen her compliments. Eloise thought of the La Senza present that Candy had bought Joel. She thought of how sexy Candy was going to look in the lingerie. And she thought of the endless list of compliments Joel would spew out in her direction. Eloise's head throbbed with jealousy and her heart ached with resentment. Her strong, loving, caring relationship with her brother was being washed away by a pretty woman and there was nothing she could do about it. Her mind spun on its axis of evil. Or was there? Maybe it was time Joel was reminded that his little sister wasn't so little after all. She was a woman. And she was a woman desperately in need of some compliments herself! An idea sprang to the fore of her mind. Maybe Joel deserved to see what his sister looked like in lingerie. Her body was much better than *bony* Candy's anyway.

178

Well, it would be when she'd lost fourteen pounds of fat.

And she'd been fitted with 34DD breast implants.

And she'd had her pubic-hair gene spliced with her head-hair gene to give her curls and bounce.

And she'd had her nails extended. (Weren't women mountaineers supposed to have short stubby finger-nails?)

And . . . anything else that would give her the edge over cute, caring, charming, cheery, cool, complete Candy.

COW!

After driving in silence for a few miles, Eloise felt the wheels of guilt catching her in the fast lane. Why did she always have to wreck things with her big mouth? She took a deep breath, then, in a sulky voice, apologized to Candy for her moment of bitchiness, following it up with a polite request to stop off at Tesco. She needed Slim-Fast and she needed it quick.

When a woman is about to show off her body wearing lingerie, to her brother, it helps immensely if she's feeling good about herself.

Chapter Sixteen

Which was the complete opposite of how Zarleena had felt about herself the day Armin asked her to parade, half naked, for him, in front of the camera. They'd been married for just four months when Armin explained over a *paratha* and yoghurt breakfast that he was unsatisfied in the bedroom and needed to spice things up a bit. Zarleena had suggested mildly that their sex life might improve if the six framed pictures of his mother could be taken off the bedroom walls and be replaced with pictures of Mel Gibson, Johnny Depp and Brad Pitt. Even Max Payne. Armin didn't take kindly to adverse remarks regarding his mother, nor the fact that Zarleena's would-be pin-ups all happened to be white men, and made a suggestion of his own, with his fist in Zarleena's stomach.

'Bollywood men spit on Hollywood men,' Armin had hollered in Zarleena's ear. 'I give you Aamir Khan, Rajesh Khanna, and there's Hrithik Roshan, Raj Kapoor, Shah Rukh Khan, all better than Tom Cruise any day. What about the legendary Amitabh Bachchan, I suppose you're going to tell me Harrison Bloody Ford is better, huh? Harrison Bloody Ford can't even speak Hindi.' Armin sped to the kitchen, opened Zarleena's purse and grabbed the Blockbuster video card. 'I'm confiscating this. No more films in the house unless they're Bollywood. Got it?'

Or porn.

Coincidentally, Zarleena had discovered Armin's stash of porn a few days before he'd forced her to do the dirty photographs; but she didn't dare mention it to him. He'd hidden the video tapes behind the boiler in the airing cupboard expecting Zarleena's arm to be too short to reach round the back. Didn't men know that there is no arm longer than a curious woman's? It can stretch for miles. *Lesbian Milk Maids*, *Spank Me Hard & Spank Me Slow*, *Skinny Dipping Licking*, and finally *Lethal Lisa Gets Laid*. All modern-day pornography starring modern-day WHITE women.

So why the interest in a naked brown woman, Zarleena had thought, as Armin closed the curtains in the bedroom in preparation for the glamour shoot. Wasn't the hypocrite getting enough pleasure from his secret porn? Obviously not, screamed the bag of sex toys that he held. Obviously not, screamed the crotchless panties lying on the bed. Obviously not, screamed the digital camera in his hand. It was the lowest point in Zarleena's life. It felt like Jack the Ripper had given her a smear test. It felt like the eyes of India were watching with disgust. It felt like she was betraying her parents. It felt like she was performing for the devil himself. It was the worst of times, it was her season of darkness, it was her winter of despair; she was going direct to hell. It was her own tale.

Her Tale of Shame.

Saturday early evening, a few minutes before 6 p.m., closing time at Bindis & Brides. Apart from Shimla finding a huge spider's web in the changing room, nothing untoward had occurred. It was a regular Saturday about to take on another vowel.

I, for Irregular.

Zarleena and Shimla began their Shut-Up-Shop ritual, each holding a lit candle.

'Un-curse our purse and fill our till. Un-curse our purse and—'

A deafening banging at the shop door brought both mantras and hearts to a standstill. Peering through the glass, with a pleased with himself grin, was Armin. The leader of the National Front was more welcome than him right now.

'Open the door, Zarleena,' Armin demanded very loudly. 'You wouldn't want me to drop what I have in my hands onto the pavement.' He came in closer, his nose flat on the window pane. 'I'll give you a clue: photographs.'

Internally Armin was sneering at the two women inside. Both were dressed in classic Indian style in beautiful, colourful *shalwar kameezes*. Amazing how Zarleena could make the effort to dress in the fashion of her own culture when she wanted to make money in her business, but when they had lived as a married couple, she was hardly seen out of Western clothes. She needed to be taught some respect.

As he watched the scene of panic through the glass, a silent movie starring his wife and her assistant, an Elvis Presley song came to mind: 'All Shook Up'. If only she'd played ball two weeks ago and fetched the gold from the bank, then these photos could have remained hidden. He began counting down from ten, out loud, in Punjabi.

'*Das . . . naun . . . atth . . . satt . . . chhe . . . panj . . . chaar . . . tinn . . . do . . .* Zarleena, let me in; I'm on one . . . *ikk.*'

The door opened and Armin, dressed in black, brief-case in hand, swaggered in as if he owned the joint, keeping his bum cheeks clenched tight as he did so, trying to make his behind appear smaller.

Shimla hovered by the phone, fingers primed, wait-ing to dial 999 at the first sign of violence. Her eyes picked up Honey's latest weapon under the counter – a syringe loaded with bleach ready to jam in the jugular. She felt safe. Out of Shimla's hearing range, Armin and Zarleena stood in a corner by the huge rolls of bright silk material used to make Indian suits.

'I want £20,000 in cash. Don't care how you get it, but I suggest you borrow against this shop and get a loan.' Armin patted the briefcase, holding it up prouder (and the right way round) than Gordon Brown with his battered red budget case. 'Amazing what glamour pic-tures will get you these days.'

Zarleena looked for the fishing hook sticking out of Armin's back as she was sure she was dealing with a giant maggot. She tried, but couldn't control the panic in her voice. 'This is bribery, punishable by prison. You'd be shaming yourself and your family.'

Armin opened the case and removed a snapshot, passing it to her. 'No, I think most people would find *that* more shameful.'

She dared not look. 'You forced me. I did what any other woman would have done when scared out of her wits. Do you honestly think that I would strip naked and do those awful acts if you weren't standing there ready to beat me if I didn't? Come on, Armin, be reasonable.'

'Oh, I'm always reasonable.' He snatched the snapshot back from her trembling hands. 'That's why I'm giving you this option. Twenty grand, in cash, or these photos will get sent to every magazine, newspaper and relative. *Including your parents.*' From his evil black case he pulled out a magazine, *Readers' Wives*, and opened it to the centre pages, where he'd already stuck a picture of Zarleena. 'This is the sort of thing I'm talking about. You'll be the most famous Indian woman in Britain.'

Zarleena felt bile at the back of her throat, and it wasn't just his Joop aftershave. 'I—'

'It's not all bad though, look,' he patted the glossy page, 'you get £200 for every photo sent in.'

'I can't find £20,000, it's impossible.'

'You should have thought of that before you sold my gold to open this cosy shop.' He dropped a couple of snapshots by her feet. 'Just a reminder of the mango pickle you've got yourself into. You've got ten days to sort this out.' He turned and walked towards the door, shouting over his shoulder, 'I'll be in touch. *Namaste.*'

And he was gone.

In Zarleena's eyes, it felt like her life had gone too.

Shimla was excused, leaving Zarleena alone to marinate in her own worry. It was only last night she had been giggling with Honey, explaining that Joel's peck on the cheek yesterday had rekindled her oestrogen boiler. It had been on pilot light for so long, she'd never expected the sudden whoooosh as the heat came through her loins. (Honey was over the moon with Zarleena's confession, she'd often worried that after Armin, her sister would never be interested in men again. It had been worth letting the sausage thrower go just to hear the news.) Then there was the divorce to look forward to, a meeting with her solicitor had been planned for Monday morning. Things had been going along quite nicely. But 'had' is a word that haunts many people. Once there were millionaires who 'had' a fortune. Bankrupt directors who 'had' their own company. And Zarleena, before Armin had arrived today, 'had' her dignity. Now it 'had' all gone to pot.

It was time for some chocolate. Knowing that stocks were low in the maisonette, Zarleena decided to pop next door to Spindlers, the tiniest newsagent's in the world. On her last visit she'd completely wiped them out of Mars bars, sending the elderly owners, Mr and Mrs Cotton into a bit of a spin. Mars bars were the official food for soldiers in the first Gulf War and as such Mr and Mrs Cotton always liked to keep a few lying around in case a soldier from the 2 Para regiment in Colchester passed through. They were not too pleased with Zarleena's greedy purchase last time (but it didn't stop them taking her money either).

'Ah, Honey, glad you called round,' Mrs Cotton began, tucking her chubby fingers into her pink pinny,

'I've been discussing your suggestion with Mr Cotton and we've decided that no, we won't be selling the *jellibibbies*.'

Honey had suggested to the Cottons that because of the extra Asian business Bindis & Brides produced it might be a good idea if they stocked Indian sweets. For example, *jalebis* (sweet, sticky, curly rings), *gulab jamans* (milk/flour balls deep fried then coated in syrup) or *burfis* (stodgy squares of condensed milk flavoured with coconut or pistachio).

Zarleena said, 'I'm not Honey, I'm—'

'That's right, dear, you're the other one. Anyway, same's the same, we don't want your type of foreign sweets. They sound awful.'

And what, acid drops don't? thought Zarleena, grabbing the last six Mars bars and placing them on the counter. God, Honey was only trying to be friendly, she fumed inside, handing over her money. And it was here that she noticed the pile of Union Jack writing pads for sale. Time seemed to stop for a second as she rolled back the memories to yesterday morning. The racist note with the words 'Fuck off back to India' had been written on the very same paper.

'Mr Cotton, these must be extremely popular with the tourists,' Zarleena said, holding up one of the pads.

'Of course,' he replied, 'we British are dead proud.' He turned to his wife. 'Dead proud we are, ain't that right, Mrs Cotton?'

'Well, have a good evening,' Zarleena said cheerfully, as she walked out of the shop, not bothering to listen to Mrs Cotton's response.

At the back entrance to Bindis & Brides, where the stocks were unloaded, Zarleena sat on the doorstep mulling over her thoughts, while munching her way through her Mars bars. There was now an icy chill infecting this warm July evening. A cold front had blown in from Zarleena's past. She needed someone to discuss this with but her parents were a no-no. Honey was a no-no. Cousins were a no-no. Even the Asian Women's Helpline was a no-no. And all for a very good reason: an Indian woman taking her clothes off for filthy pictures, no matter which way Indians looked at it, was a definite NO-NO. It was shameful, degrading, a slur on India itself, with some going as far as saying an Indian woman taking her clothes off for porn was tantamount to India itself stripping off and opening its legs to the rest of the world. Zarleena knew her white friends would have trouble believing what she had done was *that* bad, but they didn't know India, where kissing in public was taboo, where showing a bit of leg was promiscuous, where holding hands was classed as a sexual position. Where . . .

. . . where lying naked on a bed holding a twelve-inch dildo was . . . Oh, Durga in heaven, thought Zarleena, what have I done? She put her hands to her face and began to cry. How the hell was she going to sort this mess out?

Chapter Seventeen

Joel switched on Teletext on the TV to find out what day it was. He was quite surprised to discover it was Thursday. Nearly a week since he'd proposed to Candy. He smiled at the way things had turned out. Right up until Monday, the day Candy had left for Cornwall, Joel had made an enormous effort to convince her that his determined cock would remain in his pants. Joel thought about that for a moment, or, did he mean: he had made a determined effort to convince her that his enormous cock would remain in his pants? Whatever, he'd decided that he would be faithful.

In the kitchen he poured a chilled strawberry Slim-Fast drink down his throat for breakfast and nodded in appreciation. If he ever became obese, at least the dieting wouldn't be too harsh, he guessed, cracking open another can and adding it to a bowl of tinned pineapple, yoghurt and chocolate chip cookies. He walked over to the huge living-room window and stared out to the green. Eloise was going through a new phase at the moment. Some bits he liked, for example the Slim-Fast stocks in the fridge, but others gave him cause to worry, like the running through the apartment in just her underwear screaming at the top of her voice, 'Don't look!'

He watched a group of ageing ramblers edge their way across the field, taking up picnic positions not far from the castle wall. Maybe it felt good to sit next to something a little older than themselves, Joel thought, wondering why he'd never seen pictures of Ronald Reagan standing next to the Pyramids. Maybe if he lived to their age he would be content with taking the shallow slopes rather than the steep climbs. Maybe living to a hundred was a greater achievement than climbing Mount Everest in some way.

Maybe it was time to rethink his staying-alive techniques. Life was dangerous enough without making it worse. Even with the Slim-Fast he had taken an unnecessary risk by dropping the ring pull into the can, then drinking the shake, hoping that on the off-chance he didn't choke on it. He'd heard stories of men turning up in Casualty with milk bottles rammed up their behinds. Even though he didn't agree with their methods, he kind of understood where they were 'coming' from. They enjoyed the risks, the danger, the thrill, but milk bottles? God, the stupidity. And thank God for small mercies that he'd decided on strawberry-flavoured shake and not chocolate this morning.

Apart from continuing with his autobiography, Joel's work diary entries for the next few months alone was enough to scare the sturdiest Sherpa into an office job. Dangerous climbs, precarious challenges, all for the privilege of advertising Armani sunglasses, Calvin Klein boxer shorts and Pot Noodle. His creep of an agent,

Pete, had even managed to wangle an advert if Joel fell off. KC BROTHERS UNDERTAKERS CATER FOR EVEN THE MESSIEST BURIALS. PRE-ORDER YOUR COFFIN NOW AND SAVE ONE HUNDRED DOLLARS LIKE THE FAMOUS MOUNTAINEER, THE LATE JOEL WINTERS, DID. The question Joel was asking himself now was: is the risk worth the money? Could he leave Candy a widow?

His mobile blipped and Joel read the text: *Just a reminder that we are due to meet today. I hope you haven't forgotten. Dylan.*

'Of course I haven't forgotten,' Joel lied out loud to himself, then text back: *Only losers forget. What time?*

All the required information for the two brothers to meet was established via text messages. Joel was still in shock from Dylan's call last night, when out of the blue, his older brother had put aside their differences and invited Joel to his house for a chat. The rudimentary rudeness was all gone, leaving just two brothers talking down two lines. The phone line and their blood line. Was Dylan becoming his namesake? Were the times *really* a-changing?

Joel stood before the oak door to the huge six-bedroom house designed by architect Dylan himself. He could still remember the day Eloise had pointed out the plot of land that Dylan would build on. An old barn and cow shed had to be demolished before the foundations could be set. Joel had joked that the cow shed should have been left intact to house Dylan's wife, Lilly, who had never forgiven Joel for nearly killing their eldest son, Danny. The last time Lilly had communicated with Joel had been via a letter, eleven years ago, in which she had explained that he talked so much flannel that he might as well have one. In the same parcel as the letter, sure enough, she had sent him a hideous green flannel; to which Joel responded by wiping his arse with it and sending it back.

The door opened to reveal Dylan smiling uncomfortably in the hallway. It had been eleven years since the two brothers had seen each other socially and, for a second or two, an awkward silence stood between them like a mosquito door. Joel noticed a plaque on the wall that befitted his brother to a T:

Creak Free House

And it wouldn't have surprised anyone who knew Dylan that his house was, indeed, free of creaks. A perfectionist by nature, or, as he was known to the builders he employed, an Anal Anorak.

'Come in,' Dylan offered, turning to his side to let Joel pass. 'Lilly had to shoot out with the children, but she'll be back shortly. Little Robin and Charlotte are excited to meet you.'

'And Danny?'

There was a slight pause as Dylan closed the front door. 'Of course, Danny. Our fifteen-year-old rebel, he wouldn't miss his uncle for the world.'

It was like walking into a Swiss cottage. Wooden floor, wooden beams, wooden furniture. Let's hope, thought Joel, that the personalities weren't wooden. He followed Dylan into a humungous lounge, its wooden floor littered with children's toys. Joel felt a twinge of sadness. He had never been short of uncles and aunts when he was a kid, so why should Dylan's three sprogs have missed out on him? He recognized, with a glimmer of relief, a remote-controlled car on the floor, one he'd sent last Christmas to his younger nephew. Joel had suspected that his presents were always binned by Lilly. He stared at a picture of Lilly on the side table. For some reason he still thought she was a silly cow.

'So,' Joel began, settling into a plush sofa-chair. 'Shall we get this kid-killing business out of the way? I know it still grinds you down.'

Dylan sighed. 'Please, Joel, a little subtlety. You talk of my elder son as if he were an expendable soldier. Your presence at family gatherings had a marked effect on my boy. Do you know what he wants to be when he leaves school?' Joel shook his head. 'A mountaineer! Not an architect like his father or a teacher like his mother used to be, or even a lawyer like our father – his granddad. No, he wants to be like you.' He paused. 'He wants to be like the uncle who nearly killed him. How's that for irony?'

Joel had a proud lump in his throat. Danny idolized him. Not able to control his grin, he asked, 'I suppose he's obsessed with knots and Everest? Maybe he might want to come on a climb with me?'

'You don't understand, Joel, I want you to talk him out of it.' Dylan deserted Joel for a moment, bringing him a can of Coke. 'It's a damn pity you haven't got frostbite, I'm sure that would put him off. What about horrendous scars?'

Joel pulled off his sock and thrust his foot under Dylan's nose. 'Athlete's foot is all I can offer.' He grinned at Dylan's disgusted face. 'Sniff it.'

Dylan stood up, any hopes that Joel might have grown up in the intervening years were fading fast. Ever since he could remember Joel had been the joker, the buffoon, the attention-seeker. A particular incident came to mind. It was the school holidays and each evening Joel could be found in the bathroom, in the bath, practising holding his breath under water. Six weeks of practice, all so that, come school term, he could pretend that he had drowned during a swimming lesson. It would have been funny had a teacher not nearly drowned in trying to rescue him. Joel had been expelled, bringing shame to the family.

But Joel seemed to revel in shame. Dylan could never fathom the inner Joel out. Okay, so Joel was never spoilt like he was. Okay, so Joel never went to a private school like he did. Okay, so Joel was always bullied by his older brother. Okay? No, it was never okay for an older brother to bully his younger brother. Dylan always felt his own shame whenever Joel vied for attention. For that's what it was, Dylan was certain, just a young boy trying to get attention from anyone who would give it. Mummy and Daddy certainly wouldn't shower their attention on Joel, how could they, when they were busy polishing Dylan's rowing trophies and framing Dylan's degree certificates? And chauffeuring Eloise to ballet lessons. It was all about black sheep and favourites. Joel was the black sheep; Dylan and Eloise were the favourites.

In some way Dylan felt responsible for Joel's hazardous path. Maybe if he'd been more brotherly and less of a snob when they were growing up, Joel might never have needed a psychiatrist. It wasn't the questioning of

Joel's mortality that had rung alarms on the psychiatrist's couch either; rather, it was Joel's constant testing of his mortality. The very same alarm bells that, to this day, worried Eloise, Joel's parents, Candy, his mates, Pete the agent, and even Dylan.

'I haven't been the best of brothers,' Dylan began, sitting back down. 'I was quite rotten to you at times.' Joel was about to interrupt, but could see the need in Dylan's eyes, so he let him continue. 'The other day Eloise came up with a novel way of challenging my perception of you.' He laughed. 'She pretended that you were dying of prostate cancer. And I must say, it shook me to the core. To think that I only had a few months to be nice to you after treating you so wickedly over the years brought me to my senses. I want our feud to end right now, Joel. Hasn't it struck you that the reason our parents left for Florida was because of our constant bickering? Christ, we couldn't even be nice to each other at Christmas.' He jumped up, walked out of the room and returned waving a Christmas card. 'Let me read what you wrote last year, Joel: "*Dear Sour-lipped Lilly, Danny, Robin, Charlotte and Dildo Dylan. To the kids I wish you well, to the parents go to hell. At Christmas we stuff a turkey or two, but this Christmas time I say STUFF YOU!*"'

The two brothers burst out laughing. Years of tension unleashed in one huge ball of laughter. In all the excitement Dylan suggested that both Joel and he go on the webcam and speak to Mummy and Daddy in Florida, explaining that they were friends again, to which Joel replied that they would look like two queers if they did that. Which set them off laughing again, reminiscing, and generally catching up. Before long, a gabble of noises at the front door halted their discussion. Lilly and the children were back. It was time to get serious again.

Lilly did her best to appear pleased to see Joel, air-kissing him from half a yard away. Robin, the five-year-old nephew, dramatically bowed and Charlotte, the three-year-old niece, curtsied. *Jesus wept*, thought Joel, *was he living in a Brontë sister's novel? And fifteen-year-old Danny?* Joel checked for Danny. Suddenly, squeaky trainers on polished wood skidded around the corner to reveal the most enthusiastic-looking climber Joel had ever seen. The young teenager's frame was laden with ropes, pitons and karabiners. A compass swung from his neck, a heavy rucksack was on his back, an ice axe in his right hand and a pile of mountaineering books under his left arm.

'Everest, here I come. Sherpa Danny at your service, Uncle Joel.' Danny bowed as far as his climbing gear would allow. 'I *am* in total awe of you.'

And he had been ever since the day Eloise told him that his uncle was a famous mountaineer. Mummy and Daddy had refused to discuss Joel, dissuading Danny from even thinking about him. And when a young boy of just eleven is dissuaded from doing something, he normally does it. Danny had seen Joel at family gatherings many times, but was quickly steered away, via a tug of his ear, by Mummy. Danny refused to let his parents' hatred for Joel get in the way of his admiration. And so, with the aid of cunning phone calls from Eloise and mammoth sessions on the Internet, everything Danny needed to know about his famous Uncle Joel was known. What's more, much to his parents' dismay,

Danny intended to emulate his every footstep. Being a top footballer was okay, or even a Formula One racing driver, but Danny's real dream was a few degrees colder than those. His ultimate fantasy would be to stand on the peak of Mount Everest with the man he admired the most. His Uncle Joel. And he couldn't wait.

'This was what I was talking about earlier,' Dylan remarked. 'He has his exams next year and all he thinks about is Everest. Please explain to Danny that Everest is not for young boys like him.'

Joel smiled at his nephew. 'Look, Danny, I—'

'He spoke to me. He spoke to me.' Danny was now on talking terms with his hero and he swung his rucksack round to his front, pulled out a writing pad and thrust it in Joel's hand. 'Can I have your autograph, please? Could you sign it from Joel Winters, the mountaineer who tried to kill Danny Winters, please?'

Joel glared at Dylan. It was time this story was laid to rest. He went on to explain the truth of what happened that day. How Joel had been babysitting a four-year-old Danny when he decided to make the evening more exciting by climbing out of the attic window and taking him up on the house roof. With Danny fixed in place with safety ropes and harnesses, Joel popped to the ground to take a photograph of him sitting on the roof. It was at that point Dylan and Lilly returned to collect their forgotten theatre tickets. 'Where's Danny?' Lilly had asked, slightly worried, as Joel seemed to be on his own. 'Oh, don't worry about Danny,' Joel had replied. 'He's up there.' And he pointed to the roof. Upon seeing his parents down below, Danny had stood up to give them a wave, lost his footing, and tumbled halfway down the roof tiles. To his certain death if it hadn't been for the safety rope attached to his waist.

As Joel scribbled his autograph, he spoke, 'I wouldn't let a climber die with me, you lot, not on my watch. Not on my watch,' he reassured. 'And if you look on the bright side, Danny lived. So, can we drop it now? It's old news.'

'You're one of a kind, Uncle Joel, you know that, one of a kind. How you and Dad are related, I just don't know,' Danny said, leaving the room to wash his hands for dinner.

And it was at this dinner, around the family dinner table, that Joel startled himself with a thought. Here he was stealing the admiration of his brother's elder son, enjoying the feeling of being idolized, quite happy to spend more time talking with Danny about life, mountains and death, when out there, somewhere, was a son or daughter of his own waiting to be born. An extension of himself lying in limbo until he and Candy decided it was time to start their own family.

'More potatoes, Uncle Joel?' asked Danny, already spooning them onto Joel's plate. 'Energy is a must in our world. The climbers' world.'

Joel laughed. 'I think you should ask your brother before taking his potatoes, Danny, but thanks all the same.' He returned Robin's spuds to his plate, giving Danny a wink.

Was it possible for a man to become broody, Joel wondered, admiring the two younger children. Never before had he felt the urge to pass on his genes. He only ever walked through Mothercare when he wanted a short cut to the car park on the other side. Up until now, babies had seemed like a complete waste of time. But now life seemed a waste of time without them. He watched this family interacting with one another like a small orchestra, all playing out of tune, but for some reason sounding like they were in total harmony. Hadn't he once sat around a family table? Wasn't he once part of a family? And even with all the shit that had gone on, wasn't it just about the greatest thing ever? Joel watched Charlotte dunk her fingers in the gravy boat and wipe them across Robin's T-shirt. Of course, Lilly exploded, mums did that sort of thing, and dad, Dylan, sat back wondering why on earth his kids couldn't behave like normal kids, even for just one minute.

Danny patted Joel's arm. 'Sorry about my lot, Uncle Joel, they're a total embarrassment. I hope this doesn't put you off visiting again.'

Joel excused himself from the table, opened the French doors and walked onto the landscaped garden fit for a king (or Alan Titchmarsh). Waiting on the lawn, wrapped in temptation itself, was a dangerous-looking sit-down mower. If he was going to be making a phone call, he might as well make it from there, Joel thought, suddenly finding himself in the sun-warmed seat.

He dialled Candy's number, asked her what was new, then explained the 'baby' idea that had arisen at the dinner table. Fifteen minutes later he was still talking about starting a family.

'When are you ovulating? When are your eggs ready for ripening for possible fertilization?' He grimaced. 'Erm, no, let me rephrase that, that must have sounded awful. Start again. When are your eggs ready for ripening for DEFINITE fertilization?'

'And who will look after our baby when you go climbing, Joel? You've really got to think these things through. The only way this is happening is if you give up climbing and I give up any outdoor pursuits that we consider to be too risky. I'm not having a baby for one of us to die on it. No way.' Candy waited to see if any response was forthcoming; as there wasn't, she continued, 'Are you willing to give up mountaineering so we could raise a child together? It's a massive decision.'

'Hillary had children and he still made it up Everest. Can't we just have a baby, see if it works out and if it doesn't . . .'

'Put it up for adoption?'

'You said it, not me.' Joel waved away a wasp. 'I can't give up climbing yet, you know that. Not until I've done my fourteen mountains. I've only got seven left. I can't give up until I've completed what I began.'

'And I can't have your baby until you do.'

'Fine!'

'Fine too!'

'BYE!'

'BYE TOO!'

Joel switched off his mobile and sneered to himself. He'd get his baby, oh that was for sure, even if he had to impregnate Candy while she slept. Even if he had to hide her contraception pills, take her to the peak of K2 where altitude sickness would render her weak, defenceless and confused, and while she was in a state of delirium, convince her that she needed a shag to keep warm. The baby would pop out nine months later. (As long as his sperm didn't get frostbite.)

EASY!

Chapter Eighteen

Armin's new business venture relied on who was left on the Indian shelf. The men and women who, for some reason or another, had not been married off by their parents. He categorized these people as the 'Too' group. Too ugly, too fat, too short, too dark, too much like hard work. They could be funny, intelligent, brimming with personality, but it wouldn't matter a *samosa* if their appearance wasn't up to standard or their pure reputation was smeared. Gloss is the determining factor when trying to match Indian couples together, never the undercoat.

Which was why Matchmaker Armin was staring at his equivalent of a Dulux paint chart, his portfolio of 'Too' women and men, working out how to turn their unfortunate exterior into his profit. Charging anxious parents a small fee to help in marrying off their unmarriageable child was a worthy cause, something to be proud of; clearing India's shelf was a vocation that Mahatma Gandhi himself would have encouraged, Armin was convinced of it.

Armin logged off the Internet and waited for his printer to finish printing some of the profiles he'd downloaded. Pictures and personal details of potential clients. Today was Friday, only four days until Zarleena was due to hand over £20,000 for his new business start-up. Office lease, stationery, new designer suits, new laptop – twenty thousand was more than enough. He'd even thought of a name for his business in tribute to Zarleena's money: *Bindi Brides*. And he still couldn't believe how easily Zarleena had succumbed to blackmail; it was like stealing candy from a baby. From a drawer, Armin picked up a discarded photo of Zarleena in her lingerie. He smiled widely. And all because she didn't want her own profile plastered over the Internet. All because she didn't want her mummy and daddy to see what a bad Indian girl she really was.

A siren wailed outside the flat and Armin stood up to watch an ambulance scream by. These surroundings had been his home since his split with Zarleena. A one-bedroom flat, above a bookie', in downtown Wembley. Quite a come-down from the posh apartment in Birmingham where he used to cohabit with his wife. Quite a come-down indeed. If only his parents had been more reasonable and had continued to fund his lavish lifestyle in the way he'd grown accustomed to, then reclaiming his gold money wouldn't have been such a priority. The blame rested on the shoulders of his parents more easily than a fox fur around Naomi Campbell. They chose Zarleena, they forced his hand, *they* were to blame.

Money problems are like cancer of the mind.

Zarleena's brain was contaminated with worry. Where

the hell was she going to find £20,000? Legally. The bank needed both Honey's and her signature before they would even discuss a loan against the business, and her credit cards were nearly maxed out already. Zarleena lay back on her bed, in the dark, with the door closed. The happy voice of Honey talking on the phone to her new boyfriend could be heard through the wall. Zarleena imagined the future as her filthy pornographic snaps were passed from one relative to the next. 'Disgusting girl,' they would say. 'Next photo please.' 'Shocking,' they would scream. 'Next photo please.' A temple would be booked to cleanse the family. Mantras would be recited. Holy men would be imported from India to cast out the demons in Zarleena. The rupee would go down against the pound. Bindis & Brides would go bankrupt. The shame-o-metre would explode.

If only I were a ventriloquist, thought Zarleena, then I would have someone to talk to about all this. Visions of a cute green duck called Orville giving her advice on dirty pictures made her smile. He would surely be an expert on having things up his furry backside at least. But keeping her predicament quiet from Honey was draining. What she needed right now was a set of Tony Blair's spin doctors who could make her dirty photos seem like they were done for the benefit of mankind. In fact, a man of Alistair Campbell's calibre might make you believe that the photographs were helping rid the world of Weapons of Mass Destruction. Really! But without Honey to confide in, Zarleena's confidence in solving her problem was nil. And, right now, Honey seemed pretty tied up in her own life. Zarleena shamelessly listened in to her sister's private call.

'... of course, Tree, I'm talking about massive disruption here. The M1. Blocked. M25. Blocked. M6. Blocked. Imagine it, Tree, Britain's entire road system constipated by the Asian cause ... I know you're not Asian, Tree, but if you love me, you'll do it ... Well, if you like me, you'll do it ... If you want to shag me, Tree, you'll bloody well do it ... Great ...'

And Zarleena tuned off. She hadn't met Tree yet, but judging by Honey's report, he seemed nice enough. In fact all of Honey's friends seemed 'nice enough'. Maybe peace protesters made the best acquaintances. It had Zarleena thinking about her own friends. Or rather, her lack of.

Armin had put paid to most of her friendships from school right from the out, discouraging contact with her past, afraid she might tell them what a bastard he was. Armin said marriage was like a perfectly tuned radio station, old friends were just interference, background noise. Their Christmas cards were to read: *Dear Static* ... Day by day the twines that held Zarleena's past together were severed by the same bullying hands that hit her. Before long she was Johnnyinder No Friends. Her life seemed a joke and the joke was on her.

It was time to do some drugs. Zarleena reached for her chocolate stash under her bed, desperate for a fix, ready to bow down to the dark brown devil called Galaxy. Hit after hit she stuffed in her mouth, making a private appointment in her mind to meet with the stepper machine tomorrow evening. Quicker than a rush of sugar, Zarleena experienced a rush of panic. Tomorrow evening! That was another day nearer her deadline. Her stomach churned. Maybe the caffeine in the chocolate acted as a catalyst to her worry. If that were true, she allowed herself a vague smile, then Joel must worry like a man condemned to death with all those Red Bulls he drank.

Joel? Now why at a time like this was she even thinking about Joel? Zarleena grabbed clumsily at some thoughts. Wouldn't it be nice, she pondered, to have someone like Joel, easygoing, funny, kind, brave (the kitten business), sexy, to chew the cud with. Life for him seemed like a game without rules. Already, just the few hours she'd spent in his company ranked high in her all-time 'time spent with blokes' memorable experiences. In another context, one minute spent with Joel was better than an hour spent with anyone else. Oh God, Zarleena thought, I must really like him.

But there was no way she was going to get him; there were already enough hurdles to call it a steeple-chase. First hurdle, she was still married. Second hurdle, he was engaged. And the water jump, he might not even fancy her – or Indian women in general for that matter. Zarleena wondered about this for a moment. Maybe that was seeing the situation as a half-empty glass; wouldn't it be better to view Joel as half full? She could only fantasize about being his girlfriend, but she could still be his friend.

And friends were supposed to help each other out in times of strife.

Before Zarleena lost her nerve, she picked up her mobile and dialled Joel's home number, partly expecting him to be out on a Friday night. Amazingly he picked up on the tenth ring. Zarleena apologized for calling on a Friday.

'Is it?' Joel seemed shocked. 'I thought it was Thursday. Shit. I promised a group of underprivileged children that I would show them how to tie knots down at the youth hall on Friday morning. I was due to make a speech about Mount Everest as well. There was going to be a finger buffet and everything. Fuck it.' Joel cracked open a Red Bull. 'Good stuff this. I'll donate them a pair of my boots instead.' He let out a sigh. 'God, I hate letting kids down.'

Zarleena wanted to hug him. The poor man seemed gutted. It was fifteen minutes later before Zarleena was in a position to explain why she had rung.

'I was hoping that you might be able to give me some advice on a rather delicate matter, Joel. I can't really talk about it over the phone. Could we, maybe, meet up at the weekend?'

There was a lengthy pause. 'Look, I can't.'

'Well, what about Monday, then? I could take the morning—'

He interrupted, 'I mean, I can't meet you. Or any other female for that matter. I promised Candy.'

'Claudia?'

'Yeah, Claudia. I don't want to wreck things with her and if she found out that I was matey with a female she'd blow. Sorry.' He sighed again, flopping back into the vibrating chair. 'It's not like I've ever given her a reason to doubt me, she's never even caught me with a woman. Not that she could have, I don't go round sleeping with other women. No, Zarleena, I couldn't do it to her, I'd feel terrible.'

Zarleena felt her stomach sink, pulling her vocal chords down with it. 'Er . . . I . . . er . . .'

'I'm really sorry, Zarleena, but I'd be in deep shit if she found out.'

'It's okay,' she said feebly. 'I'll deal with it somehow. I didn't want to involve the police but blackmail is blackmail, even if it is by your own husband. And he did force me to do it—'

'Now hang on a minute here. Police? Blackmail? Your husband? He forced you?' This sounded like a perfect sub-plot for his autobiography. He'd change the setting to the Kashmir border, add in a few gang rapes, and rescue the heroine from the baddies just outside Everest's Base Camp. *Voila!* Joel wondered how upset Candy would become if she found out that he had needed to meet with Zarleena for research into his book. He decided the risk was worth the book sales and, more importantly, Zarleena did sound desperate, so he went on excitedly, 'When d'you want to get together, Zarleena, I take back what I said about Candy/Claudia whatever their names are, they'd understand. It's not like you and I are going to shag, is it?'

Zarleena drooled, 'No.'

'We're only going to talk. It's not like you're going to go down on me now, is it?'

'No.'

'I mean, if you were trying to get me to take you from behind I would—'

'Joel! Please.'

The meeting was arranged for tomorrow afternoon. Zarleena went to bed a different person to the one who left it that morning. If there was a solution to Armin, then she was sure Joel would be the man to find it. Only slightly worrying was the fact that when she'd explained to Joel that Armin was known to like violence, he'd said, 'I can't wait to meet him.'

The sands of Cornwall had seen many men's names scribbled in their grains. Most common of these names seemed to be:

BASTARD

Candy threw her stick to the side of the picnic blanket and stared into her best friend, Sara's, eyes. Sara may have been a nurse, but men were one of women's ailments that she couldn't fix. There was no known antidote for Bastarditis.

'Well, he is a bastard.'

The two bikini-clad women looked out to the boisterous ocean tossing about the surfers and windsurfers. They'd been coming here for years; log-fire parties in the evening, volleyball tournaments in the peak of summer; a place to escape the rot of modern life. Last year a white shark had attacked a local fisherman in his boat, gnawing a twenty-inch gash in the hull. Either that or he was so pissed on the Cornwall grog that he'd hit the rocks. It mattered not, the swimmers still swam and the surfers still surfed, for it would take more than *Jaws I, II* and *III* to change the lifestyle of born and bred Cornwallians.

The evening sun surrendered to the night and Candy and Sara wrapped their blankets around their shivering bodies, bid farewell to the foamy waves and flip-flopped up the beach.

'The rain in Spain stays mainly on the plain,' uttered Candy purposefully. 'Any better?'

Sara shook her curly blonde hair. 'Just forget it, Candy, we're stuck with a Cornish accent. Could have been worse though.'

'Could have been Liverpudlian, our Sara, I know. Imagine Brad Pitt with a Liverpudlian accent? Takes the horn out of his horniness, doesn't it?'

'Yuck!'

They giggled at various renditions of movie stars with different accents until Sara noticed that when they stopped for a breather, Candy was writing BASTARD in the sand again. If she carried on at this rate, visitors to the beach would think that there were some pretty artistic lugworms down in Cornwall.

Sara waited for Candy to finish writing, then spoke softly. 'I still can't figure you out, Candy. Of all our friends you are the most independent. You are head-strong, a go-getter, reliable. And then there is this other side to you. The side that seems to think it needs a man like Joel in her life. It takes just one phone call from him and he fucks your mind up for the whole day.' She sat down on the sand, with Candy joining her. 'I'm sorry if this sounds harsh, but from where I stand it doesn't seem like love. It's too one-sided for that, surely? Tell me, what sacrifices has he made for you lately? I don't see him offering to move down to Cornwall. I don't see him dropping everything for an emergency. Only the emergencies that turn out to be him needing sex. I don't see—'

Candy wiped away a tear. 'He loves me.'

'HA! And he proves it by sleeping with other women, does he? The Candy I know would have chopped off his dick and dumped him ages ago. Wouldn't she?'

'He wants a baby and he wants to settle down. I think he means it.'

'HA!' And it echoed up the beach. 'Joel? Mr I-Had-Sex-With-Mount-Everest-And-Made-Her-Avalanche-Three-Times Joel.' They both laughed. 'What about these other women, why can't he have a baby with one of them? Here, give me that stick.' Sara proceeded to write:

> BASTARD JOEL DOESN'T KNOW WHERE TO
> STICK IT SO HE STICKS IT EVERYWHERE

As Candy watched a seagull ballet overhead, a presentation laid on for anyone with sandwich crusts to spare, she thought of the one element that was now missing from Joel's and her relationship. Trust. Knowing that it would be easier to re-float the *Titanic* than to regain the trust she'd once had in Joel. All men should be allowed one mistake, it normally happens the first time they open their mouth, but Joel had made the worst kind, and unless she could be hypnotized to wipe her mind clean, it would take years, if not forever, before she could fully forgive him.

'I'm just a typical switch bitch,' Candy remarked, kicking her heels in the sand.

'A switch bitch? What the fuck's that?'

'Well, it means I change my mind to suit the situation. Basically, I'm a hypocrite. If things were reversed and it was you with the lying, cheating, bastard boyfriend, then I would have told you to give him his marching orders pronto. And I'm not blind, I can see the significance in the timing of Joel's proposal; he only asked me to marry him because he thought I might leave him otherwise.'

'Oh thank God for that, for one minute there I thought my best friend didn't realize that she was about to fuck up her life by marrying a pig. As long as you know.'

It really was time to go. Their two-bed flat was barely a ten-minute walk away. Or a two-hour struggle if one went via the pub. Souvenir shops, an off-licence and a mouth-watering chippy lined the steep street that led away from the beach. And on occasion the girls had been too drunk to climb the hill, ordering a taxi to take them to the top.

The flat itself was a fire hazard; Sara's fluffy toys (invariably stuffed in Uzbekistan) filled every nook and cranny except Candy's room. The eyes of characters from a hundred Disney films watched your every move. Joel had been up here many times and was always bothered by the sight of Sara in her white nurse's overall exclaiming that all men who entered their flat had to undergo a 'thorough' physical examination for sexually transmitted diseases. 'Have you seen one of these before, Joel?' she'd once asked, pulling out a huge pair of metal callipers. Joel had immediately pulled down his flies and said, 'Have you seen one of *these* before?'

Plastered over Candy's bedroom walls were pictures of children she'd met and helped throughout her many expeditions. Amongst these was a large framed photo of Joel holding on to a Union Jack flag, standing on the roof of the world, on top of Mount Everest. Asked by reporters what his proudest moment was, Joel had replied that he was most proud of the fact that he was the first man to climb Mount Everest while wearing a bra. For the first time in history the press were lost for words.

A knock on Candy's door; Sara walked in with two mugs of hot chocolate. After switching on the CD player and filling the room with the sound of the Black Eyed Peas' 'Where is the Love?' she joined Candy on her double bed.

'Okay, let's say we give Joel another chance,' Sara began, 'the odds are that he'll screw up again, you do know that? Joel is like most men who have been born extra, extra good-looking, he can't say no to pretty women. Ask yourself . . . ask yourself,' she sang along to the Black Eyed Peas. 'Ask yourself, would Joel ever date an ugly cow? *Nada*. No! But drop a leggy blonde beauty in his territory and like the predator he is, he'll pounce. Every time.'

'He can't be that bad. That would make him a—'

'Bastard. Pig. Well, why don't we test my little theory? Why not place a leggy blonde beauty in front of him and see what he does. I bet you a month's rent that he fucks her.'

Candy shuddered at the thought. Even though the plan was crude, it would certainly determine whether she could ever trust Joel again. The question was: did she even want to know? What if Joel was feeling low that day and needed a . . . shag? What if Sara was proved right? What then? Not only would Candy be out of pocket a month's rent, she would be out of pocket a fiancé. But who in their right mind would want a fiancé who cheated? There was only one thing for it.

'Let's do it, Sara, let's ruin my life.' Candy chinked mugs. 'I hope we're wrong, I really do.'

Just after bedtime in this Cornish residence, a phone blipped in a handbag. A message from Joel would have to wait until morning to be read:

21 Digits.
Candy sweetie loving you lots.
Can't wait for a cute baby to share
our love with. Keep doing hip exercises.
And don't worry about me, I'm wanking a lot.
(The sperm is always fresh with me.)
Miss you. Joel XXX

Chapter Nineteen

Saturday morning and Joel was in the doldrums. He'd been led to believe, by his agent, Pete, that writing an autobiography was going to be easy, a cinch. And it had been, until today, when the first three chapters that he'd sent off to his editor had come back with one sentence scrawled across the front sheet:

Please tell the truth!

The cheeky cow had scribbled her red-blood pen through all his stories of yak attacks, pigmy ambushes and the eat-all-you-like frozen climbers' cannibal barbeques. She'd totally removed the prologue which was a detailed account of how Joel said goodbye to his female co-climbers by having hot sex in his tent with them – it was all a bit much really. The only thing preventing Joel from paying a ghost writer to write the blasted thing was a note the editor had written on the back explaining that his writing was extremely colourful and gripping.

'Gripping,' he smiled, shivering. 'It should be, I'm a fucking climber.'

Outside the sun cooked, but inside Joel's apartment the temperature was close to freezing. In order to inspire himself to write, Joel had attempted to simulate a mountain's climate by turning the air-conditioning on full. Although it was hard work typing with his climbing gloves on, the result was an extra dimension of realism that couldn't be achieved otherwise. He took a further look at the Himalayas on the map, centralized his fingers on the laptop keyboard and proceeded with his next passage:

I'm trying not to think of what I might lose, my focus aims at what I might gain. Everest, so magnificent and yet so hunched and domineering, invites me to succeed if I dare. I take another step, then another five huge lungfuls of air, I take another step, and pathetically I cry, 'You will not beat me. I've wanted this since I was five.' And Everest answers with a gust of wind that nearly knocks me off my feet. 'It's like that, is it?' I shout, holding on for dear life. Something forces me to look to my right and over a ledge. Lying at the bottom of a rocky crevasse, like discarded mannequins, appear to be at least four dead bodies. I knew to expect this, many die on Everest, but to see death in the flesh (even flesh in the throes of death) was something my training never prepared me for. At that moment my love for Everest turns to hate. Why did the dream of my life turn out to be a murderess?

Death and mountaineering have been a happily married couple since time began. Joel was often reminded of the dangers of his chosen profession by family, friends and acquaintances, but no finer reminder existed than the vision of those four crumpled bodies lying frozen at the bottom of that gully. The memory of that sight always gave him pause for thought.

The doorbell farted, and Joel answered it still dressed as a climber. Huge plumped bright-red jacket, goggles and bobble hat, boots, waterproofs, gloves and rope. It was a wonder Zarleena didn't run away screaming.

'I clearly remember asking you *not* to wear anything sexy,' Joel said, eyeing her attire.

Dressed in a white vest top, short red skirt and white pumps, Zarleena shrugged. This was sexy? Then again, she *was* being judged by Michelin Man. She was led inside where the chill had her wishing she hadn't shaved her legs that morning. This was the perfect climate for Aunti-ji Bakeshi who was hairier than a gibbon with hormone problems. At least ten empty Red Bull cans lay squashed on the floor. A map of India was draped over the sofa, a laptop screen saver showed two cows mating, and a collection of photos, most of crisp white snow, lay scattered over the coffee table next to a huge jam jar.

'If you can't bear to watch cows having sex, Zarleena, just click the mouse. I probably wouldn't want to watch them myself either if they were sacred to me. I'll get you a Slim-Fast drink.'

Great, thought Zarleena, *now he thinks I'm fat. I shouldn't have eaten those chocolates last night.* 'Slim-Fast, sounds fantastic.' She clicked the mouse, sighed in relief because the cows were gone, but became stiff with fear when she read Joel's last sentence on the screen . . . *Why did the dream of my life turn out to be a murderess?* Before she had time to ponder the meaning, her eyes were drawn to the contents of the large jam jar on the coffee table. With trepidation she picked it up and then screamed.

Joel skidded in, saw her with the jar, and laughed. 'It's just a yak's tail. It was given to me for good luck by a Sherpa family. What did you think it was, a hairy dick?' He walked off, chuckling.

Yes. In fact she had.

A sense of normality was re-established when Joel changed into scruffy jeans and scruffy T-shirt bearing the slogan REACH THE SUMMIT BEFORE YOU PLUMMET; the air-conditioning was switched off and Joel sat on the vibrating chair with a Red Bull in his hand. The jar containing the lucky yak's tail had been placed back with the kitchen spices. Zarleena waited for Joel's gulping and slurping to cease, wondering if telling him of her predicament was such a wise idea after all. The bottom line was: would Joel laugh when he found out that she was being bribed with dirty photos? Men weren't the most sensitive of creatures. He might even ask for a few to show his mates. So why was she about to tell him? Was it as simple as the fact that she didn't have anyone else to go to? Zarleena thought about that for a moment as she relaxed back into the sofa. The answer was 'yes'. She didn't have anyone else to go to. She was as desperate as could be.

'Out with it then, Zarleena!' demanded Mr Sensitive. 'Nothing is worth worrying over so much that a woman forgets to foundation the other half of her face.'

Zarleena gave a wry smile. 'Good try, but don't you know that an average woman checks her make-up at least fifty times before she even leaves the house?'

'Really?' Joel nodded sincerely. 'Would cooking me an Indian meal take your mind off your problem?'

'I'd prefer a couple of bin liners of filthy washing,' Zarleena replied, not too sure if Joel was aware of the concept of 'helping'.

He grinned and nodded. 'Sarcasm is the lowest form of humour, did you know that? So, when we discuss your "problem" would you prefer me to leave the jokes out of it? Or, would you like some entertainment to lighten the situation? Your choice. Mmm, good stuff this.'

A loud 'moo' came from the laptop speaker, and Zarleena leaned forward to click the mouse.

'You should see the pigs,' Joel stated proudly. 'Such energy. No wonder bacon tastes so good.'

Zarleena laughed. Holy Durga, she'd never met anyone so open about sex before. Maybe that was another reason why it had to be Joel who she told her 'problem' to, at least he wouldn't look upon what she had done with absolute scorn. Rather, he'd consider it something to be encouraged.

After a few minutes of small talk, Zarleena took a huge 'now or never' breath and blurted out, 'My husband left me about a year ago. His bruises followed about a month later. The marriage itself was arranged by our parents, so there was never any love floating about. It's very bad for an Indian couple to split. *Very bad*. The relatives look upon the person who split up the marriage as someone who should go to hell.' Zarleena glanced up to make sure Joel's blue eyes were registering her words. She continued in her emotion-free voice, satisfied that Joel was listening one hundred per cent. 'Armin, my husband, decided that he would try to make me leave the marriage, so that I would be looked upon badly by our relatives. And he thought that by hitting me I would pack up my things and run away. Harder and harder he beat me, but for some reason I couldn't bring myself to leave. Even though each day I grew more petrified of him, and each day I expected a fist to be rammed into my stomach, I just couldn't leave. I couldn't bear to hurt my parents.' She paused, sipped on her Slim-Fast drink, then carried on, 'In the end he just upped and left himself. He probably had another woman on the side or something. Anyway, during the marriage, he ordered me to pose for these horrible, dirty photographs and it's these filthy bits of paper that he's bribing me with.' She wiped away a tear. 'There, I said it. He only wants £20,000 in cash by this Tuesday, or the whole of the Indian community will be sent them. I don't know what to do. And, I hoped you might.'

Stalling for time while he thought of what to say, Joel offered Zarleena a yellow tissue. 'Go on, take one; a good blow always makes me feel better.'

But what to say? He tried to remember the name of the electric shock treatment that he was threatened with, as a kid, by his psychiatrist; Dr Freshman had said it would wipe his memory clean away. Maybe Zarleena needed something that would enable her to forget this horrible episode in her life. There was a mountaineer he once knew who always had an answer to everything; he would roll up his sleeve and point to his wrist band, on which was written *WWJD (What Would Jesus Do?)* It gave Joel an idea.

'Hang on a sec,' Joel said, running through to his bedroom. He dived to the floor, reached under his bed and pulled out handfuls of lost clothes. Finally he located his encyclopaedia, checked under 'Hindu Gods', then set about making a wrist band for Zarleena out of an old sock.

He returned carrying a huge smile. 'Hold out your arm.' Zarleena obliged. 'Sorry the words are a bit lopsided but writing on a sock with a marker pen wasn't easy.' He slipped on the material. 'Every time you feel down, I want you to look at these beautiful words, Zarleena, it will make life so much easier for you.'

Zarleena examined the saggy, frayed white band, trying to read the smudged writing:

WWLKD (What Would Lord Krishna Do?)

It was a sweet gesture reaffirming that, sometimes, ignorance was bliss. Zarleena only hoped that her wrist didn't develop verrucas. She flashed Joel a look of gratitude and watched him sink back into the vibrating chair satisfied that he'd helped womankind.

After a few moments of pondering, Joel spoke, 'I need to know what we're dealing with here, Zarleena; these sordid photos, on a scale of one to ten, how bad are they? Let's give you a comparison, let's say one is Judy Finnegan falling out of her dress at the National

Television Awards. And ten is a Scandinavian gang-bang.'

'From an Indian perspective, it's ten to the power of infinity. It doesn't get much worse. Hence my husband's confidence that I will find £20,000 for him.'

Joel became thoughtful, asking searching questions about Zarleena's relationship with her husband. Was Armin rash or impulsive? Did he hide his weak character behind his bullying ways? Did he drink, gamble, or owe money to anyone? What was the worst physical act that Armin had dished out? Zarleena answered frankly, hiding nothing, opening her wounds once again. Her gut feeling that beneath Joel's larking around lay a sensible man, was proved once and for all. By the time all the cards were laid out on the table, Joel was convinced that Armin could be dealt with. But dealt with, shuffled and trumped the Joel way.

An enormous ten-topping pizza was ordered, delivered and demolished. As early evening began to draw in, Zarleena was beginning to feel at home in Joel's apartment – like a vicar in a church, or a Holy man at the Ganges or even a fat American at McDonald's. A plan took shape, one that could unhinge Armin's life, one that could help Zarleena to forget this sorry mess for good. It involved £1000, something stored in Joel's lock-up, and a heck of a lot of cheek.

'I can't take £1000 off you, Joel, you hardly even know me,' Zarleena argued for the umpteenth time.

'Like I said, pay me back when you can, as and when you can afford it.' He stood up and stretched, revealing his tight stomach muscles underneath his T-shirt.

Zarleena felt like rubbing her hands all over him. 'So, you're all clear about Tuesday?' he asked.

She nodded. 'All clear.'

Zarleena felt encouraged by today's happenings. Things couldn't have gone any better. Plus, there was no doubt in her mind now that she was attracted to Joel, and it proved beyond doubt that Armin hadn't turned her into a lesbian man-hater, as Honey had once implied after a bottle of white wine. Joel pressed all the right buttons and ticked all the right boxes. She'd never really been one for imagining having sex with a man before, but tonight she was sure would be an early one, just to fantasize about what it would be like to make love to him. He was ambitious with his climbing (maybe to a fault), he knew how to make her laugh, he was gorgeous, sexy, he had a great body, he was kind and even slightly haphazard in his manner (which made him all the cuter in her eyes).

But, he was unavailable. Zarleena would never dream of stepping on his fiancée's toes (even if she could). So, friends it would have to be then.

Not one to sit still for too long if he could help it, Joel left Zarleena alone while he took a shower. The plan was to follow him in her van to the cash-point, where he would advance her the £1000 and then split, leaving her to go home, while he spent the rest of Saturday evening down the pub with his mates, trying to turn his blood into pure alcohol, like the true lager alchemist he purported to be.

While waiting for Joel, Zarleena took up his offer of sampling the vibrating seat. Suddenly her list of essentials for the maisonette now included a chair just like this. No wonder Joel's bottom had been glued to it; it was way better than a washing machine on fast spin. Out of the blue, a bleeping noise interrupted; maybe the chair was warning her that an orgasm was imminent, or, maybe – Zarleena located the whereabouts of the bleep – it was just the answerphone connecting. She reduced the vibrations to listen in.

Joel's voice began on the machine, '*By the time you hear the end of this message, you will be that much nearer to your death. Ask yourself, am I that important in your life that you need to leave a message? Of course I am. Please leave your message and I will try to live long enough to receive it. Cheers, Joel.*'

After a beat, a man's voice began, 'It's Pete, I know you said not to disturb you on Fridays, Saturdays and the rest of the week, but I have a few jobs lined up for you. I'll reel them out. Job one, a rich couple have lost their son on Mount Gasherbrum, the chances of finding his body are slim, but they want you to do a search of his planned route, and, if successful, to bury a small box near his body and recite a prayer. Job two, a new ski resort is opening in Canada later in the year, and they've specifically asked for you to climb to a specified location and set up a small number of fireworks (it's very risky, you'll love it). And lastly, job three, another underwear advertisement I'm afraid, destination New Zealand, duration two weeks, fee extortionate. Get back to me as soon as you get a spare minute from writing that book that you should have nearly finished by now . . . Bye now.'

Zarleena raised her eyebrows. Wow, Joel really was Mr Cosmopolitan. A real-life action man. Almost a super hero. Captain Climbs, raised by a mountain to do battle with heights. His arch enemy: Frostbite Man.

Another half-hour passed and Zarleena remembered a lyric from a Blondie record, something along the lines of 'her finest hour was watching him shower', and she'd thought, yeah right, like blokes take a whole hour to shower. Well, Blondie was spot on. Joel was taking for ever. After ten more minutes of worrying whether it was possible for someone to drown in the shower, Zarleena decided to check on her missing host.

Like a mother afraid to wake the baby, Zarleena crept along the wooden floorboards that led to the bathroom. The door was slightly ajar with steam wafting through the gap. She tiptoed nearer, her heart jack-knifing, her make-up threatening to run. What if she found him dead? She shivered at the thought. Or alive and naked? She banished the vision for later viewing. Just one more step and she was right at the bathroom entrance; the shower was clearly switched off, nothing could be heard coming from within. Zarleena put aside all images of body bags, blue and white crime-scene tape, a white chalked body outline, and forensic scientists, lugged a deep breath of steamy air, then took a peek through the gap. Oh my, she thought, ogling Joel's half-naked body, if only she was sitting on the vibrating chair, then she could have called this moment 'perfect'. Joel stood with his back to the door, a large tattoo of something on his shoulder blade was virtually concealed by the steam, a white towel tied round his waist, hair wet, beads of water trekking down his dream body. Joel wasn't dead at all, just taking a phone call on his mobile and judging by his gestures, it was obvious that he was receiving an ear-bashing from a woman. He kept sticking his two fingers up at the phone, while talking. Zarleena strained her ears and concentrated on Joel's words: 'I'm not going to cheat on you, it's just the pub with Jay, Brent and Clovis ... No, there aren't going to be any women sitting with us at our table ... No, I don't feel like I need a shag ... I meant with another woman, not you ... Oh, come on, Candy, you know I love you ... Well, you tell interfering Nurse Sara to stick that huge syringe right up her huge ... Sorry ...'

Zarleena backed away and returned to the vibrating chair in the living room. No wonder Joel was in trouble, he was calling his fiancée, Claudia, by the name of Candy. Poor Joel, he just couldn't let dead Candy go. Loyalty like that was hard to find these days. She knew of a woman who lost her husband and fell in love with the pallbearer. No respect. Especially as the pallbearer was the deceased's brother.

From a brother with no respect for his brother, to a sister with no respect for her brother. In charged Eloise, making an entrance Cruella De Vil would be proud of. Except this minx wasn't after puppy furs, she was here to cause trouble. Zarleena was allowed a few seconds to admire Eloise's attire. A short, tight denim dress, just about managed to keep her bust from being launched, stilettos, perfectly applied make-up, and gorgeous long brown hair left loose to flow about her like a cape completed the picture. She clutched a camera in her hand, its light on standby (always on standby).

'Who the hell are you?' Eloise demanded to know.

'Erm, a friend of Joel's,' Zarleena replied, taken aback by the sting in Eloise's tongue. She guessed that Denim Girl was Joel's sister, there were some remarkable similarities in their features, and she also guessed that manners didn't run in their family. 'He's in the shower.'

'What, to wash off your sex?' Eloise thundered up to the coffee table and picked up an empty Slim-Fast can. 'Stealing my drinks, stealing my favourite chair, next you'll be stealing my brother.'

The two girls locked eyes like two deer locking antlers.

'Did you manage an orgasm?' Joel shouted, as he walked into the living room, now dressed in jeans and a shirt. 'It's a bloody good feeling sitting on that chair, I . . . Oh, Eloise, I thought you weren't back until tomorrow morning. Or maybe I misunderstood the understanding that we came to.' He lifted his eyebrows. 'I THOUGHT that you were sleeping over at JERKHAN'S?'

'His name is Johan, thank you. And I think you should get used to it, as he will probably be my husband one day. Your brother-in-law.' Eloise tapped her foot on the floor. 'This is all very cosy. Where does your fiancée fit in with this equation? Or, would I be correct in presuming your fiancée doesn't know about this, Joel? Tut tut. Now why don't you two scoot along while I pick up the phone and dial a certain blonde lady's number. Be a love, Joel, and tell me the dialling code for Cornwall, would you?'

'Six, six, six.' Joel turned to Zarleena. 'Sorry about my mutant sister, ever since she's been eating genetically modified foods she's been murder to live with. I'll just find my car keys and we'll go, before she turns nice.'

Joel disappeared, hoping his sister could at least be civil while he was gone. He couldn't understand what had got into her recently. Picking fights, deleting his answerphone messages, opening all his cold cans of Red Bull and spilling them down the sink (warm Red Bull – yuck), even hiring a carpenter to fit three extra bolts to the inside of her bedroom door, to, quote, 'Prevent a rampant brother from coming in and watching her undress.' No, he definitely didn't know what had got into her lately.

Eloise chewed on her thoughts. Why did women find her brother so bloody attractive? (Apart from the fact that he filled most women's physical criteria of what constituted a prefect male specimen.) It had made Eloise's job so much harder over the years. Pushing women away from him so she could have his undivided attention and be his number-one woman took an awful amount of energy and time. She was sick of coming home and finding stray women begging for Joel to bed them. Sick of it!

Staring into space, Zarleena refused to get drawn into any more confrontations with Denim Girl. Flash! Eloise focused her camera, aiming it at Zarleena. Flash! Zarleena refused to look up. Flash! FLASH! FLASH!

Eloise spoke. 'You do know that Joel has got Aids, don't you?'

Zarleena looked up, startled. FLASH!

'Perfect! What a shot. He's been infected for five years now. That's why he likes cold mountains. It slows down the virus.' Eloise grinned sweetly. 'I'd dump him

228

if I were you. There's enough sadness in the world because of Joel already; don't let yourself become another one of his victims. You do know that Joel's immune system is wrecked don't . . .' Eloise spotted Joel listening in the doorway. 'How dare you say that about my brother, you cow! Joel, she just told me that—'

Joel put up his hand for Eloise to stop. 'From today you start paying rent.' He nodded. 'Yeah, that means getting yourself a job, Eloise. W-O-R-K. Work. It's time you pulled your weight around here. Now clean up my pizza box.' He flicked a crust on to the floor. 'NOW!'

Denim Girl collapsed to her knees. 'Please, Joel, I'll be good, don't send me to work. I'll do anything. Anything. I love living off you. I'll be a nothing if I'm not a sponger. How am I going to afford my manicures? How am I going to buy my designer clothes? Please, Joel, be reasonable.'

He laughed as he escorted Zarleena to the door. 'Cheerio, sis, don't wait up.' And the two of them left.

Left Eloise alone.

First stop, Joel's bedroom. She threw back the duvet and checked the sheets for stains. No stains. To the bins to check for used condoms. No condoms. The dirty Indian woman must have taken him in her mouth. No wonder she didn't talk much, her jaw was too sore from sucking.

Eloise lay back in Joel's bed, breathing in the smell of his Echo aftershave from the pillows, seeking comfort from where he slept. She spotted his *Children in Need* jar half filled with pound coins. The sign said: RAISE

MONEY FOR CHARITY. A POUND AN ORGASM. Apparently the semi-filled jar was simply the result of a few lonely nights' worth of solitary pleasure. (That's what he'd told gullible Candy when she spotted it.) There was at least £200 in that jar. 'If I can use my bodily functions to help build a school hut in Botswana then sue me. It's my body,' Joel had often said.

Eloise huffed. Things had certainly changed in the last few weeks. Joel was now engaged, but it looked like he was cheating on poor Candy again. And along with cheating on Candy, he was now keeping secrets from his little sister. Why had Joel not talked about the new woman in his life, the pretty Indian woman who had just left? What was so special about her, apart from her looks, that he had to keep his sister in the dark? The security guard-cum-doorman downstairs had already confirmed that Zarleena had been here at least once before. Turned up in her Bindis & Brides van and didn't leave for hours. And this was the thanks Eloise got for being the instigator to the reconciliation between Dylan and Joel.

If this was thanks, then, no thanks.

Eloise slipped off the bed, turning her snooping nose to her brother's drawers and boxes. Joel always had boxes. People loved to send him stuff. Sponsors mainly. It was all hoarded away in his huge, messy bedroom and his lock-up for a rainy day. The door to Joel's walk-in wardrobe was open, virtually begging her to take a peek inside. Normal people kept their clothes in wardrobes, but Joel kept Red Bull. Resting on one of the high shelves, amongst his stash of energy drinks, was a Debenhams bag. Eloise stood on tiptoes and yanked the bag down. It was pretty obvious to her that she was going to find slutty lingerie inside – most likely for his exotic new Indian bird.

She tipped the contents onto Joel's bed and gasped. This was a step further than lingerie. This was a step too far. Joel had obviously got some woman pregnant, for staring back at Eloise from the bed were baby clothes: a dinky T-shirt, tiny blue shorts, diddy boots and a cap. This was so *not* cute from where Eloise was standing. No wonder she couldn't find any stains, all his sperm was being used to make babies. The question was: who was the mother of his child? Candy? Zarleena? Or some other secret girlfriend he'd forgotten to tell her about?

The closest Joel had ever come to being a father, as far as she knew, was when he adopted a termitarium (or in English, an Australian termite nest). He couldn't even do an adoption normally, most people opt for a dolphin or an elephant, even a person. Joel did termites and he'd been sending money yearly. He even had names for ten thousand of them. Ranging from Termite One to Termite Ten Thousand. But Joel in charge of a real baby? He'd probably eat it.

Seriously though, Eloise deliberated, did this spell the end of her cohabiting? With the baby on the way, Joel would need all the space he could. Her bedroom would be turned into a nursery. She would become homeless. Life as she knew it would be over.

It was time to give Joel's plan, whatever plan that might be, a vasectomy. After deliberating over the possibilities for at least half an hour, Eloise finally arrived at the perfect solution, the ideal remedy for being threatened with being made homeless. She sniggered to herself. How could Joel possibly throw her out if he thought she herself was pregnant? His own sister? What kind of a brother would he be if he did that? Especially as he was about to be a father himself.

Chapter Twenty

The bright July sun nearly fooled Zarleena into believing there was nothing wrong in her life on this gorgeous Tuesday. And then her stomach churned as she remembered what she was planning to do today. Like a storm from the blue her mood changed. Honey was under the impression that Zarleena was meeting a friend from the past. It wasn't a lie if one removed the 'r' in friend.

Zarleena had phoned Armin last night, while Honey was in the bath, confirming time and place for today's rendezvous. Zarleena was adamant that it had to be a public place, because she was scared he might turn violent. He asked if she had all the money and she asked if he had all the photographs. A time was set for 3 p.m.

In the BHS coffee shop in Hunterslea, Zarleena could feel her nerves loading up with fear. It was 2.30 p.m. and for the last half an hour she'd been mulling around the clothes section downstairs, convinced that every other person was a store detective, surer still that every camera was centralized on her movements. What woman, with £1000 in her bag that she couldn't spend, wouldn't act a little strange amongst racks of tempting clothes?

A heavy-set waitress lumbered past Zarleena's table grateful that the lunchtime rush was over. Her bunions were on fire today. Zarleena sipped her coffee, too nervous to eat her scone. With its family atmosphere, BHS was the perfect location for underhand dealings. Zarleena wondered how many drug deals or planned bank raids had been concocted over BHS scones and coffee. She checked her watch again – 3.05 p.m. – there was no time to back out now. Zarleena suddenly became aware of a confrontation between the lumbering waitress and a nearby customer.

'Look, sir, you can't bring in your own drink. You're going to have to buy something, or leave,' she said.

'For Pete's sake, it's only a Red Bull.' He cracked it open and swigged. 'Good stuff this.'

'I expect it is, sir, but all the same you'll still have to buy something.'

A pause, before: 'Well, how much does it cost to make a BHS waitress disappear? I'll have one of those please.'

Zarleena giggled. The waitress lumbered off.

And Armin arrived.

Dressed in his black polo shirt, black trousers and holding a black briefcase, Armin deposited himself opposite Zarleena, wondering why the chairs in BHS were so small; he could hardly fit his backside on the wood.

'I thought out of respect, Zarleena, you might have turned up wearing Indian clothes.' He worked his eyes over her tight, sleeveless, lemon-coloured cotton dress. 'Your relatives in India would hang their heads in shame at your choice of clothing. Do you detest your heritage that much? Is a *shalwar kameez* too much to expect from Indian women these days? Anyway, I'm not here to argue, this is just a business transaction. I assume you've brought the money?'

Zarleena unzipped her bag and pulled out a folder, placing it before him; she hoped Joel's plan worked.

Armin scratched his chin, thoughtful. 'What's this?'

'It's the only way you'll get £20,000 off me. It's my safeguard.'

He sneered. 'Games! I don't think you seem to understand who's in charge here, Zarleena.' His voice rose, 'Tell me, how many Indian women go missing each year? The police have more than enough to do than to get involved in Asian family disputes. Is this what you want? To suddenly disappear?' He grabbed her wrist tight. 'Is it?'

'It's not a game, I have £1000 in cash today, it's all I could get at such short notice. I promise you'll have the rest next week. I'm waiting for it to clear in my bank. Read what's in the folder. It's not a game, Armin, I promise you.'

Zarleena breathed a sigh of relief as Armin released his grip. In deathly silence he looked over the contract that Joel and she had drafted on his laptop:

I promise, on receipt of all £20,000, in cash, to return the pornographic pictures of Zarleena

Shankar, my wife, and all negatives, copies and discs. After receiving the said amount, I promise to stay away from her and never to trouble her again. I accept an initial payment of £1000 in cash today in return for my signature on this contract.

Armin Shankar . . . . Date . . . .

After rereading the contract three more times, Armin finally looked up. 'I'm impressed. You're taking me seriously. Something everyone learns to do in time.'

'Obviously I don't want anyone to know about these photographs, Armin, or I would have gone to the police already with your threats.' Her voice wobbled with nerves. 'But if you fail to honour your agreement, then I will be left with no choice but to inform the authorities. You do understand this, don't you? I want you to leave me alone after this.'

'It's easy for a man of my standing to leave a whore alone, Zarleena, don't flatter yourself.' He removed a gold-tipped fountain pen from his briefcase and began to sign. 'You've been a shit wife. I don't think there is a low enough caste for you.' He slid the form across. 'Where's my cash? And when, exactly, do I get the rest?'

Zarleena explained that his pay day would be next Wednesday. He should expect a phone call before then to confirm the time and place. She fished out the £1000 and, in an exaggerated movement, very slowly passed the notes across to Armin's vulture talon. Five seconds later Armin stood up and walked away, leaving Zarleena with a vital question: how the hell did she get to marry a man with such a large bottom? Maybe that's what £20,000 was going to be used for: liposuction. Or in Armin's case: hipposuction.

Joel waited for a minute or so and then removed his hidden camcorder from an indoor plant that overlooked Zarleena's table. If luck was on their side, everything was caught on camera. He sat next to Zarleena and kissed her on the cheek.

'You did brilliantly,' he said, thrusting her uneaten scone into his mouth. 'Hungry work being an undercover detective. Let's see how ol' lard arse came out on camera.'

She snorted. 'Thanks.'

'I meant your doughnut husband,' he explained, rewinding the tape. 'I heard everything he said; what a nasty piece of work.'

They sat discussing the next step to their plan. An idea that Dracula himself would be proud of. Prompted by her common sense, Zarleena dared to ask the question, 'What if it all goes wrong?' What if, like Armin said, she just disappeared? Joel had an answer to that one: 'You're a Hindu, right? Get the fucker back in your next life. That's what reincarnation is all about. REVENGE.' But still the worry remained.

Joel stood up. 'I'm going to have to push off now. Eloise was chucking her guts up this morning. Again. So, I'll give you a call in the week.'

'Well, I hope she's okay, sounds to me like she's pregnant. Morning sickness.' Zarleena regretted her analysis as soon as she saw the drop in Joel's jaw. 'Or . . . she might have just picked up a bug; it's very fashionable these days.'

'That blasted Johan! Don't Czechoslovakians know how to stick a bit of rubber on their dicks?'

A mother on a nearby table covered her giggling young daughter's ears. The lumbering waitress began to steer herself towards Joel and Zarleena. BHS could well do without the likes of Joel in its diner. It was time he was bunion-booted out, but before she could even take four steps, Joel had already left.

Leaving Zarleena with her thoughts.

Sometimes Zarleena felt as if she had been born one generation too early. Reminders of how Indian family life was changing popped up everywhere. Even amongst the tables of this diner there was proof of that. A trio of teenage Asian girls sat in the dead centre of the eatery. Ten years ago and they would have hidden away in the corner. A pride in their colour was worn like armour. How could anyone dare to say that they were not welcome in this country? Doctors, lawyers, top businessmen, dentists, even newsreaders: all were claimed to be good jobs, and many were claimed by good Indians. This country, which once shunned them, couldn't cope without them now. No wonder Indian kids born in Britain have a rosy future to look forward to, the gold path of destiny having been laid by the many generations of Indians before them. They have their parents to thank for this. From the moment they are born, they live indebted.

While discussing the plan with Joel, Zarleena had been aware of the trio of Asians examining the pair of them from afar. Gossiping, imagining, dissing. The Indian people have come a long way, but there are many miles to go. Why is it that whenever an Indian woman is seen with a white man any Indian family in the vicinity will drop what they're doing to stare? Two arms, two legs, one head, what's the problem? Oh yeah, too white. Zarleena could remember acting this way herself once when she was younger. An innocent shopping trip to Tesco had Honey and herself following an Indian woman with a white man around the store to find out if they were a couple. Whispering to each other, 'Check to see if the man is wearing a ring. If so, is it Indian gold?' Back then, it was a rare sight to see. It normally meant that the Indian woman had opted against the wishes of her parents and gone against tradition. In not so many words, it meant that she was a traitor.

All families who leave their own country to live in another risk exposing their children to their newly adopted country's ways. When Indian families first took up residence in Britain, Asian families were extremely controlling. They didn't want their values diluted by Western philosophies. A strict code of conduct was expected to be adhered to by all children. No parties, no booze, no fags, no sex, no dates, no going out, no Valentines, no drugs, no rock 'n' roll ... NO LIFE. And to a degree this 'no life' life worked. Most children did what they were told, waited for their parents to fix them up with a partner, and married the Indian way. Most children did. But some, for example the rebellious couple walking around Tesco, decided to flout the system, follow their heart, and so be it. Zarleena could remember her parents explaining when she was still quite young that a distant relative had run off with a white man. Then it happened again. Before you could say *chicken rogan gosh* three times, almost every family in Britain knew at least one runaway. Something had to change or Indian parents would soon see fewer and fewer of their children marrying in the way they wished.

So, the strict rules that were there to protect them from Western ways were slightly relaxed. Suddenly the life of a British-born Asian didn't seem so bad. Their freedoms were partially given back to them, their parents' trust in them reinstated, their privacy their own. Zarleena snuck a look at the trio, and sure enough, just as she had expected, they were all equipped with a mobile phone. In her day, if mobile phones had existed then, it would have been a huge no-no. Phones meant boys. Secret calls to boys; boys who couldn't wait to see what really went on inside an Indian girl's knickers. Most boys Zarleena had known in her past probably expected that an Indian girl kept spices down there or something, although she did know of one Indian girl who kept a drawing compass there, just in case she was called upon to make a perfectly round *chapatti*.

Being born a generation later would have given Zarleena more freedom. Her strict upbringing wouldn't have been so . . . strict. But, and here is where things hadn't changed, she would still have been expected to have an arranged marriage. Just like the trio of Asian girls sitting in the centre. Although, nowadays, the name has been changed. It's now called 'an assisted marriage'. And it comes with a bottom line.

The bottom line is: assisted, arranged, forced or pressurized, you still have to marry a stranger who is chosen for you by your parents.

Zarleena stood up, smiled at the girls, then left them to gossip about her some more.

Joel returned to Forest Falls Apartments to find Sammy, the doorman who rarely talked, collapsed in his seat in Reception, red-cheeked, sweaty and exhausted, fanning his face with a newspaper. A huge wall of cardboard boxes stood neatly stacked by the lifts. Boxes which would have taken only the ten minutes required to unload off the lorry, rather than the half an hour that they had actually taken, if, after every other step, Sammy hadn't been so intent on uttering the words, 'That fucking Joel and his deliveries.'

'Tired?' enquired Joel, ripping off the invoice stuck to one of the boxes. 'I've got some bottled oxygen upstairs, if you need it.'

'I'm sick of you and your deliveries,' Sammy mumbled, 'sick to the back teeth.'

Joel smiled at the invoice. 'Excellent, my Treadwell thermal socks have finally arrived.' The shipment of footwear were freebies from Treadwell for advertising their product in a climbing magazine. Joel tore open a cardboard flap and pulled out a pair, rubbing the soft material to his face. 'Pure Tibetan yaks' wool.'

'I SAID, "I'M SICK OF YOU AND YOUR DELIVERIES." I'm not paid to be your slave. I've got a bad back, you know?' Sammy glared at Joel, who was still rubbing his face with the sock in ecstasy. 'I'm sick of the number of women you bring back with you. I'm sick of the offensive slogans on your T-shirts.' He pointed to Joel's latest example: the words STUD FARM with an arrow pointing to his crotch. 'I'm sick of you telling me Red Bull is "Good stuff". I'm sick of that massive burp you do before telling me "It's good stuff". I'm sick of people telling me how lucky I am to work for a local celebratory. Celebratory, my arse! All you are is a lazy, good for nothing, over-estimated, over-paid, worthless—'

Joel butted in, 'I wouldn't finish that sentence if I were you.' He peered across the counter with confusion: had Sammy, the doorman who rarely talked, finally blown his gasket? Had all that pent-up frustration over the years finally been unleashed? He was about to query Sammy's mood further when Joel's thinking was interrupted by his mobile. He walked out to the entrance to take the call.

Sammy looked on hatefully. Oh, what a surprise, Mr Popular had another phone call. It was hard to nail why Sammy disliked Joel so much, but it most likely had something to do with everything about Joel. His looks, his youth, his wealth, his car, in fact . . . his life. Normally Sammy wished good luck on people, even clapping the TV when someone won over £64,000 on *Who Wants to be a Millionaire?*. But with Joel, ashamed as he was to admit it, he couldn't wait for the day he fell down (preferably off a high mountain). Sammy sneered at Joel through the glass and then continued with his crossword puzzle until his concentration was broken by Joel's shouting on the phone. Sammy listened in with horror as Joel yelled out the words, 'Kill the babysitter . . . Just kill the babysitter, for God's sake.'

Quickly Sammy noted the time and scribbled down some details. What Joel was wearing and what Joel was saying. Clues that the police might need if and when the babysitter was murdered. Joel behind bars was nearly as good as Joel at the bottom of a mountain.

A few minutes later Joel trudged into Reception, a pained look on his face. He glanced Sammy's way. 'I'll move the boxes later. And cheer up, it's not as if someone has died, is it?'

Sammy gulped.

Chapter Twenty-one

Three blondes in a flat watching TV. The chances that they were viewing *Mastermind* or *University Challenge* were slim. Candy, Sara and Sara's cousin, Monique, were attentively watching an episode of *Neighbours*. Instrumental in their plan to fool Joel into believing Monique was a legitimate Australian was that she spoke with an authentic Aussie accent. Any hint of Cornish coming through and he'd immediately be suspicious that he was being played. Candy was already having fears that the whole thing might backfire on her.

'What if he turns you down, Monique? I'm going to feel awful for distrusting him,' Candy said, pouring top-ups into all three wine glasses.

Monique appeared astounded. 'Excuse me. A man, turn *moi* down, never!'

Sara and Candy eyed each other. Admittedly, Monique stood out, about three foot when she took off her bra, and her waist was so petite she couldn't possibly fit in all her vital organs. And then one saw how she mistreated men, and it was obvious the vital organ missing was her heart. But as far as beautiful women went, she was as far as a beautiful woman was allowed to go. She was sickeningly stunning. Tantalizingly sexy. Gobsmackingly perfect; and, from her viewpoint, the diminishing rainforest problem was an exaggeration, because everywhere she went there were plenty of men with plenty of 'wood'.

The tuition continued. 'Everything sounds like a question in Aussie, Mon,' Sara explained. 'Like this? I'm off to the toilet? The barbeque is lit? I'm so tired? And then you add in a few extras like, "Okay, sport", "G'day", "I'm a Sheila but my name ain't Sheila". It'll get easier when you get Joel drunk. He won't know whether he's coming or going.'

'Oh, he'll be coming all right, when he sees me,' stated Monique. 'You're setting yourself up for failure, Candy; it's going to be so hard for a man to turn this down.' She stood up and twirled her skinny, five-foot-eight tanned body around. 'I was thinking of wearing my red leather cat-suit.' She purred. 'Meow.'

Candy tried to explain that the idea was to 'tempt' Joel, not to 'bed' Joel. There was a line that Monique must not cross, no matter how well the evening went. And, yes, Rohypnol tablets in his Red Bull, would be crossing that line.

'So, I have to tempt him to the point that he begs me to sleep with him and then I make an excuse to leave?' Nods all round. 'It seems a bit of a shame for me to dress up in a cat-suit just for five minutes' work,' Monique said, examining the snapshot of Joel for the millionth time. 'He's rather dishy. I expect that he's got

a scrummy, hard body, being a climber and all that?'
She peered up, crossed her bust, and in her new Aussie
accent said, 'I promise I won't sleep with him?'

Candy wondered whether she had just opened
Pandora's Box. But to be able to finally remove that
niggling doubt about Joel's fidelity for the rest of her
life was worth an evening's nail biting – she watched
Monique dribbling over Joel's photo – and she would
just have to make sure that, come Saturday, her nails
were painted in chocolate-flavoured nail polish (if they
made that kind of thing), and that included her toe-
nails.

A plan was drawn up. Nothing too flash. Joel was
due to meet with his mates, Brent, Jay and Clovis at the
Two Peas in a Pod pub, in deepest Hunterslea, for the
celebration of Brent's thirtieth birthday that coming
Saturday evening. Drink was to be followed by booze
to be followed by alcohol. A huge hangover was
already planned for the Sunday morning after.

It was Wednesday evening, giving Monique two
more days to perfect her Aussie accent and learn the
Australian anthem. Her expenses were to include the
train fare to and from Hunterslea, hotel bills for the
night, drink, food and make-up allowance, and a box
of tissues in case the Rugby World Cup got mentioned
by Joel. Nothing could be simpler.

'Sounds to me that within Joel's profession, he's
quite a famous boy. How many magazine covers
did you say he'd featured on, Candy?' Monique
questioned.

'Quite a few. You won't be able to get him talking
about them though.'

247

'Oh. And why's that?'

'Because climbing is his passion, not advertising men's underpants by sticking his arse at a camera five thousand feet up a mountain.'

And right then, Monique planned on getting inside those treasured underpants. Candy had lain down the gauntlet; the Holy Grail awaited. There was only one thing left for Monique to do: practise orgasms with an Aussie accent. She hoped that Joel was as good in bed as he was to look at. And she prayed that her orgasms didn't come out like a strangled dingo. 'Yaaeeees?'

On her bedroom wall Honey stuck an updated list of Greenpeace Activists locked away in prison. She lit a candle and uttered a short prayer for their swift release. Tree, her boyfriend, had faxed the names through earlier today, while he still had the energy: he was due to begin a hunger strike in protest against Bill Gates, and had printed out his leaflets, explaining his cause, on Microsoft Word for Windows. Tree had been demonstrating since primary school where he'd once held a class sit-in because the Alphabet Spaghetti became too cold to eat by the time he'd spelt out DINNER LADIES SUCK EGGS. His dream in life was to be offered a knighthood only to moon the Queen instead.

From the living room, the methodical creak of Zarleena pumping away on the stepper could be heard. Honey felt as if she'd taken her eye off the ball with her sister lately. A degree of secrecy seemed to have crept into the maisonette like a cold frost. And it made Honey shiver. There was nothing obvious, Zarleena still joked around at work, still acted like big sis; she even helped make banners this week for a march that was due on Sunday to demonstrate against slave wages in Indian Call Centres. But whenever Honey mentioned Joel, Armin, or divorce, Zarleena's mouth clammed tighter than a mantrap. Then there were these hush-hush phone calls, secret meetings with old friends, and middle-of-the-night texts. And what about that £1000 that Honey had come across, amongst Zarleena's underwear, when she was searching for a bra to borrow? Surely Zarleena hadn't turned to drugs? It was all a bit too Agatha Christie for her liking. A banquet of mystery with one final dish to keep the meal alive. A generous serving of racist letters. Just like the one that had been delivered last week. All addressed to Bindis & Brides, all determined to cause fear and alarm, all written, no doubt, by a depraved man. But who? Zarleena was convinced it was the weasel work of Armin; Honey was not so sure.

Coating one entire wall of Honey's bedroom were pictures of great men and women. Biko, Mother Teresa, Gandhi, Mandela, people who had made a difference. She likened modern-day politicians to kerosene, a highly flammable fuel ready to wipe out all the good that these people had done. Amongst the pictures of great people, Honey had drawn a silhouette of an unknown woman. This was supposed to represent herself and twenty-first-century women fighting for their rights. A huge multicoloured banner hung across the ceiling: SAVE OUR PLANET, LET WOMEN RULE!

The time was just 10 p.m. and Honey felt her body imploding under the feeling of tiredness. She hadn't felt this spent since having the flu a few years back.

Although it went against the grain to do so, she plumped up her pillows and contemplated an early night. Something she'd not done since leaving her parents house a year ago.

Indian people tend to go to bed as late as possible once they've left home. It may have something to do with the ancient past, where retiring for the night meant lying on a bed of nails. Or, it might simply be the fact that without parents sending you to bed early to revise for your future career as a doctor, lawyer or accountant, staying up late is a luxury to be abused. Early nights, before the watershed, are extremely common for children up to the age of twenty-six still living under their parents' roof, in case any nudity appears on TV.

No nudity on TV tonight, Honey decided to hit the sack. Today had been a non-starter from the word go. The morning had been spent cleaning up a huge spider's web in the shop, her evening martial arts class had been cancelled, and Zarleena had eaten all the chocolates in the cupboards. It was definitely time for some sleep.

ZZZZZzzz . . .

The shabby curtains to Armin's flat were closed, shutting out the noisy Wembley nightlife. Prem, Armin's cousin, had been invited over to hear Armin's gloats.

'The rich get richer, the poor get poorer.' Armin stared into his bathroom mirror and shouted back, 'But the sneaky just get more handsome.'

Spread out on a low wooden coffee table was an assortment of bowls. Bombay mix, peanuts and crisps.

A few salty snacks to line the stomach for an evening's consumption of Captain Morgan's Rum and ginger ale. The highlife. A Bollywood DVD, *Devdas*, was playing on the TV, with Russian subtitles (Armin had picked it up cheap at Camden Market), and Prem tapped along to the musical score, enjoying his favourite Bollywood movie of all time.

Armin returned to the living room and slumped in an armchair. 'India sure knows how to build women, hey, Prem?' he said, referring to Madhuri Dixit, floating about the filmset in her sari. 'It's this fucking country that turns them into sluts.'

Prem passed Armin a small glass tumbler of rum, then chinked his own against it. 'Bottoms up. Just be grateful that Zarleena's true colours surfaced when they did.' He sipped his drink. 'So, I take it no more trips to Hunterslea? You said yourself if she turned you down one more time, you'll divorce her and find yourself a good wife in India. Well, she's turned you down now; it's time to move on. You can't love a bad mango for ever, Armin; rotten flesh means rotten seed.'

Armin smirked at his naive cousin. Prem not only looked innocent with his boyish looks, neat, combed hair, smart attire and questioning eyes, but he *was* innocent. A wrap-around-your-little-finger kind of innocent.

Prem's loyalty was blood thick and, even though slightly scared of Armin, he greatly admired him too. And for good reason. Back in their mischievous school-days Armin had been the only Asian kid at Newton High School who had stood up to the racist skinheads. Prem remembered watching a hero being born when he saw Armin smash two skinheads over the head with a milk crate. 'Maybe if you wore a fucking turban it wouldn't hurt, would it?' Armin had said to them, rubbing his hands in triumph. 'INDIA rules!' What a hero.

Two hours passed and *Devdas* was still playing. Both cousins were tipsy by now, struggling to hold a decent conversation. Armin sat proudly wrapped in the Indian flag. Another Indian success story was about to materialize, and it took all of his will power not to boast of his new venture, Bindi Brides, to Prem. Even amongst the squashy inebriated brain cells of Armin's head, an idea that had formed a few weeks ago began to purify. He was finally going to be rich. Twenty thousand pounds' worth. Loaded! And just in case £20,000 wasn't enough, he'd make sure to hold back a few of the forbidden photographs – he might need a top-up bribe. He laughed out loud when he thought of the contract he'd been asked to sign by Zarleena. As if a poxy sheet of paper was going to scare him. What a joke.

'Did you know, Premmy Prem Prem that there is a good book out there written by a Muslim man on how to beat your wife without leaving giveaway marks?' Armin swigged from the rum bottle. 'Useful piece of information for you.'

Prem screwed up his face, disgusted. 'That's sick!'

'Not really. I'm all for discipline if a woman misbehaves. It's the reason God made men stronger than women.'

'So we can beat them up? Come on, Armin, you're joking, right?' Prem searched Armin's face for clues. 'You *are* joking?'

Fixing Prem with a slimy grin, he replied, 'Of course . . . just a joke.'

But was it? Rumours about Armin's fists had never really gone away. Prem had refused to believe any of it, proof was in the seeing and he'd never seen Zarleena with any bruises. But tonight's comment about a certain book added a different slant to Prem's view of Armin. Did their family really have a wife beater within its tree?

Prem's parents had often said, 'We must be on our best behaviour at all times, treat this country as you would India, and make no mistakes. If you slip up, then you slip everyone up. Don't make the English hate us.' It was about being tarred with the same brush, it was about being better than you were supposed to be, it was about living a life without shame. Today, one Indian wife beater; tomorrow, all Indians are wife beaters. And the day after: no Indian woman wants an arranged marriage because she fears the next wife beater could be her husband.

Prem thought fondly of his two younger sisters, both enjoying life, both apprehensive of their future arranged marriages. Mum and Dad would choose well, he was sure; he'd even have a hand in the decision himself, but what if? What if, just as it now appeared that he had been duped by Armin, the chosen husbands turned out to be masked abusers? How could he live knowing he had had a hand in picking the man who physically abused his sister?

'Armin, tell me straight, did you lay so much as a finger on Zarleena?' Prem asked, his voice failing to disguise his anger. 'Well?'

Armin seemed to grow before Prem's eyes. He stood directly over him. 'You dare to question your own flesh and blood? You take the side of a woman who hurt me? A woman who slept with other men.' He slammed his hand on his cousin's shoulder. 'You're just like the rest.' He walked unsteadily to the door and pulled on the handle. 'Get out, and don't come back until you're sober and ready to apologize.' Armin rubbed his eyes, faking tears. 'Families stink!'

Prem left the flat and stumbled away down to the street below. The grilled window of a shop selling cameras reflected back his troubled face. What had he done? Armin seemed too sincere to be lying. And now he'd hurt his hero.

From his pocket, he produced his mobile and dialled Armin's number. After a few rings it was picked up. Prem spoke: 'I'm ready to apologize, I'm sorry for doubting you. Please forgive me. It's just that, oh I don't know, you're too nice, too lovely, too generous and—'

Armin interrupted like a court-room hammer, 'Forgiven. That's the kind of guy I am. Short and sweet, none of this keeping you hanging around, no sulking, just a fair guy willing to forgive and forget. Why not come on back up and we'll open another bottle of Captain Morgan's . . .' Two seconds later the phone was switched off and Armin was smirking again. Oh, how easy it was to manipulate people.

Especially half-witted cousins like Prem.

Chapter Twenty-two

There was only one woman who Brent, the rich property developer and also one of Joel's best mates, hated more than Laurence Llewelyn-Bowen, and her name was Marie Antoinette. According to history, the modern-day champagne glass was allegedly modelled on her breast size. Pretty damn selfish, Brent always said, that because of her diminutive boobs, every future celebration on this planet had to suffer. Weddings, graduations, christenings, the end of WW2.

Even thirtieth birthdays.

Joel, Brent, Jay and Clovis sat around a wooden table in the busy Two Peas in a Pod pub. The olde-worlde feel of the place, with its low beams, stone walls and concrete floor was in stark contrast to the clientele it attracted who were ultra modern, top-of-the-range-mobile-phone holding, sports car driving, designer-clothes wearing and successful. Talk was never cheap in here; it was always backed up with a full wallet. A few sideways glances had already been projected towards Joel's table, where, attached to the legs of Brent's chair, were helium balloons bearing the words IT'S A GIRL (it was all the Balloons For Every Occasion market stall had left).

The four mates first met in prison. Well, that's what they called their craprehensive school. And all four seemed to have one thing in common: dicks that did most of their thinking.

Joel stood up. 'I'd like to make a small speech. That's it.' And he sat back down.

Clovis raised his A-cup champagne glass to toast Brent's thirtieth and was joined by the others. Up until a few years ago, Clovis had been known by all as Rainman. He convinced them that he was autistic because he could tell how many matches had fallen on the floor. Before long, they soon realized that he was, in actual fact, counting them very quickly. Disappointment set in; they had got quite used to the idea that at least one of them was special. Joel had even asked him, apart from Qantas, which other airlines were safe to travel on. His answer was always the same, 'Virgin, you can completely trust a good, safe ride with a virgin.'

As was inevitable in pubs and clubs, it wasn't long before a certain amount of female attention was aimed Joel's way. Not that Brent, Jay and Clovis didn't have their fair share of admirers it was just that Joel had more than his fair share, which bothered them. And always had.

'God, I wish you had a tiny dick, Joel,' Brent shouted. 'I'd go to bed a lot happier.'

Jay sniggered, then lit a fag. 'You mean to tell me that you go to bed worrying about Joel's willy? You're a sick birthday boy, mate.'

'That you two are even discussing his dick is beyond me,' said Clovis. 'It's hardly a Ferrari.'

Joel gulped his champagne. 'I beg to differ. Except my Ferrari gets serviced at least once a night, and most mornings. Sometimes even during the day.'

'Wanker!' said Brent, punching a balloon away from his face. 'Total.'

The warm summer evening was matched by the warm feeling of booze in their stomachs. Sometimes life didn't get better than being drunk amongst good friends. 'A Bridge Over Troubled Water' by Simon and Garfunkel rose above the general jabbering in the pub. Joel wondered about Eloise for a moment. Wasn't he supposed to be her bridge when she was in trouble? In just a week's time he was off to New Zealand for a fortnight to advertise underpants up a mountain. But the fizz had been shaken out of his excitement with the knowledge that, despite Eloise's protests to the contrary, she might be pregnant. Commitment was a word that Joel survived on. Cancelled was a word he tried to avoid. But maybe, for the first time in his climbing career, he would have to cancel a job that he'd committed himself to. Eloise needed him more than pants did.

Joel's mobile sang, forcing at least sixteen people to check it wasn't theirs. It was Candy wanting to wish Brent a happy thirtieth. Joel smiled securely to himself as he handed Brent the phone. Women were completely transparent at times. It was soooooo obvious Candy was just checking up on him, it was almost pathetic.

'You haven't got to worry about a thing,' Brent shouted down the phone. 'All the women in this pub are dogs!'

Female glares bearing daggers encrusted in pure venom hunted the owner of that remark. Brent would later have to explain to at least three of the women's boyfriends that he suffered from a medical condition which made him hyper-rude. In no shape or form did he look upon their ladies as dogs. God strike him dead if he was lying.

'I expect that Joel will be in bed by no later than eleven, Candy.' Brent winked at Joel. 'Seriously . . . Of course I mean his own bed. He's got a strong character, has our Joel, he'll use all his will power to fight off his sexual urges. Did I mention that this is a condom-free evening? And yes, I—'

Joel snatched back the mobile. 'He's drunk! Ignore him.'

'Just behave yourself, Joel, that's all I ask. I love you,' Candy said.

'You love me, cool. So, what are you up to tonight then?' He noticed Clovis mouthing something about returning the compliment and he quickly grasped what he meant. 'Oh yeah, Candy, and *I love you too*. Lots of loving. Only you, Candy, always only you. My love bug. My toffee fudge cake with Smarties on. My toasted syrup sandwich with . . . Hang on, Candy, Jay is trying to tell me something.'

Jay said, 'End the fucking call, Joel, you're making a complete arse of yourself. And you wonder why she's suspicious. Go on, finish off and hang up before she dumps you for good.'

The conversation was swiftly ended.

Only for another to begin. Candy quickly phoned through to Monique who was waiting on standby in the Two Peas in a Pod car park. Three well-groomed men had already come on to Monique in the past half-hour, boosting her mile-high confidence even higher. Her fake Aussie accent had been a winner with one of the men who mentioned he wouldn't mind going down under her. 'Queue up, boys,' she'd giggled to herself, 'wait your turn behind hunky Joel.'

Candy's instructions had been clear. On no account was she to sleep with Joel. Monique didn't intend to sleep with Joel, she intended to fuck his brains out. And to think her prey was just behind that pub door. She delved into her large red leather handbag and brought out a small collection box labelled BREAST CANCER, giving it a little shake.

She unzipped her red leather cat-suit a few more inches and wondered whether, if she were to give these two enormous beauties a little shake, the can would be full before last orders. And speaking of orders, she would make it her determined effort to ignore all of Candy's. How dare she expect her to travel all the way up from Cornwall on a rickety old train just to tell a man, 'No'. As far as Monique was concerned, she was one Cornish pasty that needed a good filling.

Bring it on! With a flick of her long, silky blonde hair, a pout of her luscious lips, she set her bottom to 'wiggle' mode, and entered the smoky pub. What sounded like a short burst of gunfire rang out as randy men's jaws hit the concrete floor. What sounded like a second round of gunfire burst forth when the jealous women elbowed the men in their ribs. And as if her entrance hadn't been brash enough, Monique stood there, legs apart, rattling her box, chanting, 'Save our breasts? Save our breasts?'

Before long, a queue of – surprise, surprise – men were waiting to pop in a pound in the hope that out would pop a breast. The landlord, Mr Turner, was normally quite strict about who could and who couldn't interrupt his punters with their drinking. Obviously sexy blonde women in body-hugging cat-suits fitted his criteria of helpful interruptions. Ted Turner dipped his hand in his pocket and pulled out a Viagra tablet. He doubted he would be needing the blue rascal tonight. His cock was wriggling like a python in his trousers. He decided to donate £10 to the Lady in Red's Breast Fund. And nearly creamed his pants in doing so when she tucked the ten-pound note down her cleavage.

As if a successful game of Chinese whispers had taken place, all the women in the pub seemed to be saying the same thing: 'We could all look like that if we were anorexic.' To which their partners replied, 'Well, would you hurry the fuck up and get anorexic then.'

Only one table in the whole pub were oblivious to any rise in collective hormones. Joel, Jay, Brent and Clovis were happily discussing the pros and cons of being stabbed. As yet, Brent's statement that 'I'd rather be stabbed than be buggered' was the only pro so far.

'I've got a good pro,' Joel announced suddenly. 'I'd rather be stabbed – and get this, at least fifty times in the heart – than have to shag Johnny Vegas's twin sister, if he had one.'

An eruption of laughter hit their table. Their drunkenness was now at a level where almost anything was funny. Which was quite unfortunate for the young man who had just walked in with a plaster-cast on his right arm.

'Need a hand, mate?' Brent shouted out. 'I'd sue the porn channel if I were you.'

Surprisingly, even though it was obviously painful to do so, the man in the plaster-cast managed to give Brent the *swollen* middle finger.

'Charming,' Brent muttered. 'Bloody charming.'

It had been two hours since the four mates had entered the pub. In all that time not one of them had taken a trip to the Gents', out of fear that when they were gone, either their drink would be spiked, or a chair leg would be broken, or even Superglue spread over their seat. Just your typical behaviour for a four-year-old. Joel boasted that he quite liked the pain in his kidneys as his bladder begged for release. It reminded him of being hit by the shot putt at school in PE. The PE teacher's statement to the Education Board had read, 'I didn't mean to hit him. He was disrupting the class as usual. It was meant to have gone over his head.' Joel took a quick peek under the table and, sure enough, all eight legs were crossed. By the time he peered back up, Jay, Clovis and Brent were dribbling.

'Save our breasts?' said Monique, in her husky, Aussie accent. She rattled the collection can in Brent's face. 'Save our breasts, boys?'

Brent stared at his three buddies. 'You guys!' Then up at Monique. 'Come on then, get your clothes off. Make my birthday one to remember. I hope this lot paid the full whack. I just hate it when you strip-o-grams get down to your undies, then leave it there.' He began to clap, a huge smile on his face, encouraging his mates. 'Off, off, off, off, off.'

Silence!

Grinning, Joel stood up. 'I'm going to have to go, or I'll piss myself laughing.' He made his way across the pub floor, holding his chair above his head, praying a urinal was free.

Monique watched as her catch seemed to swim away. His photographs had not done him justice. Strikingly handsome, obviously well built and a bottom that was tops. If he looked this good in just a pair of black combat bottoms and a tight grey T-shirt, her mind boggled as to what he would look like naked. No wonder Candy was worried about losing him; with women like Monique around, a man like Joel was easy to lose. She whispered in Brent's ear that she was not a strip-o-gram, just a run-of-the-mill charity worker trying to help breast cancer. With a head hung in shame, Brent invited her to sit down at the table; the least he could do was buy her a drink.

Clovis, who was both married and happy and therefore now ignoring his testosterone, was slightly suspicious of Monique. Most of the charity workers he'd met over the years smelled of mothballs and wore knitted cardigans. It was important for their image to look poverty stricken. This lass, on the other hand, looked as if she'd just stepped off her own private yacht. She even came with two inflated lifejackets crammed into her cat-suit. Although it was very unlikely that a woman like her would ever sink.

'I think accents are great,' began Jay, pouring champagne into Monique's glass. 'It saves having to tell people where you come from.' He smiled at her. 'So, where are you from?'

'Australia?' she replied. 'The Gold Coast?'

'Fan-tastic,' Brent said, offering her a cigarette which she passed on. 'Do you know Kylie Minogue? More like Tiny Minogue; she's only this big.' Brent put his hand six inches off the floor. 'Tiny, but beautiful all the same.'

Joel arrived and took in the scene. Both Brent and Jay were on the edge of their seats, like vultures waiting for a scrap of eye contact from the Blonde Babe. Clovis was busy on his mobile. And the Blonde Babe herself was just pouting. Australia this and Australia that seemed to be the conversation holding the table's attention. That and a zipper on her cat-suit that seemed to have a life of its own, moving up and down the teeth, every time she breathed.

'And isn't someone going to introduce me to this gorgeous man?' she said, tonguing Joel with her eyes. 'I'm sorry if I'm a bit direct, but I'm Australian and we Sheilas aren't known for being subtle?'

'You're shitting me,' Joel said sarcastically, as he sat down. 'I've never seen such a subtle outfit as the one you're wearing.' He smiled. 'Sorry if I'm a bit rude, but I'm an Essex boy and we Essex boys aren't known for being polite. Oh yeah, I'm Joel.'

Monique felt a challenge coming on. Joel was definitely not going to be quite the pushover she had thought he might be. But instead of dampening her spirits, it worked quite the opposite way. Anything worth chasing would make the reward sweeter. And when it came to quality sex, no one had a sweeter tooth than Monique.

It was time to see how Joel's mind worked. Monique sipped her champers and directed her gaze towards her target. 'I'm only in this country for a few more days, after that, it's back down under?' she stated. 'It will be like I wasn't even here? I mean, if I wanted to do something naughty, then now would be the time to do it?' Her eyes locked onto Joel's, trying to download the information that she was up for it if he was. 'I think it's important to say goodbye to a country properly? Don't you, Joel?'

Here we go, thought Brent; this was how it always started. A beautiful woman comes along, pretends that she's a happy-go-lucky individual who talks with anyone, and then ten minutes later, she's trying to get into Joel's pants. Even though it was his birthday, Brent decided to do the right thing and step down, leaving the way open for Joel. It's what mates were for.

'Joel, if you wanted to help Monique say goodbye to England, I wouldn't mind if you left my thirtieth birthday drink-up early.' Brent kicked Joel under the table. 'It's not like Cornwall will find out, is it? It's good to try a different-flavoured candy once in a while.' Another kick. 'Hey, Joel?'

Jay stared at Monique. 'Whoosh!' he brushed his hand over his head. 'Way over your head, Monique. Don't even ask what they're talking about. Whoosh! It's an English thing.'

Clovis looked at Joel in despair. How a man known to be so disciplined up a mountain could be so out of control with his love life was beyond him. Here was a friend who, only two hours ago, had his three best mates drawing straws to see who was going to be his first kid's godfather, and now he was willing to risk everything for an Aussie piece of skirt. Joel would certainly need a kangaroo court to help him out of this mess if Candy were ever to find out. That was assuming Joel took Brent's advice.

After sinking half a pint, Brent amused himself some more. 'Monique, you're not one of these people who can't spell "Candy" are you?' He watched her eyebrows rise. 'Because if you are, then not to worry, because just underneath Joel's T-shirt, on his right shoulder blade, above a sweet rose, are the letters: C-A-N-D-Y. Candy.' He nearly doubled over, laughing. 'It's a lovely tattoo.'

'Is it?' Joel fumed. 'Is it as nice as the one I'm getting done next week which will say "Rest in Peace Brent"?' Joel hated it when he had to threaten to kill one of his mates, but a drunken Brent was likely to press on with his innuendoes until he'd wrecked any chance Joel might have of shagging Monique, so the threat was necessary. 'Let's not turn this birthday celebration into a fiasco like last time.'

Brent saluted Joel. 'Sir.'

After a short silence, Monique leaned across and whispered in Joel's ear, 'I'm all for getting out of here soon, if you are? You're delicious?' She lingered at his ear. 'God, you smell nice?'

And this place doesn't, thought Joel, who found himself back at the Gents' for the second time a few moments later. The noise of the pub was appreciably muted by the thick door. The tall metal ashtrays were home to half-smoked spliffs awaiting their masters' return. And the mirrors by the sinks were continually polished to perfection by male punters desperate to see if their looks had improved since their last pint. It normally took eight pints before the average male in this pub was happy with the way he looked. But by that time, even Joseph Merrick would be a hunk.

Joel sat on the bog seat staring at his mobile, reading through a selection of texts sent by Candy over the last week. Loving, innocent, happy, fun messages. In some ways they summed her up perfectly. Her text this morning read:

> *20 digits. Joel, always luving u*
> *always worried u might do something*
> *stupid. Always here for u.*
> *Miss U Candy x*

'Something stupid,' Joel repeated to himself in a low voice. 'Such as?'

In the bar outside, dressed in the blood-red of betrayal herself, was a stunning woman capable of stirring up many men's desires. She looked as if she ate wedding rings for breakfast and firebombed happily married lives with her promise of illicit thrills. Satan himself would have two minds about sleeping with her in case he woke up without his horns. So why was Joel even contemplating taking her back to his apartment for sex? Cupid's younger brother, Stupid, explained to Joel how Candy would never find out. She was in deepest Cornwall, the West Country; they were up here, it was impossible for Candy to discover that Joel had been a bastard again.

But Joel would know he'd been a bastard again. And it was with this argument that Stupid was banished. Candy deserved loyalty more than ever now. And loyalty begins with the zip up. Their marriage was to be built on trust, not the cheap foundations of infidelity.

Back at the table Joel sat in his seat and quietly spoke in Monique's ear. 'I'm sorry, but I'm not one for one-night stands.'

Monique looked ahead, her face tight. 'So, you're saying "no"? This is how Essex boys behave, is it?' She placed her hand on his thigh and gently squeezed. 'Come on, Joel, I'll show you the best time you've ever had?' She thought back to Miss Goody-Two-Shoes Candy, Cornwall's answer to Sandra Dee. That straight-laced, uptight woman did not deserve this hunky man, Joel, to be faithful to her. 'The best time ever? And that's a promise?'

Brent and Jay were too busy trying to see if Brent's contact lens would float on beer to have heard what was being said. Clovis, on the other hand, was happily listening in, admiring his mate, enjoying watching the Aussie squirm. Faith in mankind was returning to Clovis. Now it seemed that even Joel could turn down a wet dream.

'Look,' Joel said firmly, removing her hand from his lap. 'If the Aussies were any good at handling balls then they would have won the Rugby World Cup. No disrespect, but, like I said, I really can't be arsed with one-night stands.'

Monique's face matched her cat-suit. A bright-red layer of skin, humbled by Joel's words, humiliated by his refusals. No man had *ever* turned her down. This was nearly as bad as coming second in the Carnival Queen contest at the Millennium celebration fair; but at least there she could put it down to a pumpkin-sized zit that had grown overnight. How the hell could Joel choose Candy over *her*? Her cousin, Sara, had mentioned that Joel's brain cells were lost up Everest, due to lack of oxygen. So he was demented. But surely even a demented man could see that she was offering herself on a plate to him. And even more annoying than that was the fact that she had had to sit down and pretend to enjoy the company of a group of pissed men, pretend she didn't understand the 'whoosh!' and even ignore Brent's assumption that she was a strip-o-gram (an assumption which would normally have been answered with a sharp slap to Brent's chops). If there was a lesson to be learned here it was this: just because Essex is filled with sex, one shouldn't assume one will get some.

Standing up to leave, Monique aimed one last look Joel's way only to find him busy looking elsewhere. She coughed, then spoke. 'Joel Winters, you'll get what's coming to you? Let's see if you survive the avalanche that I will be sending your way?' She smiled at the rest of them. 'G'day, boys?' And returned her bum to wiggle mode and wiggled herself away.

Joel eyed his mates, one by one. 'Which one of you lot told her my surname?'

One by one they shook their heads. Brent's suggestion that it might have been a lucky guess was out-ruled immediately. Clovis said that he didn't trust her from the moment she walked in. Jay, who always liked to be one up on Clovis, said that he hadn't trusted her BEFORE she walked in, so there. And Joel, whose eyes were searching everywhere, wanted to know where the fuck his mobile phone had gone.

Safe in a taxi, on the way back to her hotel with Joel's mobile in her hand, Monique studied the texts Candy had sent Joel and vice versa. How cute! Minutes later she was sending one herself under the pretence of being Joel. It read:

> *21 digits. Missing U, Candy.*
> *I'd luv to C U in a red*
> *leather cat-suit one day.*
> *Every man's fantasy.*
> *I think I've drunk 2 much.*
> *Joel X*

She pressed SEND and coated her face in a wicked smile. How dare he turn her down? This was the first boulder from his avalanche. It was time a man like Joel, who was used to climbing high, knew what it felt like to slip. Losing his fiancée might be the biggest fall Joel would ever take.

'Whoosh!' right over his head.

Chapter Twenty-three

Most Indian mothers forget to tell their daughters to take up weight-training before they get married. They forget to mention that the weight of their bridal sari, with all its heavy embroidery, beads, sequins, and gold thread work, would bring Arnold Schwarzenegger to his knees. It's hard to be a sexy bride when it feels like you're walking in three Gs of gravity. It's even harder if you've never worn one before.

Zarleena had promised to open Bindis & Brides on Sunday morning so that twenty-seven-year-old Sarina, a customer bride-to-be, could try out her bridal sari in the seclusion of the shop and away from the glare of her mother. 'Hurry, hurry, rush, rush,' were her mum's favourite words, and trying on a sari for the first time, needed less of the hurry and more of the patience.

'Sugar?' Zarleena enquired, placing the coffee tray on the counter.

'Sweetener, if you've got it,' Sarina replied. 'I can't risk too many calories before the wedding.'

Zarleena eyed Sarina's flat tummy. It looked like she hadn't eaten calories for years. Probably just existing on a diet of fear sandwiches and fear soup. Fear because her parents had ordered her to remain slim for her husband-to-be. Fear because thin was fashionably 'in' for Indian brides these days. And most definitely fear because come the wedding night she would be showing her naked body to a man for the first time and the last words she wanted her new husband to say were, 'Would you mind if I turned off the lights?'

Upstairs in the maisonette, Honey cooked a roast dinner for Tree. His hunger strike had been put on hold for him to eat, until he felt strong again, until his weakness subsided. Most impressed was Tree with Honey's curried gravy. It helped wash the curried carrots down nice and easy. Zarleena was only too pleased not to have been invited. The idea of sitting at the table with Tree and Honey while they smooched over each other was enough to put anyone off their curried roast potatoes. Especially as in between slobbering over each other, every now and again one of them would inevitably say, 'I fucking hate politicians. They're wrecking this beautiful country. Power to the people.'

'Those aren't switched on, are they?' Sarina pointed to a mounted CCTV camera in the corner, as she removed her jeans. 'It'd give me the creeps to think that some old pervert might get hold of the tape and cop off to my bare legs.'

Zarleena reassured her that the cameras were off. They had only been fitted in yesterday as an extra precaution. Coincidentally, yesterday saw the arrival of yet another threatening note. Slipped under the door after hours; weak and cowardly like the man who had sent it. Maybe Armin would get bored once he realized that she and Honey were not rising to the bait. And also, maybe, he should buy himself a good dictionary with his £1000, because as far as she knew, the last time she looked, 'foreigner' had a 'g' in it. Anyway, if Joel's plan went to plan, Armin would be out of her life in just three days' time. Good riddance to him *and* good riddance to his letters.

The red and gold bridal sari was removed from the box and rested on a wooden stool. Over one thousand hours of hard labour had gone into making this amazing silk article, only for it to be worn for about fifteen. Zarleena and Sarina looked upon the sari as if they were viewing the lost gold of the pyramids itself. No dress in history, in the opinion of most Indian girls, is quite so magical as a bridal sari. And it is with this magnificence that young Indian girls are captivated by the promise of a fairy-tale wedding. From as young as ten, all their energy is to be focused on the day of their arranged marriage. And central to that focus is the dress.

'I'm proof that Indian brides are getting older,' Sarina mentioned, watching Zarleena check the sari for any snags and missed stitches. 'It's a safe bet that ten years ago, maybe a little more, I would have been considered past it. My sell-by date gone. Only Indian men with missing teeth would be left for me.'

Better a husband with missing teeth than one who tries to smash the teeth from his wife's mouth, thought Zarleena. But she knew where Sarina was coming from. And it was a place without many dentists.

'So, how well do you know your future husband?' Zarleena said, giggling, wondering how ridiculous this might sound to a white person. 'Have you met him yet?'

They both laughed this time. Making light of the situation. Avoiding the cringing truth. And what is that truth? That Indian girls find it funny that they have to marry a man whom they know nothing about? That it's hilarious that they have to give their virginity away to a total stranger? A man who might not even believe in washing his testicles. A man who might like to light a cigar afterwards. Even a man who gets his kicks out of beating his wife, like Armin did? Or, is it that suddenly, after all the lectures from their parents, after all the weddings they themselves have attended, it dawns on them, that there is no way out, no solution that will please everybody, no happy ending, unless they do as they are expected to do: marry the man who is chosen for them. A stranger. It's the funniest joke in the world. So they laugh. Ha Ha Ha. It's the only way to cope.

But inside, come the wedding day, they sometimes cry. Zarleena couldn't remember having been to an Indian wedding where the bride looked anything but petrified. Lost. Sad. Alone. And in some ways broken. The only thing smiling was the sari.

She herself, as she walked around the sacred fire on her wedding day, felt the emotions crawling out of her skin like soldiers in camouflage. Bang! Her family was shot away. Bang! Her friends and acquaintances were no more. Bang! Her home gone. Bang! Her street gone. Bang! Bang! Bang! Her job, her old haunts, her virginity gone. All gone. And then the biggest gun-shot of all when she realized – BANG! – her life was gone.

Come morning, after the bloodied sheets are taken away (and probably displayed to the groom's mother to prove the purity of her new daughter-in-law), many an Indian girl reaches the same simple conclusion: she is now the slave of a new family and, unless she is really lucky, she will never again be allowed to speak her mind.

Zarleena helped Sarina into her sari, wrapping it around the petticoat, exclaiming how beautiful she was going to look, hoping that her husband would turn out to be the good sort. If shares could be sold in 'hope', then come the Indian wedding season in summer, the stocks would go through the roof. Hope that the match made in heaven doesn't turn out to be a marriage destined for hell. Hope that both parties had been totally honest about their past – is he really a virgin? Has she really got three degrees? Are you sure he's only thirty? (Could you explain why he has a bus pass then?) Can she really cook fifty round *chapattis* in ten minutes? Are you sure the tramlines on his arms are from donating blood and not from injecting heroin? Blah, blah, blah, blah, blah . . . A lot rides on hope.

And there is no bigger hope than the hope of an Indian bride in pleasing her new husband in bed.

'I'm scared about the wedding night,' Sarina blurted out, while walking up and down the shop in her red patent stilettos, getting used to the weight of the sari. 'I'm not a prude or anything like that, it's just I really don't know what is expected of me.' She stopped just

shy of Zarleena's feet, looking down at her pink trainers. 'Tell me to shut up if I'm embarrassing you, but it's
not like I can talk to my mother about sex.'

Are you kidding, thought Zarleena; sex is my
favourite topic . . . next to chocolate, of course. Sarina's
inquisitiveness the last time she'd been in the shop, was
making sense to Zarleena now. Questioning Zarleena
about her own wedding and the aftermath. Praying
that Zarleena's words would offer some comfort.
Hoping that Zarleena would take away some of the
dread.

'I know it might be hard,' said Zarleena, trying not
to giggle at the word 'hard'. 'But, it is your duty to
please the bastard.' Zarleena dipped her head. 'Sorry, I
don't even know him. He could be a really nice bloke.
Bloody hell, he might even be an orgasm machine.
Imagine it. Anyway, remember that he'll be nervous as
well and he'll have much the same worries as you.'

'Doubt it,' Sarina stated, plonking herself on a stool.
'How many men do you know who have spent the last
few weeks before their wedding night practising on a
banana so they get the blow job right?'

Zarleena pulled up another stool and faced her new
sex trainee. It was important to instil into Sarina's
psyche that to an Indian man on his wedding night
innocence is far more attractive than sexual compe-
tence. The last thing an Indian bride wants to hear just
after her new husband orgasms are the words, 'You
slut, where did you learn that?' But admittedly, the
times were a-changing. British-Asian women were
more in touch with their sexuality these days. Instead
of lying back and thinking of India, now they lay back

and thought of Brad Pitt. Instead of wondering what an erect cock looked like, they worried that their husband's might not match up to Johnny Donkey Man's dick in the porn magazine. Instead of Mr Patel's Cash 'n' Carry (twenty pairs of knickers for £1) underwear, they now wore Ann Summers.

But even with the changing times, the crucial role of an Indian bride on her wedding night is a submissive role: to be a shy, timid, good Indian girl. Blow jobs, masturbation, leather whips, rubber boots, sexual toys, washing machines, vibrating phones even electric toothbrushes, etc., were all a no-no.

'What about candles and things like that?' Sarina asked, sipping her coffee, enjoying her girlie chat.

God, this girl had a filthy mind, thought Zarleena. 'No candles either.'

'So, my dreams of lighting a few candles and creating a romantic atmosphere are not reasonable then?'

'Oh,' Zarleena said, wondering if it was herself with the dirty mind all of a sudden. 'I thought you meant to drip them over his naked body. Candles are fine.'

And it was with this comment that the conversation was snuffed out.

Two hundred miles away, on the south coast of England, an anxious woman could be found pacing up and down her living-room floor. If her nerves could be bottled she could have opened a brewery. Candy's Stomach Acid Cider. The battle to remain sane had begun last night with Joel's awful text message about cat-suits. She remembered a BT advert, something like 'Pick up the phone and make someone's day'; well, Joel had picked up his phone and wrecked hers. And just like the Mars Beagle 2 Lander, communications since had been zilch.

'Where the fuck are you, Monique?' Candy said, looking out of the window, getting redder by the minute. 'Why the fuck haven't you phoned me?' And, more importantly, why is your mobile phone switched off?

Sara sped in with a hot mug of camomile tea. 'Drink this, to calm yourself down a little; it'll look bad if the flatmate of a nurse has a heart attack. I'd have to fill in loads of forms.'

Candy sipped the herbal tea, trying to lower her blood pressure, desperate to think positive. Even though Monique's instructions, to phone Candy as soon as Joel turned her down, appeared simple, the truth was, at the moment, she was worrying about an unknown. Or, as Donald Rumsfeld might say, she was unknowingly worrying about an unknowable unknown and until the known knowable was known the knowingly unknowable worrying should be unknowingly . . . 'Oh shut up,' she murmured to herself. 'Monique might turn up with good news yet.'

But Monique had other plans.

Taking one's time when people were waiting for you was one of the finer pleasures in life, thought Monique, standing naked at her bedroom mirror, admiring the love bites stamped on her neck, breast and stomach. The train journey home from Hunterslea this morning had been a sultry affair, with the good-looking passenger sitting opposite her on the nearly empty train needing little persuasion to eat Monique for breakfast. 'Suck hard but if you draw blood you're a dead man,' was the sexiest line Monique could muster, considering she was still in shock from Joel's refusal to get jiggy with her last night.

On her bedroom wall a huge AO-sized poster took charge. Slap in the middle of the print was one grain of sand barely visible to the eye, and an oyster. Heading the poster were the words THINK BIG. And right at the bottom were the words THINK PEARLS. The message was lost on Monique who thought it meant that life was about men with big cocks who gifted women with pearls while making love to them on the sandy beach after feeding them oysters. God only knew what she made of Edvard Munch's painting 'The Scream'.

And talking of paintings, she smiled at the colourful picture she was about to present to Candy, of what had happened last night with Joel. She couldn't wait to explain how Joel had dipped his paintbrush in her wet palette.

After ordering a taxi, Monique waited in the plant-filled lobby downstairs, wondering if her short, black leather skirt, a flimsy, strappy pink top and matching stilettos was adequate wear for breaking bad news. In all honesty, she should be wearing a black cloak and hoisting a scythe above her perfectly shampooed hair, if she was going to be breaking Candy's heart today, but that would have been a bit grim.

'Sixteen Seafront View, please. Take the long route, if you want,' Monique instructed the taxi driver, as she attempted to fasten the seatbelt around her large breasts. 'You do anyway.'

'Whatever.'

'And you can extinguish your cigarette as well.'

'Whatever.'

The chit-chat continued at this feverish pace until the cabbie drew up outside Sara and Candy's place. Monique gasped at the meter.

'I am not paying £400 for a ten-mile ride,' she growled. 'You're a con!'

He laughed and enlightened her as to the significance in the placing of a decimal point, informing her that the fare was actually just £4.00, to which she replied, 'OH WHATEVER!' threw him a fiver and wiggled her bum away.

Minutes later she was seated on the sofa inside the girls' flat enjoying the position of authority she now possessed. She explained that she wouldn't be able to discuss anything until one, she'd had a large glass of wine, two, she'd looked over the new copy of *Vogue* she'd suddenly spotted amongst Candy's wedding magazines, and three, her migraine had subsided.

'Stop being a bitch, Mon. Put Candy out of her misery,' Sara ordered, slumping onto a large floor cushion. 'Did he or didn't he?'

Monique looked to Candy who had her fingers crossed. 'I'm sorry I didn't phone last night, but I was kind of erm . . . I was otherwise engaged, if you know what I mean.'

'I just want to know if Joel came on to you, Monique. Answer me "yes" or "no". Please.' Candy stood up and walked over to the window. The view of the car park below was nicer than the look of smugness on Monique's face. 'It's a simple question.'

'We slept together in my hotel room. I'm sorry, Candy, really.' Monique dropped her head in fake shame. 'I feel terrible about it. I've been crying all morning.'

Candy's thoughts careered out of control. One minute her mind was back in time, remembering laughing at her tabby tom cat called Custard, who seemed to have impregnated half the female cats (and attempted the dogs as well) in the neighbourhood. As Custard's master she laughed at his bad behaviour. Would God, her own master, be laughing at her now, as Joel sowed his wild seeds throughout his neighbourhood? The next minute she was peering through tears at her engagement ring; given to her by the very same hand that now stabbed her in the heart. The arguing of Sara and Monique was just hazy fuzz in the background. Candy blamed the shitty feeling she had right then on her education. Maths, English and History were good subjects, but what about Lying, Cheating, Womanizing Men? Wasn't learning about how men let you down in life more productive than knowing about 1066 or what was the square root of sixty-four? Maybe if Lying, Cheating, Womanizing Men had been on her curriculum then she mightn't have been so naive as to believe that Joel would be faithful?

It seemed like only yesterday that Joel had startled her, turning their relationship from black and white to colour in one fell swoop. They had been together for six months and their lovers' L-plates were long since gone, meaning that the initial lust phase was over, replaced by arguments instead. Candy knew by now that Joel's love was divided between her and his mountains.

So, when she joined him and a few mountaineers on a trip to North America – where Candy was going to hang around the hotel while Joel and his climbing buddies climbed Mount McKinley in the Alaska Range – it came as a massive and well-received surprise when, to the dismay of the other climbers, just before Joel was about to make the ascent up the mountain face, he opted out and chose to stay with Candy in their hotel room instead. Not wanting to leave her. Not wanting to be without her. It was the first time in his life that a woman had taken precedence over a mountain. It was only then that she knew he really did love her.

It was only now that she knew he really didn't.

Wiping her eyes, Candy turned to face the traitor. 'You weren't meant to have slept with him, Monique; you were just supposed to test him with your seduction techniques. Why?' She flashed back to the cat-suit text message Joel had sent, feeling nauseous at the vision of him sliding down Monique's zip. 'Why, Monique?'

'It wasn't supposed to have gone as far as it did. Look . . .'

Monique went on to explain how difficult it had been to get Joel's attention in the busy pub so she followed him to the toilet and offered him a blow job. He declined, so she offered him her bed at the hotel room, which he accepted. The plan was to back out at the last minute. But as with all plans, a flaw arose quicker than Joel's cock: she now fancied him something rotten.

'He was amazing, Candy, a God in bed. And if it's any consolation, he put a plaster over your tattoo when we fucked, out of respect for you.' She pulled down her top and exposed her love bite. 'He was wild; similar, I imagine, to a prisoner who had just been released from jail. Honestly, Candy, it was like he hadn't had decent sex for months. That's why I feel so terrible about all this. It should have been *you* giving him his best sex ever, not me. I hate myself, I really do!'

Candy noted that Monique's apparent regret appeared to be gilded with joy. 'And what do you think Joel will say when I ask him about your night of passion?'

'Well, he'll deny it, of course. That's what womanizers do.' Monique strummed her fingers on the coffee table. 'You don't believe me, do you? So, I lied about the rose tattoo on Joel's right shoulder blade, did I? I got a man on a train to give me these love bites, and I enjoy watching a friend of my cousin's in tears. That's the kind of woman you think I am, is it? It couldn't just be that I might be telling you the truth?' Monique jumped up. 'Sort out your own boyfriend problems in future if this is the thanks I get when you don't get the result that you want.' From her pink Gucci bag she pulled out the full charity box and handed it to Sara. 'That's for your hospital's breast cancer appeal. G'day, ladies?'

Walking back out into the sunny Cornish air, Monique flipped on her shades, dialled another taxi, and smiled. At least she had her dignity left intact this way. It wouldn't have been possible to continue living in England if the girls had found out she hadn't pulled Joel. Especially after all her boasts that Joel would fall at her feet in five minutes flat.

And as for Joel . . . he was about to make the biggest climb of his life, to save his relationship with Candy. Served him right for daring to turn her down. 'I'm not one for one-night stands,' he'd said.

Pathetic.

The nearest morgue was miles away, yet, at 16 Seafront View, Cornwall, England, it felt like someone had died. Twisting her engagement ring around her sweaty finger, Candy was aware that not someone, but something *had* died. All her dead relationship with Joel needed now was a wreath.

'Do you want me to put some depressing music on?' Sara suggested, heading over to the CD player. 'We've got the Cure, the Smiths, Pink Floyd or the Death March. Your choice.'

'The soundtrack to *The Abyss* would be better, that's where my life is right now.'

Sara stuck in the Smiths, avoiding eye contact with Candy, guilt bunching up her veins like a Sumo wrestler's cholesterol. Good friends were supposed to help not hurt. If it hadn't been for Sara's suggestion of using Monique as a test for Joel then – she stared sorrowfully at her sobbing friend – then Candy wouldn't be ripping up the pages of her wedding magazines right now. Her gran used to say, 'Cornish women are a tough breed, always losing their men to the sea.' Sara wondered what she might make of losing a man to a bimbo with big breasts in a red cat-suit. Not much.

'Monique could be lying, you know?' Sara decided, walking over to Candy and consoling her with a hug on the sofa. 'She's good at fabricating the truth when the situation suits. If it wasn't for her beautiful looks she'd be destined for a great career in politics.'

Candy wondered about that for a moment. If Monique was *lying* and she *didn't* have sex with Joel, then . . . God, that was going to be a hard one to swallow without chewing on some facts. For starters, how did Monique know about Joel's tattoo? (It was doubtful Joel had taken his top off in the pub.) And why did he send that text message about the cat-suit? Then there was this business called 'Joel's Track Record' – it was hardly the diary of a monogamous man. To top all this, why would Monique lie? She'd only get found out if she did. No, it would take more than Sara's suggestion that Monique was lying to resurrect this relationship.

The Smith's 'Girlfriend in a Coma' added ambience to an already melancholy mood. In just a few days' time Candy was due to go on an adrenalin-pumping adventure with some kids from her Outdoor Pursuit Centre. A week's trip to Canada white-water rafting and canoeing on some of the best rivers and lakes in the world. To watch these children from broken homes ignite with excitement on holidays they used to only dream about, was why Candy did it. It was hard to worry about the shit in your own life when you knew that each of these kids had been through worse.

Candy discussed what she proposed to do about Joel. Confronting him now, when, not only was she due to go off, but Joel himself was due to go to New Zealand, would be a mistake. If he fell off a mountain in New Zealand and died after they split up, she'd blame herself for destroying his concentration. Besides, after a shock like the one she'd experienced this afternoon, she would need time to weigh up her options. Maybe if she met a hunky Mountie in Canada her decision might be made more quickly.

Chapter Twenty-four

Armin sat on the wooden park bench next to a small car park. It was early Wednesday evening; he was just minutes away from being paid nineteen thousand beautiful pounds. He smirked as he watched the people in the park: an old couple walking with their white poodle, a mother with a kid, a couple with a pram, two teenagers knocking a football about. Yes, Armin smirked. He would soon be the richest man in Watermill Park. Unless, he sniggered to himself, tapping the manila envelope in his hand, unless Mohamed Al Fayed suddenly sprinted by in his Union Jack shorts (being chased by the Queen on horseback no doubt).

'What a day for a daydream,' he quietly sang, enjoying the last of the sunshine on his face. 'Not a day for a pipedream.'

He wondered back to Zarleena's phone call last night. Her instructions concerning today's meet were as thorough as a recipe from Delia Smith. *Ingredients*: Zarleena and Armin. *Equipment*: One park bench in Watermill Park, Hunterslea. *Begin*: 7 p.m. *End*: 7.10 p.m. The only thing missing was a pre-heated oven. But judging by the sweat running down Armin's neck, he didn't need one.

A woman in a tight, red, Lycra jogging suit, her pony-tail swinging from left to right, power-walked by. Armin sneered. It was white women showing off their bodies like that who gave good Indian girls bad ideas. He liked to think that Indian women from India would have more class. In fact, he compared the Indian women from India and the Indian women brought up in England to hens. Indian women from India were battery hens, well behaved, strictly confined, a servant to their master. While British-born Indian women were free-range hens, able to run wild, with too much freedom – and ulti-mately too much mouth. It was because of the free-range hens that Armin's new business, Bindi Brides, was des-tined for great success, he was sure. Indian men in the UK liked to know where their hens had been. The family of a free-range Indian girl who had been promiscuous, whose reputation in this country was wrecked, would pay handsomely for Armin to marry her off to whoever Armin could, even if that meant fixing her up with a toothless peasant goat farmer from Bulandshahr whose idea of romance was a night in for two delousing his hair. Anything to get shot of their shameful daughter.

The sound of tyres on gravel had Armin glance to the car park where the Bindis & Brides van was revers-ing into a space. He checked his watch, 7 p.m. precisely. 'I promise you if anything out of the ordinary or even slightly suspicious happens tomorrow, Zarleena, the photos get copied and passed around. Starting with your parents.' Armin's final words before the phone call ended last night. It was great to be in charge. Which was why Armin always had a problem with the film *Pinocchio*. Now, why the fuck would Geppetto, the toymaker, want liar-boy Pinocchio to be real, when it was so much more fun pulling the boy's strings? And if there was one thing he'd learned about free-range Indian girls, it was to never, ever let go of their strings. Because instead of just them falling down, they drag Indian men down with them.

Armin watched Zarleena get out of the van. So classless; jeans, T-shirt, boots and a pair of shades, she was looking more and more like a tomboy every day, it was . . . hang on, Armin's heart paused. She hadn't even shaved. How dare she turn up with two days' worth of stubble on her chin? Armin's mind was struggling with the information in front of him. And where the hell had her boobs gone? Did she take steroids now? Why was she white?

And even more importantly than that, why was she a man?

Now, if thoughts were made of energy Armin would have proved Einstein wrong right then, for all his thoughts had turned to nothing. What to think, what not to think, it didn't really matter, for coming towards him, with an angry look on his face, was – not his scared wife as he had expected – but a man who looked like he meant business. The print on his T-shirt alone was making Armin's generous-sized bowels jittery. I LOST MY COCK TO FROSTBITE. I'VE GOT NOTHING LEFT TO LOSE. DON'T UPSET ME.

Without a word, Joel sat next to Armin on the bench, pulled off his shades and held his face up to the dying sun with his eyes closed. Not so closed that he didn't notice the red-Lycra power-walking woman eyeing him up as she motored by. But closed enough.

Joel finally spoke. '*Namaste.*'

Armin made out he didn't hear.

'I fucking said *NAMASTE!*' Joel shouted. 'Where are your manners?'

The situation hinted of chaos as opposed to the simplistic Delia Smith's 'how to bribe a boiled egg' plan that Armin had been expecting. Both Armin's common sense and logic agreed that he'd been duped by his bitch of a wife. Although instinct told him that the duping had more to do with the white man sitting next to him than it did his pathetic, feeble wife. This had the hallmark of a man. But who was he? Armin's imagination took a wrong turn. What if the man was an English assassin? His accent was London; he could be a mobster of some sort. Armin could feel Joel's testosterone leaking across, edging towards battle, hopeful for a fight. This wasn't fair; if Armin had known a hoodlum was going to turn up instead of his wife he would have brought at least ten others with him, all tooled up, all dressed in the Indian colours, saffron, white and green. It wasn't fair at all.

'There are three fucking types of men I hate,' Joel exclaimed, looking directly at Armin. 'I can't stand men who beat up their partners and I can't stand men who take derogatory pictures of their partners and bribe them.'

Armin's mouth felt as dry as sawdust. 'That's two, not three.'

'And I can't stand male climbers who whinge about the cold, the fucking wankers! What do they expect up a 15,000-foot mountain? A steaming shepherd's pie and a hot-water bottle? Wimps.' Joel's anger teetered on fury, his mind imagining Zarleena suffering at the hands of this brute. 'There's no possible excuse that permits a man to hit a woman. No justification holds up to a woman living in fear of a man's fists. Scum, you are.' Holding back from harming Armin was the hardest thing Joel had had to endure since Everest. And he explained this as eloquently as his anger would allow. After calming down a little, Joel continued, 'There had better be the complete set of photographs in that envelope, Armin, that's all I'm saying.'

'Where's Zarleena?' Armin turned his head to the van. 'I don't even know who you are. I'm not handing over photos of my naked wife to anyone.' He glanced back to Joel, quickly trying to ascertain whether Joel had about him a wad of concealed notes. 'Too scared to bring the money herself, was she?' His eyes narrowed. 'You have got the money?'

Joel laughed enthusiastically. 'It's in the van.'

Armin nodded to himself. 'The van. And when exactly will I be getting the money from the van? I take it you're just the middle man. Can we not just get this over and done with? Just being in the same town as my wife makes me want to retch.'

Both men stared up to the blue sky to watch a hang-glider glide past like a pterosaur from the age of dinosaurs. Joel gained a further glimpse of Armin's personality when Armin put his hands up towards the glider, imitating a fake shotgun, and pulled the trigger twice.

'Good shot,' Joel said, sarcastically. 'Where *did* you learn to shoot like that?'

''Nam,' replied Armin, just as sarcastically.

'Really!' Joel said even more sarcastically. 'I thought 'Nam was what you ate with a curry.' He paused. 'Anyway, enough of this shit, I want to know why *you* think you deserve £19,000.'

'Deserve?' Armin appeared shocked. 'Let me ask you a question. How long have you known sweet, innocent Zarleena?' He didn't wait for an answer. 'Not long I expect. Certainly not long enough to know her hidden side. Certainly not long enough to know that she wrecked many people's lives by her sleeping around with married men. She's a thief. Not only did she steal my family's gold, but she stole their honour too.' Armin closed his eyes and shook his head despondently, saddened apparently by the false memory. 'You say you hate men who hit women, and I agree, but what about women who hit men. What about—'

Joel interrupted, 'What about the bloke who taped what you said in BHS last week? I was sitting right behind you, Armin, I heard every last word, and what's more, I filmed every word too. From the moment you sat down, to the threats you made against Zarleena, to the handing over of the thousand pounds, until the end. It's damning evidence. So don't fucking bullshit me any more.'

Because of Armin's lack of practice, being honest made him nervous. But if there was still a chance to collect the cash, then honesty was the only option. Joel was slick, there was no denying that, slick and streetwise. And he was also a sheep, a goody-goody like most of the rest. If there was one thing Armin had learned in all his corrupt years it was this: it was very difficult to pull the wool over the eyes of sheep. Armin went on to explain how Zarleena had sold the wedding gold to open Bindis & Brides; he only wanted his rightful money back, and bribery seemed the only option against a woman who wouldn't take note. Joel listened uneasily.

'I'll show you the photos and you can check that they're all there,' Armin stated, opening the flap of the envelope. 'Be warned though, pink isn't her best colour.'

Joel grabbed Armin's wrist and prevented him from going any further. 'Leave them inside. I think enough eyes have seen them, don't you?' Joel swiped the envelope and then let go of Armin. 'Negatives, discs, copies?'

'If you were to open it, you'd see it's all there. But as you can't bear to look at my wife naked, then you'll just have to trust me. You're not missing much anyway.'

Armin was led to the Bindis & Brides van, his eyes growing wide with greed. In some ways, even though he'd initially been scared of Joel, he quite liked how today had gone; it bode well for his new Mafia image, and with his extra funds he would make sure he invested in a black, double-breasted, shoulder-padded suit. Eat your heart out, Ronnie and Reggie.

Joel unlocked the back doors to the van and stood aside, smiling. 'There's your payment.'

A momentarily lapse of reason hit Armin. His eyes focused on the contents of the van. It was at times like this that he wished he'd invested in a black, double-breasted, padded pair of waterproof underpants, because he felt like crapping himself. He locked on to

Joel's excited eyes. This white man was a certifiable psycho.

Joel grabbed Armin's arm with his solid rock-climbing grip and pulled it behind his back. 'Now take a good look at that, you fucker, and think for a second. Do you want to end up in it?' Armin wriggled like a caught fish. 'Am I getting through to you, you worthless creep? My lesson to you is a simple one. Stay away from Zarleena and I'll leave you alone, or step within ten miles of her and I'll have you buried in that.'

The open wooden coffin, lined with deepest red silk, stared back into Armin's soul. The casket was worrying enough, but the soiled spade lying next to it really gave him the willies.

'You look like you've seen a ghost, Armin,' Joel surmised, enjoying the bastard's fear, just as he must have enjoyed Zarleena's. 'And no more threatening letters to her shop.' He squeezed hard. 'Clear?'

Armin agreed. He would have agreed to anything right then. He would have agreed that Indian men should always do the washing up. He would even have gone so far as to agree that women were better drivers than men.

Without further ado the two men split; Joel headed back to a waiting Zarleena at Bindis & Brides, while Armin headed back to his Wembley flat to pull down the party banners and balloons, to phone his guest list, to cancel the party he had planned for this evening in celebration of his new business venture: Bindi Brides.

His wife would pay for this. And this time it wouldn't just be her modesty that he wrecked.

294

Chapter Twenty-five

Without Honey in the maisonette, the place felt as quiet and deserted as a disused mine. Although sometimes, when Honey was on top form, and a march or peace rally was due, the place was so noisy even Arthur Scargill at his finest wouldn't have been able to make himself heard.

But with peace came thought and with thought came worry. Zarleena, armed to the hilt with worry, bored with playing I-Spy with herself, stared out through the living-room window down onto the small car park round the back of the shop which they shared with Spindlers Newsagents. Joel's black Range Rover – I-Spy something beginning with R – awaited his return, nearly as eagerly as she did. It was approaching 9 p.m., two hours since Joel's plan was supposed to have been initiated. Keeping the entire mess a secret from Honey hadn't been easy – her younger sister's inquisitive nature matched that of the Elephant's Child in a Rudyard Kipling *Just So* story – but it had been necessary. Respect from Honey was something Zarleena had worked hard for; she didn't want to lose it all over a few dirty photographs.

She checked the clock again – 9.15 p.m. – and wondered if Honey had finished smashing bricks with her head at her martial arts class yet. Zarleena looked down to the shoddy wall in the car park which was leaning over dangerously from the Spindlers' side. Maybe Honey could put her martial arts to good use and head butt it straight again. She'd definitely be oblivious to the pain considering the amount of alcohol she usually consumed in the pub after her lesson. It was quite obvious that Honey would make her black belt in drinking before she made it in karate.

The noise of a diesel engine broke Zarleena's daydream. At long last, she thought, watching Joel drive into the parking bay. Her heart played Beethoven's Tenth waiting to see if, like her nightmare scenario suggested, Joel reached into the van, tossed the coffin on his shoulder, and walked up the stairs into the maisonette like *Terminator 3*, barged into the kitchen, slammed open the fridge, pulled out a trifle and stated, 'Just like the future, the jelly is not set!' Fortunately he didn't.

But it wouldn't have surprised her too much if he had. For God's sake, the man kept his own coffin in a lock-up. A hand-carved, silk-lined, luxury coffin with all modern extras. And what were those modern extras that the modern coffin-dweller needed these days? Well, Joel had assured her proudly, just in case he were to be buried alive he had had fitted an extra-loud, 400-decibels alarm with an in-built switch on either side of his arms. A small set of ear plugs were there to prevent deafening. A Bible for light reading on his journey to heaven. A hand-painted picture of the Himalayan Mountains on the inside lid. A small canister of oxygen. Two spliffs to bribe the Devil. A confession of his sins on a collection of ten tapes. A pair of shades for when he looked into the light. A picture of Mother Teresa for her to sign. A bottle of champers and two glasses (D-cup) to share with George Mallory. The list went on . . .

Joel's reasoning behind the morbid idea of a waiting death vessel was common sense as far as he was concerned. Planning ahead, thinking of the inevitable, inviting the future into his present. Life was the unknown, but death was the known. In his line of work, death was like an extra he fitted into his rucksack. It came everywhere, and took hold at any time. To be prepared was to be fearless. If he feared death like most people then he would climb like most people, and most people didn't climb the highest peaks that God had made. And if there was anything more than anything that Joel did fear, that was turning into most people.

Besides most people didn't take enough risks.

Zarleena welcomed Joel inside and ushered him into the maisonette's kitchen, eager to hear the rundown of what had happened with Armin. Judging by the lack of axe sticking out of Joel's neck, it hadn't gone too badly. She noted with some apprehension that he was holding a large, manila envelope. Some of the worst hours of her life were hidden within that envelope, and, if it got into the wrong hands, the contents would give some depraved man some of the best hours of his. Zarleena's advice to women willing to pose nude for their men would be this: make sure you have a photograph of your man after a cold shower to bribe him back with. Just in case.

'I'll put you out of your misery, Zarleena, it went well.' Joel pulled out a stool and parked his bottom, sliding the envelope across the granite work surface. 'I've never seen an Indian go white before.'

'And you didn't hurt him, like you promised?'

Joel's face was adamant. 'Just his pride.'

The details of Joel's encounter with Armin were discussed. Zarleena was not to worry; Armin would not be troubling her again. It seemed too good to be true. But slowly, as Joel explained Armin's fear – how at one point he'd thought someone was clapping behind him only to realize it was Armin's bum cheeks smacking together in fright, how upon spotting the muddied spade in the van, Armin had begun to pray in Hindi – Zarleena's worries popped like soap bubbles. And if ever a man was a reluctant hero, then it was Joel; each time Zarleena tried to thank him, he dismissed her gratitude airily, explaining that it had only been his duty.

It was hard not to look at Joel differently now.

This was the first time Joel had been upstairs in the maisonette. The first time a true hunk had been in their kitchen. Surely the value of the maisonette would have to go up. She offered him wine, he declined. Chocolate, he declined. Biscuits, he declined. Even home-cooked *samosas*, he declined.

'You see, Zarleena, I've abused my body too much lately, it needs a rest. I can't eat or drink anything that tastes nice, for a few weeks.' He paused. 'It's a kind of fast, a taste-bud fast.' *Not to mention*, he thought to himself, *that if he turned up for his photo shoot in New Zealand to advertise their macho underwear with a jelly belly, then he'd be out of a job pronto*. 'Although, I think my dietician mentioned that I could have Red Bull. If you have one.'

She didn't, but she did have a squashy sofa they could sit on. They moved to the living room where Joel couldn't help but notice a huge framed poster on the wall of the planet Jupiter.

'You're into astronomy?' he asked, admiring the picture.

Zarleena smiled with embarrassment. 'Actually, Honey put that one up; she says it reminds her of our gran in India.'

'Gran?' Joel turned to Zarleena. 'Oh, I get it; your gran farts a lot. She's like a gas giant?' He chuckled. 'That's pretty funny. All grannies are the same though, it doesn't matter which country they come from, as soon as they reach retirement age their bowels go on overtime.'

Zarleena watched Joel, wondering to which wave-length his brain was tuned into today. 'It's nothing to do with passing wind. It's because our grandmother was known, after *puja*, for having the largest red spot on her forehead in her village. They used to say that the only thing with a bigger red spot was Jupiter. Hence the poster.'

'Respect,' Joel said, as he sat down on the sofa, pushing aside a box full of SISTERS OF SOUTHALL badges. 'At least she can die happy knowing she was the best at something.'

She sat opposite Joel on the sofa-chair. The muddied waters of the day were clearing. Honey and she used to categorize marriageable men into four groups depending on how much they were willing to sacrifice for their women:

1. *Lose a limb for a woman.*
2. *Risk their life for a woman.*
3. *Lose their cock for a woman.*
4. *Lose their life for a woman.*

Zarleena chuckled inwardly: already Joel in some ways was a category 2. He'd risked his life today with Armin and for that she felt truly humbled. Although, if she were to be honest with Honey, she had never been keen on categories 1, 3 and 4. Who wanted a cockless, armless, or even a dead husband out of choice? Which took Zarleena's thoughts to Joel's T-shirt. Surely he wasn't a category 3 as well, was he?

'Erm,' began Zarleena, nodding towards Joel's T-shirt. 'You haven't really lost your you-know-what to frostbite, have you?'

He stared at her sternly. 'Put it this way, I lost most of it, there's only ten inches left now.' Joel spread his hands out, ten inches apart. 'I'm only a third of the man I used to be.' He shook his head, as though reliving the tragic event. 'The Sherpas needed two sledges to transport my "you-know-what" down to Base Camp. Those poor huskies, God bless 'em, the weight of my monster nearly broke their backs.'

And the shallowness of the conversation was breaking Zarleena's morale. She steered the talk back to today's saga with Armin one more time, before Joel stood up to leave.

'I'll be off then.' He kissed her on the cheek. 'And if you do hear from Armin again, then ring me.'

Just before Joel opened the front door, Zarleena grabbed her moment while his back was turned to her. 'Did you look at my photographs?'

He spoke to the door. 'If I had, then I would still say "no", so, in answer to your question,' he spun round to face her, 'no, I didn't look at your glamour photos.'

Zarleena examined his blue eyes, enquiring, encrypting, endeavouring. 'Serious?'

'Deadly.'

A mixture of relief and disappointment engulfed Zarleena's thinking. Men are taught from a young age that pornography is essential to their well-being. The only thing that confuses them is why they weren't born with a third hand. One to play the PlayStation, one to drink the lager and the other to play with their built-in joystick. It's beyond most men's capacity to ignore nudity when it's thrust in their face. So Joel's respectful behaviour came as quite a surprise. Unless, she guessed worriedly, unless Joel believed that her body was so disgusting underneath her clothes that it was easier not to look. He was afraid he might throw up. Suddenly it became important that Joel thought she had a good body.

'Anyway, I never take much notice of how I appear in photographs because it's a well-known fact that the camera puts on at least ten pounds.'

Joel pointed to the stepper machine. 'Is that why you've got one of those?'

She followed his gaze. Great, she deliberated, he thinks I'm FAT. It was obvious now when she looked back at the hints, clues, signals. Right from the off he was offering her Slim-Fast in his apartment, he stole her scone in BHS (probably afraid she might add another inch to her thighs) and now he mentions the stepper machine. What next? A bucket full of amphetamines and a copy of *The Atkins Diet* book (she'd rather eat the damn thing than follow its advice). Zarleena told Joel to wait where he was as she disappeared to the bathroom, only to return with a set of weighing scales. She plonked them on the floor and stood on them, while Joel looked on quizzically.

'Shit,' she said, confounded by the obscene reading of her weight. 'Hang on, I'm wearing too much, that's way too heavy for me.' She kicked off her trainers, slid out of her denim skirt and yanked off her T-shirt. She jumped back on in just her black bra and panties. 'There,' she said, smiling down at the dial. 'Just eight stone exactly . . . *and* I didn't even remove my hair band.' *Not such a fat cow after all, am I*, she thought to herself, glancing up to Joel's bemused face; *not quite the hefter you had in mind*. 'There was a time when I used to think that eight stone was . . .' And then the enormity of what she was doing dawned on Zarleena. Standing half naked in front of an engaged man who wasn't yours was wrong at the best of times. But especially when it was only the two of them alone. And doubly especially when they were only feet away from a double bed. Zarleena felt the warm rush of embarrassment hit her like sauna steam. Admittedly, for all intents and purposes she might just have been in a bikini, nothing wrong with that, sunbathers did it all the time; but in all reality this maisonette didn't have a beach. So there was everything wrong with it. She would rather Joel thought of her as fat than thought of her as a slag.

She bent down to collect her clothes off the floor-boards, annoyed that her emotions were being batted left to right like a game of Swingball. One minute she's relieved that Joel had sorted out Armin, the next she's upset that Joel might think she's fat, then she's scared that Joel thinks she's a slag and now she's worried that Joel would suddenly burst out laughing at her body. Zarleena slipped back into her skirt, T-shirt and train-ers. Even she couldn't deny that all four thoughts had one thing in common: Joel. It was just a reaffirmation that underneath the left to right batting of the ball, the ups and downs of emotions, the only game she was playing, the only game worth playing, if one could call it a game, was love. Joel's love. But would she need to break the rules to win it? Could she ever try to steal another woman's man?

Shamefaced, Zarleena walked away from Joel into the kitchen. The answer was a big, whopping, moral, decent, respectful, honourable, sober 'NO'. She poured herself a glass of white wine and knocked it back in one. Joel hadn't spoken since she'd stripped off.

'So, this is where it all happens, then,' Joel said finally, rummaging around for things to say, as he fol-lowed her into the kitchen. 'This is where you make the delicious curries.'

'No, I make them in the bathroom,' she replied sar-castically, pouring out another glass for herself. 'You

must have heard of Chicken Toilet Masala? Or Vinda-
LOO.'

Joel nodded, she was the expert, although next time
he invited Zarleena around to cook Indian for him he'd
make sure the bog was clean of skids. He laughed at his
own joke. Maybe the dish could be called Vindapoo, or
at a push, Vindaskids.

If Zarleena's patience was the camel's back then
Joel's laughter was the straw that broke it. Was everything a big joke to him? Were other people's hang-ups
an adventure playground for Joel to mess around in?
Or, basically, was he just laughing at what he'd seen
standing on the scales? I mean, forgive me here, she
thought, aren't you supposed to make at least one comment when a woman undresses in front of you? Her
anger spiralled upwards. He was still laughing.

'WHAT,' Zarleena yelled, 'ARE YOU LAUGHING
AT?'

Seeing the flames in her eyes, Joel decided he'd give
his toilet humour the flush for the moment. From experience, he'd learned that when things were going badly
it was often helpful to mention a time when things had
been even worse.

He eventually answered, 'Erm, I was just thinking
how close the world came to ending with the Cuban
Missile Crisis, that's all.' He laughed again. 'It's a warning to all who argue. It soon escalates out of control.'

'Like affairs, you mean?'

'Yeah, just like affairs.' Joel noticed the half-full wine
bottle on the table, or, to an alcoholic, half-empty.
Zarleena was obviously having an emotional crisis, Joel
could spot them a mile away; he'd been giving them to

people since he was born – legend had it that even in the incubator Joel would occasionally halt his breathing just to stress out the nurses – but was killing off a million brain cells with booze really the answer? Or did she need a hug instead? He decided on the latter, but first he stuck a wooden spoon down the front of his jeans.

'What are you doing?' Zarleena asked, shocked. 'Does your willy need stirring or something?'

He grabbed her waist and pulled her towards him. 'This is in case you knee me in the bollocks. I thought you might need a hug or something.' He enjoyed the look of astonishment in her eyes as he held her tightly. 'Everyone needs a hug now and again.'

In years to come Zarleena would most likely tell people that this was the instant she fell in love with Joel Winters. But at the moment her mind was freaked. The sensual smell of his Echo aftershave, his day-old stubble rubbing her cheek, the feel of his muscles beneath his clothes, the calming rhythm of his breathing, the hardness of the wooden spoon digging into her pelvis. And just to wreck things: the thought of Joel's engagement to Claudia digging at her conscience. In British law, if someone finds a suitcase full of money, by rights he or she has to hand it in. In British law, if someone finds someone else's man, she can shag him. It left Zarleena in a bit of a dilemma. Especially when Joel began to kiss her.

She felt the hug becoming more than a hug, the innocence becoming less innocent, the wooden spoon becoming more wooden. Her desires becoming more intense. She wondered if kitchens got a bum deal. No one treats a bedroom as a kitchen, but here they were treating the kitchen as a bedroom. Although they do say that sex is the best recipe in the world – except for Mr Wong's boil-in-the-bag chicken noodles, of course. Zarleena's morals tried to stay in the lane next to her lust, she didn't want them racing away from her. The last thing she needed in her life right now was further complications. She felt her breathing deepen as Joel's hands began to explore. But what could be simpler than animal attraction? It defied rules imposed by different cultures. It ignored race, creed, sex, caste, colour. Zarleena's and Joel's family roots might be poles apart, but their magnetism was strong. And other people's opinions mattered as little as iron filings when it came to love.

As sexily as possible, Joel pulled out the wooden spoon or – as Joel would later explain to the underwear company in New Zealand as to why his groin area was a mass of bruises – the cheap man's jockstrap, and tossed it on the side. It was becoming a hindrance downstairs. And as every male climber knows, he may find solitude at the very top, but if he wants action, it's downstairs.

Zarleena stared into Joel's excited blue eyes; yet again her sexual thermometer rose another degree. His hands were dangerously accurate, time after time, hitting spots that forced her to moan with delight. To be touched this way was the stuff of dirty books, a pleasure that could only be described as disgustingly wonderful. Joel slid down her skirt and kicked it under the table; he was kinder with her knickers and hung them on a drawer knob. Without thinking, Zarleena unbuckled his jeans and threw them across the room; she was kinder with his boxers and hung them on his erect knob. And oh, what a knob, she ogled, no evidence of frostbite whatsoever, although she couldn't promise that there wouldn't be evidence of her teeth-bites later. Next off were tops and bra, leaving them stark naked against the kitchen cupboard. There was no way any woman would be telling the truth if she said that Joel's fantastic body couldn't turn her on. One look and you knew he would fuck you to another place. He teased her by rubbing the end of his 'monster' against her pubic bone, tantalizing, delightful and cruel, raising that thermometer again.

Breathing heavily, Joel took both Zarleena's hands in his. 'Time out, we can't continue.' His expression appeared dampened. 'I never let Mallory Junior climb into a ravine without his helmet on.'

'Pardon?'

'No condom, no action.' He kissed her on the mouth. 'And before you say anything, it's not because I think I might catch something off you. "It's always best to be safe than sorry, that's why climbers use condoms."' He chuckled. 'Sorry, I was just repeating a condom advert I did once. Pretty tacky, hey? Anyway, I haven't got one. I never assume a woman is going to be an easy lay.'

Even though Joel's mouth was rude and crude it was also very honest and that's what Zarleena liked in him. Essex charm really did exist; it wasn't something Essex boys had made up just to explain their cheeky, chappy rudeness to giddy, gullible women. However, this was the first time Zarleena had heard a man's organ being referred to as Mallory Junior; who the hell was Mallory Senior? But to the important question, did this maisonette hold any contraband condoms? The chances were high that Honey kept a few. Zarleena was sure that the noises she heard coming from Honey's bedroom when Tree was over to stay were not just Protest Practice: how many marches had she witnessed with the chant 'Don't you dare come before me, Tree'? Yeah, Honey was bound to have some.

'You want some condoms?' Zarleena asked, keen to move to her bedroom now.

'Johnnies, Durex, rubbers, helmets.' Joel smiled, thinking back to the time he'd been in India, quoting the Hindi version of condoms. 'Even *nirodhak* or *kandam*.'

'I'll be getting the *kandams*, yar,' she said, in a funny Indian accent.

The night spun on, bringing Joel and Zarleena to the comfort of Zarleena's double bed. Any guilt on their faces was hidden by the swirling darkness that flooded through the window. Sunrise might bring regret and loathing, but tonight the two enjoyed each other like a couple chosen by the Goddess of Love herself, Aphrodite. Exhausted, finally Zarleena relaxed with her head on Joel's chest; a far cry from the way she would huddle in the corner after Armin had used her body. To compare the two would wreck the moment, and in Zarleena's world, moments like this were few. She closed her eyes and hoped her past marriage would never return to haunt her.

In some ways, as corny as it sounds, Zarleena wished this night would last for ever; Joel had made her feel so special.

But this for ever lasted only five minutes longer. Like someone waking up and remembering they'd left the baby at the Watford Gap Service Station's crèche, Joel sat up shaking his head in his hands, his silhouette clearly visible. Zarleena's first thought was, Red Bull withdrawal. Joel was going cold turkey. Needed caffeine quickly. She switched on her bedside lamp, adjusted her eyes to the light, and stared flummoxed at Joel's bare back. Well, not quite so bare. Zarleena was amazed to see a huge tattoo of a prickly red rose on his right shoulder blade, with the word CANDY above it. Like a game of hopscotch her mind jumped over a few ideas. One, Joel used to be with Candy. Two, Candy was now dead. Three, Joel was now with Claudia. Four, why the hell hadn't Claudia demanded he remove the tattoo of another woman's name? Something didn't make sense, but she couldn't quite work out what it was. She watched as Joel stood up and walked to the window, pushing it further open to breathe in the warm summer air. Zarleena couldn't be too sure but she sensed that Joel was in the middle of some sort of internal fight. And she didn't feel qualified to ask the question, 'What's wrong?' More importantly, she was afraid of what the answer might be.

'Look, Joel, if you want to go, I won't be offended,' Zarleena said, wrapping the bed sheets around her, feeling empty inside. 'It's been a weird night.'

'I . . . I.' He paused. 'I think I'll just go.' He headed out of the bedroom to fetch his clothes from the kitchen.

Only to bump into Honey sitting on the kitchen stool in her karate outfit, forking a strawberry cheesecake into her mouth. 'Hi, Joel.' Her eyes inspected

Joel's physique. 'Nice body. Any chance of devising a weight-training routine for my boyfriend, Tree? He's as skinny as a . . .'

'Twig? Branch?' Joel swiped his boxers off the floor and put them on. 'Stick?' He dressed into the rest of his clothes, made idle chat with Honey for a few minutes and then headed back to Zarleena's room.

In Zarleena's bedroom, two sets of eyes that only a short while back couldn't look away from each other, suddenly were looking everywhere but at each other. Zarleena and Joel hovered awkwardly like strangers. An hour ago the room had been charged like an electric storm, now it was like a flat battery in the snow. Why did sex have to be the biggest screw-up sometimes? Dressed in a white robe, Zarleena, with the barest of smiles, walked over to Joel and handed him a small envelope.

'It's part of what I owe you, £300, and if you say you don't want it, then give it to charity. It's important to me that I pay my debts.'

He tucked it in his back pocket, kissed her on the cheek, and one minute later he was gone.

Inside Joel's Range Rover a troubled soul sat in the driver's seat. In his profession it was pretty damaging to be afraid of heights; some people, the acrophobic afflicted of the world, were afraid of heights only because they believed when they reached the top they wouldn't be able to resist the urge to throw themselves off. Was Joel the same with women? Would he have to stay away from all women from now on in case he felt he had to fuck them? It was only just over a month since he'd sincerely promised Candy he'd be loyal and faithful to her. That was less time than it took a good pack of pork sausages to go bad.

And Joel's sausage had been the baddest porker of them all.

He slipped in a CD, Grandaddy, track 5, 'Our Dying Brains', and cracked open a cold Red Bull. Candy was in Canada, thousands of miles away from the scene of Joel's crime. Their last conversation before she'd left for Toronto had been a bit strained; not argumentative exactly, but slightly edgy. Joel had put it down to pre-flight nerves and warned her, if she was afraid that the plane might crash, to make sure to ask for a seat near one of the exits: 'Remember, Candy, you've done enough for these kids already; put yourself first this time.' For some reason, which was beyond Joel, she'd mentioned that at least if the plane did crash, she would be wearing something sexy. A cat-suit of all things. Joel had replied with words he would later regret, 'Well, make sure it's a red one. The rescuers will be able to pick out your dead body floating on the Atlantic Ocean more easily that way.' After that, Candy had requested Joel didn't do anything stupid (as usual), wished him good luck in New Zealand, explained how much she loved him, then kissed him goodbye down the phone.

And now, as usual, Joel *had* done something stupid. He muttered to himself, 'Am I more stupid than the idiot American who allegedly bought Tower Bridge thinking he was buying London Bridge? Am I more stupid than the man who steered the *Titanic* into an iceberg? Or, what about as stupid as Saddam Hussein hiding in a spider-hole?' Well, not quite, Joel decided, but pretty fucking close.

Crushing the empty Red Bull can in his hand, he threw it on the back seat. He picked up his new mobile and text Candy:

> *21 digits.*
> *Candy, I Love You,*
> *More Than Ever.*
> *Love Joel XXX*

'What the fuck have I just done?' Joel hollered to himself like a madman, as he drove out of Bindis & Brides car park. 'Why can't I keep my fucking monster in its cage?'

Chapter Twenty-six

It had been two days since Armin had been able to stare at his face in the mirror. Normally he could watch himself for hours, but since the business with the coffin, shame had hung around him like a necklace made of lead. How could an Indian man live with himself knowing he feared the white man? The British had already had their day in old India with the Raj, their hands were soiled with the blood of the brown man; Indians were not to be bullied again. Wasn't the horrific Amritsar massacre, when 15,000 innocent and unarmed Indian men, women and children were slaughtered, bloodshed enough?

In a fit of anger Armin had dressed up in his best suit, slicked back his hair (without the aid of a mirror), and barged downstairs into the smoke-filled bookie's. After waiting in line for a minute or so, ignoring the stink of booze and piss, Armin faced the plump, middle-aged cashier and grinned smugly.

'Your bet, sir?' the lady asked, barely glancing up from her Mills & Boon novel.

Armin smiled and reached into his back pocket, pulling out a wad of notes. 'Yes, I would like to bet £10 that the next prime minister of this racist, bloody country will be an Indian,' he said loudly. 'With a turban.'

A titter of laughter from the gambling customers. Just what he expected. Racists, the bloody lot of them. What was most annoying to Armin was that the cashier wouldn't even take his money. The odds were, apparently, 'incalculable'. He slammed the door on the way out, promising each and every one of them in his mind that an Indian winter was coming. The English had enjoyed the Indian warmth for too long. He'd especially like to get the ignorant man who'd shouted out, 'If an Indian prime minister does get in, then I hope that my *Samosa* Tax won't go up.'

Back in his flat, with the TV on in the background, Armin was restless and stifled by his own anger. Things hadn't been going too well lately. Two days ago he'd been made to look like a complete fool by an acquaintance of Zarleena's. A white acquaintance. Now how the hell was Armin supposed to plan his revenge on this white man when he didn't even know who he was? His accent hinted he was from London so that rounded it down to a few million. He couldn't threaten Zarleena to tell him who he was because the white bully had told Armin he'd bury him if he contacted her again (and he believed him too). And, unless he was on the FBI's Most Wanted list, Armin was most likely the only one looking for him.

Stalemate.

Or was it? Armin relived a portion of the conversation he'd had with the white man on the park bench.

He remembered the guy saying, 'I have been right to the top of Mount Everest and I still haven't found a creature as cold as you.' Then there was the bloke's T-shirt with its witty climbing innuendo: I LOST MY COCK TO FROSTBITE ... and even a comment regarding his worst kind of men: men who complain about the cold when they climb. This white man was obviously a climber, and – Armin rubbed his hands together in celebration of his clever deductions – and a climber who had climbed the big one. Surely there couldn't be that many Englishmen who could lay claim to conquering Everest. The pieces on Armin's chess board were flying. It was time to log on to the Internet.

Finding out the name of this English snake shouldn't be too hard. Coincidentally, an advert on the TV, which featured a mountain, caught Armin's attention as he tapped in his password INDIA RULES on the keyboard. A well-toned, half-naked tanned, man appeared spreadeagled halfway up a snow-capped mountain. The camera zoomed in a little. The American voice-over narrated, 'Not only do Frills Boxers keep the cutest bum in, but they keep the coldest weather out.' The camera then zoomed right in to the underwear's logo. 'But you don't have to climb a mountain to prove it.'

'What a complete ponce,' stated Armin, dead jealous of the man's tight bottom, completely unaware that the man in question was none other than Joel. 'I hope you fall.' He jogged the TV with his foot as if it might make the man slip. 'Fall down, you show-off.' Moments later and Armin's attention was back on the VDU screen.

If only Armin knew, Joel didn't need a mountain to fall down, just his own dick.

Joel had been to New Zealand before so he knew for a fact that there were women there. Indeed, it was a woman in New Zealand who had crafted his tattoo. It was the land of the tattoo after all. He had explained to his mates when he'd returned to England that New Zealand was a rugged, romantic wilderness and would be a perfect backdrop to film the *Lord of the Rings*. Joel expected that it should be filmed in three parts. It would need Peter Jackson to direct it, Elijah Wood as Frodo, Viggo Mortensen as Aragorn, Ann Widdecombe as Gollum and . . . he was told to shut up. They just wanted to know what New Zealand women were like in bed. Joel had replied, 'In bed? We never used beds.' It was the same old story, and this one wasn't in three parts. Even back then, Joel was being unfaithful to Candy – maybe he was being led by the dark forces of the Ring. Well, that's what he told Clovis when he was being lectured on morals.

And one should always pack some morals, thought Joel, staring into his empty suitcase; it's not like the airlines charge extra for their weight. But which ones? He was having enough trouble deciding whether he should pack ribbed condoms or flavoured (the other climbers used to laugh at Joel when he used condoms to help keep frostbite at bay, until one of their plonkers nearly broke off). By now, after visiting more countries than Michael Palin, one might think Joel's packing technique would be first class. Well, if cramming everything in anyhow and hoping it arrives in one piece is first class, then yes, Joel's packing was like British Rail.

He plucked off a prayer flag from his window display. Faded sacred text on a scruffy red square of material. He well remembered the day this flag had been presented to him outside a small village near Kathmandu. A British expedition had been organized to climb Cho Oyu, an 8201-metre-high mountain in the Himalayas. The climbing team and Joel had just cleansed themselves in a welcome solar-powered heated shower. The last feeling of warmth they were to experience for weeks. Joel loved the locals who lived near the mountains, or as he called them, 'the Mountain People', their generosity and humble way of life was a lesson in humility for anyone arriving from the rich world of the West. After the shower the British sat around a camp fire while a young Nepalese girl, perhaps nine years old, presented them each with a prayer flag blessed by a Buddhist monk. Each flutter of the flag meant that a prayer had been sent to God to keep the climbers safe. Unfortunately one of the climbers, Chris Bouvier, accidentally dropped his flag in the fire. The young girl, with sudden fear in her eyes, motioned that Chris should not attempt the mountain. Her father returned later in the evening, the night before the team headed for Advanced Base Camp, and he too warned Chris not to climb. The Gods would not be looking out for him if he did. He was doomed. Ten days later, in a raging storm, Chris disappeared. He was never to be seen again. Ever since, Joel carried his own flag in memory of Chris every time he attempted a climb – no matter how minor the mountain.

After stuffing his suitcase with clothes, pink bra,

laptop (to continue his autobiography), boots, trainers, etc., Joel wished he could have phoned 'Dial an Arse' to help squash down the suitcase lid. It was either that or he'd have to deflate the packed blow-up pillow. The time was 12 p.m., leaving him just two hours to reach the airport. Without traffic hold-ups the journey would normally take one hour and fifty minutes, giving him plenty of time to have a little lie-down. He rested his head back on the bed and loosened his mind, thinking back to the package that had arrived yesterday morning. He'd never received a kit-phone through the post before. And what's more, a kit-phone wrapped in a pair of red-laced knickers. Puzzled, Joel had shaken out the contents, whereupon a typed notelet had fluttered to his feet. Everything made sense as soon as he read it:

Joel,
I tried to ring on your mobile phone but it kept breaking up. When I smashed it up with a hammer. Don't worry, I managed to jot down all the important numbers before I broke it. Flip, fancy your parents living in America. Maybe if you'd done what a normal man would have done and removed my sexy lacy knickers that night then you wouldn't have to buy a new mobile phone. Not to mention how much fun I'm going to have with your phone numbers. Watch yourself, JOEL! Screw You.
PS I've decided to stay in England. Pommie Land.

Joel was completely baffled as to how Monique had discovered his address. Obscene phone calls were one thing, he'd been waiting for one for years, but threatening mail, where the next package might be a bomb, was quite another. Now how the hell was Joel supposed to plan his revenge on Monique if he didn't even know who she was?

Stalemate.

Or was it? It was doubtful that a woman like Monique wouldn't have taken advantage of his mobile phone: free calls to all her bimbo friends no doubt. He hadn't reported it missing until a couple of days after it was stolen. Joel was sure that when his itemized bill came through there would be a call list as long as Monique's forty-eight-inch legs covering the forty-eight hours that she had used it. And with those numbers he would track her down. Joel slipped into a snooze.

Eloise hovered at the bottom of Joel's bed, watching him sleep. God, he was such a dishy brother. Her eyes paraded up and down his naked torso. Ever since she could remember she'd been jealous of anyone who became close to Joel. Each woman Joel dated was a perceived threat to the special bond she shared with her brother. Since Joel's engagement to Candy, Eloise's true feelings had been pushed to the forefront. At best she felt strong protective feelings towards Joel, but at worst, she wanted to kill the women who slept with him.

She adjusted the focus on her camera and took aim. Snap, a picture of his face. Snap, a picture of his chest. Snap, a picture of his stomach. Snap, a picture of the bruises leading into his boxer shorts.

Snap, snap, snap, pictures in Eloise's mind of what might have led to those bruises. Joel had returned home late on Wednesday evening, seemingly towing a large ball of dejection behind him. Eloise had fired a couple of shots across the bow – 'Got a headache?', 'Someone you know beat your K2 summit record?' – before she aimed for the hull: 'Got someone up the duff? Or has Candy dumped you? Or did a pretty woman turn you down? Or—'

'Or nothing, Eloise,' he'd replied, collapsing into the vibrating chair. 'I'm the lowest form of life. Candy doesn't know it yet, but she's engaged to bacteria. And I don't mean friendly bacteria either like that fucking Yakult drink, I mean worse than streptococcus bacteria, the nasty stuff that gives you scarlet fever and pneumonia. I'm just mankind's biggest germ.'

Eloise had stood behind Joel and begun to massage his shoulders. 'So you slept with another woman again? Don't beat yourself up all the time, Joel, it was probably her fault. She came on to you, am I right?' She'd squeezed his neck muscles gently. 'It doesn't make you less of a man to admit that you were raped. It happens more than people care to think. And let's be honest about all this, Joel, if Candy made the effort to be here a little more often, then maybe you wouldn't feel the need to share your bed with these other women.' She'd kissed him on the top of the head. 'Better now?'

Hardly. The next morning Eloise had noticed Joel's depressive behaviour worsen. His zest for life tamed by guilt. It was maddening to watch her brother shuffle around the huge apartment like an arthritic Ozzy Osbourne. Then there were these episodes where he'd just stare out of the window for half an hour at a time, peering outwards to the castle ruins. The conclusion, to

Eloise, was a no-brainer: Joel was worried to death that he might lose Candy. Guilt was something he normally avoided at all costs, but this time, one by one, guilt was hammering in the nails. It was crucifying him.

'Wakey, wakey!' Eloise softly nudged Joel's shoulder. 'You'll miss your flight.'

'What flight?' Although he'd been asleep for just a few minutes, Joel appeared like he'd been asleep for hours. 'What day is it?'

Eloise shook her head, casting her long hair backwards. 'NEW ZEALAND, the All Blacks, the Kiwis, Anchor Butter, New Zealand lamb, ring a bell?' She threw him a purple Absolute Zero T-shirt. 'I'll get you a Red Bull.'

Calmly dressed and calmly packed, Joel wandered out to the living room, resting his suitcase and climbing bag by his feet. A church candle flickered its flame on the coffee table. Eloise always lit one to safeguard Joel's journey. It was as traditional as her tears.

'Don't go, Joel, I need you at a time like this,' she sobbed into her hands. 'Have you got my money?'

Joel tried to hide his smile as he produced his wallet and gave her a bunch of notes. 'There's about four hundred there.'

She sniffed. 'And what if the boiler breaks down; we have got one, haven't we? Or what if a hurricane blows out a window, or I need a new pair of Prada shoes?' She stared in disbelief at Joel's hand-out. 'Is this all I'm worth to you?'

'If you got yourself a job, then I think you might appreciate £400 isn't as easy to come by as you might imagine. I don't want to get into this now, but I really do think that it's about time you paid your own way. I'm beginning to sound like a parent here but—'

'I'm pregnant, Joel.'

Stunned silence. You could have heard a pin fall. A nappy pin, even. Eloise watched Joel's face with amusement, his brain like the Spaghetti Junction, too much traffic, too much chaos. This was the third time Joel had hinted that she must find a job, and in her experience, when it came to hints, it was three strikes and you were out. The hint becomes a request becomes an order. Faking pregnancy, mimicking morning sickness, sniffing coal, it was a novel way of keeping her unemployed status employed. There was no way a kind man like Joel, her own brother, would expect his own sister to risk losing her baby, his niece or nephew, for a poxy till job in Waitrose. Better than that, Joel was so considerate that he might even up her allowance (for baby clothes and cots and stuff). She wondered what type of baby buggy Joel would buy her. She smirked inwardly. That's if Joel had any money left from buying sprog gear for his own baby. Not for one moment had she forgotten that her brother's wardrobe was a hidey-hole for his secret baby clothes. She wondered when Joel would have the guts to tell her he'd got some woman pregnant.

'And you're sure the baby is yours?' Joel finally asked without thinking. 'I mean, who's the father? It's that fucking Johan, isn't it?' he shouted, kicking his suitcase across the floor. 'I asked you the other day about this JERK-HAN and you said, "He's okay but I wouldn't want to marry him." But you'll have a fucking baby with him, won't you? For fuck's sake, Eloise, you're still just a kid, you're only twenty.' Joel was fuming. 'Does he know? Does he even care?' His verbal blows caught Eloise full in the face; a one-sided fight that would make a Mike Tyson v. Jonathan Ross boxing match appear even-handed. It wasn't fair to treat his sister this way. Joel pulled her towards him and hugged her tight. 'Don't cry; we'll sort this out when I come back. It's too late for me to cancel my trip, I can't let them down at such short notice. Sorry I yelled but I don't want you to wreck your life.' He brushed a few strands of hair away from her eyes. 'You only get one after all.'

Joel disappeared to his bedroom and returned with the envelope containing the money that Zarleena had given him and a copy of his latest will. He handed them both to Eloise, declaring that he would be sure to oblige with any financial help she might need in the future. Eloise's false tears of sadness turned into real tears of joy. Having a phantom baby was near enough a licence to print money. No wonder women found it so easy to fall in love with Joel. He was so generous.

Picking up his case and bag, Joel kissed Eloise good-bye. 'Oh, yeah, you will remember to send Candy that package, won't you?' he said, nodding to the wrapped parcel by the stereo. 'It's important that you don't send it before she gets back, which will be next Wednesday. Cheers.' One last hug and Joel was gone.

It was too much to expect that Eloise would wait until Joel had left the premises before she tore into the envelope that he'd just given her. The will could sit tight for now, she had cash to count. But, before she had time to finger the first ten-pound note, her eyes were fixed to a folded piece of paper, partially hidden between the money. Joel obviously didn't know the letter was there as the envelope had been sealed. Well, she thought, there was no point both of them not knowing what was written on the note. Quickly, she flattened out the Bindis & Brides headed notepaper, and eagerly devoured the words thereon:

> Dear Joel,
> I enjoyed what we did together and hope the feeling is mutual. Although, afterwards, I noticed an amount of regret on your part. Let's forget that this ever happened. On another point, I am extremely grateful for all your help, it will never be forgotten. If I don't hear from you in the next few days then I will assume you want to forget this ever happened as well.
> Zarleena

What the blinding hell is going on here, wondered Eloise. She hastily totted up the money. Why was Zarleena giving Joel £300? It was obvious from the letter that Joel had been trying out the *Kama Sutra* with Zarleena, but surely Joel wasn't charging for his performance, was he? Her brother, a male prostitute? Since when did he charge for sex? She reread the words, and lo and behold, it did seem that way. Joel *was* indeed a gigolo. Mum and Dad would be so proud.

Not!

God, her brother was so sanctimonious, a word she'd been wanting to use for years. How dare he lecture her about getting pregnant when not only was he guilty of impregnating a woman, which was bad enough, but also he'd been selling his body – by the inch no doubt – to women with more money than charm. This made her own brother a potential health hazard, a time bomb of sexual diseases. But £300, surely Joel was worth more than that? He was being ripped off. It was time for some motherly advice.

Eloise dialled through to Florida and spoke to her mother. 'Mum, I love you, but sit down, I have some terrible news. Joel is a prostitute.' A pause. 'You know who Joel is! You can't disown him that quickly, Mum.'

Mum reverted back to her English accent. 'Is this another one of Joel's phases?'

'Mum, I know you live in America, but people over here don't go through prostitute phases. This is serious. He's even got it into his head that I'm pregnant. And you know how much I cherish my virginity. I expect he'll call you soon to say that I'm a few months gone. Well, as I live and breathe, I'm not. He's sex mad, Mum, no two ways about it. Your second son is addicted to sex.'

'I'm shocked, and any good mother would be. I take it that he doesn't charge Candy for sex? I assume she doesn't know about his extra-curricular activities?'

'He tells me nothing. Just do something, Mum, before he catches a disease.'

The thought of having Joel's headstone engraved with the words DIED OF A SEXUALLY TRANSMITTED DISEASE wasn't funny. Eloise had always envisaged her brother dying heroically, up a mountain, or down a ravine; never had it dawned on her he might cop-it because he couldn't zip-it. By becoming a male prostitute his sleeping around had taken on a new twist. He'd open the floodgates to a tidal wave of STDs. She just hoped that when Joel had sex his best friend was wearing a life jacket.

Eloise spoke through gritted teeth: 'You do know he might catch Aids, don't you? YOU HAVE TO DO SOMETHING!'

'And I will.' Mum paused. 'Leave it to me and your father. It'll have to wait until Joel gets back from New Zealand, but I promise you that I'll think of something.'

After dispensing with the necessary small talk, Eloise bid goodbye and replaced the receiver. She couldn't wait to find out what Mum had in mind for Joel. Then her eyes flipped to the will. She wondered how much Joel had left her this time.

Ten seconds later an angry sentence reverberated off the apartment walls.

'That bitch Candy, he's left her EVERYTHING!'

Chapter Twenty-seven

Of all the clean environments that Zarleena could think of – an operating theatre, silicon-chip factory, the inside of a bleach bottle – nothing quite beat the cleanliness of her mother's mind. It was as squeaky as a mouse on helium. And as such, explaining to her mother about anything considered to be even slightly sexually dirty was a trial. Zarleena peered deep into her reflection in the bathroom mirror and wondered if today was the day her mother's mind would become irredeemably soiled.

It was a sizzling Sunday roaster, the perfect start to August. With all the maisonette windows open and a gentle breeze flowing, the air should have been filled with the joys of summer. Instead, from Zarleena's perspective, the air was filled with disaster. It had been four whopping days since she'd slept with Joel and written him that cringing note. How mad must that have looked to any flies on the wall? Zarleena, naked, scampering around her bedroom searching for pen and paper, scribbling quickly, praying Honey would keep

Joel talking in the kitchen, then counting out the money and slapping it in the envelope, leaving just enough time to spray her armpits with deodorant and slip on a robe before he returned. Had she had enough time to check the deodorant can, then she wouldn't have walked around for the rest of the night with starched armpits.

Honey had been over the moon that Zarleena had reopened her sex account, explaining the virtues of receiving at least one deposit a week. In some ways having sex with Joel had brought some sort of closure to her relationship with Armin. It couldn't have done Zarleena any good whatsoever to have Armin's contorted face, as he pumped his curry sauce into her, as her last sexual vision. Most women who've had a bad sexual experience would like to wipe their minds clean, like an Etch-a-sketch; covering over the memory with another memory is the next best thing.

But what about women who have had a fantastic sexual experience, like Zarleena had had four days ago. Does she, too, want to wipe her mind clean? Only if she is filled with regret, perhaps, or guilt, perhaps. Or if the bastard bloke doesn't phone her back, perhaps. Zarleena sprinkled some fish flakes over Orangeina's bowl, flicked the glass with her fingers, and watched him eat his Sunday lunch. Maybe if she could turn into a fish like Orangeina, with his short-term memory, then her life would be simpler, she thought. Then she watched Orangeina do his yard-long poo. Perhaps not!

Did she want a simple life, she wondered, tucking into a dark-chocolate Bounty. Didn't 'simple' translate as 'boring'? Her gran used to say that life was like a good curry. A blend of the correct spices makes for a better meal. A little bit of fun, a dash of struggle, a teaspoon of excitement, a sprinkling of heartache, a handful of luck, a pinch of success and, to really fire things up like life's chilli, a dollop of risk. Hey presto, 'the Happiness Curry'.

If life wasn't about risks then God would have made people physically immortal, guessed Zarleena, relaxing back into the sofa. And what she had done with Joel a few nights ago was as risky as it was frisky. If this act had been performed in India – INDIAN GIRL SLEEPS WITH WHITE MAN – it might have hit the front page. It wouldn't have been the right time to give an interview while Joel was making love to her, but if she had to, then she would have told the journalist from the *Times of India* newspaper that everything was going well, Joel was hitting all the right places and certainly this was the best sex she'd had so far. Zarleena thought back to the special feelings Joel had uncovered in her, those tiny nuggets of thrills. How he seemed to flood her body with ecstasy, forcing her to scream out in pleasure, all the time making her feel hotter and hotter. Tumbling around on her bed, sweaty and naked, with a real man, a man who knew how to touch a woman, deserved to be remembered with a blush and a smile. But Zarleena was far from smiling.

The aftermath, the carnage, the stillness of the bedroom. The dull thud of an empty heart. How could a man switch from being a Sex God one minute to a Devil the next? Watching Joel staring out of the bedroom window with total regret written over his face added another spice to Zarleena's curry. The spice of humiliation. They say each picture needs a thousand words to describe. Well, Joel's face needed only three: I USED YOU. But why? For fun? For his ego? Or was it a simple matter of Joel just needing to empty his sperm pouches?

Zarleena bit into the second segment of Bounty. Maybe she was being a little naive here. Maybe the enormity of Joel's unfaithfulness to his fiancée had only sunk in afterwards. The sex itself might have just lasted an hour, but the label 'Cheat' would last for ever. Maybe that was the look that Joel had displayed: 'Guilt'. Nothing to do with regret at all. Zarleena sighed. Did she honestly expect that she could sleep with a man, just months away from his wedding, without a bruising of some kind? In this case – she cringed as she thought back to the note she'd given him – it wasn't so much a bruising as a paper cut. He was totally ignoring her now.

A huge yawn sounded in the hall like a Zulu war cry. Honey was up, which, by definition, meant so was everyone else. With Mickey Mouse jim-jams, haystack hair and breath so bad that Hans Blix would need to be informed, Honey stumbled into the living room and threw herself into the sofa-chair with her eyes closed, moaning, 'Need coffee. Lava Java.'

A plunger of Lava Java coffee was served by Zarleena, dutiful as ever when her sister was feeling tired. Juggling her three lives, Activist, Shop Manager and Tree Lover, was eating into Honey's reserves. Zarleena lectured Honey that in order to save the world's energy problems, she had to solve her own one first. She wouldn't be able to watch the rain forest regenerate itself from a hospital bed, she wouldn't be able to swim with the saved dolphins from a wheelchair and she . . .

'I get the point, Zarleena, I'll slow down. I didn't go on a march today, did I? That's a start.' Honey swallowed a gulp of Lava Java and rolled her eyes in bliss. 'What's this news that had to wait until morning?'

Zarleena mulled over everything she'd thought about in the last twenty-four hours one more time. Keeping her true feelings for Joel a secret from Honey had been a mistake; sisters were supposed to tell each other everything, and Honey's initial feelings of betrayal were quite understandable. Zarleena explained how hard it was to admit to Honey the strong feelings she felt for Joel, a man soon to be married to someone else. It was hard enough admitting them to herself. Quickly Zarleena was forgiven, in return for a fuller explanation of what she had got up to in the bedroom with Joel.

Honey's homecoming from karate class to find a heap of discarded clothes on the kitchen floor had her simultaneously smiling and shocked. Surely there was an explanation! And then she heard the distinct sound of humping throbbing through the walls. Oh, there was an explanation all right. Her sister was having a massive overdose of sex. But with whom? Honey had searched the visitor's clothes for clues to his identity. A wallet in his jeans pocket held the answers. But alongside Joel's credit cards, driving licence and odds and sods, Honey found some other things that gave rise to questions. Why was her sister being shagged by a man who kept a photograph of a blonde supermodel (well, she looked like one to Honey) next to a photograph of Mount Everest? And why did Joel keep a morbid, virtually suicidal goodbye note wrapped around his cash? It was nearly as strange as the Pigs Can Fly lottery scratch card she'd found with a ten-pound win on it; what sort of mad man wouldn't have cashed it in? She would have to warn Zarleena to be extremely careful. Joel was strange.

Zarleena gulped the last of her coffee and went on to explain the 'news' that had to wait until morning. She reasoned with Honey that it was important for her to visit their mother today, on her own, to sort out her troubled mind. Honey, as expected, tried hard to talk Zarleena out of it, explaining, underlining, drilling into her sister that the 'news' would not be as well received as she might hope. In fact, Zarleena might be risking everything, if she were to take the trip to Colchester. There were certain things an Indian daughter didn't tell her mother and this was a classic example. Especially, Honey pointed out, especially with a mother whose mind was cleaner than a nun's.

Staring up at her old house in Colchester was like falling into a box full of memories. The joyful screams of Zarleena playing with Honey amongst her parents, cousins and friends were dusty recollections now, filed away under 'happy times'; Colchester was a great place to grow up in. Zarleena's dad had a unique way of viewing his adopted town, Colchester. Col meant coal and that was where diamonds come from. Chest was what treasure went in. So, all in all, Colchester was a lucky town. 'But, what about the "er" in Colchester?'

Zarleena had asked. To which he'd replied, 'The "er" phonetically sounds like "a" which is the grade I expect you to get in your exams.' Unique.

And so was the front garden. Mum's obsession with nature had created a colourful paradise right on her doorstep. A living art form that Indian relatives swore took them back to their motherland instantly; bright saris and vivid turbans, succulent spices and dramatic weddings, monuments, temples, even the red and gold colour of rickshaws. As though she'd dipped her brush in a rainbow and covered the flowers with a hundred different shades. All she needed now to keep the authenticity of India was for Milton Keynes council to lend her a concrete cow or two. They would look spectacular amongst the jasmine flowers, marigolds and roses.

Zarleena plucked a small orange marigold and snuck it in her clipped-back hair. With her long, satin, plum-coloured skirt, white, buttoned T-shirt and trainers, Zarleena hoped the Eastern flower would balance out a little the Western overtones of her clothes. Mum always liked her to dress in something identifiable to her roots; a *bindi*, perhaps, some *mehndi*, even a pair of glittery *chappals*. But there were limits: there was no way she was turning up wearing a *chapatti* on her head.

A coward could grow old waiting for courage to arrive, concluded Zarleena, taking a huge gulp of dogged determination and walking up to the front door. In her handbag she had, at the ready, a Bodyform sanitary towel (with wings and a cotton-like feel) to wave in front of her father in case he wanted to be part of the private chat she needed with her mother. Zarleena called it 'Women's Insurance'. And yes, it was a clean one. Dad would run at high m.p.h. whenever PMT was mentioned.

Zarleena laughed at the door. Dad had done what he said he would do. There were three doorbells. One for family, one for friends and one for salesmen. Obviously the one for the salesmen was switched off. Zarleena pressed the family bell and waited.

Mum answered, belting out a smile brighter than the garden. 'What a lovely surprise,' she remarked in Hindi. 'No Honey? Never mind, come inside. You couldn't have come at a better time, it's *Bhaji* Day. I'm host.'

Oh great, thought Zarleena, the *Bhaji* Brigade were here. Of all the times she could have chosen. She followed Mum through the long hall and out to the back garden. Twenty or so Indian women, in saris, spread out over the perfect lawn. A harmony of greetings descended from the guests and Zarleena waved kindly to them all. Since arriving in England, over thirty years ago, Mum had formed the *Bhaji* Brigade. A group of Indian women from the neighbourhood who called upon each other once a week to share their opinions, discuss their problems and generally help each other out. It began as a simple way for lonely Indian wives to make friends and had now turned into quite a powerful unit which many conglomerates would envy. Day trips to the seaside, visits to historical landmarks, even shopping in Southall. One of their main priorities was to help widowed Indian women through the pain and hardship of bereavement. In fact, some of the first women who joined the *Bhaji* Brigade were widows. And it was a proud statement to make that instead of their lives dimming away like used sparklers, they became brighter and sharper, through the help and support of the Brigade's members. The *Bhaji* Brigade stood for Truth, Honour and the Indian Way.

But it also stood for partying and feasting. Zarleena eyed the generous spread that her mother had heaped on the patio tables. If God was looking down at them right now, he would have been licking his lips. Eat your heart out it wasn't. Eat your heart into a heart attack it may well have been. Creamy curries, tightly packed *samosas*, pickles, sweetmeats, *tandoori* chicken, lamb, duck, fish. Chickpeas, *dhal*, *pakoras* . . . everything. A hand-written sign sat behind a huge pile of oddly shaped *chapattis*: NON-ROUND CHAPATTIS. A comical gesture of rebellion against all the husbands who demanded that their wives made perfectly round *chapattis*.

Zarleena picked a smallish *samosa* and placed it on a paper plate. She looked out to the farmers' fields that backed onto the garden. Just within eyeshot a large billboard stood erect in the unploughed soil. Zarleena squinted her eyes to read the sign and sniggered at the words:

WELCOME TO COLCHESTER'S ROCKY HORROR
GM CROPS TO BE PLANTED HERE.

And below the words were pictures of a two-headed sheep and a two-headed cow. Moobleating. Zarleena couldn't wait to tell Honey that her activist friends had been down to her old neighbourhood. The voice of reason was everywhere.

Mum, dressed in a beautiful blue silk sari, sidled up to her daughter. 'Your father has ordered himself a tonne of clay,' she said, spooning some mint sauce over Zarleena's *samosa*. 'He wants to build a replica of his old village and sit it at the bottom of the garden.'

'He must be a master of the potter's wheel,' Zarleena joked. 'And where is he? Salivating over the new Black and Decker workman's work bench that's just come on the market?'

'Try again.'

'Snooker,' Zarleena suggested, knowing she was correct. 'Always snooker.'

The irony hit home. Zarleena's life seemed snookered right now. And unless her mum had been taking lessons from Ronnie O'Sullivan lately, she doubted her advice would be a frame winner. The moment came to steer her mother away from the *Bhaji* Brigade and head to the seclusion of the living room.

Once inside, one by one, Zarleena's nerves began to dismantle any semblance of calm that the garden had brought her, until by the time she went to open her mouth to speak, all hell had broken loose in her stomach. Her first word should have been 'bile' because that was what was on her tongue.

Sitting next to her mother on the sofa, Zarleena took her hand in hers and looked down at the carpet. 'Maji, you are very dear to me, and I'm proud to have you as my mother, but what I have to tell you today will shock you and disgust you.'

Before Mum had time to swallow the information a

knock at the door had one of the *Bhaji* Brigade asking for the key to the shed. The English heat was too much even for native Indians and the canopy was needed to give them shade. Mum suggested they look under the elephant statue on the patio. And also asked that the others be informed she was not to be disturbed for the next half-hour or so. A second later and Zarleena was alone with her mother again.

Zarleena continued, 'I have broken an oath and need you to forgive me if you can.'

Her mother's mind was like a quality Swiss watch, ticking by slowly, but ticking by ever so accurately. No presumptions, no predictions, no prejudgements. Just the digestion of the facts and the delivery of her humble opinion. It was time for more facts.

'This oath that you have broken and the forgiveness that you seek, Zarleena, will be easy for me. You are a good girl and I know that your heart is in the right place. So, tell me it all. I promise it will not be as bad as the look on your face suggests.'

Hypnotized by her mum's kind words, Zarleena relayed her story. 'I have slept with a man who is,' she stumbled, 'who is white. And one of Britain's top climbers. He saves kittens from fires. But that wasn't why I slept with him. He is kind and considerate and . . . he's engaged to another woman. She's white as well.' Zarleena nervously scratched her hair, wondering why her explanation was coming out so muddled. 'I don't think she's saved any kittens though. But the point is this: even though I don't live with Armin any more, I am still married to him and as such I shouldn't have slept with this man. If wedding vows can't be held sacred, then what can be? I feel like I have betrayed the Eastern morals you taught me just for a quick grope of the Western morals. I'm too ashamed to look you in the eye.'

Mum let out a sharp sigh before speaking. 'This is a horror story for me, Zarleena, and one starring my own daughter. I have many questions. Why do you say this man is kind when he slept with you behind his fiancée's back? Kind people never cheat on their partners.' She focused on the fireplace. 'I, too, cannot look you in the eye for I am so ashamed of your behaviour. I will never understand the corrupt ideals that your generation has dragged into this world. Is lust so hard to control? Does a man just have to glance at you and you want him?' She shook her head despondently. 'Look at the colour of your skin, it's brown, not white, not pink, not yellow, but a proud brown and it is the colour of a proud people. I want you to promise me that you will never see this man again. I will only give you my blessing on this condition. And it's a blessing that scars me deeply.' She paused and placed her hand on Zarleena's shoulder. 'You understand my feelings on this matter. You slept with another man whilst still married to Armin, and to add insult to injury, you slept with a man who was already engaged. It's despicable.'

What did you expect, thought Zarleena, a pat on the back? A *Bhaji* Brigade certificate of excellence? This was the first time she could remember that her own mother had made her feel like a slapper. Honey had warned her not to confide in Mum for obvious reasons. The threat of disownment was never too far away even with liberal Indian parents. They cut the first umbilical cord when you're born and they cut the second when you sleep around or betray tradition. Where the second belly button goes is a mystery. Maybe it's in the heart, because that's where it hurts when they cut it.

'I promise that I will never see this white man again, and I beg for your forgiveness,' Zarleena half whispered.

'Then I suppose that I shall have to forgive you,' Mum said. 'But I need your word that you will do nothing like this again.'

'You have my word, Maji.'

'You can pick and choose whichever man you want to once your divorce is settled, but until that time you play by the rules you agreed to. You are still married to Armin until that divorce paper comes through.' She stood up to let Zarleena know the conversation was over. 'Now let us join the party in the garden. Not another word about this ever again.'

And regarding Zarleena and her mother, maybe another word wouldn't have been mentioned. But lying back on the sun-lounger with her green sari hitched up to her knees, proudly showing off her hairy calves, was a smug-looking Prakesh Kaur. Smug for two reasons. One, she'd hidden the last of the onion *bhajis* in her handbag. And two, she'd accidentally listened in to Zarleena and her mother's private conversation on the way to the loo. It was just lucky for Zarleena that Prakesh Kaur would only pass on the sordid information to her husband.

Who luckily would only pass it on to his brother.

Who luckily would only pass it on to his wife.

Who luckily would only pass it on to her sister-in-law.

Who luckily would only pass it on to her son.

Who luckily would only pass it on to his mate, Prem.

Who UNLUCKILY happened to be Armin's cousin.

Chapter Twenty-eight

Not a race to be behind the times with communications, when the Indians heard that the Chinese had invented a new way of passing on information, called 'The Chinese Whisper', they decided to go one better and invent 'The Indian Shout'. A method of distorting information to add flavour to a story, loudly. It had been five days since Zarleena had visited her mother in Colchester, five days since Hairy-Calves Prakesh Kaur had first heard Zarleena's confession, and therefore five days since The Indian Shout had been in full swing.

Prem, Armin's cousin (and right-hand man), phoned through to Armin to spread the gossip.

After a quick confirmation with each other that India was the best country in the world, Prem began, 'Check this out, Armin, I've got some news about your slag of a wife.'

'Hang on a second, I want to hear this, let me turn *Devdas* off.' Armin reached out for the remote and flicked off the DVD player. 'Continue.'

'I've heard from a reliable source that Zarleena, your slag of a wife, tried to be a member of Atomic Kitten, and the band was going bust so this mountaineering guy decided to rescue the kittens from a fiery hell. That was three years ago. The mountaineering bloke has been sleeping with Zarleena ever since. She was having sex with him while you were married to her. A white man, Armin, you were right all along. She is the bad mango of the family, not you. She cheated on you and now we can clear your name.' Prem paused. 'Long live India.'

Armin loved the story so much that he asked Prem to say it all again, but this time in Hindi. Their chat left little room for idle talk; it was all business after that, centring on what Armin was going to do next. The conversation concluded; Armin replaced the phone. It was time to break into his celebration *bhangra* dance. With a subtle shake of his hips, a lift of the shoulders and a wave of his hands, Armin bopped his way around the flat *bhangra*-style, chanting, 'Life is hotter than a frying pan, nobody messes with the *bhangra* man.'

Ten minutes later, a calmer, quieter Armin sat at his computer desk assessing the dossier he'd compiled on Joel Winters. He'd seen advertisements on TV regarding the usefulness of the Internet. Great for banking, great for stocks and shares, even great for ordering cheap books on Amazon, but what about great for fucking up people's lives. It had been exactly one week since he began his search for information on the man he now knew as Joel Winters. And in Internet time, a week is a lifetime.

Armin perused the file on Joel. Hoards of photos, news articles, profiles, facts and details of the achievements of a man quite famous within his own climbing community. And it was Joel's achievements that were of particular interest to Armin. Among the TV commercials, bit parts in films, magazine covers and articles Joel had written, there was an awful amount of net space taken up by Joel's charity work. A particular piece shone out for closer inspection. For Cancer Research, Joel had climbed a small castle ruin and stayed up there for forty-eight hours (only allowed down to dash to the nearby woods to relieve himself). The interesting fact to Armin was a paragraph that read: *To help the courageous climber through his ordeal, his sister, Eloise, brought him sandwiches and Red Bulls from the overlooking Forest Falls apartment she shares with Joel. Asked what living with the country's top climber was like, she replied, 'It's lovely to wake up to his gorgeous face and body.'* A photo of Eloise hugging Joel after his accomplishment appeared underneath the article.

Armin spread out a map of Hunterslea on his carpet and circled Forest Falls Apartments with a red pen. This would be his second hit. Then – bearing in mind Prem's information today regarding Zarleena – he would concentrate on the first hit, Bindis & Brides. Armin smirked. It used to seem like the world was in control of him, and now it seemed that he was in control of the world. It was fun being a megalomaniac.

But not as much fun as reaping the wild winds of revenge on Joel. God, that was going to be joyous. And this time Joel could bring as many coffins as he liked, because there was no way that Armin was going to be scared of someone who did charity work. If that was the case he might as well kneel down to Pudsey Bear right now and wipe his yellow, furry backside. There was no way a white man was *ever* going to scare him again. Besides, he couldn't believe that a man of Joel's standing, someone who had a reputation for helping people and raising money for charities, would risk violence against a fellow human being. No, it was not feasible. When the time came for Armin's payback, Joel would run a mile, just like the typical all-mouth and no-trousers man he was.

Armin picked up the computer print-out of Eloise hugging Joel like she was saying 'goodbye'. He wiped his finger over her pretty face, tracing the outline with the tip of his fingernail. Well, she would be saying 'goodbye' to something very soon, something she obviously held very dear, and Armin couldn't wish the day here soon enough. He reached for the red pen and neatly drew a cross over Joel's face.

It's quite hard for many families when they realize that they have got a nutcase in their midst. Eloise had been back and forth on the phone with her mother in Florida for the last week discussing various aspects of Joel's behaviour. As yet, a solution was not forthcoming. Dealing with a prostitute son who kept his own coffin and ate mouldy food, who wore a pink bra, who electrocuted his testicles, who ate fish bones on the off-chance he might choke to death and who didn't wear a seatbelt but made damn sure one was wrapped around the ever-present box of Red Bulls in the passenger seat, was not something that came up often in parenthood guides. In fact, it rarely came up in guides for the mentally retarded. Eloise replaced the receiver and continued with what she was doing before her mother interrupted her with talk of her loopy brother.

Missing Joel.

She cracked open a Red Bull then sat, engulfed in her enormous lounging clothes, on Joel's enormous bed watching a collection of Joel's TV adverts that she'd recorded over the years. As a testament to her respect for Joel's privacy, Eloise had refused to open the package he'd asked her to post to Candy. Just where he'd left it was just where it still sat. A present to a woman who didn't deserve him. Eloise had driven herself nuts wondering what might be wrapped inside. And here she was thinking about it again. Should she open it? Or, shouldn't she? Suddenly her thoughts were interrupted by the sights on the TV. Her favourite Joel advert had just come on. It begins with two mates; one is Joel, finishing a piece of garlic bread. Their gorgeous dates arrive and Joel is seen sprinting away, down the street, over the countryside and the next shot we see him, he's halfway up a mountain. The camera returns to the other mate, who pops in a Tic Tac and smiles. The message is, 'Don't run away from bad breath, attack it with Tic Tacs.' Eloise laughed as she always did. Even when Joel wasn't here he was giving her pleasure. Which reminded her of an important question she often asked herself: how much pleasure was she giving Joel? How did he look upon his young sister? She suspected he might think she was a money-grabbing bitch!

Or, even, a nosy, money-grabbing bitch. Eloise could stem the flow no further, her curiosity was leaking out everywhere. Enclosed in a top that was too big, and a pair of jeans that were too big, even a pair of slippers that were too big, Eloise walked out to the living room and with morals that were too few began to open the package meant for Candy. Carefully and meticulously her fingers peeled off the tape, giving herself a guess at each turn. A large coffee-maker? A sandwich toaster? A pair of boots? Just two more pieces of tape to go. A vanity case? Or even . . . she pulled away the last remaining piece of tape . . . or even . . . a—

'A BABY?' Eloise shouted, holding up the boxed Baby Alex Interactive Doll. 'A FUCKING BABY?'

The stashed baby clothes in Joel's walk-in wardrobe (Red Bull store) made sense all of a sudden. The cute T-shirt, cap and shorts she'd found in the Debenhams bag were now keeping Baby Alex warm. Except, she stared in disbelief at the box, the baby wasn't even called Alex any more. Joel had scribbled out 'Alex' and replaced the name with his climbing hero's, 'Mallory'. A Baby Mallory Interactive Doll. She removed 'Mallory' from its packaging and pulled off the tiny ski mask. How the hell was Mallory going to be able to speak, like it said on the box, with a mask on? And more importantly, what would a Mallory say? 'Mummy, avalanche coming.' Or, 'Daddy, my fingers are cold, have I got frostbite?'

Poked inside the baby's dinky climbing boots, along with half a bar of Kendal Mint Cake, was a folded note:

Sweet Candy,
This is not a real baby. I'm sure you've gathered that by now. But I think this proves to you how

committed I am to us having a baby. I will support
you totally. Even if you give birth to a baby that
looks like your mother.
Love you always, Joel XXX

Eloise processed the information, factoring all she knew with all she guessed. The conclusion was simple: Candy was pregnant with Joel's seed. Her gorgeous brother was about to become a gorgeous father. She was now officially involved in a 'baby' race. Except hers was a phantom baby and Candy's was real (baby Mallory would have to be the pacemaker). And when Joel found out she'd been lying, he would kick her out of the apartment.

It was at moments like this that she wished her Czech boyfriend, Johan, could speak better English. But as it stood, he was still struggling with *The Hungry Caterpillar* book, and explaining complicated issues regarding fake pregnancies, real pregnancies and living in fear of losing any bonds she had with her brother to other women, would be like reciting Shakespeare to him. It would be a tragedy. But information like this needed sharing; it was like a huge cheesecake, there was no way Eloise could munch her way through this on her own. It was time to confide in her best friend, Natalie, and drink the wisdom from her pool of knowledge. Or in real words, get pissed.

But first, she had other matters that needed her urgent attention. She changed out of her lounging clothes and into something sexy. A red mini-mini-mini-skirt, a tight white vest top and her eye-catching, bright yellow Gucci knee-length boots. With countless bangles, glittery crucifixes dangling around her neck, glossy, pampered hair and perfectly done make-up, she could walk into any open space and a nightclub would be built around her. Her motto today was 'dress up to bring down'. She headed downstairs to Reception.

More out of deviousness than anything else, Eloise dropped her keys near a huge potted rubber plant in the lobby, giving the doorman on duty an eyeful of her behind as she bent down to pick them up. It was amazing how quickly a man's face turned scarlet, amazing how malleable a man's brain became when made soft by a glimpse of nudity. Finding out information about Joel from guys still dribbling with lustful thoughts was a cinch. Who Joel had taken back to his apartment, who had stayed the night, anything that Joel got up to when she was away, was relayed to Eloise seconds after she bent over. She picked up her keys, then stood up.

'Oh, hi, El,' Sammy, the doorman who talked little, responded to her prompting, sweat trickling down his neck onto his tight collar. 'Thought you'd best know, Joel was on his mobile outside a few days before he left for New Zealand and I distinctly heard him say, "Kill the babysitter." I thought I was hearing things until he shouted it louder, "Just kill the babysitter, for God's sake." It's none of my business, but I thought you should know.' Sammy opened a desk drawer and removed an envelope. 'He also left this. He said to give it to you "only" in an emergency. I think it's about £300.'

Eloise put out her hand. 'It's an emergency, Sammy.' And she headed outside in the blazing sun to wait for the taxi that would take her to Hunterslea High Street.

She slipped on her Armani shades and sat down on the dry grass in front of Reception, placing Candy's package beside her. Today should have been about catching rays, instead it was about rescuing brothers. If Joel really did want to concentrate on a life with Candy and their baby, the last thing he needed was a list of exes wanting more sex. It was up to Eloise to work through Joel's list, one by one, warning them to stay away, beginning with the lowest woman of them all: the Indian woman who was willing to pay him for sex. The taxi arrived.

'Where to, luv?' the cabbie asked.

Eloise slipped onto the fake-leopard-fur-covered back seat. 'The brown light district, please.'

'You wot?' He turned his head, confused.

'Bindis and Brides shop in the High Street, please.'

Driving at less than 30 m.p.h., Eloise had to check to see if the handbrake was still on. The taxi driver noticed her concern.

He said, 'Yeah, sorry about the speed, luv, I'm a bit short-sighted so I have to take it steady until my glasses come through.' He laughed alone. 'Most of the road is a blur to me.'

One man's Blur is another man's Incubus, thought Eloise who spent the remainder of the journey trying to keep Baby Mallory calm through the wrapping paper. She thanked the driver for not crashing and made her way to Bindis & Brides' entrance. Eloise checked her memory, and yes, this would be the first time she'd walked into an Indian business without leaving with poppadoms, chicken korma, pilau rice and a naan bread. Although, with her nerves growing quicker than stains on a baby's bib, she couldn't guarantee that she wouldn't ask for a cold bottle of Kingfisher as soon as she walked through the door to calm her down a little.

The door chimed and the smell of incense shot up Eloise's nose. The bright colours, the vivid lights, the pleasant smells, the delicate sounds, it was as if her senses had been ambushed. How could a simple high-street shop fill you with the sensation of standing in a miniature palace? Top Shop was nothing like this.

As many sets of Asian eyes zeroed in on Eloise, a song came to mind which needed a slight adjustment. It was called 'White Girl in the Ring', and summed up the moment perfectly. Eloise found herself struck by the beauty of the Indian clothes around her; she hadn't seen so many colours since watching *Monsoon Wedding*. And the rich language that scurried through the air at a thousand syllables per minute was a hypnotic tune; powerful but enchanting in its graceful tone. There were many things of beauty in here, and if this was an Indian shop then no wonder her brother wanted to try Indian sex.

'Eloise?' Zarleena appeared from nowhere. 'I thought it was you.'

Slightly startled, Eloise checked out Zarleena's orange silk *shalwar kameez*. Was this the sort of clothing her brother would have had to remove to get to her brown skin? Or did she have one made of black rubber? It mattered not; her mission here was to stop a future, which she knew would wreck Joel's life, from happening.

Picking up a carved wooden tiger, Eloise spoke. 'Joel is going to be a father. I thought you would like to know.'

Zarleena's disappointment knew no bounds. In one desperate, naive, foolhardy moment, Zarleena had guessed that Eloise's arrival in Bindis & Brides was as a messenger of good. Not the harbinger of bad. Nine whole days had passed since Joel and Zarleena had slept together. Nine days without a word. Maybe Joel's look by the window that night had been neither regret nor guilt; maybe it was just the look of a plain bastard. A man fully in charge of all his faculties was certainly to blame for conspiring with deceit to bed a woman and discard her like a dirty dish cloth. Or, in simple terms: the bastard knew wot he woz doing. He woz using her for sex. Zarleena could tell that Joel's sister was itching to say some more.

Let's be having you then, she thought; *let's get it over with*. 'A father?'

'Just one of the thousands of things he didn't tell you, I expect.' Eloise stroked the tiger lovingly. 'You honestly didn't think that a man as good-looking as my brother wouldn't have a list of girls waiting to bed him, did you?' She moved the tiger up Zarleena's arm towards her shoulder. 'He's just like this tiger, roaming his territory, ready to pounce on the nearest available pretty woman. Only one tigress has managed to tame him a bit so far. Her name is Candy and she is the woman who bears his child, the woman who my womanizing brother is marrying next year.' She opened her eyes wide and growled. 'Grrrrr.'

What was this, a circus? Eloise the clown – all she needed now was a big top. Although, Zarleena recalled, some of the larger customers who visited the shop from time to time, had asked for *shalwar kameezes* in size 24 and above, which definitely could be classified as 'tents'. Zarleena, however, could only be classified as 'confused'. Yet again, it appeared that Candy had been resurrected. Either that or she'd never died in the first place. Zarleena thought back to the moment she had peeked at the hidden photographs in Joel's bedside drawer. Written on the back of a photo of Candy were the words: *Candy, My heart bleeds for her internally, it bleeds for her eternally*. Surely they were words meant for the loss of a loved one. Weren't they? Zarleena sifted through the many conversations she'd had with Joel, fixing her attention on the multitude of times he had mixed up the name Claudia with Candy. She'd reasoned at the time that Joel was still too grief-stricken to let go. Was there another reason? Zarleena returned to a phone conversation she'd shamelessly listened in to when she'd sneaked up behind Joel in his bathroom. Yet again she'd heard incriminating evidence: he'd said, 'I'm not going to cheat on you . . . Oh come on, Candy, you know I love you.' Grief-stricken??? Zarleena was beginning to think not. And then there was that huge tattoo on his back: CANDY. Maybe the circus also had a monkey, determined Zarleena, and in this case the monkey was her.

Zarleena gently removed the tiger from Eloise's hand and returned it to its place. 'Okay, so Joel is going to live happily ever after with Candy and their baby. Great, it's the best news I've heard all week. I was just wondering . . . why did you think it was necessary to inform me? As far as you're concerned, I'm just one of a long list of women waiting to bed your good-looking brother.'

'Well, let me pose you this simple question: when was the last time you had yourself checked out for sexual diseases? A week ago? A month? Ever?' Eloise glared gleefully at Zarleena's perplexed and deliciously worried face. 'My advice is get yourself down to a clinic A.S.A.P., get yourself on a course of antibiotics as soon as you can, hope against hope that you receive the all-clear and learn from this big mistake. Never sleep with a man who is riddled with sexual diseases like my brother is.'

'What?' Zarleena cried.

'THIS IS WHAT HAPPENS WHEN YOU SLEEP AROUND,' Eloise shouted to the entire shop. 'It's nature's way of taking care of the home-breakers.'

'I didn't know she was pregnant,' Zarleena replied meekly. 'If I'd known that—'

'What?' Eloise interrupted. 'If you'd known that then you wouldn't have paid him £300 for the privilege of being screwed by him.' She stared at her with disgust. 'What sort of woman pays a man £300 for sex? It's pukeable.'

A wall of Indian eyes peered openly into Zarleena's arena. Customers loved the upbeat mood of Bindis & Brides, but this was nothing short of rock 'n' roll. One of their own was being lectured on good morals by one of them. It was worth being late home to cook *dhal* for. Amongst the observers, Honey had watched the confrontation with mounting fury and, unable to contain her anger any more, she bolted across the floor and grabbed Eloise by the arm.

'I suggest you go to the vet's and get that tongue of yours removed, lady. I think it's cheap day for snakes on Fridays.' Honey shoved Eloise towards the exit. 'You obviously know nothing about my sister. She's not the sort to pay someone for sex, if anything people pay her, now get out!'

Eloise picked up Baby Mallory and left the shop smirking, a trail of Poison perfume wafting behind her like a car's exhaust. Part-way up the street she paused to reflect on the day so far. If Zarleena wasn't put off Joel by that little display back there, then she was more of a moron that she'd given her credit for. And here was the point of all this: while Joel was away it was of grave importance that any loose ends were tied up. Every woman that Joel had seen over the last few months would have to be scared off. Nothing was allowed to interfere with Joel, Candy and their baby. Eloise headed to the Post Office and waited to be served.

'Anything of value in there?' the clerk asked, weighing the package.

'Just a baby,' Eloise answered, giggling. 'Nothing that can't be replaced. If it shits itself in transit you won't charge the person at the other end for the extra weight, will you?'

The clerk replied rather smugly, 'I think if it messes its nappy the total weight will remain the same. I wouldn't worry about it. It's one of Sir Isaac Newton's laws of motions, I think.'

And concerning Newton's second law of motion, Zarleena accelerated in the direction of her bedroom until compelled to stop by the opposing force of her bedroom wall. It was obvious that she needed some time to herself right now. Honey was left in the shop to quell the gossiping customers. Trying to explain Eloise's outburst would need a lot of quelling.

Upstairs, Zarleena busied herself doing nothing. Moving a Hindu statue of Lakshmi, the Goddess of Good Fortune, and returning her to her spot. Picking up a Strawberry Dream from a Quality Street box and putting it down again. Plucking out the memory of the night she slept with Joel and . . . God, if only she could throw that memory away. She'd tip it in the same skip as the memory of her marriage to Armin.

She'd once looked upon Joel as a good man with a kind heart; now she saw him as a refresher course in bastard men. A low-life who had reduced her dignity to his level. How could she have been so wrong about him? Had the thousands of years of Indian parents choosing their children's partners diluted a natural instinct? Had Charles Darwin's principle of natural selection created a race of people unable to pick their own partners successfully, without the help of their parents? Had the Darwinian Theory put a stop to Zarleena ever picking a good man for herself? The idea was a little ropey. For starters, men's personalities have more sides than a dodecahedron. Which sides they choose to display depends on who they are trying to impress and ultimately who they are trying to undress. The sides Joel had chosen to display – showing support when soldier Spud became racially aggressive in Ned's Fried Fill Ups café, helping her with Armin, lending her money, easing her worries – were enough for most women to wave the white flag and surrender to his charms (and not just Indian women either). Then there were his striking looks, his fabulous body, his amazing ambitions, his unusually looong tongue. Forget surrender, the majority of women would quite happily be his POW and take any sexual torture that he could inflict on their tied-up bodies. Was it any wonder his other sides had remained so easily hidden? Zarleena had been too busy wondering what he could do to her body to wonder if he could be doing it to anybody else.

But it appeared the 'anybody' was in fact 'anybodies'. Joel had been screwing around, collecting women like coupons, cheating on his pregnant fiancée, Candy. Or was it Claudia? It might even be Candida. Who knew? The point was this: choosing her own man had been just as unsuccessful as having her man chosen for her. Zarleena felt like screaming with frustration, and in the words of Bonnie Tyler, she would have yelled, 'Where Have all the Good Men Gone?'

Zarleena peered down to the car park at the back of the shop. The newsagent's next door were having a delivery of chocolate bars. She licked her lips and then hated herself for doing so. Surely she had more to look forward to in life than a stupid bar of chocolate. And then, as if a thought had been curled up asleep somewhere in her brain, an awful idea trickled down to her cerebral cortex and gave it a good kick. Maybe her bad luck wasn't so much about the men, but more about her. Maybe she was one of those women who would always attract bad men. Abusive husbands and womanizing boyfriends. Slimy, sweet-talking men who turn nasty when they get you alone. Pig husbands who shower their women with niceties until after the wedding day, then resort to Victorian ideology, forcing the wife to scrub, clean, mend, cook, and open her legs on demand. Even mild-mannered mummy's boy-men who turn into control freaks, cracking their metaphorical whip, sticking yellow Post-its around the house filled with chores and regulations. Basically men who like to shit on their women.

Or even more succinctly put, men who were full of shit.

Chapter Twenty-nine

O ver the next seven days Eloise worked her way through Joel's phone list of 'Women in limbo', reducing some to tears, others to tantrums and one to trauma. She kept the costs down too by texting them, 'Joel has Aids, call me back on 07562 674857.' Everything was going swell. Even her mind seemed sorted now. After confessing all to Natalie regarding her obsessive protectiveness of Joel, her phantom pregnancy and her addiction to buying Prada shoes and handbags, she decided to take her best friend's advice and follow what the mixed-up Hollywood stars did when having mental difficulties: yoga. In fact, she was balancing on her head and elbows with her arse up in the air when Joel returned from his trip to New Zealand. 'This is good for the unborn baby. I'm obsessed with doing everything as healthily as possible,' she'd said, trying not to fall over. 'You should try it after half a bottle of vodka and four spliffs.'

But Joel was a broken man when he returned. Like a badly funded building project the cost of his one-night stand with Zarleena was mounting daily. For the first time in his life he'd climbed a mountain carrying extra weight. The weight of a guilty heart. His agent, Pete, ordered Joel to remain professional, nothing was more dangerous to a climber than a preoccupied state of mind. It took only one slip and Joel would be dead. Which was ironic because it took only one slip and his relationship with Candy might be dead also. Up in the heights, where even birds lose their nerves, Joel had made the decision that had torn at his insides until he returned home. He would have to confess all to Candy. This building project might be about to have the foundations ripped from under it. Something was telling him that Candy wouldn't be his for too much longer. Not helping matters was Candy's flatmate, Sara, fobbing him off every time he tried to telephone. 'Candy is out with a friend.' Or 'Candy is busy, try later.' Best of all: 'Joel, take the hint, Candy isn't available for *you* at the moment.' What hint? Joel had asked himself. And then the package had arrived through the post. One Baby Mallory returned from Cornwall with a note pinned to its head: WHO'S THE MOTHER? Was that the hint?

Confusing matters even more was the mobile-phone bill he'd requested for the phone that Monique had stolen and demolished. Joel had scanned the bill quickly – missing the most important number of all: Candy's mobile number – and was left puzzled by what he saw. Why on earth would Monique be making the majority of her calls to numbers in Cornwall? Why would a woman from Australia become transfixed by people only famous for their pasties? And if things weren't already weird enough in his penthouse, Eloise kept pleading with him to watch a few of her latest favourite films: *One Flew Over the Cuckoo's Nest*, *Nuts* and of course he just had to watch *My Brother Might be Mental*. (He was sure she'd made up the last title.)

Stagnating in his own gloom, Joel decided to take a trip to Cornwall and confront Candy face to face. Eloise had asked him not to leave her alone as she was sure a man was stalking her. She couldn't put her finger on it but, since signing up for a three-week crash course in yoga down at the local leisure centre, her wait outside Forest Falls Apartments each evening for a taxi had been infected with a fear that someone was watching her. The movement of a bush, the sound of footsteps running, the sixth sense of being spied upon. Joel turned down Eloise's request for a twenty-four-hour minder and gave her £5 to buy new batteries for her rape alarm instead.

So here Joel stood, 1 p.m., yards away from 16 Seafront View, Cornwall, three days after returning from a strained but profitable trip to New Zealand. His thoughts by now were well and truly bogged down with worry. It's no good having a history with someone you love if you can't have a future with them. Joel tapped his jean's zipper and whispered, 'You've got a lot to answer for, young fella.'

An extremely surprised Sara opened the door and trailed her eyes up and down Joel's body with displeasure. 'Let me go and get some butter for you, Joel. I bet if you put it in your mouth it wouldn't even melt, would it? How could you?'

'How could I what?' Joel tried to look over her shoulder into the flat.

Sara regained her composure. 'Nothing. Candy is down at the beach at her usual spot. If you're quick you might catch what she's writing in the sand about you these days. Bye.' And she slammed the door in his face, legged it to the kitchen and dialled Candy on her mobile, warning her that Bastard Joel was heading her way. And as a favour to Sara, could she write CRAP IN BED in the sand.

Joel walked down the steep hill, admiring the graceful seagulls as they swooped and circled in the powerful sun, their eyes searching for dropped chips, their squawking deafening. Passing a trio of tired fishermen sitting on a pub bench celebrating a decent catch with jugs of cider, Joel raised a smile as they raised their tankards, and continued his descent towards the beach.

The sandy shore was packed with tourists so lobster-red it was a wonder they weren't squirming in the fishermen's nets. Joel remembered his first ever visit to a Cornish beach. 'The tides here are lethal,' Mum had warned. 'Only paddling today, kids.' 'Sure thing, Mum,' Joel had replied and then went searching for the sign that said DEADLY CURRENTS and dived right in. Being dragged back by his ear, struggling and kicking, Joel had tried to steer his father into the area with the sign that said DEADLY QUICKSANDS. Later that night Joel did not see the sign that said DEADLY HAND ACROSS BACKSIDE. Life wasn't fair.

A beach ball landed at Joel's feet and he kicked it back to a couple of giggling teenage girls, who, in their strong Cornish accent, said, 'Corr, he be a roight bit of scrumpy man.' Joel smiled and headed up the beach towards Candy's spot. A rock pool she called 'the Red Lagoon' on account of once cutting her foot on a sharp limpet shell there. Just behind the rock pool, sitting on a large beach towel, in her white bikini, Candy soaked up the sun whilst reading a book, *The Hitch Hiker's Guide to the Galaxy*. Joel shook his head; if Candy was searching for romance in novels he doubted she would find it in characters like Zaphod Beeblebrox or Slartibartfast, although Arthur Dent, the main character in *Hitchhiker's*, did share some similarities to Mr Darcy (they were both male and both fictitious). Joel picked up a small pebble and tossed it in the rock pool, dislodging Candy from her pretend reading. He hoped that there was a decent explanation as to why she had been ignoring his phone calls. He half suspected that it had something to do with Baby Mallory. Maybe he'd come on a little too heavy for her liking. Maybe the next time he sent someone a baby dressed as a climber he'd make damn sure that they were both on the same wavelength.

Candy looked up. 'Before you give me a hard time, Joel, there were good reasons why I didn't want to speak to you.' She stood up and came over to hug him. 'It's a cliché but I needed some space.'

He pointed to her book. 'Is that why you're reading that, it's about space, isn't it?'

She laughed. 'Sort of.'

Joel watched as Candy gathered up her belongings, slipped into a pair of shorts and trainers, and flipped open her make-up mirror for a lippy top-up. Scientists say that each person will view twenty-four million images in their lifetime (discounting perverts who probably view that many porno images in just a week). Joel could swear that the image he was viewing now, a tanned, blonde, toned beauty, glazed by the sheen of the midday sun, would be the best of his bunch. He'd never seen Candy so beautiful as he saw her right then. Joel shamefully concentrated on his feet. Maybe she looked so great today because he knew the tide was about to come in on their relationship. He knew that he couldn't keep his one-night stand with Zarleena a secret any longer. He knew . . . Joel peered to the sand beneath his Nike trainers. Written in the damp grains were the words MY LOVE FOR JOEL WILL LAST FOR EVER EVEN THOUGH WE CANNOT BE TOGETHER. Joel glanced up at Candy who now had tears in her eyes. They stared at each other in silence. But many words were said.

Eventually Candy broke: 'Why did you sleep with her, Joel? You promised me all this would stop.' She wiped her eyes with the back of her hand. 'You can't love me like you say you do. You just can't.'

'But I do.'

Joel suggested they walk away from the bustle of the beach and head down to a rocky alcove they used to watch the sunset from. Generally sunbathers kept away from the area on account of the limited sand. Which made it perfect for lovers and dreamers. Joel helped Candy keep her balance over the slippery rocks, desperately racking his brain as to how she knew about Zarleena, pushing her further and further over the jagged edges in the hope that by the time they'd reached their destination, he'd have come up with the answer.

Alas he only came up with more questions. How long

had she known? Why had she left it until today to tell him she knew? What did she mean by the writing in the sand? And one more, how the hell did she get mixed up with a wanker like him in the first place? Joel pointed to a small ledge they often climbed to. It was their ledge. No one else was mad enough to climb there. Ten minutes later and they were both staring out to the bluey-green ocean, their feet dangling below the ledge, their hearts on active duty via adrenalin. The last time Candy and Joel were here they were inseparable. Today it looked like they were about to lose the 'in'.

'Do you know how hard it was for me, Joel, to hear her gloat about what you and she got up to in the bed? And I sat through it all knowing that it was me who set you up with her in the first place. I don't know who's the most pathetic, you or me.'

Joel's frown deepened. 'You set me up with her? And you were so sure that I would shag her, were you?'

Candy snorted. 'What man wouldn't? Let me see if I can think of a few reasons why.' She continued sarcastically, 'Oh yeah, she's blonde, she's skinny, she's got legs up to her armpits, cheekbones that could dice salad and oh, oh, oh let's not forget her show-stopping, main-event-of-the-evening breasts, shall we? Or was it just the red leather cat-suit that unzipped your pecker? Or maybe you just closed your eyes and got turned on by her fake Australian accent?'

Joel appeared totally gobsmacked, he could only utter one word, 'Monique?'

She elbowed him in the ribs. 'Well who the hell did you think I was talking about? Nora Rickety Legs Batty?'

Now it was Joel who needed some space to think, which was a bit difficult up here. A seagull crapped by his foot and normally that would have kept him laughing for most of the day, but right now, he was in enough shit of his own. Monique, out of pure evil revenge, had obviously told Candy that they had slept together. The phone calls to Cornwall on his mobile suddenly made sense. The bizarre evening on Brent's thirtieth birthday, was also making sense, how Monique had known his surname, virtually thrown herself at him, and then became nasty when things didn't go her way. But why would Candy set him up? Surely not just to catch him out. By implication that would infer that she didn't trust him. Now what in God's name had he done to have brought distrust into their relationship?

Apart from sleeping with Claudia, Holly, Brandy, Melissa, Alice . . . ad infinitum.

He set about putting some wrongs to right. If Candy was under the impression that Joel was unfaithful, then at least, Joel reasoned, let it be for the right woman. He began to tell Candy all about Monique's behaviour that night and how she'd stolen his phone. How he'd turned her down. How he'd slept alone that night. Candy queried the tattoo: how had Monique known about that? Joel's reply was simple: Brent. Slowly Candy's mind was turned, but doubts still occupied a few shelves in her brain. Joel suggested that they go and confront Monique together and see if Monique could lie to his face.

'There's no way she'll be able to keep up a convincing act with me standing there,' Joel said, still looking in astonishment at the text message Monique had sent on his behalf. 'Trust me, she'll slip up or maybe she'll just admit she lied. Really, Candy, you only had to ask her what I yell out when I'm coming to know she hadn't been a mile near my bed.'

Candy smiled, then slapped her hand on her forehead. 'Avalanche! I didn't think to ask her about that.'

'Believe me now?'

And she did. But she didn't want to believe what he said next. It was like the sequel to her original nightmare, *Cheated II*. Listening to Joel endlessly use the word 'honest' as he described how he'd slept with another woman made Candy's stomach churn. 'I'm being honest, here, Candy.' 'I'm only saying this because I think it's the honest thing to do.' Well, he didn't think too much about honesty when he was sticking his dick in another woman, did he? Candy asked him if Zarleena meant anything to him. Or was she just *another* HONEST one-night stand?

'She meant nothing,' Joel responded. 'Just a few hours of pleasure, that's all. Nothing to write home about.'

Now Candy had begun the dig, she plunged her spade in deeper. 'So, while you were screwing this woman, did you ever stop at any point and wonder about me? About us? Was there not a voice in your head explaining that what you were doing was wrong? That you had a fiancée? That you had plans for a family? A wedding?' Joel tried to take her hand but she slapped it away. 'Don't touch me.' She glared angrily out to the ocean. 'You don't get it, do you, Joel? I really loved you. Do you know what it's like for me when a female climber, who I've never seen before in my entire life, comes up to me on one of my trips and says, with a knowing, smug look, "Oh, you're Joel's girlfriend, aren't you?" And I smile, but deep down I wonder: is that another slag that you've screwed? Is that another woman Joel has kept secret from me? And you hear about these women who keep giving their womanizing men another chance. That was me, Joel, always loving you too much to be able to say goodbye. Well, not any more.' Tears streamed down her face and this time she couldn't slap Joel's hand away. Her eyes stared into his. 'I don't want to end this, I really don't. I don't think I can be without you. So that leaves me fucked, doesn't it?'

Joel put his arm around her and she dropped her head to his shoulder. 'Love Hurts' is a song by the Everly Brothers, and it was mainly men doing the hurting, Joel guessed. To know that he was the culprit of inflicting so much pain and hurt on Candy demoted Joel from a kind man to a demon. A man was supposed to live in harmony with his lover not harm her. Joel could sense that even after his latest screw-up, Candy was willing to forgive him. He had to ask himself the question: if he did stay with her, would he cheat on her again? A horn from a ship echoed across the water sending a thousand sea birds skyward. Joel pulled Candy tighter into his body. How could he have ever cheated on her in the first place? The only fault he could find with her, paradoxically, was that she forgave him too easily for sleeping around. Which begged the question: did he only sleep around because he knew he would get away with it? If that was the case then his demonic status had just been demoted to scum. And surely, Candy deserved better than scum.

'Candy, I love you too much to keep hurting you this way.' He laughed weakly at the ridiculousness of his comment. 'I've brought you down to the level where you needed to test my fidelity with Monique. I have cut the only bond that keeps relationships together. Trust. Because of *me* trust is an eight-lettered word. Distrust. Because of *me* you're crying. Because of *me* our future together, which once looked so bright, is snuffed out. I'm not a very nice *me*, am I? You deserve better.' He took in a clean breath of salty sea air and closed his eyes. 'Candy, I want you to dump me now. End this. And if you don't, then I have no choice and will have to end it myself.' He kissed her on the cheek. 'I can't keep hurting you. If someone else were to have treated you like I have, I would have throttled him. Please end it.'

'But I can't.'

After descending the cliff, taking the steep climb towards home, Joel and Candy stood before Joel's Range Rover parked outside the flat. The entire walk up here had been conducted in silence. Thoughts and memories stewed with ideas and questions. Why would two people so terribly in love contemplate splitting without one more go at it? Because, Candy reasoned, one of them was more terribly in love than the other. And if a partnership is to work smoothly, love has got to be equal. Joel wrapped his arms around Candy and hugged her as if this was his last cuddle.

'I'm going to count backwards from ten to one,' Joel stated, pulling away from her. 'If by the time I reach one, you haven't dumped me, then consider yourself dumped at zero.'

Candy sobbed. 'I won't do it.'

'Ten . . . nine . . . eight . . .'

She cut in. 'You're dumped!' And to solidify the agreement they both fell into another hug, trying desperately, but unsuccessfully, to stave off the tears.

So Joel was no longer a 'dumped' virgin. It was the first time in his life that a woman had given him the elbow and if he were to be 'honest' with himself, it felt quite shitty. He hadn't cried this much since finding out George Mallory didn't make the summit of Everest, but the tears felt apt. He, too, hadn't made the summit – the summit of the greatest mountain everyone is vying for. The peak of happiness.

Sara watched the two from the window as they cried into each other's arms, wondering if Candy had dropped the bombshell yet. She stared over at the Clearblue pregnancy test that Candy had taken before her escape to the beach. She worried for her best friend. The Clearblue test was positive and confirmed that Candy was carrying Joel's baby.

But nothing was really clear any more – she was positive about that.

From the fridge in the boot of his car, Joel removed two tins of cold Red Bull. They toasted each other's future and wished for the best that life could bring. It was hardly champagne, but then again it was hardly a celebration either.

'To us meeting up on a mountain one day.' Joel tapped his can to hers. 'Maybe you'll save *my* life this time.'

She looked directly into his eyes. 'As if you'd let someone save you. You'd rather die than have that embarrassment.'

Joel connected with Candy's tear-filled eyes. Would he ever find another woman who knew him as well as she did? He doubted it.

Chapter Thirty

Armin, dressed from head to toe in slimming black, smiled down at the duffel bag in the passenger seat of his car. He had proof in there that showed beyond doubt that India was better than Britain. That Indian men were better than white men. No lawyer in the land could dispute his evidence. It was irrefutable.

It was 4.05 p.m. on Thursday, and slightly worrying to Armin was that Honey hadn't left Bindis & Brides yet for her daily trip to the Post Office. Today was a tight schedule; five minutes wasted here might have a knock-on effect that could put paid to his plans for later. And he'd been looking forward to payback on Joel for too long now to have to reschedule. The High Street was hectic with the chaos of commerce. Nothing like the bubbling bazaars of an Indian town, but plenty busy all the same. Armin remembered his visits to India with joy. Relatives over there treated him with R-E-S-P-E-C-T. He'd shown them glossy photos of cars in car showrooms and pretended they were his. A postcard of Knebworth House was boasted of as his 'holiday home'. Yachts. Helicopters. Horses. A picture of South Fork Ranch from the series *Dallas* was his country estate; the men in the picture, one who looked like JR standing next to the other who looked like Bobby Ewing, were in fact just two of his many white servants. Oh, yeah, Armin was well respected in India.

It was just the bastards in this country who treated him with contempt.

Finally, at 4.15 p.m., Honey, laden down with packages, barged from the shop and up the street. He'd give it a minute, enough time to play air *bhangra* drums for a few beats. Enough time to rinse the smile off his face. God, revenge was *laddoo* sweet sometimes.

With the bag slung over his shoulder, Armin crossed the road and entered Bindis & Brides. Walking to the far corner, politely greeting the customers with '*Namaste*' en route, Armin pulled from his duffel bag a pair of heavy-duty wire cutters and nonchalantly snipped straight through the CCTV camera's wire. Without acknowledging a flabbergasted Zarleena, he walked straight to the opposite corner, humming along to the *sitar* music, and repeated the process. The shop, for all intents and purposes, was now only being watched by the occupants. Which was his next job. To get rid of them.

He made a beeline for Zarleena, stopping just by the counter. He spoke clearly but quietly, 'If you don't want any harm to come to Honey, then I suggest you do as I say. She's being kept against her will in my car as we speak. Get shot of these customers and lock the front door. I want to talk to you in private.' He fished out a fiver from his pocket and stuffed it in the ASIAN WOMEN'S HOSTEL charity box. 'Move it.'

With no choice but to follow orders, a petrified Zarleena asked the customers to leave, explaining that the man who had just entered was a security assessment officer who wished to fully check the electrics in the shop. No sari was worth getting electrocuted over. The customers reluctantly complied, leaving Zarleena alone with Armin, wondering what was hidden in his bag. Something was telling her that it wasn't divorce papers.

Armin glanced at his watch: 4.25 p.m. He had less than fifteen minutes to wreck Zarleena's life: $\frac{1}{4}$ of an hour to make her wish she'd never been born; $\frac{1}{96}$ of a day wondering how she got herself in this mess; $\frac{1}{672}$ of a week believing that . . . he checked his watch again. Oh my God, he worried; he'd just wasted another minute working all this out.

Strike One.

He struck Zarleena full across the face with the palm of his hand and she gasped in pain. 'I asked you a simple thing: to get me £20,000. But you had to kick up a huge fuss about it, didn't you? Bringing in the white man. Pleading help from the white man. What is it with you, Zarleena, isn't brown good enough for you any more?' He glared contemptuously at her quaking body. 'Stings, doesn't it, when someone turns against you? Just like you turned against the Indian race with Joel Winters.' The anger in his eyes was hewn from deep shame. 'I know all about Joel Winters, believe you me, I know all about him. He's from the same mould as a magpie. Stealing what isn't his. Stealing our Indian women. That's what he is, a thief. You would rather make love to a white thief than your own Indian husband.' He saw confusion across her face. 'Don't think I don't know all about the affair you had with Joel Winters while we were married. Everyone is talking about it. No one is on your side any more.'

Before Zarleena could manipulate the information she'd just received into some sort of sense, Armin was busy emptying the contents of his duffel bag onto the counter top. Like a man possessed he laid out small jars of colourful Indian spices next to each other. Turmeric, cumin, garam masala, chilli powder, coriander powder, fenugreek, fennel seeds, mustard seeds, cassia bark, curry leaves, bay leaves, dried mint, garlic powder and cardamoms. Enough to keep an Indian chef happy.

'I will prove to you that Indian men are better than English men. Take a good look at the spices that you see before you, Zarleena. And that's not even a quarter of the spices that I could have displayed. These spices represent India, our motherland. Varied, full of flavour, reliable, robust, enjoyable Indian spices.' He paused while he picked up the duffel bag again. 'And now let us see what English men have got to offer, shall we? Let's see how varied and full of flavour the English spices are.' He dipped his hand in the bag and rummaged around for a second or so. Then he pulled out a small green plant. 'Flat-leafed parsley! Flat just like their men! Is this all the English man can offer?' He slapped the sad-looking limp parsley on the counter. 'It leaves little doubt as to who the masters of this world are. I can't think of a good curry that can be cooked with parsley, can you?' He checked his watch again. 'We've just got enough time.'

Zarleena felt the cold nails of fear scrape down her spine. 'Time for what?'

'Well,' Armin smiled, grabbing her arm tightly. 'Time for me to have my wicked way with you, of course.' He began to shove her forward, battling against her struggles, enforcing his weight upon her. 'Let's see if I can flush that white man's seed out of you.'

He roughly pushed her into the changing room. One mirror, one wooden bench, one curtain, one framed picture of Durga, the Warrior Goddess, one frightened Indian woman and one perversely excited Indian man. Once a dressing room for wedding saris and sparkling *shalwar kameezes*, now a cubicle of terror. It was the devil's version of *Changing Rooms*. It was Zarleena's version of hell.

'Take all your clothes off or Honey gets it next,' Armin said robotically, unzipping his trousers with one hand, holding a condom with the other. 'And get a move on, wife, we haven't got time for foreplay.' He rolled on the condom. 'This is for *my* protection. I don't know what diseases you might have caught off the white man, the *gorah*.'

Zarleena knew that in times of war, spies had a cyanide capsule in the mouth to bite on to kill themselves when under interrogation, to prevent the enemy torturing secret information from them. If only she had a capsule right now, she thought, as Armin began his torture. She shut her eyes, trying to cram a happy scene in her mind, desperate to block out reality. But would she have bit that capsule if she had one here now? Would she have thrown away her life so easily? The stink of his Joop aftershave would always smell like rape to her now. The sounds of the *sitar* in the shop's background would always sound like rape to her now.

The feel of another man inside her ... would that always feel like rape to her now? Zarleena forbid her tears to fall, she screamed internally for her inner strength to prevail, she spoke to God and pleaded with him to take this moment away. Armin was determined to hurt her with his thrusts, throwing his power into every motion. But Zarleena's refusal to moan, to whimper, to even acknowledge that something was happening, was beginning to dampen Armin's enjoyment. His wife, his piece of meat, his property was behaving like he didn't even exist. And he didn't. *Armin might be raping my body*, Zarleena thought adamantly, *but there's no way he will rape my mind*.

Contorted with frustration and twisted with anger, Armin punched Zarleena in the face, ordering her to relax; her frigid body was ruining the festivities. But the pain bounced right off Zarleena's skin. Even though forced to accept that Armin was attacking her, even though she should have been down in the depths of human despair, Zarleena's mood was triumphant; Armin wasn't mentally beating her today. He might have been raping her, abusing her, even assaulting her, but there was no way he was winning.

The sexual abuse ended at last, and with a final jab into Zarleena, Armin was done.

'That was a crap shag,' he said, sneering, as he yanked up his trousers. 'Joel's welcome to you. You put *no* effort into that whatsoever.'

He watched as a bruised Zarleena awkwardly got dressed into her lavender-coloured *shalwar kameez*. Fascinating to Armin was how much she seemed to have aged in the last ten minutes. And God, did she look sulky; he was glad he didn't have to come home to that everyday any more. He went on to explain that she still owed him £19,000 which she could pay off in instalments. Likewise, today was just the first instalment of her nightmare, if she refused to pay. He told her that he would be in touch soon.

He lumbered over to the counter, opened the till and emptied the contents into his duffel bag, stole the ASIAN WOMEN'S HOSTEL charity box, then added in the spices.

'Namaste, wife,' Armin shouted as he exited the shop. 'India rules. I'll let Honey go immediately.'

He glanced at his watch: 4.50 p.m. He had less than ten minutes to reach Forest Falls Apartments, the home of his arch-enemy, Joel Winters.

Even though Zarleena had been a member since her marriage to Armin, today she was reacquainted with the 'invisible' club. A club that is full of Indian women who have suffered at the hands of their husbands but who, when they go to report the incident to their elders, cannot be heard. Nobody can hear them. Nobody can see them. In fact, the club should be called the 'nonexistent' club, because nobody wants to know an Indian woman who claims to have been raped by an Indian man. Indian men don't do that sort of thing. Rape and abuse don't exist inside an Indian household. It's a subject that leaves Indians frowning so hard you would think they'd looked directly at the sun. Maybe they have, maybe that's why they're blind to it.

After locking the shop door and displaying the CLOSED sign, Zarleena stared at her invisible self in the hand mirror and touched the invisible bruise that now throbbed from her cheek and eye. It was important that no one got to see this. Especially not Honey. She painfully applied the masking make-up and hoped that the Maybelline foundation *did* look like she was born with it. Her eyes flickered to and from the phone, wondering if she should just pick up and dial 999. Her mind at that moment was a hotbed of misery, hurt, pain and betrayal. If all men on the planet just keeled over and died right then (except her dad, of course) she would have clapped her hands in joy. If they're not hurting people then they're apologizing for hurting people. It's an endless whirlwind of misery that sucks in innocent women wherever it turns. NO MORE. Zarleena had had enough. First there was Violent Armin then there was User Joel. Third time lucky didn't compute to her brain right now. More like third time unlucky for the man in question as he watched his hacked-off balls flying through the air.

To dial 999 seemed so easy, the phone was almost crying out to be picked up. Speak to officer, have medical examination, make statement, go to court, have personality ripped to shreds by lawyers, have personal life put on show for all and sundry, have meagre chance of getting conviction because no one believes wives get raped by husbands, then hide from all relatives for mentioning the invisible taboo, 'Rape'. Indian women don't get raped.

Oh, yeah, 999 was a piece of piss. A bit like the tea they serve you whilst waiting for the police officer to call in the psychiatrist.

But what about User Joel – ignoring he was a man for one second – couldn't she call upon her knight in shining armour to sort Armin out a second time? He did say, 'If you do hear from Armin again, then ring me.' Zarleena smiled at the futility of even contemplating going down that decrepit road. What could Joel do this time? Kill him? No, Joel was as untouchable to her right now as a *hari-jan*. Besides, it had been three weeks and one day since their last contact. The lines of communication were now closed. She was on her own. He'd fucked her and used her just like Armin had.

A bang on the shop window snatched Zarleena's attention. Anxious Honey mouthed, 'Open up,' and Zarleena briskly walked down the floor to let her in. Mindful of her sister's propensity to explode over matters regarding women's rights, it was of grave importance that Zarleena explained today's revolting occurrence gradually. If she waded right in and mentioned what Armin had done, there was no telling what Honey might do; the headlines in the morning paper might read: SISTER BRUTALLY MURDERS BROTHER-IN-LAW IN ACT OF REVENGE. Or, HONOUR KILLING MAKES HISTORY – THIS TIME VICTIM IS A MAN. And if it were the *Sun* it might read something like, MODEL JORDAN BUYS NEW BIKINI. Whatever, Zarleena didn't wish prison on her sister.

Honey entered and blinked hard at the sight of Zarleena. Within a microsecond the screenplay to Zarleena's last half an hour seemed to translate across to Honey's senses. Without a word from Zarleena, Honey knew Armin had been, Armin had hurt and now Armin was gone. The only question was: how much of her sister had Armin taken away with him?

'I'm okay, really I am,' Zarleena divulged. 'Nothing a good bottle of wine wouldn't . . .' And then her tears crashed out. Wave after wave of sadness. It was a good few minutes before Zarleena could say the words, 'He raped me.' To which Honey had no answers, just a shoulder for Zarleena to cry on and a listening ear to bash.

Eloise sat on her rolled-up yoga mat on the grass outside Forest Falls Apartments, waiting for her 5 p.m. taxi. It was nice to escape from the rowdy penthouse today; Danny, her nephew, had invited himself over this afternoon to ask 'Uncle Joel' his advice on a few things regarding mountaineering, equipment and knots. Eloise was pleased to have another face in the place as Joel's face was a disgrace in her space. He'd been moping around since Monday night, after his so-called split with Candy. She couldn't take this too seriously though; they'd get back together, they were made for each other. A car horn grabbed her attention. The taxi was here.

'Where to?' the driver asked as Eloise climbed in the back seat.

She gave him the address of the leisure centre and watched out of the window as the apartments disappeared from view. Most taxis smelled of fags, this one smelled of aftershave; Eloise approved. Since taking up yoga classes two weeks or so ago, the benefits of a healthier lifestyle were becoming more blatant by the day. It was doing no end of good to her unborn phantom baby. And if she had to give her phantom baby a name it would be 'Saviour' because, since mentioning the pregnancy, Joel had lain right off the pressure about her having to find a job. She'd formed a strategy to keep the pretence up as long as possible, even going so far as to borrow a friend's scan picture to show Joel when the time came. 'If you look carefully, Joel, you can just make out its cute little hands. They look like climber's hands to me.' Oh yeah, she had it all worked out.

Except for the actual birth that is. But she was working on that.

Her eyes caught sight of a ramshackle factory she'd never seen before. She focused harder, and sure enough they were in the old, deserted industrial estate on the edge of Hunterslea, a run-down area that she'd only seen on the local news when drug addicts had ODed on crack. The driver was obviously going the wrong way. She looked to see how much he'd charged so far, expecting to see it clocked too high, but the meter was missing. And it was her heart that was charging too much at the moment. Two hundred heartbeats per minute and counting. Something was very wrong about this taxi ride – she could feel it.

Trembling, Eloise rummaged around in her Prada bag and pulled out her mobile, quietly padding in Joel's number. Please answer quickly she prayed, please!

'No signal here, Eloise,' Armin said, checking her through the rear-view mirror. 'No signal and no people.' He turned up the volume to his *bhangra* CD and tapped along with his fingers on the steering wheel. The vehicle rocked on the suspension as the wheels drove over the uneven road. 'And just in case you were thinking of diving out of the moving car, I've activated the child locks. White Trash.' He revved up the engine and shot forward. 'And remember, kiddie –' he spun the car round, bringing it to a violent stop, knocking Eloise's head against the window – 'always drive with a seatbelt on.' Annoyingly, he continued to thrash the accelerator.

Eloise was about to crap herself when she spotted the condoms on the dashboard. If she was going to be molested then she didn't want messy knickers. The thought didn't cheer her up like she imagined it might.

'You can't have sex with me, I'm pregnant. I haven't even seen your face so just let me go and I swear I won't call the police,' she pleaded above the roar of a badly cooked engine.

Armin had been waiting to say this sentence for years, ever since watching *The Sweeny* as a boy: 'You don't have to call the police, I *am* the police.'

Like a dam giving way, Eloise's tears broke. The works. Sobbing, sniffing, squealing, uncontrollable panting. A tearful outburst quite unlike anything Armin had witnessed before. Apart from, possibly, the day Pakistan announced it had developed a nuclear bomb, whereupon his own mother beat herself repeatedly over the head with a colander, screaming in Hindi, 'We're doomed, Pakistan will obliterate India.' He would handle Eloise the same way as he'd handled his mother.

And it began like this: 'SHUT UP WILL YOU, WOMAN!' He hadn't followed Eloise's movements for the last week, noting her comings and goings to and from her apartment, suffering in the buckling heat, just so he could be eligible for a hearing aid by the time the day was finished. Still she hollered like the insane. Christ, Armin fumed inside, where did she learn to scream like that? A Duran Duran concert? He slammed his hand on the car hooter until Eloise's decibels became just a sniffling whimper.

'Before you criticize my driving you should see how crap I am at hairdressing,' he said, climbing out of the driver's seat and opening the back door. 'Get out!'

Armin took hold of her wrist and yanked her to the front of the car where he shoved her hard against the bonnet. Each noise was exaggerated by the desolation of the place, echoing across the run-down landscape. Even the screech of Eloise's personal attack alarm would probably get swallowed up by the silence here (not that she would get the chance to try it, as she'd spent the battery money Joel had given her for it on a Rimmel nail polish no. 307, Grape Sorbet). Armin stared distastefully at his captured prey. She who dressed like a slut shall be treated like a slut.

'It might please you to know that you revolt me, so I won't be sexually abusing you today,' Armin stated, pulling away, confident that she was too frightened to make a run for it. He proceeded to open his duffel bag. 'But don't take it too personally: all white people revolt me. You think the world belongs to you. You think that you invented civilized living. You change the history books to suit yourselves. You understand little of honour.' With a flash of sunlight on metal, Armin produced a large pair of fabric scissors and began snapping them inches away from Eloise's terrified face, while he shouted, 'IT'S TIME FOR YOU TO ATONE FOR YOUR BROTHER'S SINS.'

Eloise pushed back against the immovable car, trying to create some space between the gnashing blades and her face. She hoped her kidnapper's actions didn't speak louder than his words. It was at this moment, as the glint in her kidnapper's eyes matched the glint of the cutting edge, that Eloise wished she'd joined the self-defence class instead of yoga. She doubted that the lotus position would inflict much damage on this man, no matter how much spiritual energy she put into it.

'I'm just going to cut you a bit and see how it looks,' Armin mentioned casually, grabbing hold of her neck with one hand and bringing the scissors in closer with the other. 'Struggle too hard and you'll lose an eye.'

She closed her eyes and began to pray. 'Dear Lord, I promise that I will never steal from my brother's wallet again. I promise you that I will come clean about the baby. I promise that—'

Armin interrupted, 'Have you quite finished, White Trash?' And she had.

Strike Two.

Almost immediately, Armin plunged the blades deep into the thick of Eloise's glossy hair, and set about hacking away indiscriminately, sending bundles of beautiful long, brown locks to the dirty gravel below. Her neck held viciously with an unsympathetic grip, Eloise's head movements were kept to the minimum. Hack. Hack. Hack. Edward Scissorhands would have been proud. Hack. Hack. Hack. Armin's hairdressing gossip repertoire was limited to 'Keep still, Bitch!' Hack. Hack. Hack. Armin admired his masterpiece. Not bad for his first attempt. Obviously nothing like a Meg Ryan or a Jennifer Aniston style, more like the village idiot's, but, no, it wasn't bad. It was TERRIBLE.

Armin released his grip from Eloise's neck. 'Tell your interfering brother, Joel, that next time it won't be your hair that I cut.' He prodded her forehead hard with his finger. 'It will be your throat. Tell him to stay well away from Zarleena, my wife. Tell him that this is his very last chance and if he messes up again I will have him killed. There'll be no getting away. I think it was Gandhi who said, "Only a tree can hide in a wood".' He paused. 'Or was that Bambi? Anyway, he can't hide from me, he is the hunted and I am the hunter. When India knocks, you answer the door. Now be on your way.' He aggressively pushed her onto the road. 'White Trash.'

After whipping off the magnetic LIGHTNING TAXI stickers from the car doors, Armin tossed them in the back seat to join Eloise's bag, yoga mat, and mobile phone, and skidded away leaving his victim in a plume of dust. If Armin's face had gears for smiling, it was in top right now, speeding along at 120 m.p.h., congratulating himself on today's success. Two strikes. First Zarleena and then Joel via Eloise. Perfect.

He was sure from now on that when the Great Armin talked people would listen.

387

Chapter Thirty-one

Danny, Joel's nephew, knelt down and generously sprayed deodorant under Uncle Joel's armpits; an act of self-preservation that should have been done an hour ago. BO was an act of violence as far as Danny was concerned and it had to be crushed from existence before it became uncontrollable. Men sweat through fear, pain, exhaustion, worry, panic, excitement and even when they're . . .

'HOT!' Joel repeated for the umpteenth time. 'I'm too fucking hot for this shit, Danny, now untie me.'

Danny pointed out that the air-conditioning was on full, and maybe Joel was suffering from hallucinations; he then counted up the knots that were keeping Uncle Joel tied to the chair. Not including the knots tying the chair to the kitchen island, Danny calculated sixty. Slip knots. Reef knots. Marline Spike Hitch knots. Sheetbend knots. Fisherman's knots. Clove Hitch knots. Triple Bowline knots. The Danny Knot. His joke, 'How much do you like knots, Uncle Joel? A lot or KNOT a lot?' was losing its ability to make Joel laugh any more. What had started, three hours ago, as an innocent lesson in mountaineering survival, had turned into an unpleasant evening of escapology.

'If you don't know how to untie me, Danny, then just use a knife to cut the ropes. I need to take a piss.' Joel was tired of the game.

'You told me, Uncle Joel, that a good mountaineer never, EVER cuts the rope of his climbing partner. It's a rule made in granite, you said. NEVER EVER EVER cut the rope. I'm only listening to the words of the master. So hang on and I'll get you a bucket to wee in.' Danny ducked from view and rummaged around in the cupboard under the sink. 'What about an old fish bowl, can you piss in that?' He stood up and helped himself to another cold can from the fridge. 'Good stuff this, Uncle Joel, real good.' He took another gulp. 'I'll tell you what this is, Uncle Joel, this Red Bull is very cooling.'

'I wouldn't know about that, would I? Because Edmund Hillary won't allow his Sherpa to have any, will he? Now, please, I'm begging you, untie me.'

'I'll call Base Camp and ask their advice.' He picked up Joel's mobile phone.

'For fuck's sake, Danny.' Joel shook his head. 'And where is this Base Camp you keep mentioning? *Yellow Pages*?'

'You're delirious, I think it's altitude sickness, AMS; hang on in there, Uncle Joel, I'll have a chopper up here in a jiffy.'

'FUCK OFF!' Joel's patience was slipping.

'It's your lungs filling up with water, that's all. You'll be dead within a few hours if I don't get help swiftly.'

Joel's head sank in resignation. He now knew why his brother, Dylan, was on Valium. He looked at the clock. It was nearly 8 p.m. Nearly time for his quarter-hourly ice down the back of his T-shirt. Every fifteen minutes since this charade had begun Danny had been stuffing ice from the freezer down Joel's back. Authenticity was his word of the moment. And in Danny's expert opinion, realism was paramount if one wanted to train for Everest in a kitchen; hence the air-conditioning on full blast. Hence the green First Aid box, the polar bear cuddly toy, a slab of Kendal Mint Cake. Hence the selection of large framed photos of mountains that Danny – who could pronounce them all perfectly in the Tibetan dialect – had removed from the walls and surrounded Joel's chair with. There was Lhoste, Cho Oyu, Makalu, K2, Dhaulagiri I, Manaslu and of course Mount Everest. Nature's skyscrapers. Some of Joel's triumphs. All of Danny's dreams.

'I was thinking about chopping my knob off, Uncle Joel,' Danny remarked, opening a kitchen drawer. 'Like those monks used to do to prove their chastity to the Lord. I want to prove my chastity to Mount Everest. Now where do you keep your sharpest knife?' He stared into Joel's unimpressed face. 'Just a joke, Uncle Joel. Lighten up would you?'

Joel examined his nephew; he seemed normal enough. Dressed like most teenagers in his over-sized Slipknot T-shirt, black baggy jeans, baseball cap and £2000 trainers. His ear, eyebrow and tongue pierced. With a padlock and chain as a belt. Just a normal, healthy teenager – who had taken his uncle hostage.

'At least you've given me the title for my next book, Danny. *How to Climb a Mountain When Tied to a Chair*. It should sell millions. Now will you please let me go before I lose my temper?' Joel's voice was weak. 'I'm begging you, please let me—'

The front door farted. Saved by the wind, Joel thought.

Danny told Joel to stay put while he saw to the visitor. There was still a lot of training to get through and he hoped that the interruption was just an interruption. He opened the door and burst out laughing. He hadn't seen anything so ridiculous in all his life. Either he'd totally lost the vibe with fashion these days, or Aunty Eloise had just turned up with the funniest-looking hairdo on the planet. He fell to the floor and held his stomach in exaggerated laughter. What a day this was turning into.

Eloise stepped over her giggling nephew and walked unsteadily into the living room to find Joel. She shouted out his name. It had been three hours since her humiliation with Armin. Too frightened even to stop at a phone box, Eloise had made the hike back, taking the open roads, avoiding eye contact with anyone. She had one thought in her tunnel vision: home was safe, get there as quickly as possible.

Home *was* safe, but where was Joel?

'I'm in here, Eloise, I need help,' Joel yelled. 'I'm trapped in the kitchen. Apparently up a mountain.'

Eloise found Joel quickly and gazed at him like a lost child. Tears streamed down her cheeks as she dropped to her knees, resting her head in his lap. If ever she needed her brother then it was now. Just give me one per cent of Joel's strength and I'll be fine, wished Eloise; he would make things better, she was sure of that.

Like a small stone hitting a car windscreen, Joel felt a tiny crack appear in his heart. His baby sister had been hurt by someone, each tear bore witness to the crime. Joel felt the crack deepen as he saw the hand mark on her neck, the bruising signature of a ruthless man, and he breathed in deeply to control his inner anger. Joel nodded to Danny who quietly began to untie his uncle. The Everest expedition was over. This was now a rescue mission. After setting Joel free, Danny disappeared to Joel's bedroom, dragging the fifty metres of fluorescent-pink rope behind him.

The two hugged tightly, Joel consoling Eloise, her tears in constant freefall. His job was to protect his sister from the bad men in this world, the depraved men who walked the streets in disguise. He'd told his parents that they had nothing to fear by living in Florida as he would keep his sister safe. Now it seemed that he'd sent his parents away on the basis of a lie. Eloise had been harmed today, that was for sure, but who had harmed her – and why? And more importantly: what form did the harm take? Joel was almost afraid to ask in case she mentioned the 'R' word. Rape.

After a while, with a glass of wine in her hand, Eloise found the courage to explain what had happened with Armin. Joel listened as she struggled to convey her feelings. How at one point she thought Armin was going to rape her, then kill her. At another point she worried he was going to slash her face. How, after facing those two possibilities, his haircut from hell seemed trivial. Almost a relief. Life seemed very precious right now.

Joel regarded Armin's latest move with an amount of unease. There was nothing new or clever in attacking an enemy's loved ones in revenge. The Mafia had been doing it for decades. Was Armin a Don from an Indian cartel? Would Joel be sleeping with the *tandoori* fish? And what made Armin so sure that Joel wouldn't retaliate? It was a risky gamble. Or, Joel considered, it was a risky bluff. He ran a bubble bath for Eloise and pored over his thoughts some more while she soaked. Why was Armin confident that the police wouldn't be called? Did he rightly assume that Joel would prefer to sort this one out on his own rather than involve the cops? Now Joel really was panicking. If that was the case, what did Armin have in store for him when the time came for retaliation? Death? Surely Armin couldn't have planned his retribution that well; even Garry Kasparov couldn't think that many moves ahead.

Danny entered the living room holding two pillows; he set them down on the sofa, then disappeared again to return with a duvet and plonked it by the pillows. Joel, watched, amazed, as his nephew tucked himself under the duvet and closed his eyes. He guessed Danny was staying the night.

'Before you fall asleep and dream of Everest, Danny, I need you to keep an eye on Eloise while I pop out for half an hour or so.' He kept his voice low. 'You know that fucker stole her handbag, don't you?' Danny nodded. 'Well, her house keys were in there. She's petrified that he'll come looking for her again. I want you to bolt the door behind me and I'll have an extra word with security downstairs. I don't believe he'd be foolish enough to turn up, but best safe than sorry.' Joel picked up his car keys. 'One more thing, I'd rather you didn't tell your father about any of this for now. Which reminds me, you'd better phone and ask him if staying here tonight is okay.'

'Understood, Uncle Joel.' He switched on MTV and flopped onto the vibrating chair. 'Fetch us a kebab on the way back, would you?'

After explaining to Eloise that he would be back shortly, Joel left the apartment, got in his Range Rover and headed for Bindis & Brides. He *had* to speak with Zarleena. There was a monkey throwing coconuts at his life and he needed to know how to shake the monkey out of the tree.

Zarleena could think of only one good thing that came from her rape today and that was statistics. Statistically, in Britain, 167 women are raped a day, which would mean that one less woman would have to go through what she did . . . until tomorrow. Which suddenly didn't make her feel so good. After taking her fourth bath, she'd resigned herself to the fact that washing an unwanted man's presence off her body was harder than washing off henna. Nigh on impossible.

It was difficult to feel feminine when someone had just stolen the woman from you, but Zarleena tried her best to get back to normal. With hair still soaked, and skin smelling of Dettol, she dressed in a pair of pink tracksuit bottoms and a tight white vest. She would have to make a compromise with reality for the time being. The bruises on her arms would be tattoos for now. And the black eye was just a mistake with her make-up. The pain in her pelvis was because she'd held her bladder too long. And the feeling of inadequacy was brought on by a sugar rush after eating five bars of chocolate, straight. Maybe, tomorrow, when the morning sunshine came through her bedroom window, she'd let the reality in with it. But until then, she would bury her pain.

Honey flicked in another CD, Robbie William's *Escapology*, and rejoined Zarleena on the sofa. Honey's vision of helping the world solve its problems seemed pretty hopeless when she couldn't even help her own sister solve hers. But how could she even begin to help her when suddenly Zarleena had changed her mind about what had happened today, refusing to admit that Armin had *really* raped her? Just because he was her husband. Just because he had done this sort of thing a hundred times before when they were married. Just because she hadn't reported it to the police. Just because . . .

'IT IS STILL RAPE!' Honey had screamed. 'HE FORCED HIMSELF UPON YOU!'

Honey's frustration, along with every other negative emotion, was directed at Armin. How could a man reduce a woman's self-esteem to the point that, when she is sexually abused, she can almost shrug it off and say, 'That's what I expected from him'? Why were so many women forced to live in fear of the men who placed the wedding rings on their fingers? Honey was well aware of the figures that shocked most people when they heard them. How on average two women a week in this country alone are killed by a current or former partner. How only three out of every one hundred domestic violence cases reach a conviction. How every single minute of every single day a woman reports an act of domestic violence. All these facts seemed to betray Honey's belief that women were not the weaker sex. Maybe it was time women started following the Williams sisters' diet? Or alternatively bring back castration and watch the re-offenders' list shrink (like their manhood).

Not happy with shocking Honey just the once, Zarleena decided that now was the time to come clean about everything. The dirty photographs, Armin's bribes and Joel's involvement. Things were getting out of, as an octopus might say, hand, hand, hand, hand, hand, hand, hand, hand. It was imperative from this moment on that Zarleena was totally honest with her sister. Their only chance of ungluing Armin's plans would be if they stuck together.

'As a last resort we can get a loan and pay Armin off, £19,000 is definitely within our capabilities,' Zarleena said, scribbling down her calculations on a notepad. '"There's your money, Arsehole, now fuck off out of our lives." It would be worth it.'

Honey wasn't convinced. 'And what if he comes back and asks for more? Once he's received his money he'll get a taste for it. We'll never get shot of him after that. No, we have to come up with something better. Besides, we can't give in to him. Not after what he did.'

With the light failing outside, Zarleena lit a couple of scented candles and set them on the coffee table, almost relieved to hide her bruised face away in the shadows. She tapped her pen along to Robbie Williams, who was still bashing out hits on the stereo. Orangeina blissfully blew bubbles in his bowl; if Robbie wanted advice on scales then fish were the best to ask. The two sisters continued to discuss their options until they seemed to have none left. Both were convinced that phoning the police would only cause more grief in the long run. As would explaining everything to their parents. They didn't have any 'hard' friends who they could rely on to scare Armin off. And Zarleena didn't know of anything that she could turn the tables on Armin with, for example, a picture of him shagging a sheep in stilettos. There was nothing left to do except worry.

And panic.

And agonize.

And fret.

There was a knock at the door.

And shit their pants.

Zarleena checked the video clock: 22.18, it was late. They both asked the stupid question, 'Who's that?' then crept to the kitchen drawer where the carving knives were kept. Another knock had the pair holding each other's arms and shaking as if they were connected to the electricity mains. It had to be Armin. Quickly they made a plan. They would answer the door together, holding a knife each. They would then stab Armin in his cold heart. Phone the police. And spend the rest of their lives in prison eating gruel and water.

They agreed to open the door on the count of three. Quietly Zarleena counted, 'One . . . two . . . three,' and aggressively yanked it inwards. Two blades shot forward, landing just short of Joel's chest. Joel fell backwards, landing just short of cracking his skull on the metal railings. And the girls stopped just short of screaming.

'Oh, my God, are you all right?' Ignoring the pain from her bruises, Zarleena flew out of the doorway and crouched over Joel, any bad feelings towards him dismissed instantly. 'Talk to me.' She turned to Honey. 'If he speaks with a slur then we've given him brain damage.' Zarleena turned back to Joel and took his hand. 'Stay with us, Joel, Honey is going to phone for an ambulance.'

He sat up. 'Just get me a Red Bull.'

The girls heaved him to his feet and, taking an arm each, they helped him to the living room, depositing him on the sofa. He requested that they turn off Robbie Williams – he'd never recover otherwise – and they obliged. Anything else, sir? And they couldn't believe the list he came up with. A home-cooked Indian meal. Two tubes of salt and vinegar Pringles. A full body massage. Goldfish on toast. Even a knighthood. Sir. The relief of the visitor being Joel and not Armin was so intense that Joel could have asked for a blow job now and had a good chance of getting one.

Joel waited for his blurred vision to clear before he spoke. 'Quite a way to greet people,' he remarked, munching on his cream cheese and salmon bagel, as he lay back on the sofa. 'Ever thought about getting a peephole fitted? Just in case you happen to slice up the pizza boy.'

Zarleena and Honey laughed as they sat down on the sofa-chairs. It was an awful thing for Honey to admit but she did feel safer with a man in the flat. But what was he doing here? Apart from eating all their food.

'Nice bagel?' Honey asked.

'Oh, yes please, just a small one this time,' Joel replied, wiping his mouth with a serviette.

'No, I mean is the one you're eating nice. Not would you like another nice bagel.' She glanced to Zarleena, then back to Joel. 'So, what brings you round here at this unsocial hour? Come to try your luck with my sister again, have you?'

'Honey!' Zarleena glared coldly through the dim candlelight. 'Sorry, Joel.'

The darkness was giving Honey more courage than normal so Zarleena decided to switch the main lights back on to keep her sister's mouth in check. The moment she flicked the switch, the injuries that the dark had hidden so well jumped into view. Joel grappled with what he saw. Part of Zarleena's face was buried beneath a swollen mass of bruising. The top of her arms were raw with grip marks, the calling card of a man with little regard for a woman's feelings. And her eyes, dipped in shame, lost in a nightmare, were the saddest sight of all. Joel watched, sick to the stomach, as Zarleena struggled in obvious pain just to walk back across the room. If Joel was sure about anything it was this: one man had booked his place in hell today.

'It was Armin, wasn't it?' Joel stated, sitting up and examining Zarleena's troubled face. 'This is why you had the knives at the door, isn't it?' He shook his head, feeling an anger burning like white-hot metal inside. 'He has got to be stopped.'

But how? They discussed Armin's track record and concluded that the only stop sign he'd recognize was when the doctor signed his death certificate. There didn't seem any alternative but to pay Armin his money and hope he stayed away after that. Joel explained his reason for being here, how Armin had kidnapped Eloise and chopped off her hair. He described how helpless and distraught she'd looked when she'd returned from her ordeal and how she'd believed that Armin was going to rape her. It was at that moment Honey and Zarleena's eyes sank to their feet. It was at that moment Joel knew that Zarleena had been raped.

And it was at that moment Joel realized that Armin was more devil than man. More beast than bastard. More monster than master. Joel felt the hate in himself fire up. If he had his way, Armin would soon be more dead than alive; and without another word mentioned, or another look angled his way, Joel knew that Zarleena wanted him to bring hell to Armin, just like earlier today, when he raped her, he had brought hell to her.

'It's like I'm diseased with Armin; everyone I meet gets infected with him.' Zarleena stood up and slowly walked to the curtains, peeping out to the darkened car park below. A shadow scuttled away from Joel's Range Rover, causing her to momentarily focus harder. Probably just a stray dog. Zarleena turned round and continued, 'Joel, you must have been asked the question: if you could go back and change a day in your life what day would that be?'

He nodded, uncomfortably reminiscing. 'Oh yeah, I've got quite a few. We were in this horrendous blizzard once, up Mount Cho Oya, the Goddess of Turquoise, and visibility was just about a metre in front of your face. Anyway, I told these lost climbers to "turn left for Base Camp", I meant to say "turn right", and we never saw them again.' He paused. 'No one ever saw them again.'

Honey put her fingers to her mouth to stop the giggles. She wasn't even sure if Joel was fibbing or not. But the mood was lifted – temporarily. Zarleena went on to explain that she would have thought that the day Joel would have changed would have been the day she came into his life: because ever since then she'd been nothing but trouble. And now, even his sister, Eloise, was suffering as a result of Joel's acquaintance with her. Maybe Joel should have turned 'left' down that shopping aisle in Tesco, all those weeks ago, instead of 'right', then possibly their paths might have stayed uncrossed for ever.

After a short while, and feeling about as useful as a gherkin in a Big Mac, Honey decided that she'd leave her sister and Joel alone to discuss whatever they needed to discuss. Besides, she had a new highly intelligent motif to design: KILL RAPISTS. She whispered in Zarleena's ear, 'Don't take sweets from womanizers. You can't trust him too much. Take a look at his wrists.' And she trotted off to her bedroom.

'She's got quite a loud whisper, your sister,' Joel said, eyeing his wrists. 'These aren't what you might think they are.'

'And what might I think they are?'

'Burn marks from when a trio of naked women tied me up and used my body for their pleasure?' He rubbed the rope markings. 'Well, sorry to disappoint you, but the burns are from my nephew. He's taking his headmistress hostage next term and he needed some practice on tying people up. He's a good kid really.'

The jokes were a smokescreen for more serious issues. Zarleena had her own tangle that needed untying; she just hoped that the answers Joel gave didn't give her heart their own set of rope burns. She moved next to him on the sofa, eager to display an air of confidence and maturity, keen to show him that Armin hadn't buckled her strength. Something deep within her shell wanted to like Joel again. Wanted him to break off the garland of distrust she'd placed around his neck. And replace it with a garland of ultimate friendship. Just being with Joel again, even under the ghastly circumstances they found themselves in, was as revitalizing as it was secure. Being with Joel meant being safe. And every woman she knew wanted to feel safe. To be protected. Maybe Joel was the yang to Armin's yin.

Or maybe, as Honey had warned, he was just a womanizer with lots of sweets. And what were Joel's sweets? His looks, his body, his personality, his charm, his confidence, his humour, his bravery, his sexiness and his wages. The quintessential walking sweetshop. 'Yes, can I have a quarter of orgasms, please, and a small bag of G-spot pleasure?' The best sweetshop in the world. It was time for Zarleena to use her acid-drop tongue and see if Joel could talk his way out of his sticky toffee mess. She just hoped she didn't end up with an aniseed-twist red face.

She swallowed hard, then began, 'I've been thinking about what happened between us a few weeks ago. What you did with me was very wrong. You used me for a quick shag.' She eyed Joel's surprised face. 'You slept with me while engaged to . . . is it Claudia? Or is it, like I expect it is, Candy? The tattoo on your back reads CANDY. I can't see another woman, apart from Candy, putting up with that.' She paused. 'I'm right, aren't I? You're engaged to Candy?'

Joel sat up from his lounging position. Candy was not a topic he wanted to discuss with Zarleena. Or anyone, for that matter. Their split had wounded him deeply and the feeble stitches holding him together broke easily at the thought of being without her. Forget the SMOKING KILLS campaign. Or the DON'T DRINK AND DRIVE campaign. One only had to look at Joel's sad face to see that he was the perfect advert for the DON'T CHEAT campaign. Some might even call it LOVE CANCER. But sad as Joel was with his own life, he could see a woman who seemed sadder with hers. And he was partly to blame. He should never have slept with Zarleena. Not while he was in love with Candy.

'Okay, I admit that I lied to you. Candy and I are –' he brushed his hand through the air – 'you know. I should have been upfront about that. It was wrong.' He challenged her with a stern look. 'But were you not also wrong to sleep with me knowing full well that I was engaged to another woman? It's neither here nor there what her name was. If I'm a bastard then you're a bastardess.'

Zarleena was struggling with this one. The bastard was right. They were both to blame, both as bad as each other. She wondered why Eloise hadn't told him about her visit. About the mini-confrontation in Bindis & Brides. How Joel was supposed to have a shopping list of sexual diseases (which Zarleena didn't believe for one minute) and Joel was supposed to be a father (which Zarleena didn't want to believe for one minute).

Whatever Eloise's reasons for not telling her brother, it wasn't Zarleena's job to put him straight about it. So she didn't. She had more important matters to straighten. Like, why hadn't Joel replied to her letter? Couldn't he have the decency to at least send her a text? Only feeble men hide away from their mistakes. Only heartless men leave their mistakes feeling like failures. Only cowardly men leave their failures feeling like—

'Okay, okay, look.' Joel's brain was swollen with frustration.

He went on to explain that he'd never received the letter. He'd given the envelope to Eloise for spending money while he was on a two-week working trip in New Zealand. There was no way he would have ignored Zarleena. And if it was of any consolation, he hadn't shagged another woman since that night at the end of July.

It was of no consolation. But Zarleena was deeply relieved that Joel hadn't just ignored her like she'd pre-sumed he had. It gave foundations to the feelings she wanted to build on. And, more importantly, it meant that she could now begin to like him again.

They chatted for a while about how the world was all amuck until, like a whale coming up for air, the sub-ject of Armin entered the conversation again. In fact he was part and parcel of what was wrong with the world. Zarleena wanted to know if Joel had any further thoughts on how he should be sorted out.

'You mean without a ducking stool?' He smiled, as he doodled away on Zarleena's notepad. 'I have got an idea how we could deal with him, but I'm going to need your trust on this. It's—'

A deafening squealing noise caused the two of them to jump. When Joel had had the super-alarm fitted to his Range Rover he'd requested the siren to be so loud that it would give the thief a heart attack. Not the owner. He leapt across to the window, threw aside the curtain and peered to the gloomy shadows below. He shouted to the emptiness, 'Get the fuck away from my car or I will come and chop you up with an axe! I MEAN IT!' He pulled his car keys from his pocket and pressed the fob; the noise ceased. 'Fuckers!'

He returned to his conversation, still staring out of the window. 'Leave Armin to me and I'll do everything in my power to stop him EVER causing trouble again. Just tell me you want me to do it and I'll do it.'

Zarleena was unsure. 'Do what?'

He looked into her eyes. 'Never you mind. Just think about a future without him. I'll be needing his phone number though.' Zarleena scrawled it down and handed it to him. 'And try not to worry.'

One friendly hug later and Joel was gone.

Gone leaving Zarleena looking down at what Joel had doodled on the notepad. Holy Durga, what had she let herself in for? This was definitely not the scribbling of a sane man. The first line read: DO WEEDS BLEED? SOON FIND OUT WHEN WE SNAP OFF ARMIN'S LEGS.

Her final thought of the day as she bolted the door was: what should I bring for Joel when I visit him in prison?

The small car park around the back of Bindis & Brides was dark and dingy with an orange Biffa skip tucked away in one corner. It was the perfect place for sewer rats to live or members of the BNP. As it happened, it was not the perfect place to leave one's car. Joel grimaced at his driver's door. In scruffy but legible writing someone had deeply scraped the black paintwork with the words: PAKI LOVER. The obvious handiwork of a racist, a bitter reminder that bygones could rarely be bygones in a multicultural society. Some people just refused to change with the times. When will they realize, wondered Joel, spitting with anger, that just like Saxon Britain, Tudor Britain or Victorian Britain, White Britain is a thing of the past.

Joel slipped in a Snow Patrol CD, track 1, 'How to be Dead', smoothly drove out of the car park and up the High Street until he turned into a side road leading to Apple Blossom Residential Home. Where, coincidentally, representatives of Saxon Britain still resided. He hoped that there wasn't a death there tonight; he didn't want his phone call disturbed by a hearse rushing past. With the engine switched off, Joel punched in Armin's number. It was now just gone midnight. Armin picked up on the first ring.

'Sorry to call so late,' Joel began. 'It's Joel here. I think we need to talk.'

'Well, talk!'

'I've got your money. All £19,000.'

A pause. 'It's gone up. It's thirty thousand now. This is what happens when you don't play straight with me. Some people call it "taking the piss" I call it "interest".'

Joel's eyes followed a black cat on a wall as it deftly jumped over a branch that lay across its path. Its agility was to be admired. Joel kept his voice calm and continued, 'Don't play games with me, Armin, I'm good at games. Nineteen or nothing. You can't just increase the money like that.'

'Oh, but I can when I've just increased the stakes. Think about your sister, Joel. Think about my hands as they touched her young skin. Next time who knows what I might do to her. Maybe next time I might just take a visit to Cornwall. It's amazing how much information you give away in your website. Candy sounds really SWEET.' Armin chuckled. 'I love sucking on sweets.'

Joel choked back the word 'bastard'. He'd sworn before making this call that Armin must only get to see the white flag in Joel, the defeat, not the order to charge. Armin must believe that Joel was weak for the plan to succeed.

'Twenty-five grand is all I can get together. Twenty-five grand and you have to promise to leave both Candy and my sister alone.'

'And Zarleena? What about her?' Armin asked, his eyes glowing green with the colour of money. 'You'll need to pay me more than twenty-five if you want me to stay away from her as well.'

'I don't give a flying fuck about Zarleena; she's more trouble than she's worth. No, I'll just stick with protecting my family. Do what you want with yours.' Joel felt his mouth go dry with guilt. Even though he didn't mean those words, just saying them felt like betrayal. But he'd learned one thing from mountaineering. Sometimes you had to lose a finger to save a life. Meaning: a few bad words now behind Zarleena's back might mean saving her from a battering later. In this case Armin was the gangrene and he needed to be chopped away.

Joel laid down his trump card, cringing inside at his words, 'You're a stronger man than I am, Armin. I don't know why I *ever* thought I could get one over you. You're a born winner.'

Armin grinned. 'Finally, finally a white man with sense. The difference between you and me is this: you have to climb a mountain to prove you are a man. But me,' he paused, 'I just have to walk down my street and everyone knows Armin *is* the man. In India I am respected by everyone. Ask yourself this, Mr Mountain Boy, how many people in India respect you? Anyway, let's talk business. When do I get my money?'

Joel explained that he would require a week or so to get the cash together. He'd call Armin and make further arrangements as soon as he had it. The conversation was at an end. Armin smugly told Joel that it was rude for an inferior man to hang up on his superiors and that he would have to wait for Armin to hang up first. Joel obliged, then angrily shouted, 'YOU FUCKER!' so loud that the cat lost its balance and fell off the wall. And one of the Saxon Britain ladies had a heart attack.

The icy thoughts in Joel's mind began to thaw with the heat of revenge. It would be interesting to see how much of a man Armin turned out to be when he came face to face with Joel again. He was sure Wayne Sleep would appear more butch.

Chapter Thirty-two

It was Friday morning; a pleasant sunny day down in Cornwall and before she left for work to save lives at the hospital, Nurse Sara was trying to convince her best friend, Candy, to have an abortion. She'd begun by reeling off a list of baggage that puts men off asking a woman on a date: credit-card addictions, possessive mothers, husband hunters, hairy armpits, sexual diseases and lastly, babies. A woman with a baby, to some men, is scarier than a woman with two heads. They see the baby as a thief, stealing their lager money to spend on nappies. And besides, they never even got to name it after their favourite football teams. Chelsea for a girl and Bolton Wanderers for a boy.

'Let me make some calls and see if we can get shot of this baby,' Sara said, gruffly combing her hair in Candy's bedroom. 'I'd say that the dominant gene in Joel's make-up is his womanizing gene. The last thing you want to do is help swamp the world with more Joels. If I were you I would abort the baby, *then* tell Joel. It's not your job to care about his feelings now.

Just like he didn't care about you while he was shagging those wo—'

'Leave it.'

Sara left it. Pregnant women were so touchy.

Centred neatly on Candy's bed was a Dr Miriam Stoppard book on pregnancy. It might as well have been a Stephen King novel it frightened her so much. But within the pages of the book the message was clear: pregnancy is the most natural thing in the world. So why did everything feel so wrong? Was it the fear of bringing up a child on her own? Was it that the baby wasn't planned? Or was it that deep down she knew she carried a part of Joel but really she wanted him whole? Something was willing her to pick up the phone and talk this through with the baby's father. She watched as Sara began counting out coppers from a small plate by her make-up mirror.

'That's another seventy-five pence towards regaining your freedom,' Sara stated, dropping the coins into a small container. 'Wards A and C are chock-a-block with sufferers at the moment; I'll try my luck with them.'

Candy asked Sara to leave the collection tin at home. She didn't think patients at the NHS hospital, waiting for life or death operations, would be too pleased to have a can rattled in their face with the words HELP PAY FOR MY BEST FRIEND'S PRIVATE ABORTION.

'Whatever, it's your baby. Anyway, tell me if you can see my suspenders when I bend down,' Sara asked, bending over.

'Yes, along with everything else.'

'Excellent, Dr Winslow should be pleased. I just hope when he ravages me this time he takes off his surgical mask. It's so hard to snog through those things. Anyway, tutty bye.' Sara kissed Candy on the cheek, threw on her cardigan and disappeared down the stairs and out of the main entrance.

Leaving just the two of them alone. With little appetite, Candy managed to nibble her way through a couple of slices of buttered toast while watching *This Morning* on the TV. Anything to take her mind off things for a while. Her emotions were dripping with hormones at the moment, making clear thinking impossible. Day-to-day her job revolved around promoting children's happiness, and the joy of their happiness was never lost on her. Surely having a child of her own would multiply her joy. Surely when you receive the greatest gift of all, the last thing you do is get rid of it. It was time to make an important call. With nerves as sharp as a tiger's claw, Candy turned down the TV and picked up the phone to dial Joel. He answered with a sleepy groan after just twelve rings. They politely asked how the other was keeping. What they had been up to. What was the weather like down their end. The price of Frosties. Normal, everyday questions.

'Who have you slept with lately, Joel?' Normal, everyday questions.

'Define "lately".'

'Since we split up. As in the last four days. That "lately".'

'Put it this way, I checked in my boxer shorts this morning and found two tiny suitcases and a note. It said, "I feel unwanted and underused. Find me some action or I'm off." Can you believe it, Candy, my willy was about to leave me? I don't know what I would have told the police. I suppose they'd want a recent photo of him and a list of places he used to hang out in. It's been traumatic I can tell—'

'I'm pregnant with your child, Joel.'

It was the biggest full stop ever. Silence shifted uncomfortably at Joel's end of the phone. Candy let the statement sink in, aware that a man's mind can play pinball with information like that. Conscious that his flippers must be frantically bashing the news around his skull, waiting for the brain to light up TILT. But rarely does he become the Pinball Wizard.

Finally Joel spoke. 'And you're definitely the mother, are you?' He laughed. 'Sorry, old joke. Jesus Christ, how did I manage that? I mean, wow, I finally beat the pill. They said it would happen one day, some superhuman man would have sperm so strong that it totally ignored the pill and went right on in and did its job all the same.'

Candy explained how she'd forgotten to take the contraceptive when she last came to Joel's apartment. Ironically, it was because Joel's confession of his affairs had screwed her mind up so much that she forgot to take the damn thing in the first place. It had nothing to do with superhuman sperm. Candy described her thoughts and ideas. Joel listened, one minute in a state of catatonia, the next in a state of heightened excitement. There was a strength in Candy's statements that Joel had never witnessed before.

'Really what I want is you,' Candy went on. 'Families normally start with three people not two. But I only want you under two conditions. One, no sleeping around. And two, you give up mountaineering for good. If I let my baby, *our* baby, get close to you as he or she would do if we were a family, then I don't want the baby's heart ripped apart by your stupid death wish. Climbing at eight thousand metres without fixed ropes and extra oxygen. *It's ridiculous.* Two conditions, Joel, or I bring Manchester United up on its own.' She paused. 'I'm not having you die on us just for your thrills.'

'I'm a hunter gatherer, Candy, I need my adrenalin rush. Mountaineering is my life.'

'Shouldn't our baby and I be your life, Hunter Gatherer? Now, I need to know what you are going to do.'

Joel hated the claustrophobic feeling of having an ultimatum thrust upon him. His freedom squeezed from his body like the juice of a ripe lemon, leaving a life without zest. Surely Candy knew that he climbed mountains to escape the chains of conformity. And now she wanted him to pack away his dreams, place his liberty in storage, and move into the world of normality. He looked at the picture of Mount Everest on the wall opposite his bed. You don't swap a majestic mountain like that for a mountain of nappy shit. He should be allowed both. Joel wanted to be a father as himself not as a watered-down version of himself. Besides, to give up climbing would be to give up his income. How did Candy expect him to provide the best for their baby by taking away his means to do so? His only true answer was the honest, cruel one.

'Financially I'll help in every way I can, Candy, but don't ask me to give up my life,' Joel said, half expecting a barrage of abuse to hurtle down the phone line. 'I wouldn't be me if I gave up my goals and dreams. I'd be Joel in a box.'

Candy's mood changed. Her voice shed its casual attire and jumped into a business suit. 'Okay, Joel, you've made yourself perfectly clear. Now let me explain a few things. Our baby is now *my* baby. If I meet a man who I fall in love with, it will become *his* baby. You will only be the father by blood. I will allow some visits but only under strict conditions. One of those conditions is this: never will you be allowed to take MY baby anywhere near a mountain. Not even a hill. In fact, not even near a high chair. If you do, I will kill you. *Capisce?* I want you out of the equation. I don't want you at the birth, at the hospital; I don't want a card from you or some poxy flowers.' She paused. 'Basically, I want you out of my life. And really I want you out of my baby's life.'

'If you want me out of your life, fine, but definitely not out of OUR baby's life. Don't bother even thinking anything like that again, Candy, because I'll fight you all the way. But with you, I understand why you want me out of your life and even why you want me to give up mountaineering. The last thing you want to have to explain to the little one is that Daddy died up K2. But please, just do one thing for me.'

'What?'

'Would you let me have first choice of its middle name? I was thinking Mallory.'

'FUCK OFF, Joel!' And the phone went dead.

Joel replaced the receiver and jumped out of bed. A build-up of nervous energy needed to be worked off downstairs in the gym. For years he'd been waiting for Candy's anger to be directed at him, searching for it like a cowboy panning for gold, and today he'd struck pay dirt with a nugget the size of a small boulder. Part of him understood her reaction, part of him was annoyed. Candy had fallen into a cliché as naturally as a lemming falls into the sea. She had become the woman who wanted to change her man.

Joel smelled his armpits to see what the weather was like. HOT. Time for a quick shower. In the living room he found Danny still fast asleep on the sofa, a book on Edmund Hillary clasped between his folded hands. Red Bull cans littered the floor along with a half-eaten sandwich, an empty Twiglet bag and a lemonade bottle filled with lager. What the hell was Danny doing drinking . . . and then Joel realized it wasn't lager. The dirty bastard. This place, with its assortment of rubbish, reminded Joel of certain Base Camps before they introduced the $2000 litter deposit which forced the climbers to clear up their mess (most of the time). He'd let Danny sleep out his Red Bull hangover and then fix him a mountaineer's breakfast of porridge. About to head to the bathroom, Joel noticed today's post at the front door. One bill, one card, one climbing magazine.

He gave the bill 'one' finger, then proceeded to open the 'one' card. Something was telling him that it might well fit in with the other ones he'd received over the last few days. And sure enough, he was right. Yet again, an ex-lover had found reason to send him a get well card. He shook his head at the contents:

Dear Joel,
Although extremely upset at the way you dumped
me – leaving the message 'Kirsty, I'm not thirsty
for you no more' on my answerphone was pretty

horrible to tell the truth – but Eloise has explained the reasons, and I partially forgive you. At first I didn't want to believe what I was hearing, a man as healthy as yourself didn't seem capable of being struck down with an incurable disease like Aids. But I followed Eloise's advice and had myself checked at a clinic (the most worrying time of my life) and thank God my result was clean. She says that you are recovering slowly but hopefully you will soon be up to six stone in weight. Eloise told me that you were refusing to take the medication. Well you must, Joel, it's to help you. I pray for you, Joel, please get well soon.
Love, Kirsty XXX 4 Ever Thirsty 4 U.

It was time he confronted his sister about this. He didn't know which was more dangerous, HIV or Eloise. Her bedroom door was ajar and as Joel walked in she quickly switched off the VDU. A guilt-ridden expression on her face if ever he'd seen one. He tried to ignore the thousands upon thousands of eyes ogling him from the photos on the wall. Especially trying to ignore the new shots of himself – how the hell did she manage to take one of him in the shower?

Before he could speak, she jumped in, 'Did you manage to contact someone about changing the locks, Joel? I'm quite concerned, you know. I don't feel safe in this apartment with him out there with my keys.'

'I'll have them sorted today.' He dropped the latest get well card on her lap. 'I want you to get back on the phone and explain the truth to all these women. You've got to stop all this interfering in my private life.'

Eloise looked a mess and she knew it but it didn't stop her feeling good about life when she was about to drop another bombshell on her brother. She slipped on a NY cap to cover her crappy hairstyle – soon to be concealed by the hair extensions Joel had promised to pay for – and prepared herself for Joel's reaction.

'So you want me to stay out of your private life, do you?' Eloise switched the VDU back on. 'That means you won't want me to show you what I found on the Internet then.' She played with the mouse on its mat. 'This slag on the screen won't matter to you then? You'll kill yourself if you don't take a peek. I guarantee that it will shock you. I couldn't believe my innocent eyes when I . . .'

Joel pretended to be pre-occupied with his climbing magazine. Until he didn't need to pretend to be preoccupied any more. He'd been stitched up. Fuck what was on Eloise's VDU screen, look what the dickheads had printed on the front of *Peaks & Summits*. He shoved the cover before her eyes, his face red with anger.

'Look at me,' he ranted. 'My career is over. I'm a fucking laughing stock now.'

Eloise examined the page. A picture of Joel up a mountain. Apart from her brother appearing even more handsome than normal, what gives? She couldn't determine why Joel should be so upset.

'What's the problem, Joel? You look fine to me. But who am I to know? You hardly talk to me these days. I'm just your little sister who takes third place behind your mountains and women.' She handed him back the magazine. 'You look great!'

'Great? Are you blind?' He slammed his finger into the cover. Eloise could have said, 'Mum put you up for adoption as a child but no one would take you,' and Joel would have been deaf to it: he was that livid. 'I'm attached to the mountain by fucking ropes. ROPES! It's one of the smallest mountains in the fucking world and they've got me attached to ropes. They promised me, they fucking promised me that they would airbrush the ropes out like they did with my tattoo. Their twatty insurance wouldn't cover me if I did the climb without ropes. I agreed *only* if they airbrushed them out. For God's sake, I was climbing mountains like that when I was just fifteen. I thought ropes were meant to save your life not fucking kill it off.' Joel dropped to her bed, dejected. 'I won't hear the end of this from my climbing buddies. "Baby Joel insists on climbing a twenty-metre cliff with safety ropes." I'll be a laughing stock.'

After hearing all the commotion, Danny burst through the door and grabbed *Peaks & Summits*. He stared in disgust at the picture. 'Shame on you, Uncle Joel, shame on you. How are we ever going to live this down?' He threw the magazine in Eloise's waste bin and stormed out, shouting, 'What a fake you are, Uncle Joel, what a fake you turned out to be.'

Eloise lay back next to Joel on the bed, wondering how to shoulder his pain. He needed a good woman at a time like this. Someone who could absorb some of his hurt. But first she had to get something off her chest. Maybe now was as good a time as any to tell him she wasn't pregnant. After yesterday's ordeal with Armin, she had promised herself and God to come clean.

She took hold of his hand, and turned on her side to face him. 'Joel, I need you to know something about me,' she whispered, watching the rise and fall of his chest. 'It's about my baby. Or, rather, the baby you imagined I might be having.' His eyes blinked open and she continued, 'There's a very fine line between being pregnant and not being pregnant. It's called the thin blue line. Well, I had a fright today when my period came. I don't think I'm pregnant any more.'

Joel appeared thoughtful, taking his time. 'Maybe the shock you had yesterday caused some bleeding, I wouldn't assume that you're not pregnant. I mean, the doctor has already confirmed you are.' He sat up, pulling her with him, suddenly very concerned. 'We've got to get you to a hospital. I'm not saying this is bad but I know bleeding while pregnant needs to be checked out by a doctor.' He kissed her on the cheek. 'It's probably nothing, don't worry.' He jumped off the bed. 'Come on. Chop, chop.'

'If we go to the hospital, will you pretend that you're my boyfriend?'

'What?'

Eloise imagined the buzz she would receive from passing women who thought that Joel was her man. The thrill of their jealous dagger eyes as they spotted hunky, fit Joel with her was worth the lie any day. Eloise dipped her eyes shyly. 'You would have to pretend that you had sex with me and everything. I don't want them thinking that I just got knocked up by some young teenager who left me to bring up the baby alone. You'll have to be the father, Joel; it's the only way I will go.' She held her breath. 'There was an awful lot of blood, Joel.'

He uncomfortably agreed and explained to Danny that they had to pop out: could he hold the fort while they were gone?

'Sure thing, Uncle Joel.' Danny sat on the vibrating chair, switched on MTV and bit into his bacon buttie. '*Ciao*.' He loved school holidays.

Speeding through the streets, Joel arrived at Colchester Hospital quicker than most ambulances would have. Putting his arm round Eloise's shoulder, he walked her into the A&E entrance, telling her not to worry, explaining that this was just a precaution. A pretty nurse opened the door for them and smiled sweetly at Joel. Eloise thinned her eyes and returned the nurse a 'hands off he's mine' dirty look.

'We're worried we might lose our baby,' Eloise said to the nurse, adjusting her cap in case it fell off. The thrill of strangers believing Joel was her man, believing that she could 'pull' such a fine specimen, was better than an orgasm. 'Gorgeous, isn't he? My boyfriend. The father of my child. You can look but you can't touch.'

After a two-hundred-hour shift there was not much the nurse could say to that. Instead, she just hurried away, to grab an hour's sleep, before starting her three-hundred-hour shift later.

Joel's feet ground to a halt in the large foyer, where the smell of antiseptic was stronger than the smell of fear. He turned to face Eloise and spoke as gently as his patience would allow. 'I can't pretend to be your boyfriend, Eloise, it's dead weird. Do you really think these hard-working nurses give a monkey's about who got you pregnant? Honestly, they've seen it all before.

I'm going to be your brother, like I am.' He took her hand and led her to Reception. 'With a bit of luck someone will see you soon.'

Soon? Eloise worried. Soon didn't give her much time to think up a believable excuse as to why she had dragged Joel all the way down here for her phantom baby. She sat in the waiting room while Joel filled out a form. A man with a real broken leg waited to be seen. And a young boy with a real eye injury also waited. Behind her a woman moaned in real pain. It was time for her to face reality.

Thirty seconds later she was dragging Joel out of the hospital, tears in her eyes, shame in her belly, a deep loathing in her heart at her own behaviour. The words 'Joel, don't freak but I've been lying about the pregnancy all along' had had the receptionist spit out her tea onto Joel's ICE IS NICE T-shirt. Outside, by the discarded wheelchairs, Joel prepared for Eloise to get a spade and start digging her way out of the shit she'd got herself into. He hoped the spade was big 'cos the pile of shit was enormous.

'Darling brother –' the beginning was puke-worthy – 'do you remember when you used to climb the tall oak tree in the park? You used to pretend that you were on top of Everest. Well, I wanted a baby so much that I too pretended. You could say that my baby was my Everest. Am I making sense to you?' She daren't look in his eyes. 'I've got a feeling you know exactly what I'm talking about here.' But Joel didn't, leaving Eloise no option but to confess all. The crux of the story was this: Joel wanted her to get a job, so she invented a pregnancy to avoid one. Simple.

Disgusted, Joel walked off towards the Range Rover; she scampered behind him. He pointed to the passenger side. 'Get in the fucking car and don't talk to me on the way back. I nearly bought a fucking cot the other day, do you know that? It was made in Tibet. I am so ashamed of you.'

They drove back in silence. A dismal beginning to the hot, sunny day if ever there was one. Joel slammed the gear stick into fourth as he thought back to the other day when Eloise had asked him to clean up the bath behind her in case she harmed the baby by bending over. How she'd left a basket of washing for him to iron. How she'd asked for extra money to buy maternity clothes. How she'd suddenly craved Indian takeaways every night. How . . . Joel swerved the car to escape crashing into the bus that had just pulled into his lane. But holding Joel back from becoming overwhelmed with anger was the thought of what Armin had done to her yesterday. Maybe – as seemed to be the case with everything Eloise did wrong these days – he'd just have to let this one go . . . for now.

Back home, Danny was on the phone to his mate. He waved as Joel and Eloise entered, shouting, 'I would have used my mobile, Uncle Joel, but your phone is so much cheaper, cheers!' then returned to his conversation.

Joel walked to Eloise's bedroom and collected the *Peaks & Summits* magazine from the bin. His agent would have to be informed about this. His reputation as a climber who used little safety equipment had been damaged. Just as he was about to leave the room, his eyes were drawn to the VDU screen in the corner. The screen that Eloise said would shock him. The screen that he'd kill himself if he didn't take a peek at. The screen . . .

'Jesus H Christ,' Joel said, taking a closer look. 'Oh, no.'

The screen that was headed: DIRTY INDIAN WHORES.

Joel tried not to look, but his morbid curiosity refused to turn his head away. Glaring out from the monitor, almost real enough to touch, were a set of photographs that could never be classed as 'holiday snaps' (unless one holidayed with Hugh Heffner). Naked picture after naked picture sprawled across the twenty-inch flat screen inviting lecherous eyes to ogle, and perverted hands to pull. Sordid shots of an unsmiling model holding a selection of toys that would make Ann Summers jealous, and a variety of positions that would have the *Kama Sutra* rewritten. Joel stared into the sad eyes of the model and he knew exactly why she wasn't smiling. He also knew who she was; and he even knew who had uploaded the images. This was yet another chapter in the story of Zarleena's marriage to Armin. This was probably the lowest behaviour Joel had borne witness to. How could Armin have done this to Zarleena? Plastering her naked body on the Net for all to see. It was an act Satan himself would have scorned.

'She looks pretty miserable to me, Joel, but I have to admit she's very photogenic. It's almost tasteful porn, if you don't mind me saying so. Very sexy. Then again, I suppose it pales in comparison to seeing her in the flesh.' Eloise stood at the entrance to her room. 'I only typed in "Bindis & Brides" in the search. Which linked up with "Bindi Brides". Which took me to a site that asked if I wanted to see a dirty Indian whore. And there you have it.' She ambled over to her printer. 'Want a print-out? I can do it on gloss if you like.'

'No, thank you,' he replied.

'How about I fetch you a nice cold Red Bull then?'

He tried not to smile. 'Please don't creep around me, Eloise, it doesn't suit you.'

'I'll get the Red Bull. It's good stuff you know.' And she disappeared.

Holding a grudge against Eloise for longer than a day was nigh on impossible for Joel. It was also impractical as she normally locked herself in the bathroom for hours until he forgave her. But what she had done this time was different. He would let her get over this nasty experience she'd received at the hands of Armin and then he'd make sure she found herself a job. No more hand-outs after that.

Joel Aid was officially over.

Chapter Thirty-three

In Britain alone, without even committing a single crime, there are literally thousands of Indian women in prison, serving life sentences, with little chance of parole. No escape. No freedom. No life. But surely in this country one is innocent until proven guilty? Surely they can't put you away for not committing a crime? Oh, but they can, and they often do; there is no solicitor on earth that can prevent an Indian woman being sent to serve her sentence. There is no law in this land that will save her. There is no escape from the prison many inmates often refer to as the prison of an arranged marriage.

Zarleena, Honey and the Saturday girl, Shimla, sat drinking Cap Colombie coffee on a quiet Tuesday morning in Bindis & Brides; it had been five days since Armin's attack, and Zarleena's visual bruising had diminished slightly, although her mental bruising seemed to become more enflamed each time she relived the awful experience. They had been discussing how their female relatives often referred to their marriage as a prison. Not a fancy prison like Jeffrey Archer's, more like one from the Deep South in old America where they worked on chain gangs. They begin their sentence the day the bride's father hands her over to her new husband. From then on she is expected to keep him happy at all costs for evermore, without so much as a single moan or back-chat. By the time she reaches sixty – 321,000 *chapattis*, 29,200 hours of washing up, 43,800 hours of cooking, 14,050 hours of sex, and five minutes of orgasms later – any dreams she had as a girl have been swallowed up by the years, any looks she had as a young woman have been beaten back by grind. It's no wonder that on the day the women reach three score years, their haggard faces are tattooed with the message, HARD LIFE. Zarleena, Honey and Shimla had seen plenty of tattoos over the last year.

Under the till counter next to a half-eaten packet of marshmallows, Honey had positioned her new weapon in case Armin decided to make a surprise visit. A bicycle pump filled with car battery acid to squirt in his eyes the moment his feet came through the shop door. He had often told her sister that he must have been as blind as a bat to marry her; well, if he came through the door, he would be. Fear was still rife amongst the girls and the sooner Joel completed his plan the better. Although they were still at a loss as to exactly what Joel had in mind. Even Zarleena's phone call to him yesterday revealed nothing. It was best, Joel had informed her, that they didn't know. It was a good answer (she didn't really want to know). It was enough of a problem as it was dealing with the guilt of double-crossing her mother – by associating with Joel after promising she would stay clear of him – without having to worry about the wrongs and rights of double-crossing her own husband.

But this was her life now, not Armin's, not her parents', not even India's, and she was going to live it her way. She'd tried the Indian way and it didn't work. Something inside felt positive about following her own map and not the yellowing map of an ancient idea. You listen to your eyes when they warn you of speeding cars and you listen to your stomach when it tells you you're hungry, you listen to your nose when your feet get hot, so why wouldn't she listen to her soul when it said 'follow her heart'. For right now her heart was telling her to trust Joel. And to trust him completely. He'd shown his caring side again, phoning every day to make sure she was okay, listening to her gas on about her worries. It didn't seem so long ago that she'd been giving him the recipe for a good Indian dinner for two, now it seemed that Joel was giving her a recipe for a good life, for keeping positive, for self-fulfilment. Her own private phone therapist with a sexy voice and a sense of humour that had her in stitches. For just these attributes alone most women would go weak with desire. Then there were his unmistakable good looks, his Greek-statue body, and his sexual prowess. It was no wonder that Zarleena fancied the pants off him. It was only a wonder it had taken her this long to realize it. A comment he'd made during their last phone chat had been roaming her brain like an out-of-control free radical. They were discussing whether choking on one's own vomit should be classified as 'drowning', when out of the blue Joel had said, 'Talking of puke, I can't wait to get my tattoo of Candy removed from my back, it makes me sick.'

Zarleena's only thought at the time had been: why would Joel have said such a thing? Her thought now was: give me some sandpaper and I'll remove it for you.

Today, in Bindis & Brides, a tortoise walked with a clock on its back; time was moving slowly. 11 a.m., and the till ring was so out of practice this morning that it rang out of tune when an Indian lady purchased a set of coloured glass bangles. Honey joked that it was so dead she expected to see a ball of tumbleweed blowing through the shop like in a scene from the Western, *Gunfight at the OK Corral*. Normally on days like these only two people were necessary to keep the shop running smoothly. But with the possibility of a visit by Armin, even three didn't seem enough.

'I'm nipping next door, does anyone want anything?' Zarleena asked. 'Crisps? Coke? Paper?' The girls declined, so Zarleena donned her shades to hide her bruises, picked up her purse and walked to the entrance. 'Back in a tick.'

Inside Spindlers Newsagent's, Mrs Cotton, dressed in her pink pinny, stocked shelves with sweets. Zarleena's entry caused Mrs Cotton to cough, which in turn caught the attention of Mr Cotton stocking cigars behind the counter. Zarleena watched as they swapped glances, guessing that they were most likely thinking 'another abused woman'. She hoped they weren't rude enough to ask her what had happened to her face. Mr Cotton descended the ladder and turned to Zarleena with a ready-made smile.

'Well, well, well. Mrs Cotton was only just saying she hadn't seen you in a while, weren't you, Mrs Cotton?' Mr Cotton eyed his wife. 'It's Honey, isn't it?'

'Zarleena,' she corrected. 'Honey is the one with the longer hair.'

Mrs Cotton stood up and straightened her pinny. 'You lot all look the same to us. No offence intended. It's the black hair and brown eyes—'

'And the dark skin,' Mr Cotton interrupted. 'Us white folk will never get used to it, Honey. Sorry, I mean, Zarleena.' He smiled wider, revealing beautiful yellow, tobacco-stained teeth. 'Now what can I get you?'

'Just a dozen Mars bars and a copy of *Heat* magazine, please.' Zarleena's eyes spotted a new cardboard sign balancing in front of the till:

ONLY TWO FOREIGNERS AT A
TIME. (INDIANS, PAKISTANIS
& SRI LANKANS). DUE TO
FOREIGNERS SHOPLIFTING.

'Oh, don't you worry about that notice, Honey; it's for the other lot. We trust you.' Mr Cotton placed Zarleena's goods on the counter. 'Twelve Mars bars and *Heat*. That's five pounds sixty-five. Let's call it five pounds seventy. Six pounds with a carrier bag.'

Zarleena was too busy thinking to hear. Something about the sign, which had nothing to do with its message, was making her feel uneasy. She'd always thought that Mr and Mrs Cotton were a bit odd, but nothing a good orgy wouldn't sort out. A bit old-fashioned. A bit backwards. A bit ill at ease with the younger generations. But she'd never thought of them as a bit racist. She delved deep in her memory, back to one of the nasty racist notes that had been thrust through their letterbox. She was sure that a spelling mistake had given rise to Honey's giggles. 'How can they insult us when they can't even spell foreigners properly? They've missed out the "g",' Honey had said. Zarleena now took another look at the notice by the till. Sure enough, the word 'foreigners' was missing its 'g' again. Twice. It could mean only one thing: she was in a shop with two racists. Two racists who couldn't even spell properly. But why were they so Johnny Rotten?

'Before I forget,' Zarleena remarked, as casually as possible. 'The police might make a routine visit to you sometime soon. Me and Honey have been receiving racist letters and they think they might know who it is.' She watched Mr Cotton nervously fiddling with some receipts. 'They said, in their experience, that racists always live close to the victim. Sometimes they even live right next door.'

Mrs Cotton dropped the box she was holding. Chocolates spilling on the floor as obviously as her guilt. She could remember a time when Hunterslea was all white. A pure town of one ethnicity. There was no chance that her daughter would bring home a 'nig nog' for tea. People knew where they stood back then.

Then, in the fifties, some bright spark in the government let the lid off the brilliant-white can, encouraging immigrants into the country for cheap labour, and now the streets were painted with beige. Didn't the English see the glint in the immigrants' eyes? Couldn't they tell that they weren't going to be satisfied with skivvy work for too long? Wasn't it obvious that, as soon as the immigrants could, they would make something of their lives? And now, she couldn't even turn the TV on without the News being read to her by one of them. She couldn't watch a soap without a storyline revolving around one of them. She couldn't even go to the hospital without being treated by one of them. For God's sake, she couldn't even buy a packet of Rich Tea biscuits from her local shop because her local shop was owned by one of them. And now the business next door to theirs was not only run by one of them but was also bringing loads more of them into town. Surely those reasons alone were good enough to warrant the threatening letters. Not to mention the disruption that the Bindis & Brides' delivery vans caused for their newsagent's; blocking them in, blocking them out. Then they let their customers use the owners' car park at the rear of the shop. It was a cheek, an insult; there was no respect from Indians these days. Was it any wonder that they had asked their son to scratch a message on the black Range Rover with the tinted windows the other night for hogging the entire car park?

Mrs Cotton eyed her husband. But to get involved with the police. Especially so near to retirement. This was one story that this newsagent's didn't want sold. It wasn't that long ago that she'd been cheering David Blunkett along when he mentioned that they were thinking about fingerprinting 'foreiners'. Now, just for loving her country too much, it might be her and her husband who would be having their fingerprints taken. She shook her head in shame. And what's worse, when they rolled the ink on her fingers, it would be her with the hands that were too black.

Trying desperately to think on her feet, Mrs Cotton, as per usual, put herself right in it. 'Let's hope the police catch them quickly,' she began. 'Nobody likes a bigot. But let's be realistic about this, the police are going to find it pretty hard to trace the culprit when all the letters have been typed.'

Mr Cotton looked thunderously at his wife.

Mrs Cotton looked sheepishly at her husband.

Zarleena looked disgustedly at the pair of them and walked out of the shop – without her Mars bars and *Heat* magazine in hand but with her self-respect intact. She hadn't mentioned the letters were typed.

Ten minutes later Honey's screech, 'I will kill them both,' vibrated through Bindis & Brides' walls. Honey, who believed more than anything that God had made all women equal and all men lesser equals, was sickened by Mr and Mrs Cotton's behaviour. Now the 'white chocolate' jokes made sense. She remembered when she'd offered to supply them with Indian sweets. 'What shall we call them?' Mr Cotton had asked, a smirk on his face. 'Bud Bud Sweets?' At the time she'd thought he was making a genuine error. Now she realized it was a genuine dig. She'd like to give him a 'Bud Bud' right up his dried-up wrinkled white arse. Let's see if he smirked then.

As Zarleena made chicken and mango pickle sandwiches for lunch, Honey and Shimla decided to design a sign of their own. This one would also go by the till. This one was also intended for foreigners. But this one would be written in defence of an unnecessary attack. The bold words were coloured by retaliation:

434

TO OUR LOYAL CUSTOMERS. THE NEWSAGENTS
NEXT DOOR ARE RACISTS. BOYCOTT THEIR SHOP
OR EAT SWEETS STICKY WITH XENOPHOBIA AND
DRINK POP FIZZY WITH BIGOTRY. THANK YOU.

Honey displayed the sign, feeling a gust of wind left over from the hurricanes her parents had had to put up with when they first arrived in the UK in the early seventies. Her father had explained the hardships of trying to fit in with a country that didn't want them. How normal, everyday problems like feeding the family, holding down a job, paying the mortgage and keeping healthy were compounded by that old chestnut called 'belonging'. He'd explained that on top of the normal worries were the additional worries. Worries that only immigrants could ever truly understand. When they moved into their first house, they didn't worry most about whether the heating worked, or whether the plumbing leaked; oh no, their first worry was whether the neighbourhood would accept them or would they have a firebomb thrown through the window? When they found schools for the children, they worried whether their kids would come home with bruises from racist bullies. And even when they went to the local shop they prayed they would come back in one piece. (Which was probably why the Asians went on to buy the corner shops.) Their struggle was a battle that would never be mentioned in history books. It would never be talked about in centuries to come. It was a private war that most would like to forget. Like a warrior returning from a bloody battlefield doesn't boast of the enemies he's slain, he just wants to get back to his family and live in peace. Similarly, the first-generation Indian couples didn't want to remember their struggles. They just wanted to live in peace.

The three girls ate their sandwiches, giggling as they waited for the first customer to read the new notice. An ancient mama-ji wandered over carrying an embroidered cushion.

'Oh no. I've made the biggest mistake of my life,' Honey exaggerated. 'She's not going to be able to read English. It's going to have to be written in Urdu, Punjabi, Hindi, Gujarati and Brummie Punjabi.' She paused. 'The sign will have to be bigger than the shop.'

They laughed – always a good way to take the weight off your shoulders.

Coincidentally, Joel was adding weight to his. In the basement of Forest Falls Apartments, Joel was busy working out in the classy but empty gymnasium. The basketball court-sized enclosure with its fairly comprehensive list of equipment was made to look even bigger by the strategic placement of mirrors. The agony of Joel's workout was thus reflected at a multitude of angles.

A sign by the bench press machine was just asking for trouble with Joel around: DO NOT USE WITHOUT A SPOTTER. Of course, Joel only used the machine WITHOUT A SPOTTER. A CD player with a set of CDs sat by the water fountain giving customers a wide selection of training music. Today, Joel had brought his own music and was training to Peter and the Test Tube Babies, an eighties punk band who loved to spit on their fans as a sign of their affection. Similar, some might say, to the farmer's egg-throwing affection that Mr Prescott misinterpreted as aggression before he flew into a rage of fists a few years back.

Hanging from a chinning bar with both hands was a good way to improve grip strength. Being that grip strength is the most important strength a climber can have, Joel spent a lot of time hanging in the basement. He'd been dangling for well over ten minutes when his mobile vibrated against his thigh. Still suspended from the bar with one hand, he answered the phone with the other. Child's play for a monkey but quite impressive for a human.

'Candy . . . What decision? . . . And this is all your thinking, is it? Nothing to do with Sara? . . . No, you're right, I never liked her . . . This isn't about me, this is about our baby . . . No, Candy, get this into your head, this baby is "our" baby not just yours . . . Naming it is one thing but this is totally wrong and you know it . . . I know it's not an "it", it's just an expression, for fuck's sake . . . No this conversation is *not* finished . . . Now you listen to me, you little bitch, you can't do this to me, I'm "its" father, for fuck's sake, and I have a say . . . Be reasonable, I must have meant something to you . . . I said "meant". I didn't say I still do. Now please . . . Oh just *fuck* off.' And Joel threw his phone across the gym – just a moment before he lost his grip and fell to the floor.

Many mirrors reflected a frustrated, angry, hurt man. A feeling of utter hopelessness, which had been steadily building each day from the daily phone calls Candy had made, threatened to overwhelm him. Five days of pleading with her to change her thinking, forget their differences, remember what they used to have together and, mostly, think about the baby growing inside her. It didn't seem a lot to ask, but the more he pushed, the more he was sure he was heading into uncharted waters; the more certain he became that this voyage would end in disaster.

The CCTV camera followed him around the gym; it was obvious that the security guard was bored. Joel walked up to the nearest camera, stood on a bench and stuck his middle finger as close to the lens as possible. A minor victory in an otherwise disastrous morning. One of those mornings which he would like to hide away, along with his other disastrous days, inside his closet – if it wasn't already filled with Red Bull and other junk. Inside his walk-in wardrobe, upstairs in the apartment, a huge ball of tangled ropes waited to be undone. It was a good metaphor for his knotted life at the moment. Nothing seemed to be straightforward any more.

Jogging home, up two flights of stairs, Joel promised himself that after a quick shower and snack, he'd devote the rest of the day to continuing his autobiography. His editor had e-mailed yesterday begging to see the nearly finished manuscript. She couldn't wait to read the chapter where Joel and his climbing buddy had celebrated Joel's birthday, eight thousand metres up Mount Kanchenjunja in the Himalayas, by using all their oxygen canisters to get a high. It was only when they'd collapsed at 8386 metres, breathless and too weak to continue, just two hundred metres from the summit, that they'd admitted, with frozen tears in their eyes, 'It was a stupid idea.' To this day, Joel couldn't bear to watch *ER* in case a patient was sucking on an oxygen mask, in which case he was likely to yell at the TV, 'Save it for the summit, you idiot.' It went down as Joel's biggest mistake. He had never relied on bottled oxygen again.

Whilst Joel had been training in the gym, two cars had parked outside the apartments. Visitors of the unannounced variety for Joel; guests of the invited variety for Eloise. Unbeknown to Joel, in the late hours of yesterday, Dylan had rung Eloise to confirm that their parents had arrived safely from the USA. The two had been in cahoots since Eloise had phoned her mother a few weeks ago regarding Joel's state of mind. Today's meeting was hopefully the beginning of the end of Joel's so-called 'odd behavioural patterns'. Mummy and Daddy had flown across the Atlantic, from Orlando to England, to sort out their son. Ridding him of his problems, they hoped, would be as easy as squeezing juice from a Florida orange – but possibly just as sticky.

Joel pushed open the door to his apartment and stared stunned at the gathering of faces before him. Like a pack of wolves waiting for a full moon they sat in silence. His parents, Dylan, Danny and Eloise. A jury with jailers' eyes.

'What the fucking hell is going on here?' Joel wiped the back of his neck with his gym towel. 'Who's died?'

Mum, dressed in white jeans and blue T-shirt, got up and welcomed her son with a warm hug. 'Please don't swear, Joel, it gives me a headache, you know that.'

He popped a glance at Dad, he looked normal enough, so what the shitting hell had happened to his mother? 'Have you got younger, Mum? You seem,' he saw Eloise running her finger across her throat indicating he should shut up, 'erm . . . you seem so, so natural. You don't look plastic at all.' He winced to Eloise.

Danny, sitting on the vibrating chair, cracked up laughing. 'It's her collagen, Uncle Joel; all Yanks have it done to their lips. That's why they talk so much shit.'

'Danny!' Dylan shouted. 'Watch your mouth.'

It was an end of the insults and the beginning of their meeting. Eloise, now with her new long chestnut-coloured hair extensions, handed out photocopies of a list she had put together of some of the women Joel had slept with in the last four years. Two sides of A4. Joel's parents gasped: look what we brought into this world.

'And I'm only scratching the surface here, people,' Eloise said, avoiding Joel's *Texas Chainsaw Massacre* glare. 'These are purely the ones he's bonked in this apartment.' She placed her sheets on the arm of the sofa-chair. 'My point is this: Aids. Need I say any more than that?'

Danny seemed confused. 'But I thought you could only catch Aids by bumming.'

'DANNY!' everyone screamed in harmony.

Now was the perfect moment for Mum to take Joel to one side and have a serious heart-to-heart. They entered his bedroom and yet again Joel heard his mother's gasp. For reasons known only to Eloise, while Joel had been busy downstairs in the gym, she had been even busier upstairs in his bedroom. Her six-foot clay statue of a naked man with the foot and a half of erect penis had been carted in here (she obviously didn't want Mum to know it was hers), a condom was placed on the pillow of his bed (ready for his next woman, no doubt), a scattering of ladies' knickers were strewn across the messy room, and on the wall above the head-board Eloise had stuck at least five photo albums' worth of photographs. All women. All exes. This time it was time for Joel to gasp.

'I'm worried about you, Joel. We all are,' Mum began, removing a climbing magazine off his duvet and sitting in its place. 'Eloise informs me that you keep a coffin in a lock-up. You wear a pink bra when you climb. You take money for sex. You still risk your life unnecessarily by climbing without ropes. And if that wasn't enough, she now informs me that you were heard conspiring with someone to kill a babysitter. What mother wouldn't worry? Do you know that your father and I were seriously thinking about getting you sectioned? We still think you're unstable, Joel.'

Memories came flooding back: a younger Joel trying to convince his parents that he wasn't mentally retarded just because he was fascinated with death. Ever since he could remember, his own demise had never scared or worried him. Something inside, call it God, call it fate, call it arrogance, whatever you call it, Joel was comfortable with his own mortality. It just seemed that everyone around him wasn't, especially his parents. Besides, back then, even as a youngster, it was important for Joel to get used to thinking about death and how to try to avoid it if he wanted to be a great mountain climber. Why couldn't his parents understand that? Why did they have to panic and send him to a psychiatrist at such a young age? Why did they have to swap all his stainless-steel cutlery for plastic? Why did they remove his laces from his trainers? Why did they . . .

One by one Joel explained away his mother's list of concerns. He wore the pink bra in case he fell off a mountain and died. He'd rather there was a newspaper headline about his pink bra than a headline about his lack of climbing skills. The coffin in the lock-up was no mystery – he just wanted the design to his own specifications. The money for sex was a mix up – he was owed the money and Eloise got the wrong end of the stick *as usual*. As for killing the babysitter: he was talking to his editor about removing the babysitter scene (the scene regarding the day he left Danny on the roof) from his autobiography. 'Killing the babysitter' was just an expression.

'I find this all a bit trying, Joel, I really do. And all the girls you've slept with? What have you got to say about them?' Mum said, pointing to the wall of women.

'I had a good time.' He stood up and checked out Eloise's montage. Smack, bang in the middle of a circle of brunettes the smile of a blonde woman shone out. A smile that used to make him go weak. The smile that now made him sick. Joel lifted Candy's photo off the wall and ripped it into four, tossing the segments on the floor. 'I really loved her.'

Mum viewed the ripped remains. She'd guessed when she met Candy for the first time that Joel would break her heart. Call it mother's intuition, but she'd been sure that the beauty of their relationship would eventually be wrecked by the beast of Joel's climbing obsession, or, worse still, the beauty of their relationship would be wrecked by the beast of Joel's death.

Either way, she couldn't foresee a happy ending. But on the question of Joel's love for Candy, she said, 'No, you didn't love her. If you loved her then you wouldn't have cheated on her.' She gave her son a pitiful look. 'Men like you fill women with dread, you understand that, don't you, Joel? You lost a good one there, Joel, you really did.'

He was about to say 'I know' then he thought back to Candy's last phone call. 'No, not this one, Mum. I made the right mistake with her, if you know what I mean. Definitely the right mistake.' He was about to reveal that Candy was pregnant, then decided against it. Joel didn't want to give his mother the hope of another grandchild only for Candy to take that hope away. 'Anyway, fancy a Red Bull? It's—'

'Good stuff, we know, Joel.' She rose up and came over to cuddle him, then wrinkled her nose. 'You smell a bit pongy; any possibility of you taking a bath?'

'No problem,' he replied. 'I've just got to rig up the toaster to the extension lead and then if you could be so kind as to toss the toaster in the bath when I'm not expecting it, I'd be much obliged.'

She shot him a look that used to petrify him as a kid. 'Grow up.'

He returned a look that used to mollify her when he was a kid. 'Love you, Mum.'

And a happy and relieved Mum departed to the living room leaving Joel to freshen up. Already the trip had been worth it. To see Dylan and Joel under one roof without the slightest bickering was a better gift than any air miles voucher could buy. For parents to watch their children tear each other apart with pointless arguments and hurtful remarks was a scenario mums and dads would try to avoid at all costs. One of the major reasons for moving to Florida had been to escape the family meltdown. Now it seemed that from the ashes of Joel's and Dylan's troubled brotherhood, a phoenix had arisen in the shape of maturity. Let's just hope, Mum crossed her fingers, that the phoenix didn't come crashing from the sky at the first sign of stormy weather. Fixed relationships were easy to break, but broken fixed relationships weren't very easy to mend.

The afternoon rolled into evening; a happy time spent catching up with news and gossip, sharing tales from across the pond. Dad was at his quietest when he was at his proudest, and tonight, as he viewed his flock, he was prouder than ever. It hadn't been so long ago that he was blaming himself for the family troubles, for having brought his two sons up so differently: private school for Dylan, comprehensive school for Joel. No wonder they had waged a war for what seemed like for ever. But now, those worries were over. Now, he watched his two boys discuss how big the needle would have to be to penetrate the skin of a rhino and he felt as proud as punch.

'I'm only guessing here,' Joel continued, as they tucked into an Indian takeaway, 'but, at a guess, I'd say Margaret Thatcher would need a needle five inches long to penetrate her skin.' He nodded. 'At least.'

The laughter and munching continued until the moment arrived for the guests to leave. Mum and Dad kissed and hugged Joel and Eloise goodnight, promising that they would spend as much time as possible with them in the coming two weeks. Dylan bid Joel farewell, apologizing for conspiring with Eloise behind his back. And Danny, who had been told repeatedly to switch off the vibrating chair while he ate, also apologized, for spilling his chicken rogan josh on Joel's hand-woven Tibetan rug. There was only one person left to say sorry.

'Night, Joel,' Eloise said, darting into her bedroom. 'Seeyertomorrow.'

He followed her in and sat down on her bed. A good indication that she wasn't going to be sleeping as soon as she had hoped. Joel was the pea and his little princess wasn't getting any shut-eye until she'd explained a few things. Every wrongdoing she was guilty of in the last month, for instance. The lies to their mother about his state of mind. The text messages to his exes pretending he had Aids. The phantom pregnancy. The weird photograph of him in the shower, etc. The money that she kept conning him out of. The . . .

'EVERYTHING, Eloise, EVERYTHING,' Joel hollered. 'This Aids business has our own mother on Prozac. How dare you tell her that I was a dirty male prostitute?' He picked up her Little Miss Naughty pillow to unleash his aggression on, only to spot – lo and behold – a picture of himself in a pair of boxer shorts staring up at him. 'What the fuck is this?' He grabbed it from the bed sheet. 'Eloise? Please tell me it fell off the wall.'

'Actually it fell out of my knickers.'

'Well, what the fuck were your knickers doing on the wall then?' He was losing it. 'I mean, why was my photograph in your knickers?'

She sighed. 'In case someone tried to rape me, silly. My friends advised me to put a hard man in my knickers. We all do it. Natalie's got one of Charles Bronson. Karen's got one of the Klitschko brothers. And Samantha's got one of Phil Mitchell from *EastEnders* – don't ask – and I've got one of you. It's just a precaution, Joel. I'd just tell the rapist to take a good look at the photo because that's the face of the man who would kill him or mash him up.' She frowned at him. 'You didn't think that . . . er, yuck, Joel, you're sick. Get out of my room! You thought that . . . that I want to have sex with you? GET OUT!'

She slammed the door behind him, jammed the three locks across, removed all of her clothes and lay back on the bed, grinning.

What a day, thought Joel, as he dived into bed; they didn't get any stranger than this. He switched off the light, closed his eyes then waited, as he normally waited, for his sister to finish with her vibrator.

God, what did he do to be lumbered with a sister like her?

Chapter Thirty-four

Armin the Great had been coaching Prem how to shoot with an air rifle on a small patch of wasteland round the rear of the betting shop. Apples, pears and mangos had been representing Joel's head. Each direct hit was rewarded with a vegetable *samosa*. Each miss was rewarded with a kick up Prem's behind. Armin's Military School for Hindus worked on the carrot and stick method of training. Or, rather, the *samosa* and kick.

'Eat up,' Armin ordered, referring to Prem's fifth *samosa*. 'We've got money to make.' He looked up at the beautiful blue sunny sky. 'Even India shines down on us today, my friend.'

It was the last Monday in August, eleven days since Armin had cut off Eloise's hair and taught his spineless wife a lesson in respectful behaviour. He'd heard from Joel a number of times since then, each call confirming that the money was being sorted, each conversation coloured with the fear of a cowardly Englishman. Armin was under no illusion though; Joel was definitely *not* to be trusted; he was white after all. Hence

447

the air rifle back-up plan. Hence the *Assassin* video they'd enjoyed last night in preparation for today's potential bloodbath. Hence the worried expression on Prem's face that his cousin, Armin, might have watched one too many Bollywood Mafia films. Prem's fear of Armin's take on reality was heightened when Armin reached into his pocket and handed him ten air rifle pellets, all painstakingly painted in stripes of saffron, white and green – the colours of the Indian flag.

'If things go wrong, these are to be used on Joel. Let him know what it feels like to have some of India inside him.' Armin patted Prem's back. 'Remember, you get five grand for helping me today, Prem. Not bad for one day's work.'

And today was the day.

Yesterday afternoon, Armin had received the call he'd been waiting for from Joel. Finally Joel had managed to sort out the money, and the meeting was arranged for 3 p.m. at Watermill Park in Hunterslea. Armin's hands had been sore ever since from rubbing them together in glee. And if there was a lesson for the white people from all of this, Armin supposed, then it was this: never underestimate the heat of an Indian.

Armin, dressed in black, and Prem, dressed in camouflage, arrived an hour early at Watermill Park. After parking the car, they casually strolled over the virtually empty green to a dense wall of bushes which overlooked the car park. With a quick check for bystanders, Prem disappeared from view, swallowed up by the thicket of green leaves. His sniper's position was unlikely to be disturbed by anything other than dogs. Armin withdrew back to his car and phoned Prem on his mobile to check they were in communicado. Everything was sweet, nothing to worry about; all was 'Go' for lift-off. Armin slipped in a *bhangra* tape and played air drums until, thirty minutes later, at 2.45 p.m., Joel's Range Rover pulled up next to him. Armin nodded to himself on noticing the extremely dark tinted windows of the vehicle. Joel was true to form here, concealing himself and hiding behind the blackened glass. Yet another sign of weakness in his character. He hides up mountains, hides behind his shades and now he hides behind the screen of his car. When Joel had stated that he was good at games Armin had hardly assumed that he was referring to Hide 'n' Seek. He wondered how good Joel was at playing Catch with an air rifle pellet.

The primary rule of aggression is to strike first. Armin stepped out of his car and stood confidently with his legs apart and arms crossed, waiting for Joel to leave the safety of his Range Rover. He was just about to deepen his smirk when he noticed the scratched paint-work on the driver's side of Joel's motor: PAKI LOVER. Armin sniggered and watched for any sudden movements as Joel stepped down from the Range Rover.

Armin spoke, pointing to the graffiti: 'There are better ways to creep around me than to write that you love Pakis, you know, Joel? It's a bit over the top. And to be perfectly honest, it's a bit of an insult as well, considering that I'm Indian. "Indian Lover" would have been much more apt.'

Joel looked at the writing, then back to Armin with amusement. 'Sorry, I'll have it re-sprayed and rewritten later. I don't want to insult you.'

Taking a quick peek to the bushes Armin noticed, rather unhappily, that his rather large bottom was in Prem's line of sight. He jiggled over a little (about two feet) to give his cousin the perfect shot if required (in case Joel tried any 'funny' stuff) and raked his eyes over Joel's clothes. Black boots, black combat bottoms, tight, black T-shirt with white writing: STAY UP ALL NIGHT, SMEAR COFFEE ON YOUR DICK. And black shades (to hide behind). He expected that under those black combat bottoms Joel was hiding two very sore knees from the amount of grovelling he'd been doing on the phone lately. 'Please stay away from Eloise', 'Please don't harm Candy', 'Please don't harm me'. The man was a pathetic loser.

'The money is in the car,' Joel said. 'Twenty-five grand and not a penny more. I want you to count it in front of me. I don't want any of this "£2000 is missing" lark.' He suddenly remembered his manners. 'Sorry about my attitude, I'm just so nervous around you.'

Armin rubbed his chin with his fingers. 'I understand, you're not the first person to say that. In India, people tremble when I walk the streets. I'm known from Bombay to the Punjab region as a man who doesn't take any shit. They call me Armin the Great.'

Climbing Everest was hard, but stifling his laughter was even harder. Joel repeated, 'Armin the Great. Suits you.'

Joel suggested, because of the privacy given by the tinted windows, that they should count the money in the Range Rover. Armin the Great agreed and swaggered over to the back door.

'What are they in, fifties, twenties or tens?' Armin asked, waiting for Joel to open up.

'Oh, erm, forties,' he replied, opening the door, and pushing Armin hard into the back seat. 'Now get in the fucking car!'

Bundling in behind him, Joel grabbed Armin around the neck and ordered Brent, who was now sitting in the driver's seat, to pull away. A side window suddenly smashed, sending shards of glass inwards. Three seconds later another side window cracked. Ignoring the mini attack of air rifle pellets, Jay helped hood a struggling Armin with a black sack, while Joel tied his hands behind his back with nylon rope – using his new favourite knot, the Danny Knot. Armin was then forced to kneel on the floor with his hooded head facing the seat. He hadn't knelt this way since he last prayed – which, coincidentally, was what he was doing now. But was anyone really listening?

Driving with a smashed window was likely to draw attention from the police; Joel therefore instructed Brent to take the country route, avoiding the main roads and limiting the risk of being seen. Apart from shouting out general directions, nothing was said by either the three mates or their terrified hostage. Just the rumbling of the diesel engine and the groaning of the exhaust as the four-wheel drive negotiated the tight country bends and narrow bumpy roads. The journey continued for a good hour until the tyres crept up a steep hill and on to the unmistakable sound of crunchy gravel, parking next to a red BMW. The engine switched off, leaving just the noise of Armin's thumping heart.

Still without anybody talking, Armin was ushered from the Range Rover and escorted across a length of tidy lawn and on to a huge clearing populated with heavy building equipment and materials. Brent's latest development plan, a project to build ten luxury apartments in the country, was at the embryo stage of progress. The builders had been given a day's paid holiday today – and when builders get a free day's pay they don't ask 'why?' So, for all intents and purposes, the site was deserted. And the chances of anyone accidentally finding their way up here were virtually zilch. Armin's pockets were emptied; his mobile, car keys and wallet were put somewhere safe.

Joel had the honour of removing Armin's hood and all three mates stared disgusted at the man who had caused so much misery. Armin felt his strength ebbing away as his eyes hooked onto the scene he found himself in. Nightmares didn't get scarier than this. Armin wouldn't have been too surprised to find Clive Barker sitting on a tractor taking notes for his next book.

Joel began, 'I'm not one for big speeches and it's not in my nature to drag out the inevitable, but this worthless piece of shit touched my sister without her permission.' Joel dared Armin to smile, just dared him. 'Forget what seedy crimes he is guilty of with his own wife. Forget that he rapes and abuses women for the fun of it. Forget that this bastard has tried to blackmail me and his wife. Forget that he leaves a trail of hurt behind him wherever he goes. Forget that he threatened to hurt Candy and said that he would cut Eloise's throat next time. Forget he's posted pornographic photos of his wife on the Internet. Forget all that?' Joel threw the black hood at Armin's face. 'Do you honestly think that I *can* forget all that? Did you honestly believe that I was going to succumb to blackmail and pay you £25,000 for you to stay away from my sister and Candy?' Joel's eyes grew large. 'And to think that you had me creeping up to you on the phone.' Joel looked to Brent. 'Do you know why I couldn't come out for a drink with you the other night?'

Brent shrugged.

'Because this piece of worthless shit had set me a Gandhi test to revise for.' Joel watched as Brent tried to muffle his laughter with his hand. 'I sat up until two in the morning revising for a fucking Gandhi test that Armin was going to make me do the following day.'

Jay turned his head away, so Joel couldn't see him chuckling.

'I had to get ninety fucking per cent or he said he was going to up the money. And because I didn't want to give the game away I had to go along with everything he said. If he'd asked me to bake a fucking cake in the shape of a turban, then I would have done it.'

'So,' Jay started, 'what did you get on the Gandhi test?'

'Oh, do behave, mate,' Joel advised angrily, then calmed a little. 'I got ninety-five per cent if you really must know. How was I supposed to know that Mahatma means "Great Soul" in Indian? That last question was a fix.'

Armin piped up, 'Everyone knows the answer to that one. In India.'

Joel smarted. 'Shut the fuck up!'

It was now time for Armin to atone for *his* sins. With Brent grabbing one of Armin's arms and Jay the other, they followed Joel around a huge pile of bagged cement, over a steep mound of sand and onto an open space beside an orange digger. Lying six feet beneath ground level, in a hole dug out early this morning, was Joel's coffin; snug, inviting and with the lid off. Armin's initial shudder at the sight was replaced by a statue-like stillness. Frozen rigid by his fear, it appeared that Armin had entered into rigor mortis about two hours too early. Joel had been in the Death Zone many times at eight thousand metres above sea level, this was the first time he'd seen someone enter the Death Zone at just six feet below ground level.

'You're a Hindu, right?' Joel questioned; Armin nodded feebly. 'Well, I'll give you a choice: you can either be cremated like Hindus are supposed to be.' He pointed to a petrol can by Jay's foot. 'Or buried alive in that coffin.'

Like a magician's assistant, Brent picked up the can and held out his lighter to Joel. 'Burn the fucker.'

Jay added his penny's worth: 'Yeah, let's torch the bastard, roast him until he melts, see his flesh drip down from his ears. I want to see him engulfed in flames, I want to hear him scream in agony and shout for forgiveness. I want fire to—'

'We get the point,' Joel interrupted. 'He is going to pay.' Joel peered down to the red silk-lined interior of the coffin. 'Death is normally a sad occasion, a time of grief and sorrow.' He looked up to Armin's terrified eyes. 'But not with you. When I saw all the bruises you had given Zarleena, I felt sick inside. I imagined what living with you must have been like. A miserable existence. To wake up not knowing if she was going to be raped or beaten or bullied: it would have seemed easier not to wake up at all. To know that the person you see the most is the person you fear the most must be a torture that only the darkest minds could devise. Evil minds like yours.' He noticed Armin's concentration waning, so clouted him around the face. 'Listen to me, you nasty, pathetic coward of a man. Picking on women, taking away their hopes and their confidence, stealing away their self-respect – do you honestly believe that this world is a better place with you around? I fucking don't.' And with that last comment, Joel smacked Armin hard in the face and pushed him into the coffin. 'I told you I'd bury you, you fucker, now have a nice sleep.'

Brent followed him into the pit with the rope and hood. Before Armin had a chance to protest, his mouth was gagged, his feet were tied and his hood was replaced. The lid of the coffin came down as swiftly as the blade of a guillotine, sealing in Armin the Great with a chilling thud. In silence Brent, Jay and Joel spaded on soil, covering the coffin, burying the wife-beater. In no time at all the ground was level again. The three mates tidied away their tools, then headed into the Portakabin for coffee, biscuits and a fag.

The dingy shelter smelled of grimy workmen, their discarded boots and overalls thrown in one corner. It also contained a filing cabinet, a box of tools, a packet of toilet roll and a table covered with architectural plans for the project.

'Nice decor,' admired Jay, eyeing the multitude of

naked women plastered over every available wall space. 'Not photos of the builders' wives, I take it.'

They laughed, and continued to laugh until they remembered that there was a body buried a few yards away. With a steaming mug of coffee each and a generous spread of biscuits the three began a serious discussion that would last over three hours. 'How much oxygen was in the coffin?' 'Who was the arsehole who shot at the car?' 'Could worms chew through oak in under four hours?' 'Did Joel really score ninety-five per cent in the Gandhi test?' And the sharpest arrow of them all: 'Did Joel have the hots for Armin's wife, Zarleena?'

Joel dunked a digestive in his fourth mug of coffee (he was missing his Red Bulls). 'Have I got the hots for Zarleena?' Joel chewed on that one. 'Put it this way, I like her.'

'But?' Brent prompted.

'But nothing. I like her. I don't like it when she gets hurt. I think she's a great person . . . Oh fuck off, you two; it's none of your business.'

Jay eyed Brent: TOUCHY.

Opening the Portakabin's door to let out the cigarette smoke, Joel stood on the steps, looking out to his surroundings. With the spectacular trees and bushes that bordered this land, Brent had sure picked a beautiful setting to build luxury apartments on. Joel stared at the plot where Armin was buried, the unmarked grave of a wife beater. His dead body would devalue this wonderful hideaway in Joel's opinion. But he doubted that Brent would be advertising that fact in his new brochures: PAY NOW FOR A BRENT HOME AND WE'LL

PROVIDE A CORPSE UNDER THE KITCHEN FLOOR FOR NO EXTRA CHARGE. (Subject to availability.) HURRY NOW, WHILE STOCKS LAST, BEFORE MAGGOTS SET IN. Joel smiled at his dark humour, then checked his watch.

'I'm going to be making a move now,' Joel stated to his buddies. 'I'm knackered, I need some sleep. Anyone want a lift?'

'So, we're really just going to leave him, are we?' Jay asked, blowing out a smoke ring. 'But he'll die.'

Brent stood up, emptying the ashtray in the metal bin. 'He'll either die or he'll run out of oxygen, don't beat yourself up about it. You said yourself that *The Vanishing* was your favourite film. Well, we've just made *The Vanishing 2*. Good, hey?'

But it wasn't good. When Jay had agreed to this 'burial' he was sure that Brent would pull out at the last minute. Never did he believe that the crime would be seen through to its end. Now it appeared that both Brent and Joel had been gung-ho serious about it all along. No wonder they had looked at him a bit strangely when he'd said that the funniest part of the day was going to be when they dug him back up. Jay eyed his two best friends. He would do anything for either one of them, but there was no way he was going to prison over someone like Armin.

'We agreed that any decision we took would have to be unanimous. I vote that we dig Armin back up now. We've had our fun and taught him a lesson. We don't know who shot at us today but no doubt they had something to do with Armin.' Jay pleaded with them both. 'Look, guys, I can't afford to throw my life away because of this. I really can't.'

Joel understood. 'You two can do what you want with him, but there is no way I'm picking up a spade to dig that fucker out just so he can carry on with his sick ways again – that's if he's still alive. I leave this up to you two. I'm sorry, but I can't bear to even look at him.' He added softly, 'Sometimes an eye for an eye is the only way. No matter what Gandhi said about the world going blind.'

He shook their hands and left them arguing between themselves like two archaeologists.

The question was: to dig or not to dig.

Chapter Thirty-five

In some ways Zarleena had a bigger question: to divorce or not to divorce.

It had been nearly a week since Joel had phoned Zarleena informing her of the good news that Armin would not be bothering her ever again. She had asked him to expand on the word 'ever', to which he'd replied, 'Never.' She'd asked him to give her a clue to Armin's fate, to which he'd replied, 'David Blaine.' She'd asked him if he'd hurt Armin, to which he'd replied, 'Expand on the word "hurt".' The conversation went round more roundabouts than Milton Keynes, with Joel forever skirting closer to the truth of what had happened to Armin and Zarleena forever backing away. Armin *was* still her husband and if he were lying dead in a ditch somewhere then she'd rather not know. Which left her in a bit of a tizzle when it came to divorcing him. She had heard that in France there were rules that allowed you to marry your dead partner; as far as she was aware there were no rules in Britain that allowed you to divorce one.

Zarleena read the headline of her Sunday paper as she picked it up off the mat: WHAT A DIFFERENCE A DAY MAKES. It was referring to the latest government scandal (something to do with a lorry load of black-cherry gateaux going missing after John Prescott visited a cake factory). Still in her pyjamas she flopped on the sofa, flicked aimlessly through the newspaper while drinking her morning coffee, and thought about her life: WHAT A DIFFERENCE A WEEK MAKES. Armin was now gone from her world and so had the bruises he'd gifted her; Honey and Tree were getting on swell – he was due to meet the parents tomorrow; shop takings were at their all-time high this week (Zarleena was sure that the customer increase was brought on by gossiping, nosy Indian shoppers wanting a look at the 'beaten-up Hindu woman') and best of all, Nestlé had released the special-edition orange-flavoured KitKat again. No more yearning in vain for its wonderful taste.

Just a yearning for something else. SEX.

Since Joel's call on Monday evening she'd not heard from him. He'd finished the conversation by offering to take her out for a drink sometime. It was as good a brush off as him saying, 'See you around.' Without even being in a relationship with him, she felt dumped. Their daily phone conversations had ceased as quickly as they'd started. On more than one occasion this week she'd embarrassed herself by sprinting through the shop, tossing customers to one side as she did so, in order to answer the telephone that might just be Joel ringing. Anyone who had rung Bindis & Brides these last five days was under the impression that the shop was owned by an asthmatic.

And yet, the only heavy breathing Zarleena wanted to be doing was with Joel. SEX SEX SEX seemed to be on her mind an awful amount at the moment. Not that she had a clue as to whether Joel was thinking the same thing. But her confusion over his behaviour was justified in her opinion. She believed that his relationship with Candy was over – that business with him wanting to have the tattoo removed seemed to prove that. Then there was his flirting on the phone, the sexual innuendoes, the compliments, the filthy jokes; he had even asked her if she could pole-dance for him over the phone. She gave it a go, but felt pretty fucking stupid when Honey came in and asked her what she was doing with the broom. For all intents and purposes it appeared that he had strong feelings for her. Zarleena aggressively flicked through the newspaper's glossy supplement; tutting over a picture of a woman before and after a nose job with the caption: LOOK WHAT FIVE GRAND DID FOR ME! – she could have got Armin to do it for nothing. So, if Joel did have strong feelings for her, Holy Durga why wasn't he picking up the phone and declaring his love? Didn't he know she was still suffering from pole-dance splinters? It was the least he could do.

Or maybe it was best he didn't. Zarleena looked at the other possibility that would explain Joel's behaviour towards her. He was a womanizer. Plain and simple. A flirt who thought nothing of telling a woman what she wanted to hear so that he could hear the words that he wanted to hear: 'Fuck me, Joel.'

Oh God, even with the negative Joel vibes, even with her instinct telling her not to, even with all that,

Zarleena still wanted to say the words, 'Fuck me, Joel.' And she didn't want to be saying them to a broom (although she did admire the length).

Saddled with his new-found knowledge, Joel lumbered around his apartment like a tired donkey while Eloise got ready in her bedroom. Sometimes he wished weeks and months had never been invented. At least then he wouldn't have to cope with the sour information that he hadn't had sex for nearly six weeks, or a month and a half. He remembered joking with the little old lady behind the counter in Boots when he purchased his last batch of condoms: 'Don't worry about the boxes' sell-by date that runs out today, Betsy, I'll have these used before sundown. And before you ask, yes, I have got a big willy.' The shame. The boxes were still in his bedroom waiting to be opened. And Betsy was still on the blood pressure medication she'd needed after Joel's visit.

Joel planted himself by the huge living-room window, hoping to take his mind off his nonexistent sex life for a moment, and watched as specks of rain appeared on the pane. The grey sky became darker as God played with the dimmer switch. Within minutes the heavens had declared war and a billion missiles fell to the ground below. Joel loved it when nature showed off (as long as nobody died, of course): blizzards, storms, hurricanes, tornadoes, avalanches. *Take note, little humans*, Nature warns, *I can have you anytime I wish*. It let people know who the real rulers of this world were. Soon the rain was so dense that the castle ruins in the distance were taken from view. It was as good a time as any to get out his laptop and finish his autobiography. Chapter 35, his last chapter.

Joel sat on the vibrating chair, turned up the power to max, and began to tap away on the keyboard. His editor had asked him to bend the rules slightly when writing. 'The truth is great most of the time,' she'd instructed, 'but sometimes the public want to hear something extraordinary. For instance, when you stood on top of Everest for the first time, your words were "FUCK A DUCK." But perhaps, something more profound would sound better, for example "It's the best high of my life." And perhaps your four-page lengthy description of the frozen faeces left behind by previous expeditions at Camp 6 on Everest could, perhaps, be . . . condensed?' (Coincidentally 'condensed' was one of the adjectives Joel had used to describe the huge, brown, snaking, man-made, curly python-like number twos).

The door farted and Eloise, dressed to the nines in a mini-skirt, halter-neck top and boots skidded from her room and across the floor to answer it, whispering to Joel, 'Be nice to him, I really like this one.'

'What's "this one" called?' Joel asked, not looking up from his screen.

Eloise opened the door and pulled in her new boyfriend. 'Meet, Luke.'

Joel peered up; Eloise had her arm hooked proudly around the guy's waist. There was something familiar about him which Joel couldn't put his finger on. And normally Eloise placed a lot of emphasis on looks. This Luke, for want of a better word, was ugly. Not quite up to the usual standard that Eloise crowed about. Maybe his sister was showing signs of maturity. Maybe life to her wasn't all about good looks and fat wallets any more. Maybe this Luke had a great personality.

'Have you seen the film *Vertical Limit*?' Luke asked Joel, his eyes checking out the surroundings. 'It shows you what real wankers climbers are.' He plucked out a fag and lit up, blowing smoke over towards Joel. 'You're a climber, aren't you? You have to be pretty selfish to be a climber. You get those Gurkhas to do all your heavy work and—'

'Sherpas,' Joel corrected.

'Yeah, you get those Sherpas to do all your heavy work. What's that geezer's name who made it up Everest first?'

'Hillary,' Joel said lethargically.

'Girl's name! Anyway, Hillary didn't get there first. I bet his Gurkha did. Selfish, the bloody lot of you.'

Joel pondered for a moment. Luke was ugly, thick and had the personality of a wet cabbage. He just hoped for Eloise's sake that the prick was good in bed.

'Just a quick word, Luke, before you whisk my sister away,' Joel said, eyeing him with a degree of inhospitality. 'Make sure you use a condom, the last thing I want is a nephew or a niece with your blood in it. Not that I've got anything against brainless orang-utans, but I don't like you. Now put out your fucking fag and stop being so fucking rude. PRICK.'

'Joel, stop it,' Eloise barked. 'We're in love. Live with it.'

Since Eloise had realized that she was losing her brother to other women, she'd set about trying to find a match. Someone as good-looking as Joel. A Joel look-alike even. Someone who would make her number one in his life, make her feel wanted again – and someone who would give her the buzz of jealous women wondering how she'd managed to bag such a sex god. Hunting through pubs, clubs, strip joints, gymnasiums and even the local athletics club she'd searched high and low to locate Joel 2. But men who were as scrumptious-looking as Joel were very hard to come by. Lightning very rarely strikes twice and all that. There was James with Joel's eyes and nose. Pete with his body and mouth. Johnny with his smile and eyebrows. Even Kenny with his ears and scrotum. But no Joel 2. Finally she had to reluctantly settle on Luke. After seven bottles of Bacardi Breezer, two spliffs and a fairground distorting mirror, Luke could just about pass himself off as Joel's uglier, uglier, *uglier* to the power of ten, brother.

Joel continued to type, trying hard to ignore the loving couple's attempt to snog in front of him as they canoodled on the sofa, their aggressive kissing more akin to bare-knuckle fighting than romance. Finally he called 'time' and ordered them to go to Eloise's room when she asked him to fetch her the squirty cream from the fridge. They both gave him the evil eye.

'If I wanted the porn channel, then I would have subscribed to it,' Joel explained. 'Except on the porn channel I doubt that you'd get the performers saying, "I love you", "No, I love you more", "No, I said it first, I love you the most".' Joel cracked open a Red Bull. 'Face it, you both *don't* love each other, you just want a shag. Now go away, you're making me sick. If there's one thing I can't stand it's young couples drooling over each other in public, it's a—'

His mobile bleeped. Joel read the words of the text message, at first barely registering their implication. On rereading them, their true meaning was met with horrified eyes. Joel knew that what was staring back from the phone would highlight this day in his life for ever. There was more bad news in just three syllables than in the whole of his 120,000-word autobiography. He tried to disguise his unease from Eloise by furnishing his face with a makeshift smile. But nothing much less than a pot of Marmite would disguise the whiteness that had spread over Joel's features. This had to be the lowest moment of his life.

Joel, slightly shaking, excused himself from the lovers and headed for the safety of his bedroom. Unfortunately there was no escape from his mind in here. In fact, the isolation seemed only to purify his anger. Joel walked to the wall diagonally opposite his bed and admired the framed picture of K2. At 28,251 feet, he'd nearly lost three fingers to frostbite up there. One in three climbers dies up K2. Joel picked up the heavy photograph and lobbed it against the framed picture of Everest on the other side of the bedroom. When two mountains collide, the fallout is immense. Thousands of glass shards burst in every direction, broken frames dropped to the floor. Joel crunched across the shattered glass to the TV, unplugged the wire then, with a shot-putter's grunt, he threw it hard against the door – half expecting Ant and Dec to crawl out of the debris (seeing as they were on the fucking thing every day). Next he kicked a box of Red Bull across the floorboards. Then, ignoring the throbbing pain in his right foot, he completely trashed his underwear drawer. Finally, he pulled the doors off his walk-in wardrobe and hurled them across the room. Now he knew what it felt like to behave like a professional footballer.

There was a feeble knock on his damaged door and Eloise poked her head around. 'You okay?' she asked, temporarily overlooking the fact that he was wearing a pair of boxer shorts as a hat. 'What's happened?'

'Nothing.'

'Nothing?' she queried.

'Sweet FA. Honestly, nothing for you to worry about.' Joel removed his boxers (the ones on his head) and picked up his keys. 'I'm shooting out. Make sure you and Luke don't use this room as a love suite.'

Eloise viewed the bedroom with doubtful eyes. She'd seen cosier bus shelters than this room, now that her brother had trashed it. But then again, she'd always wanted to make love in a bus shelter. She hoped Luke was up for it. Eloise watched Joel walk to the front door and leave. It was obvious that his mind was working overtime. Pickling in anguish. Hurting like she'd never seen him hurt before. He wore the pain on his face and although he tried to disguise it with a smile, Eloise knew, as only a sister could, that Joel had received news today that had ruptured his life. If only she was as close to him as she used to be, then she could have made him feel better.

After cleaning the maisonette, Zarleena slumped on the sofa, thinking back to her mother's advice on how to rid a house of men in less than a second: mention that you were about to spring clean. Dad would always have a friend in need of a desperate hand whenever Mum mentioned the words 'bucket and mop'. His friend back then, if Zarleena could remember rightly, was called 'Beer'. Seven hours later Dad would roll in half-cut, stinking of his friend, admiring the newly polished floor – before he vomited all over it. Cleaning was a woman's job, making a mess was a man's.

And putting the world to rights was Honey's job. Once again, on yet another Sunday, Honey, Tree and their entourage were on a march. The venue, Hyde Park, and the cause, Gay Rights for Animals. They carried a huge banner picturing a mixture of zoo animals jumping out of a wardrobe. Certain animal faces looked remarkably similar to certain MPs, which gave Honey the confidence that legislation would come quickly. Only when the world was the way Honey wanted it, would she relax.

But relaxing didn't come too easy for Zarleena either; her mind a constant courtroom drama, her thinking all over the shop. Sometimes she just wished her brain would take a dive and plunge into freefall, see where it landed, forget what was on the ground below. And these days much of her time was spent thinking about Joel, wondering if she would ever go to bed with him again.

And competing with Zarleena's sexual urges were two other urges right now. The urge to demolish an entire box of Milk Tray and the urge to watch *Grease* for the umpteenth time. Although drooling over John Travolta's tight little bottom as it wiggled away dancing to 'You're the One that I Want', while biting into a strawberry cream was almost a sexual act in itself. Almost.

Zarleena slipped in the *Grease* DVD to delay having to change out of her pyjamas. By the time 'Summer Nights' had played, she had finished a whole layer of chocolates. By 'Hopelessly Devoted', the next layer was half gone, and by the time the film had reached 'Sandy', Zarleena was standing naked under the shower, trying desperately to hose away the five thousand calories she'd just consumed, wondering if the 'beached whale' look was in season these days. After drying, she dressed in a white lycra vest top with the sequined words SIMON SAYS, and a short pink chiffon skirt; perfect wear for a summer's day indoors even though it was pissing down outside. When Zarleena's relatives had visited from India, they'd mentioned that when it rained in Britain, they instinctively wanted to run outside with buckets and saucepans to collect it. It's a good job, Honey had joked, that when the relatives from India saw a hole in the ground they didn't do what was instinctive for them to do (squat), or they'd be sent back home before their *kacchas* (underpants) had even hit their ankles. Zarleena sprinkled Orangeina's bowl with fish food, poured herself a coffee, then sat back on the sofa and continued to watch *Grease.* It wasn't too long before she was back in the fantasy land of Rydell High.

And it wasn't too long after that that reality interrupted her afternoon with a solid 'knock, knock, knock' at the front door. She hadn't ordered a pizza (although that wouldn't have stopped her eating someone else's), Honey already had a key, Armin was out of the picture and her parents were away in Leicester for the weekend. After turning off the TV, she crept over to the door, and without a peephole to look through,

Zarleena carefully, nervously lifted the letterbox inwards and stared at the rain-soaked jeans in front of her expanding eyes. *Well, blow me*, she thought; *or rather, let me blow you.* She knew that crotch anywhere. It was Joel's.

'I need to speak to you,' he said, as soon as she opened the door. 'Can I come in?'

Zarleena viewed the drenched figure before her and realized he was soaked with something far worse than rain. Misery. His blue eyes, once a furnace of mischief, were now two dull embers of pain. And his usual heart-warming smile was gone, leaving just a flat expression of sadness reflecting from his face. Feeling almost embarrassed to see him like this, Zarleena stepped aside to let him in, closed the door behind him, and without thinking too much about it, she hugged him tightly. He returned the hug with such force that she expected his clothes to be squeezed dry. And if the hug continued in this fashion, Zarleena thought, she'd have his clothes steam-ironed by her lust in no time. After a short while, she broke away and fetched him a clean towel from the airing cupboard and a baggy T-shirt from Honey's stockpile of failed demonstration wear. It read: EAT AN INDIAN TODAY (BUT MAKE SURE YOU ASK HER PARENTS FIRST). Joel smiled politely as he put on the T-shirt, quickly and roughly dried his hair, then returned to his look of dejection as they sat on the sofa.

'Read that!' Joel passed his mobile across. 'It's the top message.'

Zarleena read it through and shrugged. 'And this is what's upsetting you?' She shook her head, dumb-founded. 'It's not that big a deal, Joel, surely?'

'Big fucking deal?' He shouted: 'NOT A BIG FUCK-ING DEAL? Jesus, how cold *are* you?'

Zarleena viewed the message again, in case she'd missed something:

RED BULL HAS GONE BUST.

She knew that Joel loved the stuff, but to be this upset? It was shameful. 'Look, Joel, Red Bull going bankrupt is not the end of the world. I promise you that there are more important things in this life than a can of stimulating drink.' She paused at his vague, confused expression. 'Have you thought about trying another brand? I think Tesco do one called Kick. I—'

Joel snatched his phone from her hand and pressed a few buttons. 'You've read the wrong one. That was Brent's idea of a joke. Read this.' He handed back the mobile. 'This is the text that I'm upset about. This is the one that is driving me fucking insane.'

She scanned her eyes down the linked messages, each sentence drying up her throat, each callous remark edging her closer to nausea. And what was she supposed to say to Joel to comfort him, make him feel better? Her eyes remained steady and fixed on the text message, whilst her heart went out to him.

Joel, you said you understood the pain you put me through. You said that you were sorry. People said I was mad to stay with a man as selfish as you. You said that you would take care of me. But you didn't. You took care of all the slags you slept with instead. I've dreamed of ways that I could hurt you. Just like you hurt me. To slice you with a knife, or to push you off your fucking mountain. Or boil your testicles in molten tar. To hurt you like you hurt me with your sleeping around. Then one day I became pregnant with your child. Your offspring. Your future son or daughter. The one thing I know you dreamed about. The one thing you were looking forward to. Well listen here, my ex-boyfriend, I've had an ABORTION. I've terminated your child. HURTS, DOESN'T IT? Let's hope it hurts like you hurt me. Let's hope it teaches you to keep your cock in your pants.

You were my life, Joel, but now I've had to sacrifice a life to get you out of mine. It really hurts, doesn't it? Candy

PS I've thrown your engagement ring in the sea.

Joel tugged the phone away from Zarleena. 'I admit that I haven't been the greatest of boyfriends, but to take it out on the baby for revenge is . . .' He shook his head despondently. 'I don't know what the fuck it is, but it's definitely not right. Wasn't there a motherly instinct inside her at all? Did she really hate me that much?'

Feeling his pain, Zarleena took his hand. 'It sounds to me like she loved you too much. Sometimes I think you blokes don't understand how deeply a woman can love a man. I'm not saying that having an abortion is right, but maybe the only way she can really forget about you and get on with her life is to rid herself of everything that is you.' Zarleena paused. 'Actually, I don't know why I'm sticking up for her; she's a bitch.'

And Joel went on to explain what a real 'bitch' Candy had been over the last few weeks. How each phone conversation became an argument filled with rage and blame. Candy threatening him with abortion, arguing that it would be Joel with blood on his hands and not her if she had one. If Joel gave up mountaineering, then the baby could live. If he couldn't, then thumbs down for mini-him. No woman or child wants to take second place to a mountain. The threats of abortion became taunts which became promises and now . . . it was reality. Since receiving the text an hour and a half ago, Joel had been wandering the streets in the thrashing rain like a vagrant, fighting the urge to do something stupid, screaming at the demons trespassing in his mind. Finally, using all his will power to remain calm, he'd sat back in his Range Rover and phoned Candy. With the rain pummelling the car roof, Joel listened to her miserable excuses. Her cowardly defence. How bringing up a child on her own was impossible. How no other man would want a woman with another man's baby. How she couldn't bear to bring up a child who reminded her of Joel . . . How Daddy had paid for the private abortion. ABORTION. The worst three syllables of Joel's life.

Glancing up at Zarleena, Joel carried on, 'I made it clear that I never wanted to see or hear from her again and she burst out crying. What did she fucking expect?'

Zarleena had seen Joel's bare body before but this was the first time he'd bared his soul. She'd expected the inner workings of Joel's mind to be a core of granite. Tough and capable of dealing with life's problems. It came as some surprise to see him tearful and cut up with emotion. And it came as even more of a surprise that she found his sensitivity highly attractive. It was like finding out that Robin Hood kept a teddy bear in his arrow sack. (Or maybe it wasn't.) Zarleena continued to listen as Joel described his regrets and failings. How his womanizing days were over, how sleeping around always leaves at least one person hurt, how he'd learned his lesson with Candy. Joel confessed that deep down he knew he deserved what Candy had done. His punishment was in line with his crime. From the living room to the kitchen they nattered away, adding another coat of paint to their already colourful friendship. Zarleena thumped her chopping board on the side and began to make them both a bite to eat.

Leaning against a cupboard, Joel watched as Zarleena piled up ingredients for her quick-flash chicken curry. He smiled, thinking back to when he'd first met her in the supermarket. Even then she'd come across as an 'I'll help first and ask questions later' type of person. And today, after Candy's text, he found himself drawn towards her. Not his friends whom he'd known for years nor his family whom he'd known for ever, but Zarleena, whom he'd only known for nearly four months. There was something very special about her. And it was a thought that was doing the rounds with his emotions right now. Joel studied the master chef at work as she tossed in the spices and fried up the onions. He'd always loved Indian food, and on his trips he'd always loved India and he loved the Indian mountains. Surely, Joel considered, he wasn't falling in love with an Indian woman, was he? Zarleena turned around and lobbed him a can of tomatoes to open. He asked himself, how would he feel if he never saw her again? How would he feel if he saw her with another man? His heart seemed to abseil down his insides and land with a thud somewhere in his abdomen. Jesus, Joel sat back on a chair, what if he'd been living in denial all along regarding his feelings for Zarleena? Is that why he'd helped her with Armin? Or would he have helped her anyway? And how come, after promising Candy that he would never cheat on her again, he still slept with Zarleena? And *only* Zarleena. It was a clue that proved beyond reasonable doubt that his feelings for Zarleena were a little more than lust and looks. But, more importantly, what were her feelings for him? Did she see him as a man who cheated on women? An unreliable rogue? Would she ever risk wrecking their friendship for something deeper? Were there things about him that she would . . .

'Joel! The tomato can?' She grabbed it off him and opened it herself. 'I bet if it was a Red Bull can you would have opened it immediately.'

He chuckled, then his face became serious. 'Why did you sleep with me? Was it because you liked me, or was it because you just wanted a shag?'

Taken back by his question, she accidentally dropped the tin in the saucepan. 'Shit! I hope you like metallic curry.' She turned around, laughing. 'You want to know if I used you for sex? A womanizer wants to know if he has been exploited. Sorry, I shouldn't joke, you've had a rough day. No, Joel, I didn't use you. I thought, I mean, I think you're a really nice guy. I slept with you because I . . . erm . . .' Zarleena could feel herself reddening. 'I fancy the pants off you, okay? I wouldn't just sleep with anyone. Now, if you'll excuse me while I fish out the tomato can before the label dissolves. Thank you.' She raised her eyebrows and said, 'As in "Thank you, could you go away now, please, while I die of embarrassment",' and then returned to the cooking.

Before Zarleena had time to do anything, Joel walked up behind her, placed his arms around her waist and kissed her on the neck, tiny pecks which turned smoothly to delightful nibbles. There was no point in him romantically sniffing in the scent of her hair as it was only going to smell of curry. And equally there was no point in kissing her hands as they were only going to smell of garlic. Finding another place to kiss was going to be hard.

'Fancy taking a shower?' Joel asked.

'What, both of us together? That's such a turn-on.'

Joel smiled. 'I was thinking maybe just you.' He watched her face drop. 'Only a joke.'

Five minutes later and the pair of them were all lathered up in the shower, enjoying the feeling of their bodies connecting once again. The erotic ecstasy took Joel to a steamy high which he'd never reached before while Zarleena soaked up the sensations of having a man use her body for pleasure rather than a punch bag. She was just about to kiss him hard on the lips when she saw his eyes roll backwards and his body tense up. She knew exactly what this meant and wasted no time in letting Joel know.

'Avalanche?' she queried, bracing herself for the energy burst. 'You're about to avalanche, aren't you?'

'No,' he replied, pushing her gently away. 'I've pulled my fucking back out.'

Meanwhile, the curry burned.

With sex off the menu, and definitely burnt Indian off the menu, the only sensible option seemed to be: talking. After getting dressed, Zarleena fetched a bag of frozen chips from the freezer and carefully manoeuvred them under Joel's back as he lay in 'apparent' agony on her bed. She thought climbers were supposed to be macho. And she hadn't heard moans this loud since Mum had phoned Dad to inform him that she'd accidentally put four-star petrol in his diesel car.

'Are you positive that you don't need an ambulance?' Zarleena asked sarcastically, as she sat down on the edge of the bed. 'Once those chips have defrosted I've only got chocolate ice cream left and there's no way you're having that.'

'I'll be fine. It's a bit of a shame we had to stop though; I hate half-finished jobs.' Joel grinned. 'Or should I say half-finished masterpieces? Tell you what, why don't you continue without me. I'll just lie back here and watch.'

'And what do I get out of it?' She tried to keep a straight face.

'An orgasm? It's the least I can do.'

Zarleena used to wonder how bed-ridden arthritic men got their kicks. She now knew. She stood up. 'I expect that I'm only going to really enjoy this orgasm if I dress up in slutty lingerie?'

'Now you're getting it.'

'And I suppose to increase *my* pleasure further I should rub oils all over my body.'

Joel was moaning again. She wasn't too sure whether it was his back or something else this time. He managed to nod 'yes'. And she was certain she heard him mumble out the word 'pink'.

'Pink?' she asked, confused.

'Wear pink. You look great in pink lingerie,' he replied, adjusting the chip bag. 'In fact pink is *your* colour.'

Her eyes zeroed in on his. 'But you've never seen me in pink lingerie!'

He was about to blurt out, 'What about those X-rated porn pictures I saw of you on the Internet, you wore nothing but pink,' when he remembered that Zarleena didn't know he'd seen them. There was only one thing for it: if in doubt, do the tortoise trick. Joel pulled up the duvet and tucked his head inside.

Beneath the covers, Joel murmured, 'Did I say pink?' He tried desperately to recall the colour of the underwear she'd worn last time. He smiled as the memory blotted through. 'I meant to say blue.'

'But I've never worn blue lingerie with you either.'

Shit, Joel suddenly registered that blue was the shade of the boxer shorts *he* wore last time. 'Did I say blue? I meant red.'

Zarleena shook her head. It was all dawning on her now. 'You saw my photos, didn't you, Joel Winters?'

A sheepish Joel re-emerged from under the duvet. 'Yes. You looked beautiful though. You turned some pretty disgusting sexual positions into what can only be described as works of art.' He winced heavily at his last comment. 'I didn't sneak a look from the envelope that Armin handed me; Eloise found them on the Internet under "Dirty Indian Whores".'

'THE INTERNET!'

Why God had saved him he would never know. But save him he did, instructing the two white men to dig him from the grave. Never had he been so pleased to see a white man's face as the moment they pulled open the coffin lid. Moments later he was bundled into a red BMW and driven back to Watermill Park where he found a worried Prem, still holding the rifle, listening to *bhangra* music in his car. He'd told Prem that this day was never to be mentioned again, EVER.

That night he'd received a call from Joel with clear instructions, which Armin was only too pleased to comply with – this time:

1. *Divorce Zarleena.*
2. *Remove Zarleena's pictures from the Internet.*
3. *Never return to Hunterslea or Colchester.*
4. *Never cross Joel again (or next time you won't be dug up).*

Unbeknown to Armin, it was Joel who had saved his skin not God. As Joel had walked away from the burial scene, his conscience had come to life. Jay was right, Armin was not worth going to prison over. He'd sped back to the building site and helped his mates with the initial digging until the job was very nearly done. 'I want that fucker to think I would have left him here, so you'll have to finish this off between you,' Joel had whispered, ramming his spade in the earth and trotting across to his car. 'Let him think I'm a fucking psycho.' Brent and Jay had looked at each other. They already thought he was. 'A big girl's blouse psycho,' Brent had said, and they'd laughed, as Joel gave them the middle finger.

In his flat above the betting shop, Armin continued to chant for forgiveness.

After studying all the teachings of Gandhi, it had taken a bastard white man, as far as Armin was concerned, to teach him the biggest lesson of them all. RESPECT OTHERS.

Epilogue

Ten months later

Candy whispered in Joel's ear, 'I'm never going to close you.'

She looked into his beautiful blue eyes and smiled. God, he was gorgeous. She was so lucky to have him. Candy lifted up his top and blew a raspberry on his chubby stomach, sending Joel into a fit of giggles. She was sure when baby Joel grew up he was going to be a heartbreaker – just like his father – but it was going to be up to his mother to teach him how to treat women properly.

Another aeroplane flew over her hotel room and she automatically ducked her head. Her flight was just five hours away. After spending her entire life in England she was left with just five hours to say goodbye. Goodbye Mum and Dad, goodbye Sara, goodbye job and friends, and goodbye bastard British men.

When baby Joel was born three months ago, Candy's conscience willed her to pick up the phone and tell Joel the truth. There was no abortion, there was never going to be one. She wanted out of his life and if that meant a sick story to cover herself then so be it. The last thing she needed was for their baby to begin growing up with two parents but to end up with only one. Whether Joel died up a mountain or he had another affair, there was no way, in her eyes, that they would have a lasting future together.

So now she was booked on a flight to Australia to start her life anew with her baby. Her eyes caught sight of the magazine she'd thrown in the bin last night. She told herself not to, but she couldn't help herself and picked out the magazine to have one more read. The words inside proved to her once and for all that Joel was never the man for her. How could he have been when inside the pages of the climbing magazine was incontrovertible proof that Joel had never truly loved her.

An interview with Joel Winters after his latest expedition up Nanga Parbat, the Naked Mountain, in Pakistan four months ago. Within the article the interviewer asked various questions. What was Joel's greatest achievement? Which kind of tent did he prefer up the high mountains? Blah Blah Blah. Until he was asked, 'Why do you now climb with fixed ropes left behind by other expeditions, and oxygen? You're kind of known for your suicidal climbing methods.' Candy felt her heart rip wide open once again when she read his answer. 'I climb with ropes and oxygen now because my girlfriend, Zarleena, asked me to. I don't want to die on her. It wouldn't be fair just because of my ego.'

Candy picked up baby Joel and tried to stem the tears. 'He couldn't climb more safely for us, could he? He didn't love us enough, did he?'

Baby Joel put out his hand to grab something and Candy obliged with her finger. And boy, did baby Joel have a strong grip. His father would have been so proud.

But his father would never get to know he had a son.

A son named Joel Mallory Tenzing Hillary K2 Greenwood.